An Unfinished Death

Dee Henderson

****

Contact the author/publisher:
Dee Henderson
P.O. Box 13086
Springfield, IL 62791
dee@deehenderson.com
www.deehenderson.com

current printing revision: December 16, 2017

****

Connie August, a Christian combat medic, one who had experienced healings and miracles on the battlefield similar to those in scripture, wasn't looking to make waves back home now that she was retired from the service. She opened Connie's Pizza and settled into her chosen community, wanting to be herself, content to lead a small group of paramedics, doctors, nurses and chaplains who were studying the scriptures and sharing their experiences from across the Chicago area. Ryan Cooper, CEO of a religious-affiliated private hospital, had seen too many of Chicago's children die from gun violence, young mothers die from cancer and random illness take both the young and old. He wanted the vibrancy of God's healing to be a predictable experience again. A friend introduced them at a party. He wanted to understand what she'd experienced. She wanted him to give a chaplain friend a job when he retired from the service. They struck a deal that would change both their lives and soon begin to reverberate across Chicago. This is Ryan's story, Connie's, but mostly it's God's story, a God who is still amazing in his goodness.

****

Let the adventure begin…

Prologue

COMMANDER JOE BAKER

The chapel was quiet. Located on the grounds of the pentagon, in part of the rebuilt building after the 9/11 attacks, it was both a memorial to the lost and a place of reflection; the presiding chaplain served over all the military branch chaplains. A holy place, Commander Baker had always thought. Nodding to the Army corporal on the protective detail for the Secretary of Army, Joe walked past the corporal, toward the front of the room. The civilian who led the Army was seated in the first pew.

The Secretary of the Army looked up from the New Testament he was reading, closed it and slipped it back into his suit pocket. “Thanks for coming, Commander.” He motioned to the pew beside him.

“The SA calls, curiosity itself would get a naval officer to say yes to the meeting. Army and Navy can be like salt and pepper up close.” Joe took a seat and tried to relax beside the man whom tradition dictated was due as much deference as any man in the pentagon, Joint’s Chiefs to Defense Secretary. “What can I do for you, Sir?”

“For now, a conversation, listen to a request and consider if you wish to take on what it might entail.”

“Okay.” Joe didn’t need to ask if it was a sensitive matter, the SA had gone across services and asked to meet here rather than his suite of offices.

“You wear the Silver Star.”

Joe nodded. “Eight years now, Sir, back to when I was young enough to think a day at the office was the front line of the most current war. I acted with valor because it was that or die on the battlefield. I’m proud of it and also aware I wear it mostly by good fortune—the wounded soldiers with me lived, as did the civilians we were trying to protect. I could just as easily have become one of the white gravestones at Arlington and received it posthumously."

"You speak with the humility that marks the men who wear that award."

"We learned it. As did those among us who were worthy of the higher Valor awards, the Service Cross, the Medal of Honor."

"It's because you understand that mindset that I asked you here. But a couple more qualifying questions first, before I explain what I need. How do you like retirement?"

Joe smiled. "It's another kind of world compared to the service. When I was on extended leave between missions and home, there was still the duty and uniform, the call to be ready. Now it's my wife enjoying our time together and a serious amount of deep sea fishing, with some excursions volunteering to lead youth on wilderness adventures. Retirement overall still rather feels like I'm waking up on the moon."

The SA chuckled. "An apt analogy. Retirement eventually comes to us all. Commander, you're also a religious man."

"I am. I've been a believer in Jesus Christ since my youth."

"Good." The SA let the conversation pause, seemed to come to a decision, for he nodded before he spoke again. "Good. I come from Baptist roots myself. Four people I trust have independently recommended your name to me. Three from within the service, one outside it, a woman who wrote a book you would be familiar with. I asked her to confirm that religious heritage of yours was still an active faith."

Ann Falcon had been one of those recommending his name. It wasn't common knowledge that one of her early books was really his story, but enough people knew, that it might get mentioned when his name came up. "Alright, Sir. You've got my attention."

"Out of one battle, have come recommendations by a field commander for two Medals of Honor, six Silver Stars and an assortment of lesser awards."

Joe leaned forward. It was rare to see a Medal of Honor awarded, let alone two from the same battle.

"In the early morning hours of March 19th, 2016 in Quiam province, Afghanistan," the SA continued, "a forward operating base was overrun by Taliban fighters. US soldiers and afghan troops retreated to the remains of a nearby destroyed village and a convoy diverted to assist them. Over a period of six hours, order was restored, the enemy was killed, fled or was driven from the battlefield. There were sixty soldiers involved in the firefight, twenty-eight from the FOB and thirty-two from the convoy, in addition to air support brought in to assist. Twenty-three soldiers were injured during the course of the engagement.

"We knew it would be a significant battle with the potential to trigger those kind of valor numbers even before the fighting ended. So even as the narrations of events were being written to make those Medal of Honor recommendations official, the pentagon had swung into action, event records were being gathered, including drone footage, air and ground radio traffic, all after-action reports. We have a remarkable amount of video data given the number of drone resources and air force assets involved. We began in-depth interviews that same evening. The collection of evidence from the area was thoroughly done—even as investigators were still coming under sporadic mortar fire.

"That comprehensive package of evidence is now in the hands of the award investigators. Consideration for the various awards is proceeding through the review process, both MOHs look likely to be revised to the Distinguished Service Cross, one Silver Star may be upgraded to a Service Cross, two lowered to a Bronze Star with Valor."

"Yes, Sir, that would be expected," Joe replied. One thing the military was particularly good at was standardizing the process of awarding the Medal of Honor, the Distinguished Service Cross and the Silver Star—its top three awards of Valor. Award investigators set a high bar, weighing the merits of the actions taken against the criteria for the award, evaluating if the actions taken were more appropriately due a lesser award. He'd been stunned to learn his own actions had held up to the level of a Silver Star. It had taken 16 months for his own award package to work its way through the reviews to the Secretary of the Navy. This battle the Secretary of the Army was describing was now a year old, so awards for it, given the numbers under review, would probably be about midway through the review process.

"Traveling with the convoy were a chaplain and a combat medic. Both are being recommended to receive the Silver Star. The soldiers who walked away from the battle have unanimously agreed everyone lived that day in large part because of the actions of those two individuals. Commander, I need you to independently look at the evidence regarding these two individuals and make a recommendation privately to me. Do their actions merit the awarding of the Silver Star to one or both of them?"

"Sir?" Joe was surprised at the request, for both the investigating officers and the award board of review had long experience with making just that kind of evaluation and judgment call. To bring someone independent into the process was highly irregular, not unheard of, but usually involved only situations where foreign personnel serving with US troops were involved in the narration, had been saved by the actions of a US soldier, or had otherwise been involved in the act of valor. A representative of their country's military would often request review of the incident and it was granted as a courtesy. But to add an independent investigator from a different branch of the US military wasn't at all common.

"There are rare circumstances involved in this situation." The SA offered two personnel folders.

Joe opened the first. Chaplain George Whittier, 52, married, one son, one daughter, fifteen years with the army, with an impressive list of rotation dates, this was a man who had repeatedly volunteered to see combat rather than take the occasional state-side placement. Joe understood that impulse, as his own personnel record would have a similar look.

He opened the second folder and paused. "The combat medic is also a *she*, Staff Sergeant Connie August," he mentioned, impressed. "This would be only the third Silver Star awarded to a woman since the second world war."

"You know your history."

"I do. This is why you're going across services."

"One of the reasons," the SA agreed. "They were getting shot at while treating the wounded in an active firefight so straight heroism under fire is part of this. The award investigators and review board are well qualified to weigh that part of the record, the valor shown during the firefight, do their actions rise to the level of a Silver Star or are they more appropriately due a lesser award. It's the rest of what happened that we're not sure how to assess. What's causing consternation is what the full event record indicates happened after the shooting stopped."

"Make a leading point and stop..." Joe assessed. "I'll follow you over this cliff. What happened after the shooting stopped?"

"Commander, the evidence suggests they raised one or more soldiers from the dead."

He was a religious man, he'd seen one miracle on the battlefield his unit never spoke about outside of the six who had been present, but Joe wasn't ready for that statement. "No joke."

The SA shook his head. "No one along the chain of command keeps smiling after they see the evidence. This is as serious as it gets. Something truly odd happened that day."

"You want to know if they did a miracle and if that qualifies for a Silver Star."

"Basically—yes. These two individuals are being considered for a valor medal, in part, because of events which happened hours after the shooting stopped, which would make this an unprecedented decision.

"There is a curious lack of information coming from those who would have been in a position to see or know details. It's my belief we weren't supposed to notice the rest of the story. The battle dynamics, the field commander's recommendation for the MOH's, triggered data aggregation that otherwise wouldn't have happened. Those on the ground were hoping this stayed unseen and unnoticed."

The SA's comment walked him to another cliff edge and simply dropped him over it. "So this may not be the first time something unusual has happened around one or both of them."

"I'm thinking not. And isn't that also an interesting chestnut? Do you really want to open that box and look?"

The SA leaned back, his body language suggesting the bulk of the matter had been presented. "I can't ask the chaplain's service to investigate one of their own for possibly having done a miracle. Nor do I wish this to be an Army matter only if I am about to award only the third Silver Star to a woman since the second world war. If you raise one soldier from the dead, does that rise to Silver Star material? It's just one person, so maybe not. What about if you raise four? And just what exactly *do* you write on the award citation?"

If it wasn't the SA making that remark, Joe would have glanced at a calendar to make sure this wasn't April 1st, April Fool's Day. "You aren't exaggerating."

The SA shook his head. "Watch the video for yourself. I know I've got four soldiers walking around alive whose best explanation for what happened is paperwork error."

Joe laughed.

The SA smiled. "I'm not saying you aren't going to find an explanation that might look something like that. But I'm not joking about the mystery.

"I want you to talk to people off the record, look at the raw data, interview both individuals, find me more to work with and give me a recommendation. You'll treat the religious question with respect, both for personal and profession reasons. You wear the Silver Star. If one or both of these individuals deserves to also wear it, you'll make a strong case on their behalf with credibility behind it.

"Whatever happened that day was of a breadth it couldn't stay hidden. Was it what it appears? And if it was, how long has that been happening? I need the bigger picture. Probe any part of their history you think is relevant. Your security clearance is high enough I'll clear you to see anything you ask to see for the duration of their careers. The chaplain is still on active duty at Fort Benning, GA, has put in his papers to retire in July. She's been out of the army now for seven months.

"I'm willing to send you back to Afghanistan, across this country, wherever there is someone you think would be helpful to speak with in person. You'll be my investigator on this matter, one without active duty complications influencing what you might decide to tell me. You don't need to write down your report, deliver it verbally if you prefer. Just move me from where I am now closer to the truth before I have to make a decision.

"If I were to ask those who report to me to look into this, they would be trying to read the inflections in my voice, do I want them to make this go away and confirm nothing happened? Or they'll find something but simply come back with 'it's unclear, Sir' because they won't want to go out on this limb and tank any chance of their own future promotions by placing their judgment in question by others."

"A reasonable assessment," Joe judged. "I'm retired and no disrespect intended, but what the Army thinks of me is useful only in inverse. If the Army thinks I went off the deep end saying a miracle happened, my Navy buddies are going to insist all the more I'm right. I win either way."

The SA laughed. "I figured as much."

"How much time do I have?"

"If you can get an answer you're comfortable with in 90 days that makes my life marginally easier. The official recommendations for this group of medals likely arrives in July, but could be slowed until December."

Joe realized he'd already decided he wanted this mystery to be his. "People will either talk to me or they won't. I can make progress in 90 days, with the caveat my wife can travel with me. Otherwise this long vacation I'm proposing to take isn't going to get a good reception."

The SA smiled. "Granted. Try to keep the number of people you include in what you're thinking to a minimum, but it's understood you're going to need to discuss this with people, both inside and outside the military, with the working assumption it actually happened."

"The truth has a ring to it, Sir, you know it when you hear it. I'll see what I can find for you."

The SA offered an envelope that had a name and phone number written on it. "Travel authority, the access cards you'll need for this battle footage and the phone number for my handpicked aide whom I've yet to stump with a request. Just tell Peter what or who you need to see and he'll make it happen. He's expecting you to be in touch."

Joe nodded and pocketed the envelope. "I'm glad you called."

The SA's smile widened. "Retirement was getting that boring?"

"You've no idea." Joe stood and offered his hand, took his leave of the SA. He walked out of the chapel in a thoughtful mood. He'd meet his wife for an early lunch—she'd traveled with him from Texas to D.C. so she could sightsee while he took this meeting, convey the general news of what was going on, then spend his afternoon looking at video to see for himself what had caused this stir to begin.

Soldiers had stories, most never spoken about outside close unit buddies. Angels walked among battlefields. He'd seen one during his years deployed, brilliantly bright, armed for battle, wielding a sword, a fearsome sight that made a soldier tremble. A flash of that sword had triggered a rockslide allowing them to escape a deadly ambush. Others had tasted clouds so dense their enemy walked by ten feet away unable to see their position. A few had heard the cries of the demons as a rush of enemies poured through a smaller unit, killing most who were present. Joe accepted as more probable than not, something had happened during the events of March 19th, 2016. Finding someone who would talk about what had happened… that might be the real miracle.

1

RYAN COOPER

Ryan Cooper enjoyed the parties Ann and Paul Falcon hosted at their home on the occasional Friday night. He had met architects and artists, children from the local elementary school, more cops of various law enforcement flavors than he had realized were out there, the occasional foreign exchange student and an assortment of restaurant chefs, building contractors and city employees. The parties were occasions to mingle with city of Chicago residents who came from non-intersecting realms. Even the Governor had been known to stop by. Ann didn't consider it a good party unless there were as many kids and dogs as adults, though she had it thoughtfully arranged so quiet conversations could happen as easily as group video game adventures.

In his line of work, the week never really ended, for weekends brought some of the most critical incidents into his hospital ER. Spending a Friday evening with friends was still worth starting even if he couldn't count on ending the night here. The diversion the hours brought to his life were well worth the investment of his time. Ryan paid the cab driver and was glad for his coat as he made the short walk to their building on now thankfully snow-free sidewalks. It might be March 15th, but spring hadn't pushed aside winter yet.

Paul had asked him to come by early so he could show him the memorial wall plans before the party got underway. So many had died in Chicago over the last decade due to the violence that wasn't ending. The FBI was quietly trying to figure out how to become a community level resource for neighborhoods which had given up on the Chicago Police Department. Honoring the lost was one of the ways to say they hadn't been forgotten, to show tangible goodwill. As the head of the Chicago FBI office, Paul Falcon had initiated most of those efforts, the memorial was his political and personal skills at work, the groundbreaking planned for as soon as the weather cooperated.

Rebuilding trust with the community was the goal, serving as a mediator the means, but to even get there more bridges had to be built. Ryan could help Paul in small ways. His hospital had treated some of the gunshot victims in the last year and the chaplain's network, the family service groups, had first hand contact among the grieving families. Those connections matter when you were asking people to sit down with each other, to consider talking with law enforcement.

Ann and Paul's home occupied the fourth floor of an old brick warehouse in downtown Chicago, transformed decades before by Paul's grandfather. Ryan gave his name to the building doorman, offered a wave to the camera and security unlocked so the elevator could stop on their floor. As the elevator headed up, Ryan changed his phone to vibrate mode and moved it to his shirt pocket near his heart. A serious emergency at the hospital would get his attention. It was a Friday night in Chicago. Five people on average were going to get shot tonight. Mercy Hospital wasn't a trauma one hospital, but they got their share of the casualties. The reality was it had become the norm for Friday nights and no longer stopped parties from being planned, or people from going on about their lives. The simple awareness of that reality sat heavy on him.

Twenty minutes of serious conversation with Paul, then set it aside and shift to something lighter and filled with laughter. Ryan knew Ann was hosting these gatherings mostly for Paul's benefit, to lessen the weight of that FBI job. He was personally looking forward to th food, the guests and the four hours of socializing with being for a hospital related purpose. There would be quality art to enjoy for Paul was a serious art

Paul's sister Jackie had created one of the nicer restaurants in town, she would often have arranged the catering; and it was inevitable that Ann would introduce him to someone among her friends she thought he should meet as a potential date. Ann liked matchmaking and was rather good at spotting who would click as a couple.

The doors slid open and Ann was there to meet him with a smile. "Ryan, I'm so glad you could come this evening."

"I'm early."

"You're not the first early guest." Ann hugged him in welcome. "Paul's taken the dog for a brief last walk, he'll be back momentarily. He'd like to show you the memorial wall, get your input before everyone arrives. Come in; let me take your coat. Coffee? I've got hot or iced."

"Iced coffee sounds perfect."

She hung up his coat and led the way into the spacious kitchen. She gave him a concerned look as she fixed the drink. "What's been going on with you? It looks like it's been a hard month."

Because she was someone who would uniquely understand, he tugged out his wallet and offered her a picture. "Jessica. She was shot in the chest. We lost her fifteen hours later. She was 12." He offered another picture. "Anthony. He was shot in the head and died in surgery. He was 9." When Ann had looked at them, quietly nodded, he slid the photos back into his wallet. "All the Chicago area hospitals had tragedies this month. Those two were ours."

"I'm truly sorry, Ryan."

She'd worked homicide for a lot of years. She understood the way the faces remained long after the situation was over. "The weight gets heavier every month. I hate it when we do all we can and still lose a child."

"Did you really do all you could? Did someone pray to raise them from the dead?"

He looked over to see a woman wearing jeans and white knit top enter from the living room.

"Jesus raised a 12 year old girl once before. God's got a soft spot for kids; their angels always see his face. And he's got a commandment against murder. Did someone bother to ask God to raise them from the dead?"

Her question stunned him. "No. Not that I know of at least."

"Then you didn't do everything you could do. If Jesus did it before, the odds are good he would have liked to do it again had someone asked him. But no one asks, you just decide it was a tragedy. Mercy Hospital has deep religious roots. You should be the leading experts on the subject of what Jesus does today in regards to healing the sick and yes, raising the dead. Instead, you look like you're going prematurely gray with the stress of the CEO job rather than deploying every resource at your disposal."

Ann stepped between them, into their line of sight, to cool off the conversation. "Ryan Cooper, Connie August. And maybe now is a good time to mention it's a Friday night party before the fireworks truly get started."

The woman lifted a hand. "No need, Ann. Soapbox closed. I'm just tired of God getting the bad rap for something that wasn't his doing."

Ryan knew when truth slapped at him and was a smart enough man to accept it. "Point taken. Someone should have asked." Given the pain the deaths had caused so many people, someone certainly should have asked and in more than a perfunctory way.

"I've got hors d'oeuvres to pull out of the oven. Settle this nicely, you two."

Ryan couldn't remember the last time he'd felt a punch of words quite that hard and found himself walking across the room just to see where the conversation might go next. "Chaplain? Bible Professor?"

"Me?" she asked surprised and laughed. "For the last eight years, a Whiskey 68." She stepped back into the living room and picked up her glass from the side table, empty but for the ice.

"A combat medic?"

Connie paused on her way to refill her glass to give him another look. "Not many recognize the MOS—military occupational specialty code. A whiskey suits the profession at times."

"I can imagine."

"I like the sound of it, rather than the drink and the fact it tends to make religious people wince. I'm neither politically nor religiously correct, nor particularly concerned with being so."

"I'd say that's refreshing, but I've already gotten sliced by a pointed remark tonight."

She lifted both hands. "Cheap shots over for the night. Losing kids is tough. Goodness knows my stack of photos runs deeper than two. I had an errant mortar round land on a girl's school the second tour, killed nine in the courtyard while they were playing soccer. But you can be sure it was the last dead child I saw that I didn't try to raise from the dead." She headed into the kitchen after their hostess. "What am I drinking, Ann? It's not bad for punch."

"That cut glass pitcher on the end."

The moment to follow up on that comment of Connie's was interrupted as Ryan heard Paul arrive, the ding of the elevator opening, the sound of dog feet trying to find traction on entryway marble, the single deep bark as the animal realized company had arrived.

"Hey, Ryan," Paul stepped into the living room with hand outstretched. "I'm delighted you could join us tonight."

"Glad to be here, Paul."

"I think you'll enjoy the evening, it's going to be a good gathering."

"Sure about that last part?"

Paul turned at the casual question to see the woman coming behind him. "Connie! It's about time you made one of our parties." Paul promptly picked her up off her feet and swung her around. "It is *great* to see you. If I wasn't married, I'd be asking you."

"You're full of blarney is what you are Paul."

He laughed and lowered her back on her feet. "Where's your date? I need to meet this guy. I'm past ready to vet him for you."

She smiled back. "Setting up for a concert. And he's been well vetted by friends of yours who are equally nosey."

"That's good to know. Sam's going to really be annoyed he wasn't here tonight when he hears you came."

"The nice thing about being stateside, I can say 'another time' and it's likely there will be."

"I hear you're up for a Silver Star."

"There's paperwork flowing through the bureaucracy for a lot of us. I'd rather have avoided the episode than get pinned for it afterwards, you know how that is."

"I unfortunately do. You've met Ryan?"

"I have. But I haven't met him." She nodded to the dog watching them with obvious curiosity.

"This is Midnight, we call him Black—Ann's dog, though he's been bribed with enough bacon that at times he pretends he's mine."

"He's a good fit, all manly big guy." She knelt to stroke her hands through thick black fur and the dog promptly rolled over to get his belly rubbed.

"Now he's in heaven. Don't slip away on me, Connie, I want to catch up later. Come on back, Ryan. I've got the landscape drawings I want to show you in the office."

"Sure."

Ryan followed Paul, amused by the greeting he'd witnessed. Paul was not an overly expressive guy, so that friendship went back a lot of years.

Ryan tracked Connie down an hour later, found her in the hallway by the stairwell to the studio, discussing strategy with a group of middle age boys immersed in creating their own action adventure with toy soldiers and toy cars across a landscape of inverted pans and stacked books now turned into a mountain range.

"You need to hold this high ground and watch for a sneak attack. They'll try to come through this pass but in a way that will confuse you, they'll start some kind of diversion to get your attention away from this point."

Connie was aware he was listening in, but mostly ignored him after an initial glance. She walked the boys through how a squad would move to cover for one another and watched as they began another rolling maneuver.

"I need something better than MREs, guys," Connie said, gesturing to the stack of Oreo's beside her, "I'm taking a food pause." She rose gracefully. "Let me see if Ann's got extra hot pad holders. They will work perfect as landing pads for the helicopters."

Ryan was content to follow behind as she maneuvered through the crowd, fixed a plate from the buffet table and carried it into the kitchen, began opening kitchen drawers looking for hot pads. He leaned back against the kitchen counter and ate another stuffed mushroom, chose the moment they had the kitchen to themselves. "Did you succeed?" he asked idly, but with nothing idle about the question. "In raising a child from the dead?"

"I don't discuss what I've seen on a battlefield, Ryan. Even for the sake of making a point." She crowed with success when she found the right drawer and tugged out four squares. She stepped back to the hall with them. "Try these, guys."

She returned to pick up her plate. The conversation from the party crowd drifted into the kitchen in snippets of understandable remarks. Ryan picked up Connie's glass and refilled it for her as she dug into the nachos on her plate. She nodded her thanks. He made an observation. "Nice tan. I meant to remark on that earlier. Given it's winter, it makes a statement."

She grinned. "I like it. Years in the sun rather baked it on."

"Answer me one question."

"One." She scooped up jalapeno dip with a melba toast round.

"Want a job?"

She gave him a long look and laughed. "Thank you, but no. Can I have your flags?"

He offered her the long toothpicks with curled ribbons on top that had pinned meatballs and cheese cubes together.

"Thanks."

She headed out of the kitchen. "Boys, I've got the pendant flags we need for capture the flag. Who wants to be the blue force and who wants red?"

****

Ryan carried his glass into the kitchen, threw away the stack of party plates he'd gathered up, slid silverware into the dishwasher. The last of the guests were leaving in groups as the evening drew to a close. Ann was rinsing off the cake platters. Ryan picked up a towel to dry them and to give himself a private minute with her. "You throw a nice party."

"Thanks. It looks like you and Melinda were having a good conversation."

He gave her a gentle nudge with his shoulder for the matchmaking she'd done and picked up another platter. "I liked her," he agreed. "It's hard not to like a preschool teacher who knows how to fold paper into swans and baby bunnies. I figured out we actually went to the same middle school, even remember a few of the same teachers. We've been crossing paths for decades without being introduced, which rather dates me. You've known Melinda awhile. Care to clue me in on why she's not got the steady boyfriend right now, or the husband?"

"Her parents went through a nasty divorce and she stepped back from thinking she wanted to get married herself, took herself off the available list and spent a few summer breaks touring Europe."

"Yeah, that fits and is helpful. We're having lunch Sunday."

"Good. She's a nice lady, Ryan. Your mom will like her."

He laughed at the additional note. "I'm sure she will."

Ann brought over the trays of remaining cookies. "You'll take a box of leftovers for the hospital staff?"

"Sure."

She boxed cookies and pastries for him. "I'm also glad you got to meet Connie, despite the fireworks."

"She left early."

"Her date, Jason Lasting, plays in a band on Friday nights, so she cut out early to join him."

"My heart is still bleeding from the slice of truth I got handed, but I admit, it feels better to have sorrow for what I didn't do, than just carry the grief. The years of losing kids have been tearing me to shreds, Ann. It feels like I just got walloped by God with a slice of truth and told to quit grieving and do something about it. It's weird, having a conversation as if that's a normal thing to do, to ask Jesus to raise the dead. Connie rather shocks your frame of reference."

Ann picked up one of the cookies and leaned back against the counter to offer reflectively, "Ryan, I spent a career working homicides. I listened to the families grieve, I worked the murder and it never crossed my mind to think about the situation as God saw it. God hates murder. I was standing in a situation brought about by evil, with someone dead who shouldn't be dead. How many of those people was Jesus desiring to raise back to life, if only a Christian had been willing to act? It never crossed my mind to pray for them and ask Jesus to raise them from the dead. That's my regret, Ryan. It never crossed my mind.

"I can think back over names and faces and I know in my heart that number is more than a few. Jesus healed someone dead for four days. Most victims I dealt with had been killed only a few hours to a day before. I should have had the understanding and the faith to ask. Instead, I walked by oblivious to what God might want to do in the situation. I use to think God put me in that profession because justice matters deeply to him and it does. But I think I missed the entire second half of why God put me there. It was to restore life to victims who shouldn't have been dead—and I dropped that ball, didn't act, didn't even consider it. I was likely the only Christian present in a percentage of those cases. If someone was going to ask God to raise them from the dead, it was going to need to be me."

"In cases of murder it seems obvious now, considering the question, that it wasn't God's will for them to be dead."

Ann nodded. "God is sovereign and in control. But it doesn't mean what he wants to have happen is getting done. He gave us responsibility. We don't act, it doesn't get done."

"How did you and Connie meet?"

Ann gathered up the pitchers to rinse out. "You know I've written books about friends in the military."

Ryan nodded. "I've read them."

"My circle of friends and friends of friends, runs deep that direction. We got introduced and have stayed in touch. Paul actually knows her better than I do. She helped him out with a family situation a couple yeas ago. How she handled it convinced me if I ever got in trouble, she'd be in the top three for whom I'd turn to for help. I was glad to hear she was coming back to Chicago after she retired from the military. She's from here originally."

"Just between us Ann, has she done it? Has Connie raised people from the dead?"

"I know the army is dealing with more than one situation it can't explain. I know there are guys who are walking around who shouldn't be given what happened on the battlefield. There's a chaplain she worked with, a George Whittier. They buffer behind each other, downplaying their part and attributing what happens to the other, but neither one really talks about the details of what they've seen. I know the retired officer the Secretary of the Army has asked to help sort out the questions. I can give you some names, if you want to hear the stories from the soldiers themselves. One of them said an IED blew off his leg, but he woke up in the field hospital with both legs intact, being treated for some minor burns and a bad headache. Those kind of stories and rumors of others like it have been floating around for years. George has been an army chaplain for fifteen years. Connie served as a combat medic for eight. I think they met, clicked and have looked at the deaths in war and said this isn't right and they set out to do something about it. Connie's the type to be bold, so yes, I think she probably has succeeded more than once. She's neither confirmed nor denied it. But she doesn't talk like its theory to her."

"Mind giving me her contact information?"

"That would be her decision, but I can tell you where she'll be tomorrow morning."

"That will do."

2

CONNIE AUGUST

The early Saturday morning crowd had filled the tables at the coffee shop and created a short line at the counter. Connie joined the line, tugging off her gloves and dug out the money she'd pushed into her jacket pocket for this stop. Ryan Cooper was at a table by the window eating a cinnamon roll and drinking a mega-size cup of coffee. She'd never seen him in this particular coffee shop before, though Mercy Hospital was only about six blocks north.

"Your usual, Connie?" Linda asked, finishing with the customer ahead of her.

"Yes, thanks." She laid three dollars on the counter.

Ryan walked over to join her and she put two and two together. She had known that remark was going to boomerang on her and it just had.

"Ann said you'd be here between 8 and 8:15."

"I'm becoming worryingly predictable. Good morning, Ryan."

She accepted the sweet roll and the medium dark chocolate coffee from Linda, nodded to the collection jar to donate the change. "Thanks, I'll see you again Monday."

"I'll be here," Linda agreed cheerfully.

Needing to stay on schedule, Connie turned toward the door and Ryan opened it for her. She nodded left. "I'm walking that way. I'm on the way to work and on a clock. Connie's Pizza is open Monday thru Saturday."

"Your place?"

She heard his surprise and realized no one had told him. "I like being my own boss. And you're not here to talk pizza. Why are you here, Ryan?"

"I have a question."

They maneuvered around others on the sidewalk. When she turned east on Voss street the pedestrian traffic cleared making it easier to walk together. "Ask it."

"Some background to it first. My family goes back four generations with Mercy Hospital. I can count over a dozen in my extended family history among its surgeons, doctors and nurses. I'm one of the few that doesn't have a medical degree, rather a business degree. I've been CEO of the hospital for seven years now.

"My uncle is the chaplain at the hospital. I asked him last night if he'd ever prayed to raise the dead. He surprised me by saying he had, a few times. He hadn't been successful in those prayers.

"Walter's a guy who loves people, is a good pastor, hospice leans upon him heavily. The chaplain's office gets high marks for patient and family comfort, they create hope in patients, expectations for recovery, numerous prayers have been said for and with patients for their recovery. He's developed within the chaplain's office a volunteer program around 50 people strong who make sure patients have someone who visits them and prays with them.

"We see results of prayer in the lack of post-op complications, patients not spiraling into more serious problems, patients recovering maybe a day or two faster than you would otherwise expect. But more definite healings, miracles, they are sporadic in the hospital history. You walloped me with the reminder it doesn't need to be that way. I am convinced there is more to healing for today than most Christians understand. And a religious-affiliated hospital should be at the vanguard of that understanding if we're doing our job properly. At a minimum, I want Mercy Hospital to return to having the repeatable capacity to heal the sick by prayer."

"Prayer doesn't heal the sick. Authority does."

He stopped at her correction. She paused her stride too, so she could look at him as she added, "Jesus never prayed for someone who was sick. He healed the sick, he raised the dead, but he never prayed for them. Check the gospels. Prayer is what you do before you walk into the situation which needs you to act. It isn't how you heal."

"Teach me. That's my ask. You clearly know the subject matter in a way I don't."

"Ryan." It wasn't the response she expected, nor what she wanted to hear. She resumed her walk to stay on schedule.

He matched her stride, settling in beside her. "What about James 5:14-16? It's such a cornerstone passage to what the hospital does through the chaplain's office that I can easily quote it. 'Is any among you sick? Let him call for the elders of the church and let them pray over him, anointing him with oil in the name of the Lord; and the prayer of faith will save the sick man and the Lord will raise him up; and if he has committed sins, he will be forgiven. Therefore confess your sins to one another and pray for one another, that you may be healed. The prayer of a righteous man has great power in its effects.'"

"What about it?"

"James instructs us to pray for the sick. That passage is why I'm so frustrated that we aren't seeing more definite healings at Mercy Hospital. We should be."

"There's enough there to get it done," she agreed. "Look closer at the instructions. Pray over him. Anoint him. The prayer of faith. The prayer of a righteous man. Are you sure all of those are talking to God? Over him implies standing beside him looking down at him and speaking. Of faith implies something inside the heart of the person speaking. A righteous man implies a specific type of man and scripture makes it clear you aren't righteous by your own works. Anoint him with oil brings into the picture the Holy Spirit and an action showing an active faith. The prayer, 'God, heal this man', may be sincerely said words from a well meaning volunteer, but it's rarely going to get the job done. 'God, please don't let him die,' is similarly sincere, but it's rarely going to get the job done either."

"You know this stuff in a way I don't and desperately want—need—to know it. Teach me."

"I'm not a teacher."

"Then let me ask you questions and you can give me what answers you know."

"My verbal way of dealing with this topic is to gush information like a burst dam and watch it flatten someone," she replied, knowing reality. "You want the guy who taught me. Who, by the way, is also a chaplain, a patient man, quiet spoken and a good teacher. He'll be retiring from the service later this year. When he arrives in Chicago, I'll make a point of introducing you. He and his wife are moving back here to be near his grandkids. Your uncle and George Whittier are likely the same in temperament and the type to become good friends."

"I'll take the introduction and look forward to meeting him. But I still want your help. I'm hungry, Connie. I'm tired of having patients die whom Jesus would have healed. Not to mention the equally deep desire to see the deeds of Jesus again, the blind see, the lame walk, the deaf hear, the maimed made whole."

"You don't want much, do you?" She shifted her coffee to free a hand to get out keys. "That's my place." She nodded down the block. And she wisely chose not to try and answer him. She understood that hunger, had some answers, but she didn't think she wanted to step into teaching him. She had enough people in the role of students right now.

She gave him credit for accepting the shift of topic with good grace, he turned his attention to where she had nodded and studied the business with interest. This street was old Chicago, when buildings were brick and tall and joined together by common walls, the storefronts narrow. Connie's Pizza was at the end, a tailor shop on one side and an alley on the other.

"I like your place."

She smiled at the mild remark offered before he'd even seen inside. "My uncle began the business back in '57. It was Nick's Pizza back then. The building came to me in his will as his favorite niece. I rented the place to a cookie shop while I was in the army, then reopened it as Connie's Pizza when it was time to retire."

At the storefront, she visually ran a check. The alley was clear of debris, the front window sparkling clean, the sidewalk swept. She could mark those items off her morning list. The homeless in the area had adopted her business and paid her back in goodwill for the pizza she shared without charge. She unlocked the front door and stepped in ahead of Ryan, turning on lights.

The chairs were still upside down atop the tables, picked up the day before so she could mop as the last step in closing. She would open at 10 a.m. and it was 8:35 a.m. As long as she got the oven switched on by 8:40 a.m. she was in good shape, with enough time to finish prep with a few minutes to spare before the door sign turned to 'open'.

"Where's your staff?"

"You're looking at the staff. This is a one person operation. And I've got a routine that is timed to what needs done. No offense, but our conversation is over for now."

"Can I stick around while you prep? I'll stay and have lunch."

"Don't you have somewhere more important to be?"

"No. I've still got questions and I'm the boss of my time."

"I'm the boss of mine, too and I'm about to cram the equivalent of eight hours of work in between now and three p.m. After that, I'm going home to silence for two hours before I decide what my evening will be. And before you ask, no I'm not offering you that time. I've got tentative plans for this evening."

"Understood."

"There's a used bookstore two blocks east that opens at 9 a.m. which has comfortable seating inside to encourage people to linger. Go away until 10:15. If I'm not packed at the opening you can ask one or two questions while I prep pizzas."

"Thanks."

"The odds I'm not packed on a Saturday are slim. This is my busiest day," she warned.

"I'll still take it."

****

RYAN COOPER

Satisfied he had gotten from Connie what he could, Ryan tugged out his phone to see if Margaret had time for a drop-in guest to stop by. If not, the bookstore would suit him.

Connie didn't know him. Didn't know how accustomed he was to dealing with obstacles and figuring out a way around them. Didn't know how serious he was about learning what she knew that could help him. He'd been asking God for a breakthrough and he'd just met someone who understood the topic from experience. A combat medic. It made sense, if there was ever a place where urgency for answers and faith would cross over into breakthrough, it was in a war zone.

"Good morning, Margaret. How's my honorary grandmother this Saturday?"

"Ryan! It is a pleasure to hear your voice."

She sounded like she was fighting the start of a cold, her voice was more raspy than normal. "Like some company? I'm in your area."

"Of course. I just put on coffee."

"Pour me a cup and I'll see you in about five minutes."

He pocketed his phone and headed east. On Saturday's he made it a point to see as many family members as he could. Margaret was family, even if she wasn't a blood relation, loved by the entire Cooper clan.

****

As directed, Ryan arrived back at Connie's Pizza at 10:15. There were two customers entering ahead of him. Ryan pulled open the door after them and the sound of music and voices, the rich aroma of melted cheese, hot tomato sauce and spices, baking bread, met him.

The narrow entryway was set off by a half wall, the other side of the room filled with the tables. Connie's was already busy, several tables had customers. The interior was old, but sparkling clean. The tables and chairs basic metal painted a gloss white with red trim. Connie was assembling a pizza at a long counter ahead of him, an open kitchen behind her showing a commercial conveyor belt oven and three refrigerators. There was a menu of sorts on the wall above her, a list of pizza ingredients. To the right of her work area was a buffet table with warming lights and six large pizzas on it.

She looked up from her work at the sound of the door chime. She subtly shook her head, then gave him a smile. "Welcome, I'm Connie. Looking for some good pizza? You've found the right place." Her hands full of pepperoni slices, she nodded toward the other end of the counter. "Help yourself at the pizza bar. I'm taking requests on what to create if your favorite combination is not there. There's a couple breakfast pizzas in the mix if you prefer that over lunch. Hot Italian sausage and mushroom is coming out next. Drinks are self serve, too."

She didn't want it known they were acquainted, that much was clear. Not knowing why, he tamped down his annoyance and for now went along with it. He nodded his thanks at the information.

"If you like the meal, there's a donation box by the drinks, a dollar a slice covers the costs. If you're light on cash, feel free to eat on the house, as I've got plenty of pizza today." She scanned the room. "I'd recommend laying dibs to one of the window tables, as I hear we're about to get invaded by the neighborhood boys on the community basketball team."

"I appreciate the news."

He moved to the pizza bar and picked up a plate, realized two of the generous slices would cover the plate and started with a slice of the supreme. The drinks on offer were iced tea, lemonade and coffee. There was a heaping plate of large chocolate chip cookies beside the donation box. He settled at a table by the window with his pizza and iced tea and relaxed. It was early for lunch, but he'd been up since five. He was ready for an early lunch.

He watched Connie work while he ate, still puzzled by her waving him off. He liked businesses, how they ran, what made them unique. It was early for the lunch cycle, but Connie's had attracted a dozen customers already with the breakfast and lunch options. She made a fine pizza, he decided after the first bite. Good and hot, likely pulled out of the oven in the last ten minutes. The pizza and its price would certainly bring back repeat customers. He watched the flow of people as he ate, nearly all locals who knew each other from the way they greeted one another.

No waitress staff, no one bussing tables, just one person in the kitchen. It made business sense. If the donation box wasn't pilfered and folks were honest, she'd cover her costs and make a reasonable profit. She slipped a tray of bread sticks into the flow of cooking pizzas and coated them with garlic butter when they came out. The aroma of baking bread was itself enough to make customers hungry.

Connie shifted tasks, bringing clean plates to the buffet counter, hauling used plates into the kitchen and disappearing with them. She was back a minute later with pitchers to top off the drink fountains. A commercial dishwasher, run all of the plates through after hours—she must be doing the back kitchen work herself too. He admired what he was seeing.

He went back for more pizza, selected a slice of what looked like four kinds of cheese and one thick with pepperoni, picked up one of the chocolate chip cookies for dessert.

She knew her customers, her laughter was part of the backdrop. The music wasn't a radio station—no commercials—the changing songs a nice variety, some contemporary pop as he heard the band Triple M begin a song, some Christian music, some country. She had put together a nice eclectic playlist.

The boys from the basketball team streamed in as a group. There was never a lull, either in customers, or the number of pizzas she kept bringing out to the buffet, swapping empty pans for hot new offerings. It became obvious as a half hour passed that his table was going to be needed for incoming customers.

She caught his attention and did a come up wave of her hand. He cleared his table for another customer to use, slid a large bill wrapped by a one into the donation box and picked up a second cookie to take with him. He walked up to the counter as she switched to using an ice cream scoop to dip out more cookie dough onto a tray. "Not admitting you know me?" he asked quietly, still puzzled.

"A very nice hypochondriac seated at table two just left with her sister. Your line of questions would have set her nerves all a flutter and she's inquisitive enough she'd put together your hospital connection. From that point on, you'd be in serious trouble if ever spotted again. I was gifting you with some peace."

Ryan smiled. "Then accepted and thank you."

"Find the bookstore?"

"Filled in the time visiting a friend in the neighborhood."

"I'm afraid this isn't going to be a good time to handle questions and if I'm this busy now, it's only going to get more so in the next hour."

"I can see why you're busy. It's good pizza."

"Thanks." She sent the tray of chocolate chip cookies through the conveyer oven, returned and switched back to prepping the next pizza. He mentally did some math and realized there must be a thousand prior ones behind the speed at which she created that supreme. She was not chinsey with ingredients as the cheese mounded on. “The food’s also offered at great prices. You’re making a profit?”

She smiled at the question. “I’ve been in the black since the second week I was open. Low overhead helps and I don’t mind the pace of the work. I’m still enjoying the first year novelty of running my own business. I’m curious. Who did you go see? Your friend in the neighborhood.”

“Margaret Voss. And before you ask, she’s no relation to the guy they named the street after a hundred years ago.”

“Okay. We’ve not been introduced.”

“You’d like her. Margaret is a young 77. Tends toward sweaters with roses on them; lost her husband ten years ago. She’s my unofficial grandmother.”

Connie nodded. “I’ll introduce myself when I see her in the neighborhood.”

“Appreciate that.” Two more customers had come in while they were chatting, one had left and Connie made a point to smile a greeting, share a nod goodbye. It was time to head on, he was interrupting the flow of her business. As he took a step back, she stopped him with an offer.

“I’ll move up my morning by fifteen minutes. You can meet me at the coffee shop at 7:45 and I’ll change the route of my walk to pass by the hospital. We can talk on the walk and we’ll part ways there. It’s what I can offer, so it’s basically take it or leave it.”

“I’ll take it,” he replied promptly. “And I’ll see you Monday.”

“Take a couple cookies to go, more are coming out.”

He glanced over his shoulder at the laughing boys clustered around four tables they’d pulled together and had to smile. “Another time. You’re going to need every one of them soon.”

“They do like to eat. Sorry it got this busy.”

“Don’t be. Your place is the definition of a neighborhood gem locals love.”

He lifted a hand in farewell and headed out, well satisfied with his morning. Connie was a woman not afraid of hard work. And the hook had set, she'd volunteered a way she could help him. That was the definition of success in his own line of work. Those minutes of a morning were going to be priceless to him. He wouldn't abuse the gift, but he'd make full use of them.

Sole proprietor. Proud of her business. Mid-thirties. Family ties to the location and she owned the building. She'd stay put and be a gem in this community for decades to come. He glanced at the hours on the door as it closed behind him. Open ten a.m. to two p.m., closed on Sundays. He'd pay her a second visit when he was again in the area. This was the kind of place where you slipped an extra fifty in as a tip and it benefited an entire community. That opening remark, to eat on the house if cash was light, hadn't been added for his benefit, it was part of the welcome introduction she'd given to every first time customer who had come through the door. She was feeding the hungry and doing it with a smile, regardless of the cash in their pocket. She probably had some regulars slipping her a few extra dollars when they could for that very reason.

Ryan headed back to the hospital to pick up his car, mentally rescheduling his Monday morning. "Thanks, God," he said softly. He felt lighter than he had in months, just with the hope that answers were coming.

3

Ryan arrived at the coffee shop at 7:40 a.m. Monday, loath to be the one who was late. Connie entered at 7:44, waited through the short line and asked for her usual. She joined him with a smile. “So you took me up on the offer.”

He held up his own coffee. “Alert and ready, teach.”

She laughed at his reply. He held the door for her and they stepped outside. Connie tucked her scarf tighter around her jacket collar and took a long drink of her coffee. “It’s cold. Let’s move briskly.”

Ryan agreed with both remarks and set a pace that would warm them up with the exercise. They headed toward the hospital. She glanced over with surprise as he held out his phone angled to her.

“I’m recording the conversations,” he explained, “audio only, since the video would just jump around. I don’t want to ask you to repeat something you’ve already told me—you would find that annoying—and this way I can share the conversations with people later when I’m trying to explain something you said. They can hear it in your own words.”

“Thinking ahead, I admire your confidence. I just hope your hand doesn’t freeze and you drop that expensive phone.”

He laughed. “I’m good, I promise.”

“I can’t take you where you want to go, Ryan, without teaching you how to get there. So we’ll call this lesson one. Let’s start with scripture.

Bless the LORD, O my soul;
and all that is within me, bless his holy name!
Bless the LORD, O my soul,
and forget not all his benefits

"Where am I quoting from? Do you know?"

"I don't know the passage. It sounds like the Psalms," Ryan replied.

She nodded. "I'm quoting Psalm 103. This is a Psalm of David. There are three things it's helpful to remember about David: He is the anointed King of Israel, the Holy Spirit rests upon him and the New Testament calls him a Prophet. There is no one similar to David in the bible for the prominence God gives him as the example for who Jesus will be. Jesus is referred to as the Son of David, one who sits on the throne of David. God calls David a man after his own heart; Jesus is God's 'beloved son with whom I am well pleased.'

"David is not just speaking to the nation of Israel in this Psalm. God is using David to speak to all his people across all the ages: to the Jews under the first covenant of the law and to both the Jews and Gentiles under the second covenant which ushered in the church. This Psalm describes what God will do through Jesus. God fulfilled bringing us these benefits through Jesus. Listen to the opening verses:

Bless the LORD, O my soul;
and all that is within me, bless his holy name!
Bless the LORD, O my soul,
and forget not all his benefits,
who forgives all your iniquity,
who heals all your diseases,
who redeems your life from the Pit,
who crowns you with steadfast love and mercy,
who satisfies you with good as long as you live
so that your youth is renewed like the eagle's.
(Psalms 103:1-5)

Connie paused a moment to let him reflect on the verses, then said, "Bless the Lord O my soul and forget not all his benefits. How many Christians can name them? How many Christians understand, trust and believe those are God's benefits to them? Listen to the list again:

> who forgives all your iniquity,
> who heals all your diseases,
> who redeems your life from the Pit,
> who crowns you with steadfast love and mercy,
> who satisfies you with good as long as you live
> so that your youth is renewed like the eagle's.

Connie went quiet so he could think about what she had said. Until she had quoted the passage, he couldn't remember hearing it before, though he knew he had read through all the Psalms more than once in his life. He shifted his phone just enough to flip open the bible app and find the passage, read it again and pinned it for quick reference.

"Are you healed right now Ryan?"

He took a moment trying to figure out how to truthfully answer her question in light of his last physical. After about five seconds she simply reached over and patted his jacket sleeve. "How can you successfully ask God to give a gift of healing to someone else when you aren't even sure he has given it to you?"

Connie's words were a lighter punch than last Friday's comment, but they connected. He had to offer a rueful smile. "Point made."

"I'll let you redeem yourself. Answer me these questions. According to Psalm 103, who forgives everything you have ever done wrong?"

"God."

"Who heals you?"

"God."

"Who redeems your life?"

"God."

"Who crowns you with steadfast love and mercy?"

"God."

"Who satisfies you with good always?"

"God."

"What's your part in having those benefits?"

He tried to carefully answer. "Not forgetting them. Knowing they are my benefits. Wanting them. Accepting them."

Connie nodded. "Good answer. Not a single one of those benefits comes because of your own works."

She gave him time to think about it as she finished her coffee, then remarked, "God gives really spectacular free gifts. It would be good if we knew what they were. We perish for lack of knowledge. Lack of knowledge of God's word and faith in God's word. We basically don't trust the God who wrote those words. We can't list his benefits. We don't believe them when we hear them. And then we wonder why we struggle as Christians."

She glanced over to kindly smile at him. "You really want lesson two?"

He laughed. "I admit, I'm going to feel like a piece of swiss cheese by the time you get done skewering me with truth, taking me through what you know, but I'm not walking in this cold because I want the easy teacher who grades on a curve. What's lesson two?"

"You are a brave man. Exodus 15:26b. 'I am the LORD, your healer.' We'll get to it tomorrow."

The hospital was up ahead. They were about to part ways. He reluctantly shut off the recording. "Thanks, Connie. This was very helpful."

"If you show up for coffee tomorrow, you can expect to be asked what your five benefits are."

"Homework. And you say you're not a teacher."

She laughed. "Goodbye, Ryan."

She turned away from the hospital in the direction of her pizza shop. Half a block away, she turned. "Hey, Ryan." He slipped off the earpiece, having started the conversation playing back so he could go through it again. "What's that way?" She pointed west toward the other buildings in the hospital complex.

"Beyond the clinic buildings, mostly parking lots and the hospital rehab center, the garden park." The clinic buildings where doctors saw patients were hospital owned but mostly leased out to physician groups.

Connie looked at her phone judging the time. “Give me six more minutes and let’s circle as far as the garden park. I’m getting nudged pretty hard to say one more thing.”

“Sure.”

He walked back to join her and set a new recording to start. He led the way toward the garden park and, conscious of the time limit, didn’t interrupt to ask what she meant by that nudge remark, filing it away to ask later.

Connie began with a comment. “There’s a scripture in Hebrews that is a warning the Holy Spirit directed Paul to write to believers:

Take care, brethren, lest there be in any of you an evil, unbelieving heart, leading you to fall away from the living God. But exhort one another every day, as long as it is called “today,” that none of you may be hardened by the deceitfulness of sin. For we share in Christ, if only we hold our first confidence firm to the end, (Hebrews 3:12-14)

“I need to offer an important comment about God. He’s righteous and he’s made us righteous like him. We hear that word, but it often goes by as a concept and doesn’t always sink in. I’d like to make it practical. Listen to these attributes of God.

This is the message we have heard from him and proclaim to you, that God is light and in him is no darkness at all. (1 John 1:5)

Every good endowment and every perfect gift is from above, coming down from the Father of lights with whom there is no variation or shadow due to change. Of his own will he brought us forth by the word of truth that we should be a kind of first fruits of his creatures. (James 1:17-18)

God is not man, that he should lie,
or a son of man, that he should repent.
Has he said and will he not do it?
Or has he spoken and will he not fulfil it?
(Numbers 23:19)

And the word of the LORD came to me, saying, "Jeremiah, what do you see?" And I said, "I see a rod of almond." Then the LORD said to me, "You have seen well, for I am watching over my word to perform it." (Jeremiah 1:11-12)

"That last one is a play on words; the Hebrew words for almonds and watching are a single letter apart. God was giving Jeremiah a visual way to remember his point," Connie explained.

"That's God, as the Holy Spirit Himself would have us see Him. God is light. God keeps his word, He performs it. God does not lie. I like how God's interactions with us illustrate that. Listen to what a verse says about his relationship with Sarah.

The LORD visited Sarah as he had said and the LORD did to Sarah as he had promised. (Genesis 21:1)

"God is faithful, he keeps his word, he does not lie," Connie stressed.

"Got it," Ryan replied.

She smiled. "Do you? Because God equips us to be the same—to be faithful, to keep our word, to not lie. He's made us righteous like himself." She paused and then shifted the conversation the other direction. "Now I want you to switch from thinking about God and righteousness, to the devil and evil.

He [the devil] was a murderer from the beginning and has nothing to do with the truth, because there is no truth in him. When he lies, he speaks according to his own nature, for he is a liar and the father of lies. (John 8:44b)

The thief [satan] comes only to steal and kill and destroy (John 10:10a)

The reason the Son of God appeared was to destroy the works of the devil. (1 John 3:8b)

"See clearly the difference between God and satan?" Connie asked.

Ryan had to smile at the question she had set him up to answer. "I do."

Connie nodded. "Good. Then let me make a very serious point: one of the deepest errors we can ever make in our Christian walk is to think God isn't telling us the truth. Don't ever offend God by thinking he is like satan. God does not lie. We can have questions, wonder about things and need help from God to figure out our experience in the light of the scripture; that's growing up in Christ. But saying something God wrote in his word isn't true is to call God a liar. We are so painfully wrong in our thinking about our God at times that we have to be reminded of the most basic fact that God does not lie."

Ryan registered her point and more seriously nodded.

Connie thought for a moment then added, "It helps if we see the picture of just how stark the difference is between God and satan. For one thing satan is not God's equal, satan is a created being, an angel; whose parallel would be the angel Gabriel or the angel Michael. Satan is not all knowing, not all powerful, not able to be everywhere at the same time. God is all those things.

"Satan went from being an angel of light standing in God's presence leading worship, one of the three chief angels, one of the most beautiful beings in all God's creation, to stumbling, letting in pride and scripture says iniquity was found in him. God hurled Lucifer out of his presence and changed his name to satan. Satan's sin was to want the worship that was due only to God. That pride has consumed satan. All that was beautiful in him has turned to only darkness as he's now outside of God's presence, outside of God's light.

"A man, consumed by sin and evil thoughts, dies and his evil dies with him. Our darkness is limited to what accumulates in a lifetime. Satan never dies. There has been no end to his ever-increasing darkness. Satan has thoroughly become the evil one. The angels who fell with him have become demons as they too now live outside the light of God. At the last judgment, satan and the demons will be cast in the lake of fire for eternity to remove their evil from creation.

"Man thinks a little darkness is no big deal, we all have sinned; God's grace will cover us. And His grace will, but it is designed to pull us out of that sin and darkness spiral, not to make us comfortable with some darkness left in us because we're too lazy to renew our minds and put on Christ. God calls us to be children of light.

"We listen to God's word, but do not hear the truth, when our hearts have grown hard. The truth doesn't register with us. What God is saying, it doesn't sink in. That's the warning the Holy Spirit had Paul write. Don't harden your heart. Guard against doubt. Questions are fine and good and how the Lord teaches wisdom. Admitting you don't understand something is a humble move which lets God guide and teach you from that point to find and understand the truth. But to close the door to the word of God with a thought 'that's not true' can be one of the most devastating self-inflicted injuries you can do to yourself.

"God is righteous, a God in whom there is no darkness. Don't ever offend God by attributing to him the darkness which is in satan. Satan is a liar. God is not. What God has written in his word is true.

Bless the LORD, O my soul;
and all that is within me, bless his holy name!
Bless the LORD, O my soul,

and forget not all his benefits,
who forgives all your iniquity,
who heals all your diseases,
who redeems your life from the Pit,
who crowns you with steadfast love and mercy,
who satisfies you with good as long as you live
so that your youth is renewed like the eagle's.
(Psalms 103:1-5)

"And with that, I'm two minutes past my stretched time and going to have to move like lightning. Sorry," Connie said, already moving away.

"Go," Ryan urged.

She tossed her empty coffee cup in a trash barrel and set out at a comfortable run toward her shop. Ryan watched the grace of her movements. She'd spent years running, that stride wasn't a self-conscious woman trying to run for exercise. Combat medic. He reminded himself with the title just what her life had been like for eight years.

Ryan realized he hadn't shut off the recording and did so, glad he had that extra eight minutes recorded.

He turned back to the main hospital building and wondered aloud, "God, how many times recently have I just assumed the reason my experience wasn't yielding results was because you were speaking in a generalized way? I'd read that 'the prayer of faith will save the sick man' and mentally add on the word 'sometimes', never facing the fact I was calling you a liar by doing so. My head and my heart hurt right now and that was only about 25 minutes with her. Forgive me, God, sincerely, for not believing your word means what it says. I asked what the problem was and you just held up a mirror to show me part of the problem is me."

The Holy Spirit had sliced clean, Ryan was grateful for that. Delivered the blow but not pressed on the weight of the guilt after his eyes opened. Ryan slipped in the earpiece and replayed Connie's words as he turned toward the hospital main building to listen to it again, using his bible app as he walked to locate the scriptures she had quoted.

Greek and Hebrew were rich languages, to get English to give the same nuances in meaning as the original scripture texts took more words and it was useful to hear how three or even four translators rendered a passage. Ryan found Connie had memorized passages mostly from the Revised Standard Version. That translation was a little older than the New International Version he primarily used. The timing made sense, RSV had been widely used about the time she would have been in high school; it had probably been her first personal bible and the one she had been memorizing scriptures from since her youth.

He'd be wise to start some study notes for these conversations as they were going to be rich in verses if this one was typical. She wasn't just quoting scripture, her statements themselves were often referencing scripture. These were going to be very useful walks.

****

Ryan Notes / conversation one / additional references

My people are destroyed for lack of knowledge (Hosea 4:6a)

Now war arose in heaven, Michael and his angels fighting against the dragon; and the dragon and his angels fought, but they were defeated and there was no longer any place for them in heaven. And the great dragon was thrown down, that ancient serpent, who is called the Devil and Satan, the deceiver of the whole world -- he was thrown down to the earth and his angels were thrown down with him. And I heard a loud voice in heaven, saying, "Now the salvation and the power and the kingdom of our God and the authority of his Christ have come, for the accuser of our brethren has been thrown down, who accuses them day and night before our God. And they have conquered him by the blood of the Lamb and by the word of their testimony, for they loved not their lives even unto death. Rejoice then, O heaven and you that dwell therein! But woe to you, O earth and sea, for the devil has come down to you in great wrath, because he knows that his time is short!" (Revelation 12:7-12)

He who commits sin is of the devil; for the devil has sinned from the beginning. (1 John 3:8a)

4

Tuesday morning Connie walked into the coffee shop at 7:45 a.m. and Ryan simply said "Connie" and nodded to his table. He'd remembered her standing order and bought it for her before she arrived to save her the time in line.

She accepted with a grateful smile, took a first sip of the coffee and let him hold the door. "I wasn't sure you would show after round one with me."

He smiled. "What can I say, I'm a man who knows what's good for me can occasionally sting. I can take hearing truth, even when it's personally convicting." He made an observation, wondering how she'd take the personal remark. "You look particularly tired, Connie," he mentioned, concerned.

"A long night," she replied, "which makes the coffee even more appreciated." She didn't explain further. She nodded to his phone. "You'll need the recording today, this lesson has branches. Exodus 15:26b. 'I am the LORD, your healer.' How many names does God give himself?"

She went straight to the topic of the day and he switched to follow her, glad he knew this answer. "Seven. I AM the Lord who sees you. I AM the Lord who provides. I AM the Lord your victory, something like that. The other three escape me."

She nodded. "In Hebrew the names were like hyphenated words, they weren't such a mouthful as the English translations. They're like us saying one of our titles is CPA, Doctor, Pilot, Lawyer. The title is a statement of our training and skill, what you can expect us to be an expert at doing. God's names are self-given statements about himself. Unlike how we would say 'I am a writer', or 'I am a doctor' and its part of who we are, but not the whole of us, God's names are more like facets of his being, a deeper statement of who he is all the way through. And

God says one of his names is 'I AM the Lord your Healer.'"

She ate part of the sweet roll with obvious pleasure before she continued, nodding her thanks for that breakfast. "God tells his people that name at the time of the Exodus. They've left Egypt and are heading across the wilderness to the promised land. God is ready to pile on them good gifts, to give them, in his own words, 'great and goodly cities, which you did not build and houses full of all good things, which you did not fill and cisterns hewn out, which you did not hew and vineyards and olive trees, which you did not plant' (Deuteronomy 6:10b,11a) It's a pretty cool list. That's our God, how he thinks when he says 'I'm going to bless you.' We underestimate today what God's idea of being good to his people looks like. Anyway. Even before Israel gets to that promised land, God has started blessing them by announcing this one of his seven names."

She glanced at him, curious. "Why do we think we have to talk God into healing people? He likes healing people. God basically hung out a shingle that said, 'I'm your doctor, appointments are free' and wanted anyone who got sick to come see him.

"And where did we get the idea that God stopped being himself?" Connie asked with wonder. "God didn't change his name after a hundred years and say, 'I've had enough of this, no one comes and I don't really like healing people anymore anyway.' No, the Father says about himself in the Old Testament book of Malachi 'I the LORD do not change' It's Malachi 3:6a. He's always been a God who defines himself as 'I AM the Lord your Healer.'"

Connie drank more of her coffee and Ryan chose not to interrupt with a comment, as time on this walk was all too brief.

"David was King of Israel around roughly 1,000 B.C.," Connie mentioned. "So the Exodus goes back to something like 1,500 B.C. One thousand five hundred years after God says 'I AM the Lord your Healer', Jesus shows up and heals every person who comes to him of *every* disease and says 'I'm only doing my Father's will'. That's a pretty amazing picture. God the Father clearly hadn't changed his name in over fifteen hundred years.

"Jesus healed people because the power of the Holy Spirit rested upon him. The Holy Spirit is God. And God likes to heal, its one of his self-given names. After the resurrection, Jesus returns to heaven and the Holy Spirit arrives more broadly on earth with the birth of the church. He's here to dwell with us and be in us, those who believe in Jesus, forever. Now what do you think the Holy Spirit would like to do for you and me and everyone around us? Heal us. The Holy Spirit with us today is the exactly same Holy Spirit which descended from heaven and remained on Jesus. And right now he's walking around earth with us marveling at all the sick people we simply let walk past."

Connie paused their conversation and Ryan realized she was studying the people coming their direction, taking to heart her own words. She let ten people walk by, then quietly said, "Headaches, flu, back pain. And we walk right by without offering help in Jesus' name."

She shifted from that remark back to her topic without explaining further and Ryan nearly interrupted. He needed more time with her than these brief walks were giving him, because he heard the confidence in her remark that she could in fact help those passing by be healed. He was so incredibly hungry to understand how to do just that.

"God is a triune God, three persons who are one," Connie continued. "God the Father, God the Son, Jesus our Savior and God the Holy Spirit. God is three persons and yet one, the trinity. In the New Testament, the Holy Spirit is also called the Spirit of God, the Spirit of Jesus and the Spirit of Grace. Think of the Holy Spirit as the innermost part of God. If you want to know God's heart, just look at what the Holy Spirit is doing. And scripture says it's by the Holy Spirit we are being healing today.

If the Spirit of him who raised Jesus from the dead dwells in you, he who raised Christ Jesus from the dead will give life to your mortal bodies also through his Spirit which dwells in you. (Romans 8:11)

"God likes to heal. If he didn't, he would have said so. Instead, he made healing one of his very names. We need to get a clear look at that truth and let it plant itself firmly in our hearts. The Father doesn't change. He never will. And Jesus, who is the image of the Father, doesn't change. He never will, either. Hebrews 13:8 says 'Jesus Christ is the same yesterday and today and for ever.'"

Her phone rang and she ignored it. They were almost at the hospital. "God encourages us to get to know him, to realize that because there's no variation of change in Him, we can trust what we learn to always be true. God is reassuring us that every little bit we figure out about Him is going to be true forever. God likes to heal people. He will like to heal people for all eternity. That's the lesson for today.

"We do not have to convince God to heal someone. He's been the God who wants to heal us for the last three thousand five hundred years, ever since he announced His name to us. He hasn't changed in his willingness or desire or power to do so. The problem the church is dealing with is not with God. It's in us."

Connie stopped walking, for they were at the hospital corner, but didn't immediately turn toward her pizza shop. "For homework, Ryan. You know enough now to be dangerous to the kingdom of darkness. You know God's name. I want you to think about that name until you trust it. Then I want you to go use it.

"Choose a volunteer patient willing to learn with you, someone with a good heart who can laugh with you, relax with you. After you have both listened to this conversation, pray for each other. Put your hand on their arm and say, 'In Jesus' name, I give God the Father, who wants to heal you, permission to heal you by the Holy Spirit. And I give God the Father permission to heal me by the Holy Spirit as well. Amen.' Amen means 'So be it', it's like the gavel of a judge coming down, rendering, declaring, what is to be, into existence. After you've both prayed that for each another, just say 'thank you, God' and trust him to do exactly what you've both asked. I want you to both experience healing as well as experience giving it.

"I want you to anticipate God's answer and come with expectancy into every new day. You put a seed into good soil. The word of God planted in your heart by a faith-filled prayer. You're now watching what grows. Don't speak a single word of judgment – 'I don't think anything happened', 'I don't see anything different', just shut your mouth and watch day by day what changes. In a week, you can tell me what you've observed. If healing hasn't appeared visibly by then, we'll have another conversation."

"I've got someone in mind," Ryan mentioned, thinking about Nathan Dell. "Thanks, Connie."

"Remember God likes to heal. We're his sons and daughters and he loves to use us to bring that good news to people. Thanks for the breakfast," she added, as she turned toward her business. "I'll see you tomorrow."

"I'll be there." Ryan closed the recording and walked on to the hospital.

He was coming to understand the problem in him. He knew the information. He had heard 'I AM the Lord your Healer' before, but hadn't put it together as she had, to see the arc of that truth across the scriptures. To *see* God, the Healer. Ryan thought back and felt ashamed of the way he'd handled that verse in the past. When someone he prayed for didn't get healed, he reminded God He was the healer, as if God had forgotten and didn't look further for the source of the problem. He reasoned he just hadn't convinced God to heal the person. Connie had just kicked the legs out from under that stool. God's character hadn't changed and never would. God was still the healer who liked to heal and always would be. The problem he was dealing with wasn't with God.

"God, I'm impatient to see results change, to see many patients healed. I'll accept Connie's homework assignment and see Nathan Dell this afternoon. Teach me, Holy Spirit and let this lesson from today sink in deep. I'm truly sorry, God, for all the times I've doubted your willingness to heal. Every failure has just sunk my skepticism in deeper, but I learned the wrong lesson. I thought I had to convince you to heal. Ouch. Have I ever been buying into a lie satan was selling. I got your character wrong and from it has come a host of self-inflicted errors. I repent—my thinking just changed. I've seen you with Connie's help and I know your name. You're my God and you like to heal people.

"Connie's right. I know enough now I can be dangerous to the kingdom of darkness. And my hope is rising fast. Keep lighting my path, Dad. Keep healing my heart and correct my thinking. I can feel confidence building, faith and the certainty things are going to change in my experience. I will see people healed. You are very willing to heal people and you're going to use me, because I'm your son, to show people your love for them. This is turning into a very interesting set of conversations."

****

Ryan located related scriptures as he listened to the audio again that night, adding them to the notes he was making.

Ryan Notes / conversation two / additional references

The seven names God gives himself
God is our Righteousness
God is our Peace
God is our Guide / Shepherd
God is our Physician / Healer
God is our Provider / Source
God is Ever Present
God is our Victory

On the last day of the feast, the great day, Jesus stood up and proclaimed, "If any one thirst, let him come to me and drink. He who believes in me, as the scripture has said, `Out of his heart shall flow rivers of living water.'" Now this he said about the Spirit, which those who believed in him were to receive; for as yet the Spirit had not been given, because Jesus was not yet glorified. (John 7:37-39)

And I will pray the Father and he will give you another Counselor, to be with you for ever, even the Spirit of truth, whom the world cannot receive, because it neither sees him nor knows him; you know him, for he dwells with you and will be in you. (John 14:16-17)

But the Counselor, the Holy Spirit, whom the Father will send in my name, he will teach you all things and bring to your remembrance all that I have said to you. (John 14:26)

When the Spirit of truth comes, he will guide you into all the truth; for he will not speak on his own authority, but whatever he hears he will speak and he will declare to you the things that are to come. He will glorify me, for he will take what is mine and declare it to you. (John 16:13-14)

5

Wednesday morning brought a burst of mild spring weather. Ryan changed his order to an iced coffee to celebrate and shared a snack sack of donut holes with Connie as they walked, doing his best to keep his phone far enough away from the sack so as not to pick up the noise of rustling paper.

"How does God do stuff?" Connie asked. "God is Spirit, he's invisible, he lives in an invisible world called heaven and yet he made the visible one. What does the bible tell us about how God does stuff? How does the invisible affect the visible?"

Ryan offered one verse that came to mind. "In creation, 'God said, "Let there be light"; and there was light.'"

Connie nodded. "Genesis 1:3a." She held out her hand and the sunlight highlighted her skin. She turned her hand and let the light play across her palm. "God speaks and things happen in the visible world. I'm showing you one of the most beautiful examples of that right now. Look at the light landing on my hand. God's first recorded words, 'Let there be light' and I'm basking in his words right now. I can trace the light and the warmth I'm feeling directly to God's first words recorded in Genesis. That is astonishing. And it's a profound truth into understanding what scripture is and how it works. The word of God creates tangible reality in the visible world. We're still enjoying the words He spoke at creation.

"God's words have always had power in them. What God says happens. 'Let there be light'; and there was light. God speaks and what he says comes to pass. One of the keys to understanding God and our relationship with Him is to understand how the invisible and visible are linked by words.

By faith we understand that the world was created by the word of God, so that what is seen was made out of things which do not appear. (Hebrews 11:3)

"Lesson one, God doesn't lie. It's more than a moral statement about God, a statement of his righteousness, though it is that. I actually think it's impossible for God to lie. His words create and do what he's spoken. To lie, God would have to speak a word without power in it. I don't think it's possible for God to speak a word without power in it. God speaks and his words make stuff happen in the visible realm. God speaks and what he says comes to pass.

"Now Jesus comes to earth, sent by the Father. Jesus comes to earth as a man. He has emptied himself, literally set aside his power as God. Jesus is a man with a human nature like ours. Yet Jesus speaks and what he says comes to pass. 'Peace! Be still!' And the wind and waves obey him.

And he [Jesus] awoke and rebuked the wind and said to the sea, "Peace! Be still!" And the wind ceased and there was a great calm. He said to them [his disciples in the boat with him], "Why are you afraid? Have you no faith?" And they were filled with awe and said to one another, "Who then is this, that even wind and sea obey him?" (Mark 4:39-41)

"Jesus is a man, but he's acting a lot like God. His words are impacting the visible world. Material things obey the words of Jesus. Why? How's that possible?"

Ryan didn't try to answer, recognizing Connie was unfolding a thought with the questions.

"Jesus is using words like God uses words, to change the visible world by what he says. Jesus is a man of like nature as us. When he's ordering things around, he's doing so as a man. The key is that Jesus is also the Son of God, a man born of the Holy Spirit, with the Holy Spirit resting upon him. Jesus' words were causing stuff to happen by using the Father's power, by drawing on the family connection. Jesus has the authority the Father has, because he is a son.

"Jesus didn't have to be adopted to be that son. He was God's first-born son. His standing as a son of God was sufficient for the man Jesus to be able to act as God does, for his words to have power, even though Jesus as a man was just as limited as we are.

"Jesus told Peter to 'Come!' and Peter walked on water. Jesus spoke a word of command and in that word was the power of God to do what that word said.

"There are two types of men in the world, walking around on earth. Fallen men, whose words have no power. And born-again men, adopted sons of God, born of the Holy Spirit, whose words have been restored to power. Believers will use words the same way Jesus uses them.

"...For truly, I say to you, if you have faith as a grain of mustard seed, you will say to this mountain, `Move from here to there,' and it will move; and nothing will be impossible to you." (Matthew 17:20b)

"We are the adopted sons of God, we have the Holy Spirit dwelling in us. Jesus is impressing upon us that God will treat us as true sons. Our words will cause things to happen. Just as God's words create and do what He has said, just as Jesus' words create and do what he said, our words will create and do what we say.

"There is a reality to how God does stuff and how a son of God does stuff. And that's our reality now. When Jesus says your words move mountains he is not being figurative. Jesus was showing us how a son of God does stuff. We use our words. 'Nothing will be impossible to you.' Jesus is being literal. Jesus means exactly that, with all the implications those words *nothing* and *impossible* convey. Our words now have power because we are children of God. True sons.

"To understand prayer, you have to realize you are not speaking powerless words that a fallen man might say. You are a true son of God and your words have the power to change the visible world. We have been adopted; we are sons of God. We have authority in our words when they are spoken with faith."

She looked ahead and stopped. They were at the hospital. Yet another morning was ending with a thought of massive substance being offered and she was going to simply leave it there. Ryan wanted the next five sentences, the next five paragraphs, but it wasn't fair to make her late to work. "Thank you Connie." He closed the recording. "I'm looking forward to the rest of this conversation."

She smiled. "It does go interesting directions. Goodbye for now, Ryan." She turned away to jog toward her shop.

****

Ann brought lunch with her, lasagna from Saputo's and Ryan gladly stopped reading emails long enough to join her at the table in his office.

"Paul wanted me to give you that," she said, as she nodded to an envelope. "I think you can mark the funding that you need for the rehab pool repairs off your list. One of the Olympic athletes who now swims professionally, coaches others, was looking for a like charitable cause. The topic came up and Paul remembered your need."

Ryan opened the envelope, read the letter and glanced at the check. "I'm going to thank the giver personally and gladly accept. You'll convey my thanks to Paul?"

"Sure."

Ryan found them more napkins. "How's Gina?"

Ann opened the foil wrapped package of bread sticks. "Doing great. She goes home tomorrow afternoon, her twin girls will likely go home on Saturday. You have very nice staff working the maternity wing."

"I gladly accept all compliments on their behalf. We try." Ryan tasted the lasagna and it was even better than his memory. "So what else brings me a good lunch and your company?"

"Curiosity. So did you meet up with Connie?"

Ryan nodded as he reached back to his desk for the drink he'd left there. "Saturday, yes I did. We've been connecting every day actually. I meet her at the coffee shop, we talk while we walk, part ways at the hospital so she can head on to work. Or more accurately she talks and I record the conversation on my phone, while I try to grasp as much as I can the first time I hear it. Connie says she's not a teacher, but she's actually rather brilliant in the way she densely packs information together."

"I think she's accustomed to choosing words of impact. 'No bleeding. No infection. No pain. Just healed, in Jesus name,'" Ann murmured as a quote. "The medic's prayer. I realized recently it originated with Connie, or possibly with George who taught it to her. They needed something powerful in ten seconds or less when they were handling an IED blast with numerous casualties. They'd race through the casualties to assess and pray the medic's prayer for each, then prioritize on the one who was going to die first. I'm told by people who know the details no one in that division died from an IED blast after they began using that prayer."

Ryan glanced to the metrics on his wall and would love to see a few of those charts drop to zero. "She hasn't mentioned that prayer yet, but it makes sense, given the situations they were dealing with."

"If its not private material, could I ask if you'd be willing to share copies of those conversation audios? I know it would be fascinating material to hear."

"Sure. Connie knows I'm recording them so I can share them with interested individuals. My uncle has been listening to them and my brother. We've been keeping the topic in the family for now."

He sent her a copy of those on his phone.

Ann confirmed receipt with a nod. “Thanks.” She put her phone back away. “Connie’s got a group she teaches, Ryan. Tuesday nights, sometimes Thursdays.”

“Really… she hasn’t mentioned that either.”

“It’s invitation only from what I hear and much like AA. You don’t talk about it. Mostly, I think, so she doesn’t get peppered by questions from those who hear only bits and pieces and want to challenge something they’ve heard.”

“You know the group exists how?”

Ann shrugged. “A friend cut out of a gathering early, another begged off an invitation and I know the building manager where they’ve occasionally gathered. Pieces filter together when you spent too much of your life as a detective. It’s hard to shut off the habit.” She picked up a breadstick and smiled at him. “So tell me about Melinda. How was the date Sunday?”

“Now I hear the real reason you stopped by.” Ryan thought about the three hours they had spent together. “She is a delightful woman.”

Ann laughed at the way he said it. “I knew it! You’re interested.”

“We’re going boating next Sunday. We’ll freeze, I’ll get seasick, but her brother has a fishing boat charter up north and wants to meet me. I said yes because two hours in the car both directions is more valuable than an evening at a nice restaurant where you linger over coffee and desert. I want to know what she’s like when she’s cold, wet and tired. That’s when you meet the true woman.”

Ann laughed with delight. “You are taking this question very seriously.”

“I guess I am.” Ryan reached back to his desk and picked up the modified calendar Janet had given him that showed his evening commitments for the next 90 days. He handed it to Ann. “Date time is at a premium.”

She scanned the three pages. “Ouch. You’re saying yes to all the invites Paul and I send regrets to. I get the donor relations obligations, but you’re going to be social chit-chatted into a coma with some of these. What's MWG?"

"Meeting with God. Janet's clearing me some evenings to study. Connie is landing truth after truth and I need to go back to school. She's busting my chops is what she's doing."

"You're enjoying it."

"Yeah. I am. She's like a crash course in what you should already know about God. I haven't had a chance to ask her yet who taught her, but it's like tentacles of knowledge running various directions."

"I'm going to guess that answer is mostly her chaplain friend George Whittier and the rest is self-taught. She likes to read. And she has the time, as she doesn't watch TV."

"Seriously?"

"Don't hold me to it, but mention anything related to television shows for the last ten years, common knowledge stuff and she's a total blank, even current news isn't particularly followed. She's simply too busy to care."

****

Ryan arrived at Connie's Pizza at 2:50 p.m. Wednesday, grateful to find the lights were still on and caught motion inside as Connie set chairs up on tables, preparing to mop. He leaned against the brick of the building and waited for her to finish the wrap up.

Jesus, she needs to say yes and I know what I'm asking. Help me. His prayer had the edge of desperation to it, mirroring his thoughts and why he had made the decision to leave the hospital and drive over.

The door opened at 3:05 p.m. Connie stepped out humming a tune and stopped with surprise when she saw him waiting for her.

"I've got a 10-year-old girl dying of cancer. Help me."

Connie studied him for a long minute. She used her key to lock the door. When she turned back to him, she didn't say no, so he took part of his prayer as answered.

"My time is particularly packed today Ryan. It's going to need to be no introductions to people, no extra conversations, no lost minutes to other things."

"I can do that," he replied promptly.

"Then let's go." She turned to walk in the direction of the hospital.

"I drove over, Connie." He unlocked his car, grateful he'd been able to find an open spot on her block and held the passenger door for her. "Thanks for this."

"I haven't done anything yet."

"You're coming."

He checked traffic and pulled away from the curb. "Do you want to know any particulars about her history?"

"What's her name and what's her relation to you?"

"Joy Ellen Patterson. Her father is a good friend of a surgeon on staff. I've known the family casually for the ten years since Joy's birth."

"The parent's names?"

"Dan and Amy."

"That's enough to know for now."

He started a recording and set his phone between them. "What you were talking about this morning, our words have power because of the son relationship we now have with God. Tell me more." He was asking her to pray for someone dying of cancer and expecting her to do something about it. He intensely needed to understand what she knew about prayer.

"Ryan."

"I won't hold you to being eloquent about it, just tell me what comes to mind about the topic that you think I should know."

She shifted in her seat to better see him. "We're in a relationship with God now, it's not a piece of paper, a *'young man you should sign a different last name now'* kind of formality. The God who created and rules the universe just adopted us as his sons and daughters. Every being in the invisible world just sat up and took notice. One of the first gifts God gives us is authority of position: we are sons of God. As sons, we now share God's way of operating. We have authority in our words. God gives us the right to have what we say. I can give you the scriptures easier than a lot of words right now. This is not my best time of day.

"...For truly, I say to you, if you have faith as a grain of mustard seed, you will say to this mountain, `Move from here to there,' and it will move; and nothing will be impossible to you." (Matthew 17:20b)

"...And whatever you ask in prayer, you will receive, if you have faith." (Matthew 21:22)

"You want to know what God considers fair game to do with your words, just look at Jesus. He always did the will of the Father. He came as a man, the first-born son of God, he had the Holy Spirit with him. He's using his words to change the visible world. And in particular he's going after sickness and disease. Jesus hates the works of the devil, he came to destroy them and he's doing so using his authority as a son. A good summary is in Matthew:

And he [Jesus] went about all Galilee, teaching in their synagogues and preaching the gospel of the kingdom and healing every disease and every infirmity among the people. (Matthew 4:23)

"When Jesus is healing every disease and every infirmity what he's doing is giving people the reality of what the gospel of the kingdom means, he's showing and giving people what he's just been teaching and preaching. That is his entire ministry, talking about the kingdom and then giving it to people. For example:

Now when John heard in prison about the deeds of the Christ, he sent word by his disciples and said to him, "Are you he who is to come, or shall we look for another?" And

Jesus answered them, "Go and tell John what you hear and see: the blind receive their sight and the lame walk, lepers are cleansed and the deaf hear and the dead are raised up and the poor have good news preached to them. And blessed is he who takes no offense at me." (Matthew 11:2-6)

they brought him [Jesus] all the sick, those afflicted with various diseases and pains, demoniacs, epileptics and paralytics and he healed them. (Matthew 4:24b)

Connie used her fingers to list the points she wanted him to remember. "Jesus healed everyone of every disease. He's showing people the Father, the one who said I AM the Lord your Healer. He's talking about the kingdom of God and then giving it to us. We're Jesus' disciples. Jesus said in John 20:21a 'As the Father has sent me, even so I send you.' Jesus expects us to be doing what he did, tell people about the kingdom of God and then give it to them.

"A disciple is not above his teacher, nor a servant above his master; it is enough for the disciple to be like his teacher and the servant like his master." (Matthew 10:24-25a)

"Truly, truly, I say to you, he who believes in me will also do the works that I do; and greater works than these will he do, because I go to the Father. Whatever you ask in my name, I will do it, that the Father may be glorified in the Son; if you ask anything in my name, I will do it." (John 14:12-14)

"Those verses from John are wonderfully reassuring—you will also do the works I do—it's a promise we can lean against, we have Jesus' word on it, we will do in Jesus' name what would otherwise be impossible for a man to do. But Christians rarely see what else that verse is. It's actually a warning. If you aren't doing my works, you don't believe me. He said follow me and be like me.

"Jesus would like to remind you of your new title, 'Hey, you're my Ambassadors. It wasn't theory, it's an actual job with works to do. He who believes in me will also do the works I do. Go heal the sick, raise the dead, cast out demons. You are an adopted son of God. The Holy Spirit is with you. I'm right there, for I will be with you always. Stop watching satan kill, steal and destroy. Act. Give me something to work with. Go stop what the devil is doing.'

"Jesus has decided what he does now on earth he will do through us, so he can teach us how to be who we really are, adopted sons of God. It's like Aaron who spoke for Moses. No one mistook who they each were. I don't heal, God does. He just needs someone to show up with faith and speak from delegated authority so he can do what he desires to do.

"The centurion told Jesus, 'just say the word and my servant will be healed.' He said that because he understood authority. Whatever Jesus said, that is what would be done. Jesus called that confidence—that knowledge of and in, his authority—great faith. We need to trust Jesus' word to us that we now have permission to speak in his name. I know Jesus' authority over disease and death. So I give Jesus something to work with. I trust and know I have authority to speak in his name and I speak with the confidence that what I say in his name is what is going to be done."

Ryan pulled into the parking garage at the hospital and felt again the frustration of not having just one more minute, two more, so she could give him the next paragraph of that thought. He parked near the elevator on the lower level. "Thanks, Connie." He closed the recording. "Joy's in the ICU."

He took Connie up to the 5th floor. Staff noticed him, several spoke to him, but he smiled, politely gave only a word or two and moved on, trusting Connie to follow him. He circled around to the ICU and coded in the security number to unlock the door to the family only waiting room. A glass wall similar to the neonatal unit let family members monitor what was happening inside the ICU outside of the brief minutes every couple hours when bedside visits were encouraged.

"Her parents are in with her now," he said, nodding to the fourth bed. Dan and Amy were holding Joy's hands, talking to her, though she could only give subtle squeezes of a hand in reply. She was on a ventilator now and death was so close her color had already begun to shift. First had come the cancer, then chemotherapy and radiation had ravaged her body, trying to defeat the cancer killing her, they were in the last stages of losing the fight. He nodded to the marked door. "We can go in this way. Thoroughly wash your hands, try to minimize what you touch, but it's not necessary to glove and gown up."

Amy wiped away tears and leaned down to kiss her daughter.

"This won't do," Connie murmured. "Ask her parents to step out and the nurses to give me a few uninterrupted minutes, preferably get the parents out of this room as well—take them for coffee, a walk, to the chapel to pray with you, something."

"I want to be there."

Connie simply gave him a look. "Do you want my help or not?"

"How long?"

"Make it twenty minutes. I'll wait here, read a magazine, be family for another patient, so you can bypass the introductions with her parents. Just let the nurses know I'll be in momentarily."

She didn't want him to take the time to explain her presence and he didn't want to raise the parent's hope by trying to explain why he thought Connie praying might help when their prayers, his, others, had yet to bring the help Joy needed. He went to join her parents to do as Connie asked.

He took her parents for a walk, prayed with them, talked through how staff would handle the evening, having already made arrangements so they wouldn't need to leave the hospital to get some rest themselves. He returned with her parents twenty minutes later, washed up with them, came into the ICU. Joy was asleep and alone. He paused the ICU chief nurse. "Connie?"

"She stayed about 5 minutes with Joy, then said to tell you she'd see you for coffee tomorrow morning."

"Thanks."

6

After a last check with ICU on Joy's condition—asleep, holding steady—Ryan went home just after nine p.m. knowing he'd be called if she took a turn for the worse. Walter was with the family. He dumped his wallet on the dresser, stepped out of his shoes, tugged the oldest sports shirt from the chest of drawers and with relief hung up the suit.

"God, hope tonight is at war with the reality of a history of cancer losses. Knowing someone who believes in you with great faith has prayed for Joy is why I have hope. Reality is I can give you the names of those in similar situations to Joy who have died. It's good to talk about the subject with Connie. My heart is grabbing hold of her words and hope is springing to life, yet reality is like sand rubbing against my skin. I don't want to speak words of doubt with you tonight, to not anticipate a good outcome, but there is the fact I'm struggling tonight to believe this can turn around, that prayer can do this. Without calling you a liar, or what Connie has explained being wrong—I can feel the truth in how she describes Jesus—I need you to open my eyes to see why I don't have much confidence in you. Is it simply the reality of so many situations similar to tonight that my entire soul has already braced for bad news and doesn't want to let hope get traction? I'm carrying home the reality Joy may die tonight and am bracing for that event. I don't want to take it anymore, God. I'd rather go shovel snow in Alaska than deal with more kids dying on me. You can take it as given if Joy loses this fight and dies tonight, I'm going to ask Connie to come pray for her before the doctors officially call time of death. Whatever you'd like to say tonight, I'm listening as best I know how."

He got a cold soda from the kitchen and headed into his home office. He'd known when he went to get Connie this afternoon this would be the result. Hope, warring against reality, with him uncertain which way this fulcrum was going to tip tonight. Would he have the guts to brush himself off if Joy didn't make it and go back to listening to what else Connie said without the doubts piling up?

"I didn't intend to put her on trial and implicitly, to put you on trial, God. It's simply the situation that arose. I want to process what happens with wisdom and learn from it. Joy's won't be the first death to cancer where we lost the fight, but it would be the first loss since hope was sitting in my heart with an expectation we could turn things around even this close to death. Jesus, you didn't have failures. That would be a very nice place to reach. I don't want to endure another one. I need to ask Connie how many she has prayed for without seeing the result she asked. I should have let her set my expectations earlier. Connie… she just speaks with such confidence, you know when you're with her it's a sure thing and then the reality begins to flow by and I admit, I'm not standing on rock right now, confident in what's going to happen. Help me, God."

He needed to study, to get his mind back in the scriptures and give the Holy Spirit some room to work. It was the last thing he wanted to do, setting himself up for a steeper fall, but it was the most important thing he had to do. Connie had spent 5 minutes with Joy and left. He didn't think it was because she had looked at the situation, said I can't do anything, said a perfunctory few words and left. She'd come to the hospital because he asked, prayed for Joy and left because she was satisfied she'd done what she came to do. He desperately needed to understand that confidence she had, how it had built in her.

Ryan listened to the day's two audios and he added notes late into the night, relieved as time passed and his phone stayed silent. He dug deep for fresh insights, reading through the gospel of Matthew. Jesus had healed, not as God, but as a man who had the Holy Spirit with him. Jesus had been healing everyone of every disease out of that trust relationship he had with his Father. Doing it as a man, one who was a son of God. Realizing Jesus was modeling what adopted sons of God would also do Connie had fearlessly moved that direction herself. Ryan had been praying for a breakthrough in understanding, when it had been here all along, waiting for him to see it. God had held up a mirror for him to see the problem in himself. Now God was shining a light on the scriptures, helping him see and understand what he had only read before. Connie was basing that confidence of hers on what she found in Jesus' life. It felt good to absorb the words of scripture, even if he was still struggling to grasp their implications. He didn't have that confidence she did yet.

****

Ryan Notes / conversation three / additional references

And he [Jesus] went about all Galilee, teaching in their synagogues and preaching the gospel of the kingdom and healing every disease and every infirmity among the people. (Matthew 4:23)

So his [Jesus] fame spread throughout all Syria and they brought him all the sick, those afflicted with various diseases and pains, demoniacs, epileptics and paralytics and he healed them. (Matthew 4:24)

And when Jesus entered Peter's house, he saw his mother-in-law lying sick with a fever; he touched her hand and the fever left her and she rose and served him. (Matthew 8:14-15)

That evening they brought to him [Jesus] many who were possessed with demons; and he cast out the spirits with a word and healed all who were sick. This was to fulfil what was spoken by the prophet Isaiah, "He took our infirmities and bore our diseases." (Matthew 8:16-17)

When he [Jesus] came down from the mountain, great crowds followed him; and behold, a leper came to him and knelt before him, saying, "Lord, if you will, you can make me clean." And he stretched out his hand and touched him, saying, "I will; be clean." And immediately his leprosy was cleansed. And Jesus said to him, "See that you say nothing to any one; but go, show yourself to the priest and offer the gift that Moses commanded, for a proof to the people." (Matthew 8:1-4)

As he [Jesus] entered Caper'na-um, a centurion came forward to him, beseeching him and saying, "Lord, my servant is lying paralyzed at home, in terrible distress." And he said to him, "I will come and heal him." But the centurion answered him, "Lord, I am not worthy to have you come under my roof; but only say the word and my servant will be healed. For I am a man under authority, with soldiers under me; and I say to one, `Go,' and he goes and to another, `Come,' and he comes and to my slave, `Do this,' and he does it." When Jesus heard him, he marveled and said to those who followed him, "Truly, I say to you, not even in Israel have I found such faith." And to the centurion Jesus said, "Go; be it done for you as you have believed." And the servant was healed at that very moment. (Matthew 8:5-10,13)

And behold, they brought to him a paralytic, lying on his bed; and when Jesus saw their faith he said to the paralytic, "Take heart, my son; your sins are forgiven." And behold, some of the scribes said to themselves, "This man is blaspheming." But Jesus, knowing their thoughts, said, "Why do you think evil in your hearts? For which is easier, to say, `Your sins are forgiven,' or to say, `Rise and walk'? But that you may know that the Son of man has authority on earth to forgive sins" – he then said to the paralytic –

"Rise, take up your bed and go home." And he rose and went home. When the crowds saw it, they were afraid and they glorified God, who had given such authority to men. (Matthew 9:2-8)

And behold, a woman who had suffered from a hemorrhage for twelve years came up behind him and touched the fringe of his garment; for she said to herself, "If I only touch his garment, I shall be made well." Jesus turned and seeing her he said, "Take heart, daughter; your faith has made you well." And instantly the woman was made well. (Matthew 9:20-22)

And Jesus went on from there and passed along the Sea of Galilee. And he went up on the mountain and sat down there. And great crowds came to him, bringing with them the lame, the maimed, the blind, the dumb and many others and they put them at his feet and he healed them, so that the throng wondered, when they saw the dumb speaking, the maimed whole, the lame walking and the blind seeing; and they glorified the God of Israel. (Matthew 15:29-31)

And he [Jesus] went on from there and entered their synagogue. And behold, there was a man with a withered hand. … he said to the man, "Stretch out your hand." And the man stretched it out and it was restored, whole like the other. (Matthew 12:9,10a, 13b)

And when they had crossed over, they came to land at Gennesaret. And when the men of that place recognized him [Jesus], they sent round to all that region and brought to him all that were sick and besought him that they might only touch the fringe of his garment; and as many as touched it were made well. (Matthew 14:34-36)

Now when Jesus had finished these sayings, he went away from Galilee and entered the region of Judea beyond the

Jordan; and large crowds followed him and he healed them there. (Matthew 19:1-2)

And the blind and the lame came to him [Jesus] in the temple and he healed them. (Matthew 21:14)

7

Ryan was waiting outside the coffee shop Thursday, holding a carry container with their coffees and a sack with breakfast, as Connie approached. "I tipped Linda an extra dollar and said you'd see her tomorrow," he mentioned, eager to share his good news. "Joy's sleeping comfortably. Her vitals are good. They took her off the ventilator this morning. She's breathing comfortably on her own."

Connie simply smiled and took the coffee and breakfast he offered. "Good."

"You expected this."

"Of course. God does excellent work. I actually don't think he can do sloppy work, it would violate his perfection. There are all kinds of things God can't do: God can't lie; God can't do sloppy work; God can't not love us, for he *is* love and his steadfast love will continue forever."

Ryan smiled at the way she said it. "Thank you for helping her. It's a big deal, seeing this improvement. Teach me the rest of it, Connie, what you did and how." He knew he was in the early hours of watching a miracle unfold and the one who had brought it had needed only five minutes.

"It's not complicated, Ryan. Jesus heals because it is the just thing to do. Having taken our sins, death has no more claim on us. Jesus heals to restore justice."

She ate more of the sweet roll and wiped sugar off her mouth with the back of her hand. "Linda has a bakery source for her breakfast rolls who is a creative genius with yeast and sugar." She smiled at his laugh and went back to their topic of the morning.

"Of all the reasons God could heal us—he loves us, he's our creator, he enjoys being merciful—the reason scripture says he heals us is because Jesus' shed blood has forgiven all our sins and not just ours, but the sins of the whole world. Death which followed sin into the world has no claim, no legal right, to touch us anymore. Sickness and disease are simply the visible signs death is beginning to destroy life. And our God is a righteous judge.

"When we rebelled and sinned, satan had rights, because we gave them to him. Jesus paid the penalty for that sin, crushed satan and freed us, so there's no legal claim death can make against us anymore. With God, healing is a matter of justice, as much as it is a matter of compassion and love. Death is touching this person and he has no legal right to do so." She shrugged. "So it's… 'In Jesus' name, death, get your hands off Joy.' He does. He doesn't have a choice in the matter. The judge has ruled.

"There are different kinds of faith and different kinds of prayers, that's a conversation of its own, but faith when it comes to healing is, at its core, knowing the ground you stand on. You can heal anyone in the world by knowing what the righteous judge has already ruled on the matter. Amen is 'so be it', it's the judge's hammer coming down, enforcing the matter. Jesus heals people because he has dealt with sin. You bring the healing by speaking that verdict in his name."

It was a bigger answer than Ryan had expected to hear, so big it was astonishing. She gave him a moment and smiled. "Listen to the scriptures, you'll see it:

> ...sin came into the world through one man [Adam] and death through sin (Romans 5:12a)

> by one man's disobedience [Adam] many were made sinners, so by one man's obedience [Jesus] many will be made righteous. (Romans 5:19b)

> If, because of one man's trespass [Adam], death reigned through that one man, much more will those who receive the abundance of grace and the free gift of righteousness reign in life through the one man Jesus Christ. (Romans 5:17)

as one man's trespass [Adam] led to condemnation for all men, so one man's act of righteousness [Jesus] leads to acquittal and life for all men. (Romans 5:18b)

"Do you see it, Ryan? Jesus' act of righteousness has led to acquittal and life for *all* men. Acquittal *and* life."

She paused to give him time as he turned his phone, opened the bible app to Romans and read the chapter. "I'm seeing the verses in a way I hadn't before," Ryan replied, realizing he needed some serious study time in Romans.

Connie smiled. "Let me take you to the punch line, Ryan. 'forget not all his benefits, who forgives all your iniquity, who heals all your diseases,'" she quoted from Psalms 103:2b-3. "This is how those benefits were given. Jesus forgives us and makes us righteous; he heals us and gives us life; and he does both for us at the cross."

Ryan looked over, startled. She'd just neatly sent him straight back to lesson one. He looked at the verses in Romans again and saw it now. *Of course.*

Connie nodded, seeing his comprehension. "At the cross Jesus forgives us and makes us righteous, to reconcile us to the father, then he heals us and he gives us life, to restore to us what is just. Jesus gives us both righteousness and what righteousness looks like. By one man's act of righteousness there is acquittal *and* life for all men.

"Jesus, at the cross, forgave every man's sins, not just ours, those who would believe in him, but the sins of the whole world. And he gave life to *all* men, because once he removed everyone's sin, he then defeated the death that came into the world through sin. Sickness and disease are simply the first visible stages that death has begun to destroy life. That's why Jesus spent his ministry years healing everyone of every disease and telling people 'your sins are forgiven, go in peace.' Jesus didn't care in which order they received his gifts, healing first, or forgiveness first. Jesus was showing what the kingdom of God looks like, what he was about to do on the cross for everyone. He was giving us the tangible reality of what it means to be forgiven of sins, to be healed, to have abundant life. Then Jesus went to the cross and he paid the price for that abundant grace to pour out upon the whole world.

"God sent his son to that cross in the hope that mankind would accept the love poured out and on display in Jesus. That's the good news of the gospel. God acted first. The most powerful words ever recorded on earth are those at the cross, "It is finished!" Jesus yanked back the earth from satan and rescued mankind. The kingdom of God restores us to who we were before sin and death entered the world. It's the brilliance of God on display.

"Jesus has forgiven and healed every person in the world. He's done it at the cross for the whole world in advance. It's a free gift of his grace. 1 Peter 2:24 says two things happened on that Friday. 'He himself bore our sins in his body on the tree' and 'By his wounds you have been healed.' Both are past tense statements. Both are inclusive of all of mankind. The Greek word translated wounds is literally the stripes of scourging.

"It wasn't necessary for Jesus to get scourged in order to go to the cross, shed his blood and die to atone for our sins. So why did God the Father ask his son to go through that additional suffering? That scourging was brutal. God loves his son, He wasn't adding cruelty without a purpose. Jesus endured that scourging, he let his body be ripped apart, so our bodies could be restored from disease to health. There was a payment necessary to remove what death had done to us and Jesus paid it in full. There was no other way to restore us. That is the act of a very merciful Savior. The cross was equally cruel and also necessary, for it was the only way to make full payment for our sins. There is a powerful exchange going on. Jesus became our sin and died in our place so we could be made his righteousness. Jesus suffered in his body with the scourging so we could be healed of what death was doing to us. He made the full payment for both and then proclaimed with authority 'It is finished!' Both the complete forgiveness of our sins and complete healing of our bodies are finished works of what Jesus did for us on that Friday when he died on the cross."

She gave him a moment to think about it as she drank her coffee, then added, "Jesus doesn't make healing contingent on us, but on his work done on our behalf. Jesus spent three years healing everyone who came to him, showing us the Father's will. He's the same yesterday, today and tomorrow. He's doing the same work on our behalf now that he is on the throne. Jesus doesn't care what kind of life you've led or what you've done. If you come to Jesus, you get healed. It's a grace gift.

"The Holy Spirit who was with Jesus as he walked on the earth has been poured out upon all flesh now that Jesus is exalted in heaven and is reigning on the throne. We're healed by the same Holy Spirit as those who Jesus' touched while he was here. The Holy Spirit was poured out not because of our works or goodness or deeds. He has come as the evidence that Jesus is on the throne. The Holy Spirit dwelling in and with us is the proof text that Jesus is alive and ruling.

"Healing is a free gift we receive from Jesus' grace; we don't earn it or deserve it. He heals us because he loves us. The same with forgiveness of sins. Healing and forgiveness are free gifts available for everyone. Come to him, ask him and he heals you. He forgives you. It really is that simple. He'll heal before you believe in him, he did it all the time for people, as a proof text that he loves you. Jesus said believe me because of my words, or believe in me because of the works I do in my Father's name, just believe in me.

"It's beautiful, how God set up the gospel. The greatest news on earth is God's goodwill toward men. He forgives all our iniquity, heals all our diseases, redeems our life from the Pit, crowns us with steadfast love and mercy and satisfies us with good for as long as we live so that our youth is renewed like the eagle's – and that Friday, the cross, is how he did it. What looks like the weakest moment in history is in fact God's magnificent act of redemption and restoration of mankind. God did his part in advance, in hope that men would accept that free gift of abundant life."

Ryan had been looking to understand where Connie's confidence rested and it took less than twelve hours for God to hand him a conversation with the answer. Connie had found the cross and what God had done there in Jesus and built her confidence upon it. That truth had become the rock under her feet.

Connie smiled as she watched him thinking. "It's finished. That's the brilliance of how God did this. That fact puts to rest a lot of questions, like whether healing ended in bible days or not, because the correct answer is everything ended in bible days. Today it's just a question of do we want to receive what has already been done. Jesus smashed everything satan would ever do in all of time, freed us of every sin we would ever do in our lives, healed us of every disease we would ever face, opened the door to eternal life and did all of it on a specific Friday, on a cross, in the year A.D. 33. God isn't bound by time, he took the sins and sicknesses of all generations who would ever live and laid them on his son.

"Matthew quoting Isaiah says Jesus 'took our infirmities and bore our diseases.' (Matthew 8:17b). It's why Isaiah, looking ahead to the cross, says 'by his stripes you are healed' as a prophecy, but Peter, looking back at the cross after it has happened, says 'by his wounds you have been healed,' past tense. Isaiah saw it coming about 700 years in his future, while Peter knew it had happened in his past on that Friday in A.D. 33.

"Infirmities are the weakness and frailties that come as a result of being sick. What we think of as aging is actually mostly infirmities we live with because of accumulating disease. Jesus took both our infirmities and our diseases and got rid of them for us. He took all our sins and put them into a grave. Jesus is the one 'who forgives all your iniquities, heals all your diseases and renews your youth like the eagle's'. By his blood we are forgiven of our sins, by his body we are healed of our diseases and by his death and resurrection we have abundant eternal life. It's wonderful.

"There are two scriptures that encapsulate it which I love:

> and he [Jesus] is the expiation for our sins and not for ours only but also for the sins of the whole world. (1 John 2:2)

> He himself [Jesus] bore our sins in his body on the tree, that we might die to sin and live to righteousness. By his wounds you have been healed. (1 Peter 2:24)

They were coming back to the main hospital building and Connie slowed her steps. "The beauty of that is amazing. Jesus has crushed satan. Jesus now holds the keys of death. Jesus has reversed everything that sin and death brought into our lives. 'I have come that you might have life and have it abundantly.' God does all things well. And it is all a free gift from his grace, a lavish free gift. Those who choose to believe what Jesus has done have abundant life now and eternal life forever, for the just shall live by faith."

Ryan wanted to take every detail of this conversation back apart and think it through, for the conclusions astonished him. Connie was reading it right and yet he'd never realized it until today. He would have said God healed people because he loved them, cared about them, but he had not before realized the reason was connected directly to that Friday and the cross. Every healing for every person in the world had already been accomplished, it just needed to be accepted; and what a thought that was to grasp!

Connie stopped and nodded west. "That has to be it for now, I need to go."

"Let me walk with you on to Connie's Pizza," Ryan offered. "We're just getting started on something that's critically big."

Connie considered it, but shook her head. "I've things to do on the rest of the walk, Ryan. We'll keep talking; it's just going to need to be another time."

"Can I come by at closing, walk you home?"

She hesitated and he pressed. "Please?"

"The most tired hour of my day I spend with Jesus, not people. It's going to have to be another time."

He could appreciate the wisdom in those words and told himself to take a step back. "Tomorrow morning, then."

She smiled as she nodded. "I'll see you, Ryan." She turned away from the hospital toward Connie's Pizza.

****

"Paging Dr. Blue. Dr. Blue please pick up a house courtesy phone." The summons came mid-afternoon, the Dr. Blue reference the name used by every CEO since the hospital had been founded. Ryan found the nearest phone and took the page. "Yes, Janet."

"There's a Connie August here to see you. She said she'd be at the garden park until four thirty if you're available. If not, she'll see you tomorrow morning for coffee."

His surprise rippled at that news. "Yeah. I'll take that drop in meeting. I'll turn my phone back on, but everything but emergencies hold until after four thirty."

"Will do, Ryan."

He took five minutes to wrap up his conversation with the head of orthopedics, picked up an extra jacket from the valet group, walked out the front hospital doors and headed to the garden park.

Connie was sitting on one of the four benches in the center circle of the garden park, head slightly tipped back, eyes closed, relaxing in the sun. He'd just been given a gift.

He wasn't going to ask why. She had been giving him time of a morning she could have used to sleep, now time she would have otherwise used to rest after hours running the pizza shop by herself. He started a recording and set the phone on the bench between them. "Hello, Connie."

"Ryan." She opened her eyes and smiled at the move. "You're going to get tired of listening to my voice one day, but I'm glad you're doing the recordings. When the day arrives I finally ask 'do you have any questions?' maybe I won't have to repeat much."

"I'll be well versed with what you have said, even though I may not have grasped it as thoroughly as you have a right to expect and hope."

"It comes with time. George was a patient teacher. I'm learning how to be in my own way."

He passed on the best news of his day. "Joy is stronger even in the last few hours. They'll be moving her from ICU sometime tomorrow at this pace."

"Thank you, God," Connie murmured as she nodded. "I'm glad, Ryan."

She shifted on the bench and tugged a small New Testament from her back pocket. She offered it. "If for some reason we never finish these conversations, you should have it. George Whittier taught me from it. His notes on the categories are indexed in the front."

Not expecting such a gracious gift, Ryan opened it, curious. Underlined verses, different colors of highlights, George had turned the New Testament into a teaching textbook on various topics. "Thank you, Connie."

"It's been through years of combat so those words have been well tested. I'm not as complete a teacher as George, you'll find it useful to look at his way of presenting a topic."

"I'll put it to good use," he promised. "Does this mean I should worry about you saying our time is done?"

Connie smiled. "At some point I'm taking back those morning 15 minutes, but it won't be in the near term."

"I've appreciated every minute," Ryan reassured.

"Consider this a continuation of this morning's conversation if you have time."

"I do," Ryan replied and settled in to listen.

"Jesus secured the five benefits God has for us on the Friday he died at the cross. By Jesus' shed blood we are forgiven of our sins, by his wounded body we are healed of our diseases, by his death and resurrection we have abundant life now and eternal life in God's presence forever. God designed it so the benefits flow to individuals through that cross. Paul says the word of the cross is literally the power of God to us who are being saved. Communion is how we participate in the cross and receive its benefits."

Communion. Ryan found himself both surprised and not, by where this conversation was flowing. He hadn't understood this either. He would have sighed, but it no longer surprised him that there were entire layers to his faith that he hadn't grasped, that Connie had either figured out or herself been taught. The benefits were at the cross, so communion would be the logical connecting thread.

"Some scriptures to start with that set the foundation," Connie offered.

For I received from the Lord what I also delivered to you, that the Lord Jesus on the night when he was betrayed took bread and when he had given thanks, he broke it and said, "This is my body which is for you. Do this in remembrance of me." In the same way also the cup, after supper, saying, "This cup is the new covenant in my blood. Do this, as often as you drink it, in remembrance of me." For as often as you eat this bread and drink the cup, you proclaim the Lord's death until he comes. (1 Corinthians 11:23-26)

And the Holy Spirit also bears witness to us; for after saying, "This is the covenant that I will make with them after those days, says the Lord: I will put my laws on their hearts and write them on their minds," then he adds, "I will remember their sins and their misdeeds no more." (Hebrews 10:15-17)

in Christ Jesus you are all sons of God, through faith. (Galatians 3:26b)

For as many of you as were baptized into Christ have put on Christ. (Galatians 3:27)

We were buried therefore with him [Jesus] by baptism into death, so that as Christ was raised from the dead by the glory of the Father, we too might walk in newness of life. (Romans 6:4)

May the God of peace himself sanctify you wholly; and may your spirit and soul and body be kept sound and blameless at the coming of our Lord Jesus Christ. He who calls you is faithful and he will do it. (1 Thessalonians 5:23-24)

"There is only one place in the New Testament that talks about why Christians get sick. The Holy Spirit told Paul to write the Corinthian church and tell them what the problem was, why they were getting sick, chronically sick and dying early. It's in first Corinthians eleven. The Holy Spirit said it was because they weren't taking communion properly. They weren't taking it in a worthy manner and they didn't understand the difference between the body and the blood. Jesus' blood was for the forgiveness of sins, while Jesus' body was broken for their healing. They thought both his body and blood were for the forgiveness of their sins. They weren't discerning the parts of communion as being separate gifts. But scriptures show the body and the blood have different functions:

the blood of Jesus his Son cleanses us from all sin. (1 John 1:7b)

By his wounds you have been healed. (1 Peter 2:24b)

"They didn't understand what Jesus had done for them, how to receive the life he had given them. They were acting as if communion was a ritual, nothing of present meaning to them but a history note in their gatherings, not realizing it was the transmission method for Christ's life to them."

Ryan didn't wince, but he would have raised his hand and admitted he hadn't understood that either, though it was obvious to him now as she said it. Communion had been a time to be sorry for what he had done, to apologize for the sins that had made it necessary for Jesus to go to the cross, to thank Jesus for taking his place and saving his life. All well and good. He'd understood the blood of Jesus cleansing him from his sins, but couldn't remember ever thinking about Jesus' gift of his body as a unique fact involved in his healing. If it had even been taught, the lesson hadn't registered with him. How many years of communion had it been without understanding the full picture? Thirty? Ryan pushed away the sadness of that to focus on what Connie was offering with this conversation.

"Jesus understood what communion would be to us and was talking about it in depth even before he went to the cross. Listen to some statements of Jesus:

I am the bread of life. (John 6:48)

he who eats me will live because of me. (John 6:57b)

the bread which I shall give for the life of the world is my flesh. (John 6:51b)

unless you eat the flesh of the Son of man and drink his blood, you have no life in you (John 6:53b)

He who eats my flesh and drinks my blood abides in me and I in him. (John 6:56)

"Jesus was talking about communion. With communion we proclaim Jesus' death and resurrection until he comes, but it is much deeper than that. Communion is when we come into union with Christ. As Paul expressed it in 1 Corinthians 10:16, 'The cup of blessing which we bless, is it not a participation in the blood of Christ? The bread which we break, is it not a participation in the body of Christ?' We come into the divine exchange with Jesus during communion."

Connie gave him a moment to consider those words, then held out her hand and let the sunlight brighten her skin. "Look at the light I'm enjoying. I am present day experiencing God's word 'Let there be light' spoken at creation. Likewise, when I take communion I am present day experiencing Jesus' words from A.D. 33 'he who eats me will live because of me.' Jesus was speaking the Father's words by the Holy Spirit, for Jesus said 'I have not spoken on my own authority; the Father who sent me has himself given me commandment what to say and what to speak.' (John 12:49).

"What Jesus was describing with communion was the Father's design for how we receive what the cross does for us. The act of eating the bread is to be done with the words in mind, 'I am the bread of life', 'This is my body for you', 'By his wounds you have been healed', so that we eat with faith (trust) in those words and we receive that life offered. Likewise, when we drink the cup, it's to be with the words in mind, 'this is the new covenant in my blood'. That new covenant that says, 'I will be your God and you shall be my people. I will remember your sins and their misdeeds no more.' Communion is incredibly powerful when taken with understanding faith.

"God likes symmetry. Adam and Eve brought sin and death into the world by what they ate. God arranged his answer so that what we eat, the bread that is his son's body and what we drink, the cup that is his son's blood, would reverse what sin and death have done to us. God turned the act of eating that was disobedience, into an act of obedience which sets us free.

"Jesus' words 'he who eats me will live because of me' are carrying the power of life with them. When we participate in communion, discerning the difference between the bread and blood, receiving both gifts – forgiveness and healing – communion accomplishes what God the Father designed; it brings to us life. God's word is living and active. It always has been. And it means what it literally says, 'he who *eats* me will live because of me'. Healing is in the bread of communion. And we have mostly missed seeing it.

"By taking communion without understanding, seeing it as a ritual without practical meaning in their lives, the Corinthian Christians were setting themselves up to be sick, chronically sick and to die early. They weren't receiving what communion was designed to bring them. They were not seeing it as a living act. They were not discerning the difference in the two gifts, the body given for their healing and the blood given for their forgiveness.

"It's the same for us today. If we don't take communion discerning both the body and the blood and come to communion to receive life, we are cutting ourselves off from the ongoing life that is intended to keep us healed and healthy for the rest of our lives."

Connie paused, turning her hand to watch the sunlight highlight her spread fingers, before lowering her hand and looking over at him. "As I understand scripture, communion is the primary way God heals and keeps Christians healthy. The laying on of hands is the primary way God heals unbelievers—he uses an act of faith by a believer to help an unbeliever. The word of authority and the prayer of faith work equally well to heal both groups."

Ryan nodded at that useful summary.

Connie shifted on the bench, her voice turning even more reflective. "God, in Christ, finished his perfect plan. The five benefits of being God's people—he forgives all our sins and heals all our diseases, being the first two—

came through Jesus and the cross. They flow through communion to us. The benefits are grace gifts. We don't receive any of them by our works. Not many people realize you can't, by your works, be healthy. To try is to actually guarantee you won't be. But that's a conversation for another day.

"'...the word of the cross is folly to those who are perishing, but to us who are being saved it is the power of God.' (1 Corinthians 1:18b) Jesus dealt with sin, sickness and disease for us. It's his victory. It's not our ongoing fight. The battle is finished. We need to let that light get into us. We need to know the truth, for the truth sets us free. If you're sick, a good place to start is to take communion with every meal, come into union with Christ by faith and receive from him life.

"Jesus said he came 'to seek and save the lost.' (Luke 19:10b) We need to let him. The world is lost because they haven't understood forgiveness, they think they have to work to earn it rather than receive it as a free gift. Christians are mostly lost because they haven't understood how to be healed and made whole. The answer for us is the same as for the world, come to Jesus and receive grace for all our needs.

"Saved in the Greek is so comprehensive a word it is hard to list all the meanings in English—delivered, forgiven, healed, made whole—saved is being restored fully to life. We tend to only think of forgiveness, when God has provided so much more. All our needs in life are answered in Jesus. Second Corinthians says even the money we need comes directly from what Jesus did for us that Friday. Our answers run straight through the cross. It's Paul's core message, 'by grace you have been saved through faith' (Ephesians 2:8) We need Jesus, to see with understanding him both crucified and resurrected. After that we need to open our eyes and realize Jesus is now a King. And Kings rule. But that's also a conversation for another day."

Connie went quiet for a long moment and Ryan could see the tiredness in her pressing down after a long day of work. He chose to silence his own questions. Now wasn't the time.

She glanced his way, offered a sad smile. "We have a bad habit, Ryan. When one of those benefits isn't reaching us, we come up with theories for why God's word isn't true. We don't ask him what the problem is and press through to the answer he has for us.

"It grieves God's heart to see people sick when Jesus paid the price to make everyone healthy. His heart aches to see how many will go to hell when Jesus paid to save everyone's life. God told his sons, us, to share the gospel. This generation of the church, we've mostly forgotten what that good news actually is."

Ryan didn't try to find words to describe what he was feeling. It was her most somber message so far, even as the content was some of the richest. He'd never seen the connections before. And the conviction he felt was like the Holy Spirit had taken fire from God's altar and let it fall on him. "We're that Corinthian church."

Connie nodded. "We're the generation of Christians who are sick, chronically sick and dying early."

He quietly closed the recording, thinking it through. "I need to start bringing communion to the Christians in my hospital every day."

Connie's smile lightened. "You'll get there, Ryan, but not in a day, or even a few days. The Corinthian believers were taking communion and it wasn't profiting them because they didn't understand it. You've got to know the word, get it in your own heart, train a few others, bring communion to people and in the method of sharing communion raise their understanding so they can participate with faith."

"I'm a man who can, with God's grace, figure out how to do that. Thanks for giving me the extra time today."

Connie offered a tired shrug. "Jesus said, 'let's take a walk' and I said 'okay'. We ended up here. If I'm going to sit and enjoy your garden, even while it's mostly still in winter stillness, I figure it's only fair I give you something back."

"Where to next?"

"Home."

There was one question he felt compelled to ask on behalf of others. "Would you be willing to walk through the hospital with me one day?"

"That's a question for another day, Ryan."

"Alright. Today more than ever has me understanding how badly I need more of your time. I'm been thinking about that problem. I hear you teach a class. I want in."

"How'd you hear?"

"Ann."

Connie smiled. "Not much slips by her." She considered the request, but shook her head. "No. It wouldn't be fair to the seven in the group. They've been around me for months now, have a foundation of scriptures I've talked about that goes deeper than yours. Your questions would naturally backtrack. You're at different places."

He had already anticipated that would be the answer, so pressed for his fallback. "Give me two hours. An early dinner. An evening. Give me one evening. One block of time long enough to get more than the top of this iceberg described. I'll listen, so will my recorder."

"My schedule, my life, is busy Ryan. You want a chunk of time, then I need a chunk of time behind it to decompress from that conversation and a lot of other priorities in my life end up squeezed of what should have been theirs. I'm not willing to add what you're asking of me. Maybe in a few weeks when something clears off, I can make that a different answer."

"What if I hire someone to do the clean up after you turn the sign closed, you sit and supervise and give me that hour?"

"You want the most exhausted hour of my day? Think again, Ryan. I applaud the way out of the box suggestion, but that's not the answer."

"How much time do you need to finish the core of what you most wished I knew? A couple days of simply talking? I don't have to grasp it all right then. I can listen to the audios over and over until I understand it."

"Why this Ryan, why now?"

"Desperation. Ann mentioned the medic's prayer you used. Simply grasping things like that could transform the hospital metrics I see every day."

She considered that and bobbed her head. "I concede you've got a valid point. But trying to speed up what is a process rarely works and this is a process, Ryan. For you, as much for me."

"Would you be willing to try and see? What about taking a day off work? What's the price for that? Put a note on the door, 'I'm sorry, we will be closed on Monday' and give me that Monday? I'll make it financially worth your time."

She was going to say no, he could see it coming. "What do you want? We'll make a trade. What I want for what you want. There has to be something."

She was quiet for nearly a minute and he didn't interrupt. If she offered something, they'd eventually be able to find a solution. He needed her seeing this as her problem to solve, too.

"You aren't going to like it," she finally said.

"Try me."

"I can give you some audio blocks of time, record some things at odd hours of my day you can listen to and we can talk about later, if in return, when George gets to Chicago, you give him a job at the hospital in the chaplain's office. You let him do his thing. I want him comfortable in civilian life, with options he'll enjoy for his time as he makes the transition. Occasional time, regular part-time, full-time, it changes around to be whatever he prefers and it is a guaranteed job for five years."

"While conceptually, sure, the guy who trained you is someone I most certainly want on staff, I can't commit blind. I've never met George. But I can say if I can't give him a job at Mercy Hospital, I will find him a job or series of jobs in the Chicago area that suit his time and interests."

"He can't know it's our deal. You're helping a retired army chaplain because it's the right thing to do."

"You introduce us, I'll take it from there," he promised. "I'll like the guy Connie, if only because you clearly do. I've got no problem helping a military veteran find a job. Part-time, full-time, whatever suits him. You can hold me to it."

She nodded toward his phone. "You really want more of this?"

Ryan smiled. "Connie, you dangle raising the dead, healing the sick and being effective in prayer, in front of me. If I didn't intensely want what God had taught you, I'd be an idiot and God wouldn't have wasted your time on me thus far. You're too valuable to him as a resource given what you know. I want it all. I refuse to settle for a piece, if it's possible to have it all. We've got a deal, if that's what you want in return."

"It's what I want."

He offered his hand to seal the agreement. "See you for coffee in the morning?"

She smiled. "I'll be there. It's nice, the fact I haven't paid for breakfast lately."

"My own small version of thank you."

"It's been appreciated."

****

As he walked back from the garden park, Ryan copied the audio file over to his archive of their conversations, eager to share it with Walter and Jeff, then made a video call to his office. "I'm back, Janet. What did I miss?"

"We're cruising without problems so I'm going to say the rare word 'nothing'. The garden park isn't your typical location for a business meeting. You're dating Melinda and seeing Connie?" she asked, amused with him.

Well acquainted with her interest in his personal life, he simply laughed and offered, "Dating Melinda, talking with Connie. She's got a boyfriend of her own, a Jason Lasting."

"The worship leader at Lake Christian Church?" Janet asked, surprised.

"You know him?"

"We're talking serious heartthrob in looks and voice. I'd heard he was officially dating, but I hadn't heard who he was seeing."

"And you'd know this why?" he asked, equally amused. "You're married."

"But half of HR is not. Several attend there. It's the closest church now that they've bought and converted the old Macy's building. There are reasons it is drawing crowds. Jason is one of the reasons."

"It's nice to have a piece of news I didn't know. I'm shutting off my phone once I walk into the hospital, so page if you need me."

"Will do."

Ryan hung up with Janet and out of curiosity, found the Lake Christian Church website. Jason Lasting was a founding staff member and served as the worship leader. Ryan started the video from last Sunday's service. Jason had been gifted both in looks and in voice. He did a nice job opening the service. And was probably not an idiot, Ryan thought, given he'd met Connie and made a move there before someone else snapped her up.

Ryan shut off his phone, satisfied with the information. Connie was mentally exhausting him, he could only imagine how Jason had adapted to being around Connie as a lifestyle, but only a fool would have passed by her, a wise one would have stopped to figure out how to come up to her speed. Ryan was doing his best to catch up with her. She was simply at times far ahead of him in what she understood about the scriptures. Combat medic, he reminded himself. She'd had to learn it fast for soldiers were dealing with traumatic injuries and dying around her. Those eight years had burned something intense into her. He was on the receiving side of eight years of battlefield training. With each passing day he realized the blessing God had handed him was quite a bit larger than he'd first realized.

****

There was a note from Janet on his desk atop a received invitation. Ryan picked it up as he finished the soda he'd bought from vending. He'd been working his way up through the floors of the hospital, making himself available to anyone with a question or comment and taking notes on items staff needed him to tackle for them. He was preparing to end his evening at the hospital and head out to a social engagement hosted by long time hospital donors, then much later than he would like, finally head back home so he could tackle what would be a late night of studying. The fact Janet had gone home told him the day had ended up here still in decent order.

He read Janet's note. "I thought the name Connie August sounded familiar. I located this in the folder of invitations you did not accept because the date conflicted with one you already had. – J"

He picked up and opened the white card with gold trim, found a neat script note inside, the card probably run through a printer, with a signature at the bottom.

An invitation from combat medic Connie August to a dinner discussion about the bible and healing today, for those in the medical field. Participation is limited to twelve. Those accepting thus far include paramedics, doctors, nurses, a surgeon and a chaplain. RSV by September 15th if you would like to join us. Dinner at 6 p.m., discussion begins at 6:30 p.m. and ends promptly at 8 p.m., moderated by Connie August.

The invitation was addressed it him personally. He'd turned her down six months ago. Ryan felt literally sick seeing what had happened. "Jesus, how many more gifts from you have I managed to miss in my lifetime?" he whispered. He could have had the Tuesday evening conversations, the occasional Thursday ones, with a group who were living this material out and had been for the last six months. Connie was giving him a crash course through it trying to catch him up to where he would have been had he simply not made this error. An unforced error at that. "What happened, Jesus?"

He had a sinking feeling he knew. He hadn't prayed about which invitations to accept, just looked if the night was free and filled in dates. He would have seen the conflict in dates and simply declined this one without praying about the matter. Had he asked the Holy Spirit for the yes and no's this night would have remained open and Connie's would have been given the Holy Spirit's approval as where he should attend.

He propped the invitation against his terminal as a reminder not to walk into any more unforced errors. The breakthrough he had been praying for had been in his mail in September and he had missed in. It was a sobering reminder. The answer had come and he hadn't recognized it. "Thanks for saving me, God, with a do-over."

He was too busy to know the Word as he should, too busy to hear God's voice and he wondered why he was floundering. That mirror God was holding up was showing a man who needed his eyes opened in more ways than one. For his own sake, he had to change those facts.

****

Ryan headed to his study when he got home just after ten p.m., needing time to work through what had happened today. It was a good thing that he liked to take notes, liked to study, to think. He'd come to recognize when the Holy

Spirit was driving home a truth and this was one of those moments. Connie was breaking open ground in the scriptures he had read right over in the past and the Holy Spirit was using her words to help him see what he hadn't grasped before.

Ryan Notes / conversation four / additional references

For the word of the cross is folly to those who are perishing, but to us who are being saved it is the power of God. (1 Corinthians 1:18)

And many followed him [Jesus] and he healed them all and ordered them not to make him known. This was to fulfil what was spoken by the prophet Isaiah: "Behold, my servant whom I have chosen,
my beloved with whom my soul is well pleased.
I will put my Spirit upon him,
and he shall proclaim justice to the Gentiles.
He will not wrangle or cry aloud,
nor will any one hear his voice in the streets;
he will not break a bruised reed
or quench a smoldering wick,
till he brings justice to victory;
and in his name will the Gentiles hope."
Then a blind and dumb demoniac was brought to him and he healed him, so that the dumb man spoke and saw. And all the people were amazed and said, "Can this be the Son of David?" (Matthew 12:15b-23)

I [Jesus] am the bread of life. (John 6:48)

"I [Jesus] am the living bread which came down from heaven; if any one eats of this bread, he will live for ever; and the bread which I shall give for the life of the world is my flesh." (John 6:51)

Truly, truly, I [Jesus] say to you, unless you eat the flesh of the Son of man and drink his blood, you have no life in you; (John 6:53b)

He who eats my flesh and drinks my blood abides in me and I [Jesus] in him. (John 6:56)

As the living Father sent me and I [Jesus] live because of the Father, so he who eats me will live because of me. (John 6:57)

The cup of blessing which we bless, is it not a participation in the blood of Christ? The bread which we break, is it not a participation in the body of Christ? (1 Corinthians 10:16)

For I [Paul] received from the Lord what I also delivered to you, that the Lord Jesus on the night when he was betrayed took bread and when he had given thanks, he broke it and said, "This is my body which is for you. Do this in remembrance of me." In the same way also the cup, after supper, saying, "This cup is the new covenant in my blood. Do this, as often as you drink it, in remembrance of me." For as often as you eat this bread and drink the cup, you proclaim the Lord's death until he comes. Whoever, therefore, eats the bread or drinks the cup of the Lord in an unworthy manner will be guilty of profaning the body and blood of the Lord. Let a man examine himself and so eat of the bread and drink of the cup. For any one who eats and drinks without discerning the body eats and drinks judgment upon himself. That is why many of you are weak and ill and some have died. But if we judged ourselves truly, we should not be judged. But when we are judged by the Lord, we are chastened so that we may not be condemned along with the world. (1 Corinthians 11:23-32)

He himself [Jesus] bore our sins in his body on the tree, that we might die to sin and live to righteousness. By his wounds you have been healed. (1 Peter 2:24)

If the Spirit of him who raised Jesus from the dead dwells in you, he [God] who raised Christ Jesus from the dead will give life to your mortal bodies also through his Spirit which dwells in you. (Romans 8:11)

"O death, where is thy victory? O death, where is thy sting?" The sting of death is sin and the power of sin is the law. But thanks be to God, who gives us the victory through our Lord Jesus Christ. (1 Corinthians 15:55-57)

And Jesus went away from there and withdrew to the district of Tyre and Sidon. And behold, a Canaanite woman from that region came out and cried, "Have mercy on me, O Lord, Son of David; my daughter is severely possessed by a demon." But he did not answer her a word. And his disciples came and begged him, saying, "Send her away, for she is crying after us." He answered, "I was sent only to the lost sheep of the house of Israel." But she came and knelt before him, saying, "Lord, help me." And he answered, "It is not fair to take the children's bread and throw it to the dogs." She said, "Yes, Lord, yet even the dogs eat the crumbs that fall from their masters' table." Then Jesus answered her, "O woman, great is your faith! Be it done for you as you desire." And her daughter was healed instantly. (Matthew 15:21-28)

Afterward he [Jesus] appeared to the eleven themselves as they sat at table; and he upbraided them for their unbelief and hardness of heart, because they had not believed those who saw him after he had risen. And he said to them, "Go into all the world and preach the gospel to the whole creation. He who believes and is baptized will be saved; but he who does not believe will be condemned. And these signs will accompany those who believe: in my name they will cast out demons; they will speak in new tongues; they will pick up serpents and if they drink any deadly thing, it will not hurt them; they will lay their hands on the sick and they will recover." So then the Lord Jesus, after he had spoken to them, was taken up into heaven and sat down at the right hand of God. And they went forth and preached everywhere, while the Lord worked with them and confirmed the message by the signs that attended it. Amen. (Mark 16:14-20)

****

The one a.m. hour found Ryan in his kitchen fixing a toasted cheese sandwich and drinking the last of the milk. His brain was tired, but it was a good tired. He had it grasped now, he thought; he'd begun to put his mind around Jesus' words, 'I am the bread of life.'

In the conversation with the woman who was not an Israelite, seeking help for her daughter, Jesus had referred to healing as the children's bread. Jesus had viewed healing as part of what God's people would have daily, it was their bread, a staple of life. Jesus had come as the bread from heaven to be that source of life, to bring that healing.

By his blood there was forgiveness of sins, by his broken body, healing of disease, by his death and resurrection, new life. Connie had given him the lines he could understand and the Holy Spirit had begun adding color to the picture, adding layers of details, bringing the scriptures alive. It felt good to be on the same page with God, to have learned something tonight that came simply from time with the Holy Spirit, learning together. He was going to need a lot more nights like this one. That was okay with him. He wasn't lost without answers anymore. He was simply walking a landscape that was new to him. One he hadn't seen before.

After the simple meal, Ryan fixed communion for himself and spent twenty minutes going through his notes, reading through Jesus conversation with his disciples, beginning with the words 'I am the bread of life.' There was life in this act of communion, a participation in what

Jesus had done on that Friday ending at the cross and Ryan saw the connection now.

It felt both odd and perfect, taking communion after his meal. And he determined for his own sake, that it would be a daily practice now. Not as a ritual, but as an important exchange of life with God. He needed this. His spirit was comfortable with the decision, even though his mind was still sorting out the implications of what it meant to participate in what Jesus had done. It was a remembrance. It let him repeat with faith the words of life Jesus had used to describe the bread and the juice. It let him express his faith in what Jesus brought to him. It was a time to say thank you to God. For now that was where his understanding could take him and it was enough to begin there. He wanted the abundant life Jesus had come to bring him and the scriptures showed it flowing through the cross. That much he did understand.

"Tomorrow, God, I want more. I don't want you to stop teaching until I have at least seen all the terrain. It may take months of thinking about parts of this before I grasp it all. By your Holy Spirit enlighten my eyes to understand what you're teaching. Please show me the full picture, then come back and deepen the colors. If I thought I was hungry to understand before, it is nothing compared to right now, as I begin to see. Connie's raised the dead, the more I hang around with her the more certain I am that is also in her wheelhouse. She knows this stuff, its not theory with her. For that reason please give me more, more time with her in conversation, more scriptures getting mentioned, let her be the guide to the terrain you've shown her so I can hike around with you over the next months learning this too. I'm not so naïve to think everything in how she expresses a thought is perfect, but I'm wise enough to recognize when truth is slapping at me and go do the studying and thinking necessary. You're my teacher, the Spirit of Truth. You're the one who brings everything into sharp clarity. You appointed preachers and teachers for a reason, to get our eyes to open and see what was out there. You answered a deep ‘need of my heart’ prayer by sending Connie across my path. I want it all, God, everything you’ve taught her. Please put the necessary pieces in place so that happens. In Jesus’ name, that’s what I’m asking, God. Amen.”

8

Ryan covered a yawn Friday morning as he pulled open the coffee shop door for Connie. He'd been arriving five minutes early, but that pattern had just been broken as he'd chosen to sleep in They stood through the short line together and walked back outside, both drinking coffee for the needed caffeine.

"Now you're the one looking particularly tired," Connie mentioned as they began their walk.

In reply, Ryan simply turned his phone, flipped to his calendar, set it to show the last 30 days and handed her the phone. "Blue are the evening scheduled events, mostly donor relations."

She looked at all the blue and gave a small laugh. "Ouch."

He accepted back the phone with a good natured shrug. "The CEO's job is hospital management, but it's also watching out for our survival. Endowment donations and straight gifts to the non-profit help us offset shortfalls when patients can't pay, or the state is running behind on paying its bills. We are very efficient at holding down costs. One of the best in those metrics in the state. But we still need donations to keep us in the black. It's been lean recently as corporate donations tend to be a percent of their profits and business has been down ever since the last recession."

"You're good at raising money."

"I try to be. The mission of Mercy Hospital has been baked into my DNA by all my family ties. People respond to that story, join in partnership with us." He set up a recording for their walk.

"There's a concert tonight, at the Keller auditorium in the former Chrysler building," Connie mentioned as he did so. "It's going to be loud, 1,800 people, a general audience target, with Jason and the band from Lake Christian Church performing. They'll be doing a mix of music, some Christian, some country, giving short testimonials, mostly introducing Jesus to an audience that doesn't know much about him. You're welcome to come if you like. I'll be leaving from Connie's Pizza about five thirty to walk over, as parking is impossible on full concert nights. There's no need to decide now, if you show up, you've decided to come."

"I'll consider canceling what's on tonight so that I can, if only because I just heard the opportunity to seize another walk with you." Ryan held out his phone, having begun the recording. "Would you talk to me more about Joy and what happened?"

"Sure, it dovetails nicely into what I thought would be today's topic." Connie gestured with her coffee. "You've seen most of it already, Ryan. Visible sickness and disease is death beginning to destroy life. Jesus is alive. He's King. He's forgiven all sin. He's now holding the keys of death. All authority in heaven and earth has been given to Jesus. Notice who has no authority anymore? Satan. Death. They no longer have a legal right to touch a person. Knowing those facts, I brought the King's reign to the situation. 'In Jesus name, death, get your hands off Joy.'

"Death leaves when you tell it to, Ryan. It's what Jesus meant when he said 'I will give you the keys of the kingdom of heaven' (Matthew 16:19) What are the keys Jesus is holding? The keys of death and hades. The right to bind on earth what has been bound in heaven, the right to loose on earth what has been loosed in heaven.

"We are announcing the judgment of the King. We're the spokesman who speaks with the delegated authority of King Jesus. We speak his will, in his name and it's done on earth as it is in heaven. We're not making up what we personally think might be interesting to have happen; we're acting with authority because we're under authority. He wants his will done on earth, as it is in heaven—and that's the whole ballgame. There's no sickness in heaven. And the earth is now under Jesus' full authority.

"'By his wounds you have been healed' is a statement of fact. Jesus is the Victor in this massive collision of kingdoms which occurred. Jesus has decided that he will act on earth through the words and actions of his disciples. He waits for us to step into our responsibility. Healing simply requires us to go deliver what Jesus has done. We're announcing the victory of the King over sickness, disease and death."

Ryan found the kingdom collision description very helpful. "Would you describe the prayer you said? I wish I had been there to get it recorded."

Connie laughed softly. "For that reason alone, I'm glad you weren't. You would try to copy my words rather than give your own. I told death to get his hands off Joy in Jesus' name. I rebuked disease in her body and told it to get out. I blessed her in Jesus' name. I asked the Holy Spirit to fill her, to give her his overflowing abundant life. I asked Jesus to comfort all who entered her room. Then I asked the Holy Spirit to teach and guide all her caregivers while Joy was their patient. I said Amen, which means 'so be it'; it's like the judge's gavel coming down. Then I said thank you to God, because I knew God had just done what I asked. And because we both enjoy it, I sang God a song of thanks as I walked home and celebrated in advance what would unfold in the hours to come.

"I exercised faith, Ryan. The words I spoke came from my heart. Came from the truth I know. I said what was going to happen and the Holy Spirit gave my words authority because I am an adopted son of God. Everything in the invisible and visible world reacted to my words and complied with the orders. Death took his hands off her. Disease left. Life flowed into her. Healing prayer isn't difficult, you simply have to know what the will of God is on the matter of healing, then go speak from his delegated authority as a son of God. Jesus healed everyone of every disease—that's the standard. We are to go and do the same.

"Sometimes it helps to close my eyes and simply put my attention on Jesus, rather than look at who I'm seeking to have healed. The invisible is the real and lasting world; this one we see is changeable. The invisible world is the truth, God's domain. This world we physically see is more like facts. It is real – you can touch, taste, see, smell and feel it – but it is changeable. Facts can be changed. God's truth, his kingdom, never changes.

"The invisible world created this visible one. The laws of the invisible world are more powerful than the laws of the natural visible world. The invisible world is the parent and the visible one the child; the child obeys the parent. Think of it this way. Gravity is a powerful law. But the law of lift can enable a plane to fly, as if gravity didn't exist for the plane. In the same way, spiritual laws don't negate natural ones, they simply come in over them and can do something which natural laws can't do.

"God heals by both natural laws, our immune system kills a germ, for example and by spiritual laws. Jesus speaks and a blind man sees – that's a spiritual law in action. God is quite comfortable healing in either way, for he created both the visible and invisible worlds, natural and spiritual. They are all his methods and laws and ways of working. It's not just natural laws which work on earth; it is who is speaking and acting that gives a law its effect.

"Think of a miracle as a healing which happens in a compressed time period. Or one which requires an act of creation to occur, a blind eye now sees. If the healing comes through a natural law which God energizes, or by a miracle, a spiritual law is applied, that is up to God. I know the truth I am speaking. In Jesus name, this person is healed. I know what healed looks like and that is where my confidence rests. What I am speaking in Jesus' name is what God has done for this person through Jesus' grace. I know what the outcome of being healed looks like.

"I was praying over Joy, but mostly I was simply taking action as the spokesperson for Jesus. I already knew what he wanted done, so I did it in his name. I spoke to death. I spoke to disease. I spoke to the Holy Spirit and to Jesus and said what I wanted to happen. I wasn't ever really asking God would you like to do this thing I'm asking? I simply directed. I'm humbly gracious when my words are directed to the Holy Spirit, to Jesus and curt with death and disease, for I know to whom I'm speaking. But I never really asked anything during that prayer, I simply said what would happen. And said Amen confident what I said I received. We're now watching it unfold and become visible. Joy will grow stronger until she's healed, barring anything intervening which squashes the prayer I said. Which itself is a topic for another day.

"I acted as Jesus would have in that situation. He would have phrased things differently, but Jesus is fine with my personality shaping how I choose to express his words and will. The gospels of Matthew, Mark, Luke and John sound like the guys who wrote them, but all are the inspired word of God. I speak from the comfortable footing of knowing who Jesus is and what he wants done in this situation. If I'm not sure, I go talk to God until I am. Asking prayer, petitioning prayer, looking for understanding, that's what you do before you enter a situation that needs you to act. Healing is an action, a proclamation, a direction. In Jesus' name, I say what is to happen."

Connie gestured toward the garden park so their walk could continue another six minutes, granting an extension she'd have to make up from her own morning schedule. Ryan gratefully nodded his thanks and turned that way with her.

"That prayer for Joy is what the Holy Spirit does. He teaches us to do what Jesus did by both explaining where the authority comes from and how we are to use it. The Holy Spirit teaches us how to get our footing. It's like the first time we stand up on a surfboard. It helps to have someone coach you through it. God did not give us a spirit of timidity but a spirit of power and love. The Holy Spirit teaches us how to get things done, how to bring the kingdom of God to earth using Jesus' name. The Holy Spirit is the one called alongside us, he's our helper, he's God who is bringing healing. He simply chooses to work with us rather than independent of us.

"Jesus never prayed for someone, he simply healed them. That was the most striking thing I noticed as I went through the gospels after George and I started talking. Jesus prayed all night on occasion. He valued prayer. But he understood that something else was needed from him when he was dealing with sickness. He said what would happen and it was done. He had authority as the son of God. He destroyed the works of the devil not by petitioning the Father to act, but by stating what the Father wanted done and the Holy Spirit gave his words power. Jesus was a man like us, speaking with the authority of a son of God, with the Holy Spirit resting upon him. That's the definition of a believer today, an adopted son of God, the Holy Spirit with us and dwelling in us.

"I'll often ask the Holy Spirit when I'm with someone, 'what else do I need to do?' I'm looking for insight into what he sees. Sometimes you tell infection to die; sometimes you tell white blood cells to multiply in numbers. It's not unusual for the Holy Spirit to give ideas that use the knowledge you have of anatomy or disease so you give very specific directions. I've heard surgeons tell specific ligaments to heal, specific blood vessels and because they are speaking in Jesus' authority, that's what happens.

"We grow more confident the more we do. It's like a child with training wheels on their bike, who will wobble at first without them, but then finds their balance. How you learn is by doing."

Connie paused and smiled. "By the way—the Holy Spirit teaches children to say healing prayers easier than he teaches adults. Children expect they can learn things they haven't yet mastered; adults have already decided they can't do it. An eight year old who knows Jesus is King can order cancer to get out in Jesus name easier than an adult.

They know a King's name is all powerful and still grasp with a child's faith the understanding that the invisible rules the visible. Supernatural things happening are still within a child's comfort zone.

"You learn how to do stuff in the kingdom of God by looking to Jesus and what he did, by reading the book of Acts and watching the early church thrive using Jesus' name to act." She paused and Ryan could see her searching for how to sum up what she understood.

"It comes back to the basic fact the word is living and active. The Holy Spirit wrote the word and is your personal teacher. He explains it in ways you can understand. He knows how you are perceiving a lesson. He knows where you've grasped the truth as he intended and where your understanding is partially there and when you're simply not seeing and understanding something he wants you to know. That's okay. It's the Holy Spirit's job to teach you everything you will need to know about being a Christ follower. He'll keep coming back to a lesson until we understand what he wants us to grasp.

"When the Holy Spirit looks at us, even when we are 100 years of age, we're still going to look young to him. The Holy Spirit has volunteered to be with us for eternity and his name isn't going to change. He will still be our teacher and our guide, our comforter and our helper. The one called alongside to be our advocate, when we are a million years old. That's why Jesus says you need to be a child to enter the kingdom of God. You need to still be willing to learn, to take risks, to trust the God who is teaching you. Who is working with you to help you grow to maturity. To trust his good heart toward you. They know what they're doing. We have to let them—the Father, Jesus, the Holy Spirit—be God and if they say jump, we jump. You learn by doing. It's the definition of who we are, his people obey his voice."

Ryan was fascinated by that explanation. "Thanks, Connie." He needed to let her head on to work without further delay, but the extra minutes had been priceless for him. "I'll join you before five thirty if I'm coming to the concert," he promised.

"There are concerts most Friday nights, if not this one, I'll invite you again," Connie reassured and turned toward work with a wave goodbye, moving into a comfortable jog to make up her time.

Ryan closed the recording, well satisfied with the morning's conversation and walked on to the hospital to start his work day.

****

"Dr. Blue, please pick up a house courtesy phone. Dr. Blue, please pick up a house courtesy phone."

Ryan heard the page as he entered the radiology department, recognized the voice and stopped to take the call. "Yes, Dr. McKellan."

"You asked to know when Margaret's cultures were back. She's got this year's flu strain and a mild ear infection. She was prescribed the right antibiotics, has been on them since Tuesday evening. She received her flu shot November 28th, so will have some immunity already built up. It's going to be a mild case of the flu. She has a follow-up appointment scheduled for Monday at 2 p.m."

He'd been right to worry, that raspy voice had been an early symptom of something more serious. They had been receiving patients into the hospital with this year's flu strain since early December. "I appreciate the news." He was listed on Margaret's health care records in place of next of kin and was her power-of-attorney for health care, as she didn't have family to fill that role.

"Liquids to avoid dehydration, move slowly to avoid dizziness, take Tylenol for the fever and body aches and most valuable of all, rest. She gave me that prescription even as I began to remind her of it. She'll call if symptoms worsen. She's a sensible woman. It's been taking about ten days to run its course."

Ryan thanked the doctor and continued on to his meeting. Someone from the Cooper family had been checking on her daily this week and would continue to do so. Prying her out of her home to stay with one of them would take better negotiating skills than he possessed. He was grateful to hear that expectation it should be only a mild case of the flu. He already planned to see her tomorrow to assess firsthand how she was doing and take over whatever she might need. He walked a fine line with her independent spirit. She wasn't one to like him hovering, but he could love on her as he wished.

Ryan smiled. Even if the title was honorary, she was the definition of a grandmother. It was good to have family. He prayed for Margaret again as he headed to his meeting. He needed to ask Connie the different between praying for someone in person versus praying for them without their knowledge when you heard a need existed. He suspected there was a difference in effectiveness, but that was mostly a guess on his part. He planned to dose Margaret with both, for she was in the personal circle of those he desired to make sure stayed well.

9

COMMANDER JOE BAKER

The rain sweeping across Texas was now heading north and it was with relief that Commander Baker switched off the windshield wipers for the final time and drove toward the rainbow now stretching across the sky. Texas was home, but he lived on the gulf and it was a long drive to the Texas panhandle without much to see but open road and pastureland, most of it still thirsty even after the rain showers. This land had suffered years of drought and was only beginning to recovery. The native grasses were beginning to grab traction again and the cattle were being allowed to slowly increase in numbers, bringing back the economy of the area.

Joe had collected plenty of information about his two Silver Star candidates from soldiers across the nation, having elected to start working his way through their careers from the first days to the present, following the rumors. He had been talking to people who had served with them, crossed paths with them, been helped by one or both of them. Primarily speaking to those who had left the service so he could push for candor and had mostly heard it. Those who had remained reserved hadn't surprised him, given what Joe suspected they weren't saying. Doctors wouldn't break confidentiality without permission, but the rumors out there were credible.

The end of his task was turning to the events of March 19th, 2016 the SA had asked him about specifically and filling in what had occurred during those last hours in the assembled record. Joe had a pretty good idea how to answer that question, but suspicion was not facts. He had located the man whose first hand account would be very useful and wanted their conversation done before he rejoined his wife. She hadn't wanted to join him on the short hop over to New Mexico to interview a retired major, nor on this detour across the state. She was already packing for California and soon after it Chicago. If this conversation and the remaining few after it went as Joe expected, he would soon be heading north so he could meet Connie August in person for the first time.

****

Ed Bolt was still a young looking 25, out of the army now four months, having joined up after high school graduation so he could get hands on training repairing trucks and other heavy equipment through the army trade schools. Joe found him working at an auto mechanics shop in Crosroads, Texas and had deliberately not called to alert him to expect the visit.

Ed wiped his hands, held down the lever to lower the vehicle lift and bring an older model Oldsmobile back to the shop floor. "No disrespect to the navy, Commander, but this army vet doesn't have much to say about the matter that's going to help you."

Joe rolled over a stool and made himself comfortable, he wouldn't be leaving without details and he could be as patient a man as a situation required. "Talk me through that day, March 19th. I know you've told it to other people, but tell it to me again. You're the only one who can put me into the scene of what happened at Charlie base. I've got video for much of the rest of it. What I don't have is that first hour back at Charlie base. Hearing it, seeing it, through what you saw is uniquely helpful to me. The army can't award recognitions without first hand accounts of events. You've nominated guys in your unit for citations yourself, you know the process."

"Which is why I know this is a waste of time. My story hasn't changed since the last four times I told it."

"I like to say the truth has a ring to it, you know it when you hear it. Humor me and I'll let you change the tires on that military issued ride. No self-respecting mechanic should have let out the motor pool given the condition those tires are in. I'll be doing the next guy who has to drive the vehicle a huge favor, saving him from having a blow out on a highway."

Ed considered the car. "The paperwork to get reimbursed will bury you."

"My problem, not yours." Joe held out the keys, serious about the offer. "You can work while we talk. What I want is every detail of the day as you remember it. You're no longer active army, so there's no possible repercussions coming your way. If you saw something odd, you say it."

"I appreciate the caveat, but won't need it." Ed studied the afternoon sky outside the open garage bay, thinking, looked at the car Joe had parked by the office, nodded and reached for the keys. "Let me bring in that death trap. You really did get handed a lemon."

"Tell me about it."

Ed backed out the Oldsmobile and pulled in Joe's motor pool car. When it was on the lift and raised so the weight was off the tires, Ed pulled over a stool and reached for a lug wrench.

"Let me tell it this way. I worked in the motor pool at Charlie base. It's a big base, housing for soldiers, full repair shop, the field hospital was on base, medical flights came and went all hours. The only thing we didn't have was an active air squadron, they were flying out of the airfield to the north. The larger artillery mostly rolled in, refueled and passed on through. We were the hub for other units. We were a 'find it here' service nexus. You needed a haircut, we had the only barber chair in the province.

"We'd been hearing updates throughout the day on the battle. The convoy diverted to assist the overrun FOB was returning to Charlie base after a seven day circuit through the area. They were our guys. We knew the vehicles were going to be in all kinds of conditions when the fighting was contained. So we spent the afternoon loading supply trucks with what they might need at the scene of the battle.

"The fighting ends. We came in with trucks bringing in water, food, fuel, replacement tires, engine parts, mechanics. Those vehicles that could be made drivable, we got on the way back to the base to be fully repaired. The others deemed fixable, we would haul back using what was basically an improvised tow truck rig. We park our trucks as directed, unload gear, get to work. I was helping secure a vehicle we'd decided to haul back when my name got called; they needed a driver for the mortuary run.

"It's the one job you don't want to get tapped to do. Its both so solemn and something of a target. The unit of those in the firefight normally designates someone to ride with the deceased. The enemy likes to drop mortars on the vehicles carrying the dead to add insult to injury. To cut down on that, the vehicle used is selected randomly out of the general transports. I got pointed to the truck they'd chosen—basically its any of the personnel trucks that has been fitted with the cot securing tie bolts—and handed the clipboard with the paperwork to sign.

"The combat medic and chaplain walked over as I was filling out my portion of the paperwork. 'Our work here is done, so we're going to catch a ride back with you.' I nod my agreement. Sign off on the paperwork. Figure they were mostly coming along to provide moral support for the soldier accompanying the bodies back to base. I then learn the accompanying soldier won't be riding with me. He'll be driving one of the escort vehicles instead, providing firepower if needed, as manpower is short. That works for me. I get in the truck, the other vehicles join up with me and I drove back to Charlie base as part of a six vehicle group.

"When we reached the field hospital, the escort gave me a salute, but didn't stay. He did a u-turn and joined up with two flat haulers to escort them back out to the scene. It's going to be dark within three hours and whatever is going to get done at the site needs finished well before then. I pull around to the east side where the mortuary is located, park and go in to report my arrival. The chaplain and combat medic come in to get coffee.

"I signed in reporting 4 + 2, four deaths + two riding with the deceased.

"The mortuary team went out to bring in the bodies, only to return saying the truck is empty. I go out with them thinking they went to the wrong truck, as there are several parked on that east side. I walk over to the truck I drove and the truck bed is empty. It's as neat as it would have been had it just been signed out of the motor pool. I'm shocked. It's not like someone is going to carry away four bodies in the middle of a secure field hospital within the ten minutes max that truck was unattended. So we go check with the other mortuary teams. Did someone see my truck arrive, already bring in the deceased? That draws an absolute no and the man handling the paperwork on all bodies entering the cold room insists he's checked in only one guy in the last hour.

"The chaplain and combat medic are still drinking coffee. I check with them. 'I was told I was bringing 4 KIA and the 2 of you, plus an escort driving with us.'

"The chaplain says, 'The total is right, but the others just headed over to the after-hours club, very much alive. You have names for the KIA?'"

I read the 4 names from the paperwork.

"That's them. Try the after-hours club."

"I find the 4 named individuals alive and well at the after-hours club, playing darts. They obviously aren't dead. It's a paperwork error. So I let it go.

"Other soldiers that were part of the convoy begin arriving back on base. Confusion roils things. These guys were supposedly killed in a vehicle explosion. Yet they are present and accounted for and obviously fine.

"One of the four is shaking his head. 'I don't know what to tell you, Sergeant. After the casualties were transported, we got pointed to a truck and told to clear the scene, return to base. The order made sense as our vehicle was one of those totaled in the firefight. The chaplain and combat medic caught a ride with us because their work was done too. We got back here probably half an hour before the rest of the unit rolled in.'

"Battlefield confusion. That's my answer. The guys were fine, were told to clear the scene. They had crossed over to the truck and gotten in back, were waiting for a driver to get assigned. Someone thought the guys were among the dead because their vehicle was destroyed and they weren't around to be seen.

"I know I was driving the truck and I know the soldiers whose names I was given are all standing there fine. There wasn't anything unusual about the trip."

"Drone footage shows their vehicle hit by mortars, its explosion and later four body bags being carried over to the truck you were assigned to drive," Joe said mildly.

Ed set down the wrench. He hadn't been told that part before, the shock Joe saw was a fresh reaction to the news.

"That makes no sense. Are you sure it was to the truck I drove? These guys walked over to play some darts. They didn't have a scratch on them. It's not like they were CIA spooks or something, pretending to be dead so the enemy would see them loaded into body bags. We're talking regular army, guys 22 to 24, who were glad to get back to home base. Glad to have come through the firefight without getting shot.

"I know their names got on a casualty list out at the battle scene. And I remember the three hours that evening of rolling back slap reunions. Those at the scene had heard their names were on the casualty list and they were now rolling in to find instead the four are fine. The unit went from having lost four guys, to everyone having lived through the firefight. I never heard a good explanation for the mix up on the names, how it happened, but it was classic battlefield confusion."

"Did you ever hear anything whispered, any rumors, that maybe something happened?"

"Like what, Commander?"

"Anything. Did the four ever say anything which struck you as unusual?"

"Nothing I ever noticed. The guys were probably at Charlie base another five weeks before their unit rotated out to take over security at the airport. I know the interviews were detailed regarding events during the battle, who was up for what citation and award. It wasn't like the battle got forgotten. There were a lot of injured who went through the field hospital. You'd see the four guys in the mess hall, working weights in the gym. They'd shrug when asked. Yeah, they remembered the mortar hitting their vehicle. And wasn't that a shame as it was the newest vehicle in the convoy, the only one with a still reliable CD player. They'd totaled the best ride rather than the oldest. They were calm about it. They talked about others who had been injured, stayed abreast on how they were doing. They were mostly getting bored, as their unit had been taken off convoy duty as it was undermanned temporarily. You need to tell me what you're looking for, Commander, because I don't have any idea what you're after."

"I'm mostly listening and collecting impressions," Joe replied, not willing to get drawn into answering that. He closed his notebook, satisfied with the conversation. It was time to ask four soldiers what they might be willing to say, then Connie and George. He was heading to California next.

10

RYAN COOPER

Connie had said 5:30 p.m. Ryan got away from the hospital in good time so he didn't have to rush on the walk, grateful the day was mild weather. He'd been able to ditch the suit for casual clothes in his gym locker and was ready, he hoped, for what the evening would be. Connie was just stepping out of the pizza shop as he arrived. She was in matching jeans to his, a sweatshirt and jacket not unlike his, much older tennis shoes. She had a backpack slung over her shoulder that looked like it was combat medic gear.

Connie smiled a welcome and mentioned, "It's the medic's motto, be prepared. People listen to me when they see the gear and there is some medical stuff at the bottom. Mostly I'll be pulling out my concert night special resources as needed – chocolate chip cookies, water bottles, earplugs and the softest seat cushions you've ever experienced should they be needed."

He grinned at the news. "I'm glad to know I am traveling with a professional concert go'er."

"The music is great and I don't mind loud, I've been traveling through war zones, but this many people in one place can be a bit goofy. They do a good job screening alcohol out at the entrance checkpoints, but a crowd this size gathers, there will be those selling hazardous refreshments for palmed ten and twenty dollar bills. A general audience brings with it everything that can imply. I normally end up having to deal with someone who took something they didn't expect, as if the music isn't a high enough." Connie glanced over at him and grinned. "Still game to come?"

"And to think I gave up a suit and tie and a rather formal dinner party for your company. It has all the markings of a fascinating evening."

She finished locking up and nodded east. They set out for the concert venue. "All part of the human story. I'm sure you've seen your share of rave parties gone bad."

"More than a few."

"This won't come anywhere near it. We're the relatively tame crowd, the spiritually curious and the lapsed Christians who don't want to think of themselves as so strung out they can't remember which concert they've come to see."

"Seriously, you thought this was my speed of an evening?"

She laughed. "You are rather easy to wind up, Ryan. I'll deal with someone who tripped on the stairs and thinks an ankle might be broken, or if we're really lucky, a woman in labor who thought the music and movement might finally get the kid to pop out. Nothing particularly serious. And having now warmed you up to fear the worse, what actually is our evening is going to be boringly normal and you are going to be mildly disappointed when it turns out to be just a lot of loud music and screaming people."

"I've been reverse psyched by an expert," he realized.

"Pretty much. I offer all my guests info on the exit doors and permission to call it an early night without fear I'll think you have no taste in music."

"Now I'm just getting dared to leave early," he noted, impressed. "You do this a lot?"

"I choose my target audience for Friday nights with care. No offense to Jason, but I've heard their core songs a dozen times, whereas my chosen audience guest is getting the new experience. A girl has to have some fun. My date is on stage for about three hours and I'm the front row left faithful girlfriend. We've all got our roles to play tonight."

"I'm mostly your entertainment," Ryan realized, amused.

"You'll be more of a challenge than most. I tend toward the teenage girl who ends up having a major crush on my guy. You'll be a departure from the norm."

Ryan could feel the weight of the last week peeling off him with the way this conversation was going. "Thanks, Connie."

She smiled, understanding his reaction. "You're welcome." She nodded at his phone. "But I'm a realist; you didn't give up your dinner party for my sense of humor."

"That's true." He took a deep breath, let it out and clicked on a recording, prepared to do his best to keep up with her topic for the evening. "Okay. Where are you taking me this evening?"

"The topic for tonight's walk is faith."

She gave him a moment to mentally shift gears to that particular subject. He nodded, already thinking this was going to be an interesting walk.

"So let's start with a couple scriptures:

faith comes from what is heard and what is heard comes by the preaching of Christ. (Romans 10:17b)

without faith it is impossible to please him. For whoever would draw near to God must believe that he exists and that he rewards those who seek him. (Hebrews 11:6b)

"Christians often think they have to come up with faith, that it's something they have to mentally will themselves to have. 'Okay, I've convinced myself these verses I wonder about are actually true, so now I'll hurry and pray with faith.' They try to stay on that mental balancing beam long enough to pray and hopefully get their answer from God before their doubt overwhelms the faith they had worked up. They've missed a major point of truth and have also moved themselves back under the law, thinking they have to work to get faith.

"Faith is a gift given by grace; like the forgiveness of sins, it's free and it's something that is from God. Faith just comes in a unique way. You receive faith by hearing the word of God. You hear the word and it's like faith is sticking to the letters. Faith comes to you by what you hear, it's brought to you by the word of God. This living active word of God changes us by something that comes along with the word.

"Faith comes. Faith arrives. Faith shows up. Keep reading the word of God, hearing it, thinking about it, quoting it back to yourself so you can hear it with your ears as well as read it with your eyes. There will be a moment where you'll suddenly realize 'I get it, I understand this, I trust this,' and you'll realize faith has shown up. Our mind is renewed with the truth of the word, while faith accumulates in our heart as we understand the word. Both the word of God and faith are alive, they are powerful things which change us by their presence. Faith is quiet in its arrival, but powerful in what it will then want to do. You'll move mountains after faith has arrived and will do so without doubts. Scripture is full of that intersection of having faith—trusting God—and that faith propelling you to go out and do stuff.

For time would fail me to tell of Gideon, Barak, Samson, Jephthah, of David and Samuel and the prophets – who through faith conquered kingdoms, enforced justice, received promises, stopped the mouths of lions, quenched raging fire, escaped the edge of the sword, won strength out of weakness, became mighty in war, put foreign armies to flight. (Hebrews 11:32b-34)

"Because of their faith, they went out and did things. The start of the next verse – 'Women received their dead by resurrection' – how cool is that? Faith is powerful. Faith also allows us to stand firm with God. Even when the situations unfolding around us seem like crushing defeats, faith gives us God's perspective. It's critical to our success that we understand what faith is, how it comes, what it does and how it does what it does. Christians are to both know God and be active because they know God. Christians are to be doers of the word. You can't just mentally believe and think that's a living faith. Faith is either active doing works or it has died. And a dead faith isn't going to get you into heaven. Mental knowledge alone is death to us. To know, but not be doing, means we are only deceiving ourselves.

"Faith is completed by works. Faith gets traction in us and finishes transforming us only when it is active. Muscles that atrophy can't lift anything. Muscles which are worked daily can move weight with ease. Faith is similar. Faith which is alive is doing things and growing stronger with use. We are to 'be' Christians—it's identity, character—but it's also 'be doers', it's who we are in motion, it's what we're doing in our lives. As James says, we are blessed 'in our doing'. We will be people showing our faith by our actions.

"Follow it in the scriptures:

receive with meekness the implanted word, which is able to save your souls. But be doers of the word and not hearers only, deceiving yourselves. For if any one is a hearer of the word and not a doer, he is like a man who observes his natural face in a mirror; for he observes himself and goes away and at once forgets what he was like. But he who looks into the perfect law, the law of liberty and perseveres, being no hearer that forgets but a doer that acts, he shall be blessed in his doing. (James 1:21b-25)

Do you want to be shown, you shallow man, that faith apart from works is barren? Was not Abraham our father justified by works, when he offered his son Isaac upon the altar? You see that faith was active along with his works and faith was completed by works and the scripture was fulfilled which says, "Abraham believed God and it was reckoned to him as righteousness"; and he was called the friend of God. You see that a man is justified by works and not by faith alone. And in the same way was not also Rahab the harlot justified by works when she received the messengers and sent them out another way? For as the body apart from the spirit is dead, so faith apart from works is dead. (James 2:20-26)

By faith Sarah herself received power to conceive, even when she was past the age, since she considered him faithful who had promised. (Hebrews 11:11)

As the outcome of your faith you obtain the salvation of your souls. (1 Peter 1:9)

"A living active faith wants to do something. It sees needs and opportunities and internally nudges you to act; 'let's pray for that person to be healed, invite that person to church, sign up for the youth leader training, answer that opportunity to give to the missionaries in Chile.' Not every opportunity that crosses your path is something you raise your hand to and say yes. There are ones that Jesus has in mind for you, those that hit a passion that just resonates inside you. You say yes and your faith gets excited and dives in and your actions blossom into good works. That's a living faith. You find life challenging, stretching, fun, you're growing like mad and relying on God and lives are getting changed – you're tasting living in the kingdom of God and it feels really good to you. You want more of this. You're coming alive as a Christian because your faith is flourishing."

Connie paused as they reached a major intersection with turn-lanes in all directions, with crowds waiting at the cross-walks for the signal to change to walk. Two people riding bikes slowed to coast between stopped cars and make a turn. "I've experienced traffic jams and crowds in every country I have ever been in, most without the stop lights to help organize matters and can't say I have ever gotten use to them," she mentioned. Once they were across the intersection, she picked up where she had left off.

"Anyway…the opposite of a living faith is dead faith. Faith that is dead has no works. People don't plan to end up in the situation with dead faith in their heart, but it happens frequently. Jesus was constantly on his 12 guys for having no faith, for letting their faith die, you of little faith. Tending to faith is our responsibility. It's critically important that we watch to make sure our faith doesn't die. Faith dies because it gets suppressed, poisoned, or crushed. Those problems deserve some detail, but I'm not going to go that direction tonight. I'll sum up this first part with a verse:

We are bound to give thanks to God always for you, brethren, as is fitting, because your faith is growing abundantly and the love of every one of you for one another is increasing. (2 Thessalonians 1:3)

"That's what you want to see when you look in the mirror. Faith comes as a grace gift as we read the word. Faith lives in our heart and it's our job to tend it, to let that faith do stuff. Where people misunderstand Christianity is they think being a Christian is a lot of their own effort, that it is a lot of constant hard work. In fact, God is doing the work. That new life inside you is powerful. Faith comes when you read the word and that faith is alive: it is constantly nudging you, 'let's go do this', 'let's go do that' – the impulse isn't coming from you, it's coming from faith. There's an eager joy in it, an anticipation, 'that looks challenging and fun, let's go dive in and do it'. If you cooperate with what is welling up inside you, your faith gets you involved in stuff and you blossom as you tackle things that require God to show up.

"Nothing is more thrilling than doing something and realizing God is with you in the doing. It has become a supernatural thing. If you don't suppress what God is doing, you will grow and flourish very quickly. Your faith rockets up into sturdy mature trees. You'll easily say yes to harder and harder challenges because your growing faith is more than a match for what is needed.

"It's uncomfortable trying to hold back faith from acting. There's a constant tension inside as your spirit and soul wrestle for control of who you will be. One side or the other always wins. You become like Christ, or you kill this new life inside you and turn back to the world. God doesn't let you hug the middle. Over the course of a lifetime, the only ones who endure to the end are those who have elected to become like Christ."

They were within sight of the concert venue and the sidewalk around them was flowing with people heading that direction. She nodded to the recording, signaling she was done for now.

"Thanks, Connie." Ryan closed the recording.

"I like this topic. The next conversation is back to being practical; this was more theory. I previously assumed people understood faith, but it's an area where there is often more misunderstanding than clarity. It's hard to talk about praying with faith if you haven't realized faith itself is a grace gift from God."

"I'll look forward to that conversation, too. They've all been helpful, if in different ways."

"I haven't forgotten where you want to go, Ryan," Connie mentioned, "to the big questions of opening the eyes of the blind, the lame walking, raising the dead, doing supernatural stuff, but for that conversation to be useful to you, I have to show you how to get there."

"How close are we?"

"A week."

He was startled enough he stopped walking, causing people behind him to have to rapidly react to avoid bumping into him.

Connie turned back toward him and smiled. "I didn't say you would have understood it to the point you have faith to do supernatural things, but yeah, about a week."

He felt like he'd just done a belly flop. Without implicitly saying so, she was saying she had raised the dead, opened the eyes of the blind, done the supernatural in Jesus' name. "Okay. That just motivated your student quite a bit."

She laughed. "Come on," she waved him to start walking again. "Concert venue, good music. Learn to love worship, Ryan and people who don't know Jesus yet. This is where Jesus hangs out on a Friday night. This is his kind of crowd."

Ryan fell back in step beside her, hoping he was ready for where she was taking him, both this evening and in the coming week.

11

"Would you like me to pray for your ears to stop ringing?"

Ryan laughed at Connie's kindly worded question. He gladly pitched the earplugs he had worn into the trash can at the entrance. A full moon was out. "You were absolutely enjoying every minute of that concert."

"I like loud music."

"The percussion was enough to make even Ben vibrate." The six-year-old son of the band member playing the keyboards had progressively lost his hearing since age four, was now profoundly deaf, but he'd been having a great time without needing to hear the music, able to dance around in the open area between the front row and the stage, using the crowd as his own visible music to enjoy.

Connie smiled. "That's a boy who will have no trouble falling asleep in the car on the way home."

"You've been praying for Ben's hearing to return."

"Of course." Connie retrieved the last cookie in her provisions and broke it in half to share. "I will pray for you until you are healed and if you die before that happens, I will pray to raise you from the dead." She said it with a smile, but she wasn't joking. "Ryan, a simple rule of thumb: if it's good, it's God, if it's bad, it's the other guy. The thief comes to steal, kill and destroy. Jesus comes to give abundant life.

"Satan stole Ben's healing. It's like a slap in the face to the band. He couldn't knock one of them out, so he went after a family member. Ben will get his hearing back because that's God's will in the matter and one of God's benefits to him. In the process, I'll learn how to do something I didn't know how to do before.

"By watching Jesus, I've learned never to look at a problem and think that's just the way life happens, or that a problem is permanent. Nothing in the visible world is permanent, it all gives way to the invisible world's verdict.

"His parents are probably the key that opens the lock, as parents have a very unique authority over what occurs with their children. Music is part of it, too, I think. To bring Ben to the concerts is one of the recent impressions both his mom and I got when praying for him. I know the atmosphere of praise is powerful and when the gospel is preached by music, by testimony, the Holy Spirit is very active in the crowd. Ben can't hear the music, but he enjoys the concerts. And if what I suspect has happened, Ben's got an afflicting spirit affecting his hearing; spending Friday nights at a nearly three-hour-long loud concert glorifying Jesus, has been the most miserable hours of that demon's existence to date.

"The woman in the synagogue who was stooped and bent over, couldn't straighten, Jesus set her free of the affliction and said satan had bound her for eighteen years. Jesus said 'enough!' and ended the woman's suffering and she was able to stand up straight again. She had an afflicting spirit binding her. Something similar is probably happening in Ben's case."

Connie gave him a thoughtful look. "I can see the discomfort; I'm treading into topics you don't normally consider."

Ryan could think of several ways to answer that but chose to simply shrug. "I'll adjust."

She smiled. "Most of what you deal with in healing the sick is going to be disease, something death brought in, that needs removed. But occasionally that approach yields no answer. Don't give up; instead, step back and consider what else might be going on. It's worth solving that puzzle when it presents itself. Think of Ben's situation as an advance level course, a topic I wouldn't have normally introduced you to this early. Jesus removed unclean sprits as well as healed the sick and often the presenting symptoms looked similar. The Holy Spirit helps us figure out what we're dealing with. The final outcome is the same, the person is healed." Connie shifted the backpack and pulled out another water bottle. "You were a good sport to come tonight."

"If I missed these opportunities, I'd miss getting glimpses into that range of topics you are sorting out when to discuss. And I'd miss meeting the Bens in your life."

"Let me give you one key that you might have enough to recognize now. Ryan, when you think of Ben, do you think of him as deaf?"

"He is deaf."

"That's a fact, but its not who he is. I see Ben, a normal hearing child, who has a problem blocking his hearing."

Ryan felt her words register as a solid punch. "I think of him as deaf. You think of him as hearing."

Connie nodded. "When you tie the label of the disease and the person together, you can, without realizing it, subconsciously agree with the fact the situation is permanent. It makes it incredibly hard to pray with faith once you've internalized that what you are dealing with is a permanent condition.

"A key to healing is to see the person in front of you as God does, healthy, normal, thriving with life, who temporarily has – name the condition – which needs to be removed."

"That gem right there was worth the concert."

Connie laughed. "Good. Because I'm about to test just how good a sport you are and ask if you'd like to join me for the next Friday night concert, too."

"I'm already planning to clear the evening so I can be there. I'm impressed with Jason," Ryan remarked. "He had that crowd willing to listen to the story of Jesus' life, without feeling like they were getting a sermon. I haven't heard that much theology about who Jesus is in most church services, let alone a general audience event."

"The nearly three hour time span helps and the mixed in country music," Connie mentioned. "You want to spin a tale of a life in need of a savior, just drift along with a cowboy theme and take the opportunities the music presents. Jason's a story teller by nature. I talk in conversation chunks about what faith is, while he simply tells a story of a guy who chose to believe."

They reached the street sidewalk and Connie paused. "You've earned the right to decide the direction from here. Want to walk to the hospital and your car? We can talk on the walk."

"How about your place, I drop you there and then I backtrack to the hospital? It's not like I don't have things to think about that could use the time."

She nodded and turned south. "We can just walk if you like. There's a point where you've earned the right to say that's enough for now."

"I like listening to you Connie. You're like this entirely different universe compared to where I normally circle."

She laughed at that image. "Okay, then let's finish the topic of faith tonight and I'll try to make it worth your while."

Ryan obligingly tugged out his phone and started a recording.

"Let's start with two scriptures:

And Jesus answered them, "Have faith in God. Truly, I say to you, whoever says to this mountain, `Be taken up and cast into the sea,' and does not doubt in his heart, but believes that what he says will come to pass, it will be done for him. Therefore I tell you, whatever you ask in prayer, believe that you have received it and it will be yours. (Mark 11:24)

In the morning, as he was returning to the city, he was hungry. And seeing a fig tree by the wayside he went to it and found nothing on it but leaves only. And he said to it, "May no fruit ever come from you again!" And the fig tree withered at once. When the disciples saw it they marveled, saying, "How did the fig tree wither at once?" And Jesus answered them, "Truly, I say to you, if you have faith and never doubt, you will not only do what has been done to the fig tree, but even if you say to this mountain, `Be taken up and cast into the sea,' it will be done. And whatever you ask in prayer, you will receive, if you have faith." (Matthew 21:18-22)

"What is faith? It's the ability to 'believe that you have received it' (what you've asked) before it is in your possession. It's confidence that what you ask God is what will be done.

"Jesus asked a blind man, 'What do you want me to do for you?' He said, 'Lord, let me receive my sight.' And Jesus said to him, 'Receive your sight; your faith has made you well.' And immediately he receives his sight.

"A woman who had a flow of blood for twelve years says, 'If I touch even his garments, I shall be made well.' She comes up behind Jesus, touches the fringe of his garment and immediately her flow of blood ceases. Jesus turns and tells her, 'Daughter, your faith has made you well; go in peace.'

"Notice it was the blind man's own faith, the woman's own faith, that made them well. Jesus didn't need to add his own faith to get these healing miracles done. Their own faith was powerfully sufficient.

"The blind man came to God, said what he wanted with faith (confidence, trust) that he would receive what he said and he promptly received it. The woman healed of bleeding, acted with faith (confidence, trust) that she would receive what she had said and she promptly received it. These are teaching pictures for how our own faith operates. We ask Jesus for what we want, Jesus answers us 'receive it' at the time we ask, for he is the 'yes' to every promise of God and what we ask then shows up in our visible lives. You have faith (trust, confidence) that you will receive what you ask, that what you say is what is going to happen. You ask God for something and it shows up because you believe it will."

Ryan had heard the prayer of faith discussed many times, but her explanation was among the most precise. He nodded his thanks to Connie for that description.

She turned the topic a bit further. "God is the only being in the whole universe who can say 'ask me for anything and I'll give it' and not be lying."

Ryan smiled as Connie headed straight back to lesson one. She was delivering on her promise to offer something interesting tonight.

"God knows the end from the beginning. God has considered every possible request you will make over your entire lifetime, the entire tree of possibilities and has decided yes, I'm willing to give her everything she might ask. So God writes in his word to you, 'whatsoever you desire, when you pray, believe that you have received it and it will be yours.' (paraphrasing Mark 11:24 KJV). God has seen and pre-approved what we want to bring to him.

"Jesus reaffirms the 'anything you ask' breadth of God's offer by adding his own intent to do the same when he sits on his throne in glory, 'whatever you ask in my name, I will do it.', 'if you ask anything in my name, I will do it.' (John 14:13a,14) And just to be sure we get his point, God writes to remind us 'with God nothing will be impossible.' (Luke 1:37b) and adds for our sake, 'and nothing will be impossible to you.' (Matthew 17:20b). A son of God speaking a word with faith is given what he asks, what he says is what he receives. That is God's gift to us as his sons.

"There is really only one natural limit to what you can ask. It has to be something which exists in God's kingdom. You can't ask for a guy to be your husband when he's currently married to someone else, you can't ask for his present wife to die early—those would be examples of the other kingdom.

"Faith is not wishful thinking. 'I wish God would do this thing for me.' Faith is realizing what God has already done for you, what is sitting in the kingdom of God with your name on it and asking to receive it, to have it move from the invisible world to the visible world. The promises of God are descriptions of what is already done for you. You're forgiven, healed, delivered, blessed. Simply ask God with faith for what you desire from him and it moves from heaven to earth. God doesn't make this process of receiving difficult. God likes blessing people. The more childlike you are in heart, the easier you simply go run up to your papa and ask for what you want."

The intersection ahead was snarled, the stoplights, having experienced some kind of malfunction, had reverted to emergency mode and were blinking red in all directions, turning the intersection into a four-way stop. Ryan was grateful for the full moon, for neither of them were wearing particularly bright clothing easy for drivers to see at night. Connie paused as they judged traffic and wove between cars to cross the street, then simply continued her thought.

"So how do we get that faith (confidence, trust) for whatever we might ask? We've talked about how faith comes from the word of God. Faith arrives, shows up, comes to us, by what we read and understand. The specific faith for 'whatever we might ask' comes in part from these verses on prayer, from the promises we read in scripture which relate to the specifics of what we need—resources, health, direction, peace—but it also comes from understanding a comment the Holy Spirit makes about God.

> his [God's] works were finished from the foundation of the world. (Hebrews 4:3b)

"This is an incredible statement about God and very useful to us when it comes to prayer.

"Let's take a simple example. You ask me for something. If I tell you I will do it and you trust me, you wait for me to act, so you can have it. Time passes. You start to wonder if I forgot, or if there was a problem, or if I just haven't gotten around to acting yet. Your anxiety rises, not because you don't trust me, but because it's important to you and it hasn't happened yet. You start debating, should I ask again? I don't want to imply she isn't trustworthy and I don't want to find out she did forget and be disappointed in her because she wasn't as faithful as I thought she was. Mentally, it turns into a mess. That situation happens all the time between people. And because that's how we've learned to think about people, we find ourselves, without intending to do so, thinking that same way about God. We asked for something, it doesn't show up immediately and we spend our lives anxious about what he did with our request.

"Scenario two – you ask me for something. If I tell you I have done it and you trust me, you simply wait for it to show up. You have 100 percent certainty it's done. You are confident it is on its way. You know I ship things by armored guards, so it's not getting lost in its delivery.

"By understanding God's works are finished from the foundation of the world, you can live in scenario two and have 100 percent certainty that what you've asked him has been done for you. Before it shows up, you are already writing the thank you note to God and preparing for what you'll do when your answer is in hand, because you know he's done what you asked. We have confident trusting faith in something that is already done, even though it hasn't shown up yet, because we believe the one who says I've done it and we know it is on its way. Listen to the verse again:

his [God's] works were finished from the foundation of the world. (Hebrews 4:3b)

"God gives us this special gift in his word, this assurance, so our lives could be peaceful in every circumstance. Life is not unfolding in a haphazard way, with God running back and forth between people and events trying to get things to work out. God is now at rest, having completed all his work. He has finished everything we need, answered every prayer, even the arrival date and time of what we have asked for has been taken care of and finished; it has all been done since the foundation of the world.

"God sees both the beginning and the end. God sorted out every detail of what would happen across all of time, what you would ask, what he would do and how he would do it, wrote 'The End' on the story, then has come back to chapter one and is now going through the story with us. We see stuff happening real time. Producer God is seeing it unfold as he wrote the story, with all its intricate details, enjoying your surprise and delight as things happen, knowing nothing has been dropped, not even the smallest detail in the story. Our lives have been fully considered and planned for in great detail. God delights in blessing us with every answer to what we ask him.

"We pray, hoping God will come through for us. God is like, 'I finished that one. Yep, that one is finished. Yep, that one, too.' If we don't pray, those answers will not come into our life. If we pray, they are guaranteed to come into our lives. How are they guaranteed? God has already done them.

"God does not lie. God does not write 'whatever you ask' without already knowing every request you will make. God has figured out how to do – and he's done – all that you will ever ask him.

"So just ask him for stuff, accept he's given it to you and relax. You'll have what you have said. It's done. Jesus lived like that. It's fascinating to watch his comfort with the world around him. Multiply bread to feed thousands? It's hand me the meal, say a simple blessing and 'okay guys, hand it out.' Lazarus has been dead four days? It's 'Lazarus, come out!' and not said in kind of a whisper so people wouldn't notice if he says it and nothing happens. It's a loud voice so all those present hear him tell the dead to wake up. That is confidence in God in action. Jesus trusted his Father. So should we. That's Jesus' message to us once we're adopted sons of God.

"'Whatever we ask' is huge, because we have a huge God. We miss something if we lower the size of his offer to something that seems reasonable to us. God is an intricate, detailed, lovely and powerful God handling the universe and all creation. God wants to fulfill what seems to us to be impossible requests to show us himself, his own nature and capacity. He doesn't need to come down to our capacity, he needs us to come up to his. Trusting him and asking him for things which allow him to be himself in your life is honoring God and who he is, it's letting him do God size things for you."

Ryan's phone recording their conversation suddenly vibrated in his hand, catching him by surprise. He hadn't taken it off mute after leaving the concert. He recognized the incoming number as the endowment group president and declined the call. If it was good news, he'd enjoy it tomorrow, if it was bad news, it would be even more important for him to understand what Connie knew about faith. "It can wait," he murmured to Connie who had paused while he handled the call.

She nodded and continued her thought. "God can tell David, a thousand years before Jesus comes to the earth, write down that they will gamble to decide who gets my son's clothing. A thousand years later Jesus dies on the cross and the soldier's are throwing dice to see who will take home Jesus' tunic. Which came first, God seeing the soldiers would throw dice, or the soldiers throwing dice and God taking note of it? Our lives are expressions of our free will, but God knows what our free will is going to choose to do. Knowing isn't causing. The two can co-exist without violating our free will, or God's omniscience.

"God can say what will happen twenty-six years from now and quote everything you will say that day, because he already knows what happens. He isn't making it happen in the sense he's controlling your free will, he's simply been in the future already and experienced that day. To him that future is present knowledge.

"We are living life thinking it is unfolding new. God is living life with us having seen all of it already. He incorporated everything we would ask him, everything we would do, everything he would do and shaped the plot to end up with the joyful marriage of his son Jesus to the radiant bride the church, with evil defeated and cast into the lake of fire.

"God relishes people who grasp his delight with them and how willing he is to answer prayers. Ask, knowing God has already finished his work to give you what you ask and you will receive what you ask. That confidence is faith. What we ask has been done. We are now just walking into the experience of it.

"The future is new to us. But it's a finished work to God. When God says 'whatever you ask in prayer, believe that you have received it and it will be yours.' (Mark 11:24b) God is telling you what he has already done in the future – it's what we've asked him for with faith."

She paused to give him a moment to think about it, then turned the subject slightly again. "We're skeptics, 'whatever you ask, that can't be true'. So we don't believe God because that statement seems impossible to us. God is trying to jar us out of that doubt in who He is so we can see the fact that it is true. God doesn't lie. Jesus' question, 'when I return, will I find faith on earth?' is poignant for a reason. Even most Christians don't believe God is telling them the truth with these verses. We live in hope we have that good of a God, while inside doubting that we do, when God would have us live in confident certainty, knowing we do have a God who is that good. God lets you have the life you pray for, that's the hidden gift in this conversation about faith.

"It's very much like the prayer of authority, when you understand you have authority in your words as a son of God, you speak and things happen. When you ask for something in prayer with faith, something similar is happening. Faith is connecting you with God's answer. Faith is triggering, it is putting into motion, it is causing what you asked to come about. You've met the one condition God places on having whatever you ask – you've asked him with faith."

Connie paused there and Ryan nodded his thanks, noting the time on the recording, as she'd just connected together the pieces of what made prayer powerful. He'd want to listen to this section again as a priority.

He'd moved the phone off mute and it chimed as a message arrived. Recognizing Jeff's ring tone, Ryan stopped walking, even as his phone chimed twice more in quick succession. "My brother, our chief ER doc. Hold on." He scanned messages. "He's about to spend quite a bit of money on a helicopter flight for a newborn preemie born at the scene of a car accident on interstate I-294." He sent back a quick okay. He resumed the recording that had been interrupted and offered Connie a smile. "You say yes, then figure out how to pay for it."

"I can imagine that gets interesting to budget."

"The one thing reliable about emergencies, they always happen. I'm enjoying this conversation on faith, Connie. I thought I understood faith and prayer, but I'm finding listening to you, I understood it at a top level, but not the substance of it. The prayer of faith is powerful, that connection to what God says he's already done for you."

"It's very powerful. A practical example – you pray like the blind man did, 'Lord, let me receive my sight'. You have faith (confidence, trust), when you pray, that you will receive what you have asked. So you say 'thank you, God.' and you go your way confident your sight is going to show up. Sure enough, you pick up something to read, can't make out the words, take off your glasses and you can. You prayed for sight, knew it was given when you asked and it arrived. You don't need glasses anymore. It's a prayer said that is directly within God's will. Jesus redeemed us from the curse of the law and one of the many things listed in the curse of the law is blindness. The thief (satan) has been stealing your vision. You can ask for your sight back and receive it. You ask for what you want with faith and you will have it. The delivery time, the arrival time varies. When your heart stays confident 'I asked with faith and I have received what I asked', what you asked for will always show up.

"If there is a delay, ask God what is going on; he knows. Don't simply decide your prayer was a failure. You can kill the arrival of your own answer by closing down your faith and saying 'I guess it's not going to happen'. Guess what – God will honor your words – 'it's not going to happen'. If that's your decision, that's what the result is. Sometimes the delay is God shaping you to be able to handle receiving what you've asked. Sometimes God is moving around people, your boss, your spouse, or arranging a series of events, or in this last example, changing the shape of your eye and the curvature of your eye lens. The variety of how God delivers your answer to you is as unique as our prayers themselves are.

"God expects us to live okay with mystery, confident in Him, even when we don't see what is occurring. We can trust there are things happening and our prayer answer is in motion. An enduring steady faith is what God is forming in our lives, because nothing is impossible to those who have been trained to ask and walk and live by faith.

"…whatever you ask in prayer, believe that you have received it and it will be yours." (Mark 11:24b)

"…whatever you ask in prayer, you will receive, if you have faith." (Matthew 21:22b)

Connie paused walking to sum up the topic. "You have authority by position, (you are a son of God) and you have ability to do by faith, (your trust in God). You speak with authority (I am a son of God speaking under delegated authority) and with faith (I trust God that what I'm about to say is what is going to happen) and you get results.

"Jesus spoke with faith when he said 'Peace! Be Still!' and his words carried with them the power to accomplish what he spoke. We're to live like that, knowing our words always yield what we say. God intends our lives to be ones of vibrant prayer, asking him for what we need and Him answering our requests. We are royal priests under Jesus and we function in that role by faith-filled prayers and actions inspired by that faith."

"Thanks, Connie." It had been a deep enough subject that Ryan was glad she'd come at the topic a few different ways. He was going to need to re-listen to this conversation, for every section had carried something that felt profound as he listened to her.

"I really like this topic," Connie said comfortably. She didn't resume walking.

"Oh! This is your home."

Connie smiled. "Yes."

The block-long brick building had once been a row of narrow and deep storefronts a hundred years before. Each storefront was now a private home, the sidewalk windows replaced with matching color brick and higher windows fitted with unique curved stainglass designs. Ornately fashioned metal work guarded colorful front doors. Connie was standing at the brief walkway to a front door which was a deep olive green, a painted 76 on the red mail box.

"It's a nice neighborhood," he decided, nothing predictable about where she had decided to live and that suited her. "You've given me a huge amount to think about tonight."

"It gets easier from here. You've seen the big boulders, faith being the last truly big one. From here it's mostly implementation and conversations about how pieces fit together."

"I'm ready for easier. Are you still up for coffee in the morning?"

"I open Connie's Pizza on time regardless of how late the concert nights go, so I'll be walking by my favorite coffee shop for breakfast. You want to be there at 7:45 a.m. I'll be there."

"Then I'll see you in about eight hours. Thanks for this, Connie, all of it, earplugs, chocolate chip cookies, meeting Ben and Jason…"

She laughed. "I'm counting on that good humor when you tell me tomorrow your ears are still ringing." She unlocked her front door and waved goodnight. He turned to walk back to the hospital and his car, glad for the time to think about all that had transpired over a long day.

****

Ryan didn't want to end the day without adding to his notes, keeping up with the conversations, as another would be coming tomorrow. He gave himself half an hour before he shut off the lights and started his notes on faith.

Ryan Notes / conversation five / additional references

His divine power has granted to us all things that pertain to life and godliness, through the knowledge of him who called us to his own glory and excellence, by which he has granted to us his precious and very great promises, that through these you may escape from the corruption that is in the world because of passion and become partakers of the divine nature. (2 Peter 1:3-4)

the righteousness based on faith says…the word is near you, on your lips and in your heart…; because, if you confess with your lips that Jesus is Lord and believe in your heart that God raised him from the dead, you will be saved. For man believes with his heart and so is justified and he confesses with his lips and so is saved. (Romans 10:6b-10)

For whatever is born of God overcomes the world; and this is the victory that overcomes the world, our faith. (1 John 5:4)

You do not have, because you do not ask. You ask and do not receive, because you ask wrongly, to spend it on your passions. (James 4:2b-3)

12

Saturday morning brought showers and the surprising realization he didn't have Connie's phone number. Calling the number for Connie's Pizza only got him a cheerful recording which detailed the location and hours she was open.

Ryan drove over to the coffee shop and hoped for the best regarding limited parking. He saw Connie walking toward the coffee shop carrying an umbrella, in no particular hurry compared to other pedestrians, looking actually quite comfortable decked out in warm waterproof boots and a long water slick jacket with hood, black gloves. He flashed his light and caught her attention, then lowered the passenger side window. "I'll give you a lift to Connie's Pizza in exchange for a cup of coffee there," he offered, ignoring the impatient driver behind him. Connie collapsed the umbrella and joined him in the car and Ryan chose to also ignore the gesture the driver behind him made for the thirty second pause.

"Thanks." She clipped on her seatbelt and lowered the hood, ran fingers through her hair, didn't seem bothered by the rain that had gotten past the umbrella. He circled the block to get back to Voss street and turned toward Connie's Pizza.

"I realized I didn't have your number."

"How's your memory?"

"For numbers, pretty solid."

She gave him her number. "I would have called the hospital and relayed a message if I was canceling on you."

He nodded. "I appreciate that. I wasn't sure if you walked to work every morning because it's simply good exercise and convenient, or if you do it because you don't have a car in Chicago. Not many do who live this close to downtown, preferring cabs or a ride-share."

"I drive an older pickup truck but don't bother to get it out of the garage unless I want to use it for three or four days. There's no parking where I live, but I can use the alley by the business when I wish."

"I'll park in the alley then, if you don't mind."

"I'd recommend it," she agreed.

"What color truck?"

"Blue. Flag blue, not the lighter blue of a summer sky."

He smiled at the image of her in that truck and thought it suited her.

"Before I forget," Connie tugged a flash drive from her pocket, "I did your homework for you. A long audio titled Saturday and also some shorter ones."

"Thanks. I'm stunned you had time to do this." He slid the flash drive into his shirt pocket for safe keeping.

"I couldn't have predicted when the ten and twenty minute gaps would show up, but there have been a few I captured for you."

He glanced over, relieved she looked less drawn than she had a couple days before. He knew her last night had been on the brief side. "Do you mind if I ask a personal question?"

"You can ask anything you like. I'm good at saying no comment. Just because you ask, doesn't mean I'll answer."

"I can live with that." There wasn't a particularly good way to ask this, so he just said the words. "How'd you sleep last night? Are you seeing a few hours of decent sleep a night, or is it still choppy? Combat medic to civilian—that's got baggage coming home with you."

She looked surprised by the question, then quietly touched, as her smile softened. "My mind is reasonably tranquil, Ryan, but thank you for asking. I'm about where most combat medics would be ten years after they leave the service. Jesus and I have a routine with memories of events that lets him sort them out for me. It's rare to need to deal with a particular memory more than a few times. And I have had George around, if not monthly, on a regular enough basis I could always get a few hours of his time. He is the best I've ever seen for helping soldiers process the mental toll being in the military creates. He now trains most of the chaplain corps on the process he uses.

"Being at peace doesn't require peaceful surroundings. Once you learn that truth, the war zone with bullets flying, the bumper-to-bumper traffic with snarled impatient drivers"—she nodded out the window—"or the quiet evening at home, can all be accommodated. I choose not to be afraid and that dramatically reduces the stress. I choose to relax and that drastically improves my ability to come up with creative decisions in any situation. I have to be busier, both mentally and physically, in a combat zone than when I'm at home lying on my couch, but I can be at peace in either place. My life is under my control even if you're trying to cause me problems. I don't have to accept what you're doing. I've got God with me and I can deal with this world however it needs to be dealt with. I literally have the peace of Jesus; he's given it to me.

"Besides, I'm immortal, Ryan, eternal. What do I care if I die today? I feel sorry for whoever has to do the paperwork, but there are no dangling threads in my life that are unfinished. I've told Jesus how many years I want to live. If I die before that date, he's going to prompt someone to pray to raise me from the dead. They may ignore the prompting, but Jesus is good at answering my prayers by whatever means are necessary. He'll figure something out."

They were at Connie's Pizza, so Ryan parked and let Connie open up the shop, get lights on, turn on the oven and start the coffee, before he asked the first of the questions burning to be asked. While she did those items, he set down the chairs off the tables for her. He chose a table near the drink counter when he was done and took a seat. "You can choose when you want to die?"

"Sure. This is like lesson ten material so you'll just have to let me say what I say and wait for me to explain some of it." She settled comfortably in a chair opposite him and slipped off her boots. "I can give you until 8:40 thanks to the enjoyable drive, but there's other stuff more important I think you should hear today."

"I can accept that."

"God gives man free will. There are very few things God doesn't let man decide. You can't decide when Jesus comes back, the Father has reserved that decision to himself. You can't decide that I will believe in Jesus, that's my call, not yours. Everything else? Pretty much up to us.

"Joshua decided the sun wasn't going to go down. So it didn't go down. Elijah decided it wasn't going to rain on the earth for three and a half years. So it didn't rain. David decided God should have a house to live in. God was content with his tent. God said I chose the man and the man wants to build me a house, so I'll go along with that plan. God threw himself into the endeavor with great passion and made the dedication of the temple David's son Solomon built the high point of Israel's history. There's never been a point of more splendor or glory in the Old Testament. God loved that house because to build it for Him was in David's heart. That's worship expressed in a tangible way and God loved it.

"By the way—have you ever read the first tabernacle blueprints, the tent God called home before the temple was built? God loves details. 'Hey Moses, here's the blueprint for what I want my tent to look like, down to the color of the thread in the curtains.'" She laughed at the image her own words created. "And as you read, you realize every one of those details was telling us something about Jesus and the unfolding plan bringing us salvation. God loves symbolic pictures of truth.

"Anyway. From those three examples which God recorded in scripture to show us where the boundaries are of our free will, I'd say that God is letting man have enormous say in what unfolds."

Connie rose to get their coffee and brought two full mugs over to the table. "The length of our life is not set in stone in God's book. God says you're appointed once to die, but he doesn't say when. God knowing the date of your death is different from him setting it. All your decisions are factored into the date he knows.

"Hezeki'ah said I don't want to die. God said because you prayed, I'll add 15 years to your life.

"People tend to forget God's first command with promise — if you want it to go well with you and you want to live a long life on the earth, honor your parents.

"You can ask to live 120 years on the earth and God will let you. Adam lived like 900 years. The reason we can't live more than 120 years now is that God changed the limit after the Noah flood, said I'm done with men living 600, 800 years, thinking nothing but evil thoughts. I'm setting a new limit on mankind at 120 years.

"Moses, who spoke to God face-to-face, was as righteous as a man could become under that first covenant. Guess how long he lived? 120 years.

"Scripture says Moses' eyesight was not dim, he was in good health, he climbed a mountain the day he died. God told him 'you're going to die today, so go climb that mountain, look at the promised land and then I'll take your breath away and you'll sleep with your fathers.' Moses dies at 120. Don't bother to ask for 121 years, because God's already said no. But 120 is fine.

"Paul was wrestling with when to die, torn between the beauty of heaven or the usefulness of his ministry on earth. He decided to stay longer on earth in order to keep ministering to people.

"It's like dying without a will and so the state decides what happens to your stuff, or you make a will and decide for yourself what will happen to your stuff. If you don't tell God when you want to die, then other people may choose the date. Satan may try to step in with a date. Or your own actions will accumulate and cause your body to stop functioning on some unpredictable date. When you tell God when you want to die, he'll answer your prayer and adjust your death date to match your prayer request. That doesn't mean you are a passive spectator to the process. If he says don't take that plane flight, you have to adjust your plans and not get on the plane. Life is still walked out together on how to get to that date you've asked Him to set. You cooperate with God so He can give you your request. But that's how God answers every prayer. We pray and we cooperate. God will let you decide when you die."

She leaned back in her chair, relaxed. "I'm surprised more people don't make this decision for themselves. They fret and worry about what might go wrong, 'maybe I'll have an accident and I'll die this year,' when they could have just set a date with God for the year they turn 97 and know they don't have to worry about the question. Death won't come until then, unless they tell God, 'I've changed my mind, I want to die when I'm 85, I'm tired of earth, all my friends have passed away and I want to go to heaven sooner.'"

"Connie, who taught you this? To choose the age you want to die?"

"George. He was talking to one of those 23-year-olds in the army, a young man who has just realized how close he came to getting shot and killed while on patrol that day. The young man is terrified of going back out on patrol come morning. He's certain he's going to die, he's never going to get married, have kids, have the life he's dreamed about; why was he so stupid as to think the army would be an adventure?

"George, in his calm chaplain way, listens to him for a while, then gives him a piece of advice. 'Relax, son. If you die, I'll pray to resurrect you from the dead.'

"The advice spread like a wildfire. Word gets around the unit. You need a DNR to stay dead. Otherwise, George was going to yank you from death back to life. A DNR in our parlance is Do Not Resurrect. And the corollary spreads just as fast: If you're a Christian and not too worried about dying because death gets you to heaven, you'd better file a DNR with George so you can stay there once you arrive.

"The change was like night and day. They turned into one of the most fearless units in the army. No one was afraid to die anymore. And no one did. They all headed home together eighteen months later when their tour finished."

"How many did George pray for?"

Connie smiled, but simply got up to get the coffee pot and refill their mugs. "You'll need to ask George that question. Somewhere in that stretch of time, George explained choosing the age you want to die and it had the same effect in a more permanent way. Rather than rely on a person to be there to keep his word—George being there to pray—you could just agree with God on the date and let God sort out details to get you to that age. If someone needs to pray to raise you from the dead, God will arrange for that person to be there when you need him."

"You really are comfortable with the idea of raising the dead being more than just for bible times, or a one person every hundred years rare event in Christianity."

"Answer me this, Ryan. Who holds the keys of death?"

He thought for a moment. "Jesus."

Connie nodded. "Revelation 1:18b. 'I have the keys of Death and Hades.' Who said 'whatever you ask in my name, I will do it,' said it twice in the space of 2 verses?"

"Jesus."

"Does Jesus lie?"

He smiled as she walked him straight into her first lesson. "No. Jesus does not lie."

"Jesus always did the will of the Father. And Jesus raised the dead. Scripture names 4 of those individuals and there were probably more given Jesus' comment to John's disciples. So people can die early, before it's the Father's will. Jesus was setting things right by raising them from the dead. He didn't stress over it. 'Little girl, get up.' 'Young man, I say to you rise.' 'Lazarus, come out.' It wasn't hard.

"Peter raised the dead. He prayed, then turned to Tabitha and said, 'Tabitha, rise.' She opened her eyes and when she saw him, she sat up.

"You know who else believed in raising the dead? Abraham. He took Isaac to the mountain top to kill him because God said to sacrifice his son. But Abraham told his servants we will be back, plural. He believed he would kill Isaac and God would raise him from the dead so that they would both return together. His descendents would be born through Isaac; Abraham had God's word on that. So if a resurrection is what it took for God to keep his word, then a resurrection would certainly happen. Abraham had a fearless confidence in God. He was a man who had taken into his heart the truth that God does not lie. He *never* will.

"Eli'jah and Eli'sha both raised the dead. One of the most fascinating resurrections ever recorded involves Eli'sha. He's lived his life and died, been buried for some months. There's another funeral happening in that cemetery in the spring. A marauding band of enemies is seen and the people attending scatter. The guys officiating at the funeral look around for where to put the dead man. Eli'sha's tomb is the nearest. They cast the dead man into the grave of Eli'sha and as soon as the man touches the bones of Eli'sha, he revives and stands on his feet." Connie laughed. "Now that's a quandary. What do you say to the dead guy who is now alive? 'Run! They're going to kill anyone they catch.' If he doesn't run fast, the man is going to die twice in the same twenty-four hours. That's just really bad timing." She chuckled. "Anyway…

"God himself obviously believes in raising the dead. God the Father was foreshadowing with Abraham and Isaac what He himself would do with Jesus. The Father would one day sacrifice his own beloved son then resurrect him and use that act as the means to save the entire world.

"People haven't stopped dying early, Ryan, before it's the will of the Father. Just look at the children dead of gunshot violence in Chicago. None of those deaths are the Father's will. The thief came to steal, kill and destroy and we let him.

"The real question is—why aren't we doing the will of the Father like Jesus did? Jesus came to destroy the works of the devil. Jesus hasn't changed. He uses us now; we are his co-laborers. We are the body of Christ here on earth.

We aren't passive spectators. It's our job to bring about the Father's will on earth using Jesus' name. When we see someone who died early, we should set things right by raising them from the dead."

"It is fascinating to listen to you. You really are comfortable with this subject."

"Had we arrived at it in the correct order of lessons you wouldn't be surprised at what you heard today, nor why I'm comfortable with the subject." She tipped her mug toward him. "You missed it, didn't you? I don't mean that question in an 'I'm disappointed in you' kind of way, but I'm always puzzled why it happens. In all the conversation going by you on the topic you've been most interested in, you still missed the answer you've been eagerly wanting to learn."

Ryan went still. "Keep talking, please."

"Ryan, who wants to do God's will? Think about that for a moment. It's not a trick question. Who wants to do God's will?"

She stayed quiet.

"God," he replied, catching the edge of what he had missed.

She smiled. "People get scared thinking this is too hard a prayer to tackle, not realizing that it is actually the easiest prayer of them all." She held up her hand and used her fingers to take him through it.

"Someone dies early. Satan has killed a person with disease or other means. It's a situation that is clearly outside of God's will.

"It's God's desire that this person not be dead. The only way they are going to be alive is if God raises them from the dead. So God wants to raise them from the dead.

"Now you enter the picture. It's you and it's God and it's a dead person.

"Who wants this person to be alive? God. And who wants his will to be done on earth? God. The Holy Spirit is God on earth; his name literally means 'one called alongside to help you'. He's with you to do what He Himself, God, wants done.

"So you find the courage to speak and you say, 'God I'd like you to do what you desire to do on earth. I ask you to give this person back his life.' Then you turn to the person and say, 'in Jesus' name, wake up.'

"And the person opens their eyes."

She gave him a moment then smiled. "Listen to it again in slightly different words.

"Someone dies early. It is God's desire that this person not be dead.

"God wants his own will to be done on earth—the Lord's Prayer— 'your kingdom come, your will be done, on earth as it is in heaven.' Jesus has all authority in heaven and on earth. Satan has none. Death has none. Jesus holds the keys of death.

"Now you enter the picture. It's you and it's God and it's a dead person. The Holy Spirit is with you; God isn't off somewhere else, he's literally right there with you.

"Ryan, God desires to do his own will. In this situation, how hard is it going to be for you to have success? God is with you wanting to do what he himself desires, he's just decided to work with you to get it done rather than work independent of you. He's given you the privilege of speaking for him. You have to pray. That's it. If you understand the situation you're in, you can simply turn to the person and say 'in Jesus' name, wake up.'

"Or you can pray with more words, 'God, this person died early. God, this isn't your will, you want this person to be alive. God, do what you want to do on earth. Raise this person from the dead.' and you turn to the person and say, 'In Jesus' name, I now tell you to wake up.'

"A few words or a few sentences, either way, God is raising that person from the dead. They wake up because God wants them to be alive. God wants to answer this prayer.

"We see a resurrection as hard. God sees it as, 'I resurrected my son, now who do you need resurrected? I just need a name.' The Holy Spirit breathes on someone and they are alive again. We do the speaking and say what is going to happen. God does the doing."

Ryan sat forward. He'd seen it now and even more, had heard her confidence. "Connie, how many people have you raised from the dead?"

"More than you, less than George."

He felt himself grinning.

He had one critical question. "Who has died early? How do you define it?"

She laughed. "A good question," she admitted. "I have a few rules of thumb: Any young person. Any mother or father of young children. Anyone who dies before their parents. In Luke 7, the funeral procession, a man has died. Jesus sees his mother, a widow, in the crowd and Jesus has compassion on her and raises her son from the dead.

"Anyone, of any age, who I think wasn't a Christian and would go to hell if they stayed dead. God's will is that none would perish. I've already got God's word on the fact he doesn't want this person dead under these circumstances. That's the easiest prayer of all. 'Death, in Jesus' name, get your hands off this person.' Then tell the person to wake up.

"Anyone under 120 years old who desires to live a long life on earth. In general, I won't pray to raise a Christian who is 90 years or older unless I know them and they have told me they want to live to 100 or 120; then I'll pray to raise them from the dead. People have a right after a certain age to just let their decision be their own.

"Anyone in those categories dead less than 14 days. God doesn't want people sitting by a grave three months after someone died asking God to bring them back to life. Grieving needs to be allowed to begin and run its course. 14 days is enough for word to arrive that someone has died and for me to travel to where they are if that's necessary. Less than 4 days is putting God in a box smaller than his willingness to act; more than 2 weeks is creating some chaos with the answer and God isn't a God of chaos. I asked for a number and God said 14 days, so that's where my own comfort level rests."

"Why haven't you been doing this quietly around Chicago since you got here? Why haven't you asked a hospital if you could pray for every person when they die before the hospital physician pronounces someone dead and gives an official time of death, before the families are notified of the death?"

She didn't answer him.

And Ryan got his eyes opened. "Oh! You have been."

He ran through the implications of that. "And I'll answer my own next question. It's not your job to pray for every person who dies in the world, or even in the Chicago area. God has a body of believers. God has some he wants you to pray for and others are someone else's responsibility."

Connie nodded. "My way of handling this is mostly learned wisdom. Jesus healed everyone who came to him and everyone his Father sent him to heal. I follow the same model. If you die in my vicinity, I'm going to pray to raise you from the dead. Otherwise, I go where God sends me. God isn't whispering so softly I miss his directions. When God has someone he wants me to pray for, he'll make sure I know the where and when.

"I have a responsibility to train others, to share what I know, just as George taught me and I am doing that with a small group that can put that training to immediate use—paramedics, a surgeon and the like. I didn't choose you, but you managed to nominate yourself. Mostly I'm training the group how to heal the sick, so people get well rather than die. That's actually harder to teach than how to raise the dead."

She shifted back in her seat, sat quietly, gave him time to think about what she'd said. "Ready for the best part?"

He was stunned to realize there was more. "Sure."

"God wants his will to be done on earth. That's actually the secret to everything, Ryan. When you pray for something God wants, who is the one who most desires to answer your prayer? God.

"You may deeply want your prayer answered, but God wants to answer it with a passion to the depth of his being. It's his will, his own desire and he's been longing for you to pray so he can answer you.

"God respects man's free will. God gave us the responsibility to pray. If we pray, God will answer. God will do his own will on earth with joy. If we don't pray, both we and God miss out.

"All the promises God has written in scripture are things he wants to do. They are his desires. We like those promises because they are good things we'll enjoy. But to God, those promises are his personal desires, what God personally wants to do. He's aching for someone to pray and ask him so he can answer. God will not do his will on earth without us. He has committed himself to us being part of the process for how he will rule over the earth. So he longs for people to pray. It gives him joy when he can answer a prayer and deliver one of those promises to earth. We co-labor with God. Want to thrill God's heart? Pray his promises.

For all the promises of God find their Yes in him [Jesus]. That is why we utter the Amen through him, to the glory of God. (2 Corinthians 1:20)

"I've got it, Connie," Ryan said, not finding words to better express what he was feeling, it was so intense.

She smiled. "I know you do; I can see the truth reflecting in your expression. You're going to have fun these next few weeks stepping into praying with God over all kinds of stuff. Go for it. Nothing is more encouraging than praying and getting answers.

"I'd like to offer one piece of advice. There's a reason Jesus would heal someone and then promptly tell them not to say anything, not to tell anyone. Discretion is useful when you step into healings and miracles. Not to hide giving God glory, but to keep the public from descending upon what is actually a private matter between the individual healed and God.

"Pray for people. Pray about situations. But do it quietly. Just you and God for now. Try not to be noticed by your staff, pray when people are asleep if you can. Let answers flourish and people thank God for good things happening and try your best to keep your fingerprints off the situations. You need time, Ryan. You want to limit how many people you have to convince not to say anything. Simply don't be known and that problem disappears. Your uncle will be a good resource, draft along behind him. A chaplain can be an explanation for about anything that happens."

"A good suggestion."

"I'm sorry I'm out of time. I need to get started on the prep work."

Ryan stood and pushed in his chair. "Connie, it was the best conversation I can remember ever having about God."

"I'm glad you're soaking this stuff in like a sponge. You were ready to hear it, Ryan. That's why it's connecting now. And it's why God rather pushed you onto my calendar." She laughed. "This wasn't at all what I thought the topic should be this morning."

"I want the rest of it, all the lessons you've got to share."

"We'll get to them," Connie agreed. "Take your time with this material. Remember you're in a marathon with God, not a sprint. He's got a lot he wants to do with you, but this is a process. Let God set the pace, lean into the fact you are working together. God arranges situations. It's not a big deal to God, healings and miracles are like 'would you pass me the salt?' kind of requests to Him. Learn to see them like God does and relax, you're just cooperating with what God wants to do, what he already desires to do. He's going to arrange the situations and nudge you inside how he'd like you to pray. You just find the courage to obey the

Holy Spirit's voice and speak into the situation what needs done."

"That's good advice, too. I'll do that, Connie."

She walked him to the door, showed him out and locked it behind him.

The rain had paused, the clouds overhead were still gray cast, but it had turned simply windy damp. Ryan looked at the time. 8:45 a.m. She'd managed in under an hour to convince him he could raise the dead and given him the confidence to actually try. He shut off the recording and immediately made a duplicate copy.

"God, there aren't words rich enough for saying this thanks. Wow."

****

Ryan scrapped the plans he had for his Saturday so he could have time to think about this. He needed to get his notes done so he could walk through the conversation in detail. Then he needed to get the audio to his uncle and brother and arrange a conversation with them. Taking an hour now before he went to see Margaret was probably best. Ryan elected to take a back table in the hospital cafeteria, offer a smile and an 'I'm not here' to staff who happened to see him and used his phone bible app to search out the passages their conversation had touched on so he could see it for himself.

Ryan Notes / conversation six / additional references

The reason the Son of God appeared was to destroy the devil's work. (1 John 3:8b NIV)

Then the LORD said, "My Spirit will not contend with humans forever, for they are mortal; their days will be a hundred and twenty years." Genesis 6:3 NIV)

Moses was 120 years old when he died, yet his eyesight was clear and he was as strong as ever. (Deuteronomy 34:7 NLT)

On the day the LORD gave the Amorites over to Israel, Joshua said to the LORD in the presence of Israel: "Sun, stand still over Gibeon and you, moon, over the Valley of Aijalon." So the sun stood still and the moon stopped, till the nation avenged itself on its enemies, as it is written in the Book of Jashar. The sun stopped in the middle of the sky and delayed going down about a full day. There has never been a day like it before or since, a day when the LORD listened to a human being. Surely the LORD was fighting for Israel! (Joshua 10:12-14 NIV)

Elijah was a human being, even as we are. He prayed earnestly that it would not rain and it did not rain on the land for three and a half years. Again he prayed and the heavens gave rain and the earth produced its crops. (James 5:17-18 NIV)

Elisha died and was buried. Now Moabite raiders used to enter the country every spring. Once while some Israelites were burying a man, suddenly they saw a band of raiders; so they threw the man's body into Elisha's tomb. When the body touched Elisha's bones, the man came to life and stood up on his feet. (2 Kings 13:20-21 NIV)

In those days Hezekiah became ill and was at the point of death. The prophet Isaiah son of Amoz went to him and said, "This is what the LORD says: Put your house in order, because you are going to die; you will not recover." Hezekiah turned his face to the wall and prayed to the LORD, "Remember, LORD, how I have walked before you faithfully and with wholehearted devotion and have done what is good in your eyes." And Hezekiah wept bitterly. Before Isaiah had left the middle court, the word of the LORD came to him: "Go back and tell Hezekiah, the ruler of my people, 'This is what the LORD, the God of your father David, says: I have heard your prayer and seen your tears; I will heal you. On the third day from now you will go up to the temple of the LORD. I will add fifteen years to your life. And I will deliver you and this city from the hand of the king of Assyria. I will defend this city for my sake and for the sake of my servant David.'" (2 Kings.20:1-6 NIV)

By faith Abraham, when God tested him, offered Isaac as a sacrifice. He who had embraced the promises was about to sacrifice his one and only son, even though God had said to him, "It is through Isaac that your offspring will be reckoned." Abraham reasoned that God could even raise the dead and so in a manner of speaking he did receive Isaac back from death. (Hebrews 11:17-19 NIV)

Abraham offering Isaac as a sacrifice / full passage / Genesis 22:1-18

Children, obey your parents in the Lord, for this is right. "Honor your father and mother" – which is the first commandment with a promise – "so that it may go well with you and that you may enjoy long life on the earth." (Ephesians 6:1-3 NIV)

For to me [Paul], to live is Christ and to die is gain. If I am to go on living in the body, this will mean fruitful labor for me. Yet what shall I choose? I do not know! I am torn between the two: I desire to depart and be with Christ, which is better by far; but it is more necessary for you that I remain in the body. Convinced of this, I know that I will remain and I will continue with all of you for your progress and joy in the faith, so that through my being with you again your boasting in Christ Jesus will abound on account of me. (Philippians 1:21-26 NIV)

Then one of the synagogue leaders, named Jairus, came and when he saw Jesus, he fell at his feet. He pleaded earnestly with him, “My little daughter is dying. Please come and put your hands on her so that she will be healed and live.” So Jesus went with him. A large crowd followed and pressed around him. … some people came from the house of Jairus, the synagogue leader. “Your daughter is dead,” they said. “Why bother the teacher anymore?” Overhearing what they said, Jesus told him, “Don't be afraid; just believe.” He did not let anyone follow him except Peter, James and John the brother of James. When they came to the home of the synagogue leader, Jesus saw a commotion, with people crying and wailing loudly. He went in and said to them, “Why all this commotion and wailing? The child is not dead but asleep.” But they laughed at him. After he put them all out, he took the child's father and mother and the disciples who were with him and went in where the child was. He took her by the hand and said to her, “Talitha koum!” (which means “Little girl, I say to you, get up!”). Immediately the girl stood up and began to walk around (she was twelve years old). At this they were completely astonished. He gave strict orders not to let anyone know about this and told them to give her something to eat. (Mark 5:22-24, 35b-43 NIV)

Soon afterward, Jesus went to a town called Nain and his disciples and a large crowd went along with him. As he approached the town gate, a dead person was being carried out--the only son of his mother and she was a widow. And a large crowd from the town was with her. When the Lord saw her, his heart went out to her and he said, “Don't cry.” Then he went up and touched the bier they were carrying him on and the bearers stood still. He said, “Young man, I say to you, get up!” The dead man sat up and began to talk and Jesus gave him back to his mother. They were all filled with awe and praised God. “A great prophet has appeared among us,” they said. “God has come to help his people.”

This news about Jesus spread throughout Judea and the surrounding country. (Luke 7:11-17 NIV)

As Peter traveled about the country, he went to visit the Lord's people who lived in Lydda. There he found a man named Aeneas, who was paralyzed and had been bedridden for eight years. "Aeneas," Peter said to him, "Jesus Christ heals you. Get up and roll up your mat." Immediately Aeneas got up. All those who lived in Lydda and Sharon saw him and turned to the Lord. In Joppa there was a disciple named Tabitha (in Greek her name is Dorcas); she was always doing good and helping the poor. About that time she became sick and died and her body was washed and placed in an upstairs room. Lydda was near Joppa; so when the disciples heard that Peter was in Lydda, they sent two men to him and urged him, "Please come at once!" Peter went with them and when he arrived he was taken upstairs to the room. All the widows stood around him, crying and showing him the robes and other clothing that Dorcas had made while she was still with them. Peter sent them all out of the room; then he got down on his knees and prayed. Turning toward the dead woman, he said, "Tabitha, get up." She opened her eyes and seeing Peter she sat up. He took her by the hand and helped her to her feet. Then he called for the believers, especially the widows and presented her to them alive. This became known all over Joppa and many people believed in the Lord. Peter stayed in Joppa for some time with a tanner named Simon. (Acts 9:32-43 NIV)

I [John] turned around to see the voice that was speaking to me. And when I turned I saw seven golden lampstands and among the lampstands was someone like a son of man, dressed in a robe reaching down to his feet and with a golden sash around his chest. The hair on his head was white like wool, as white as snow and his eyes were like blazing fire. His feet were like bronze glowing in a furnace and his voice was like the sound of rushing waters. In his right hand he held seven stars and coming out of his mouth was a sharp, double-edged sword. His face was like the sun shining in all its brilliance. When I saw him, I fell at his feet as though dead. Then he placed his right hand on me and said: "Do not be afraid. I am the First and the Last. I am the Living One; I was dead and now look, I am alive for ever and ever! And I hold the keys of death and Hades. "Write, therefore, what you have seen, what is now and what will take place later." (Revelation 1:12-19 NIV)

13

"Thanks for bringing these by, Ryan."

"It's my pleasure Margaret." He stepped into the apartment with her, where the heat was in the eighties and he promptly sweltered in the jacket he wore. "Are you sure there's nothing else you need?"

"Tangelos, bananas, milk and the prescription. I'm well stocked for a siege, but was running out of perishables."

Her voice was less raspy and her color was good, though that could be more low-grade fever than health. He didn't ask how she was feeling, for he knew her permanent answer by heart, she was always fine, even if she felt miserable. He glanced around the living room and all looked in order, she'd felt well enough to straighten the magazines and carry dishes to the kitchen, to neatly stack her knitting supplies beside her chair.

The blanket and pillow beside the recliner were normally in the spare room, it looked like she'd been napping and nesting in the recliner in front of the TV. At a guess, it was easier on her breathing to be elevated than lying down. A glass of iced tea and another of the juice she favored were on coasters by the recliner, she was taking the doctors orders to stay hydrated seriously. Ryan saw his mother had also been by, he recognized the basket with the blue trim she used to carry pies and casserole dishes. "Walter asked if you'd give him a call this afternoon," Ryan mentioned, choosing not to treat her as an invalid in tacit recognition of her pride.

Margaret nodded as she unpacked the sack on the kitchen counter. "I'll remember. Would you like to stay for coffee?"

If he said yes, she would insist on also fixing him something to eat and he didn't want to tax her energy. He didn't like the sound of her cough, but it was strong and clearing her lungs. He put together the evidence he could see and was satisfied her flu had indeed been stopped at a mild level. She mostly needed more rest and time for the upswing of recovery to grab hold. "I've a meeting at one with the guy giving me an estimate to replace the backyard fence where that tree came down in last month's wind storm," he replied, "and Jeff asked me to take his wife's car into the auto shop for him. Another time? Monday perhaps?"

"Of course."

She came back with five dollars for the co-pay on the prescription. He pocketed it with a smile. She'd let him bring by the occasional groceries as his gift, but was a stickler on paying her own prescription costs. "I want a hug before I go."

She laughed and obliged him. She'd been the hospital's receptionist for decades, then a mainstay in the chaplain's volunteer office. The CEO of the hospital making a house call suited the situation. He loved this woman and the years of history he shared with her. "Call or text if you need anything else, I like fussing over you. And call Walter. He's got the volunteer schedule confused again. He misses you being in the office." She wasn't going to have time to feel old and forgotten, unneeded, while the Cooper family was around.

"Your uncle is a wonderful man, but organized he is not," she agreed. "I'll straighten it out."

She looked to be stable and on the road to recovering and that was good news. He didn't feel comfortable asking if he could pray for her and wasn't sure why, if it was the fact she was his honorary grandmother, was family to him, was older. He wasn't ashamed of the fact he wanted Jesus to heal her, that he was asking for that, he just didn't know how to open the subject without it being awkward. So he settled for the hug and said goodbye and planned to stop by again on Monday.

On the walk through the building and outside, he whispered, “What happened, Holy Spirit? Did I back off because I didn’t want to embarrass her, embarrass me, with the request? This is Margaret; she’s family to me. Did I back off because that was the right thing to do? Read my heart in this situation and tell me what happened, because I’m clueless. I went over confident I could pray for her and heal her and didn’t pray for her in person. What gives with that?”

He was honestly puzzled with his own actions. He’d been praying for her since last Saturday when he first heard the raspy voice. Since last night’s talk on faith, he had prayed with bold assurance to kill the flu virus she was fighting. Had he not prayed today because the problem was already solved? Or had he not prayed because something about introducing the subject had tripped him up and he had in that instant changed his mind about praying with her in person?

It would have been hard to pray out loud the new way he’d want to word the prayer given she hadn’t heard Connie’s audios. She wouldn’t have understood “In Jesus name, death, get your hands off Margaret.” That felt like part of this. He didn’t think Margaret would be comfortable with him praying for her in that fashion, so avoided doing so with her. He would have wanted to explain before he prayed, so as not to surprise her and that would have taken considerable time. Ryan returned to his car parked in one of four visitor slots for the building and went to do the two errands on his list, planning to return to the hospital later in the afternoon to link up with Walter on the chance he’d had time to listen to the audio by then.

The expectations of the person being praying for, how did Connie deal with that? It seemed logical that you didn’t want to startle the person you were praying for with what you prayed. How did she explain what she was going to pray before she prayed it? Connie had mentioned there would be upcoming conversations about implementation and Ryan thought he'd just walked into one of those classic situations.

"Jesus, I'm glad by your wounds Margaret has been healed, that this fight for her recovery is finished and you're the Victor. I agree with you and say thank you for that gift of grace and accept it on her behalf. In Jesus name, I command the flu virus in Margaret's body to cease replicating and to immediately die. In Jesus name, I tell her body to relax, rest and recover strength. Margaret, you are healed by Jesus. Walk into that experience now and enjoy being well. Amen."

The wording felt awkward but the authority in the words felt right, the confidence of faith that he understood she had been healed and he was bringing what had been settled in heaven to her. But he had questions. When you prayed for someone without being present with them, without their knowledge you were praying, how effective were those prayers compared to being with them and in agreement with them, on how and what you would pray? That was going to be an interesting upcoming conversation to have with Connie.

****

Ryan tapped on the door to the chaplain's office late Saturday afternoon. His uncle was lacing up his tennis shoes, a sure sign he was on the way to play basketball with the guys in the rehab wing. The wheelchair league was a powerful therapy in its own right.

"Fascinating audio, Ryan. Absolutely fascinating. You need to hire that gal for the hospital," Walter advised.

Ryan smiled. "I think she enjoys her present life too much to agree, but it's certainly been on my radar. Can I catch you after the game for a conversation?"

"Come find me. I'm hanging around until eight as Marla is having the ladies over. Figured I would walk through ICU, do some praying there, now that I've got some more ammunition to use against death."

Ryan loved the attitude. He hoped Walter was the first of many around the hospital who were going to react in just that way to the audios and teaching notes he wanted to put together. "I'll find you later," he promised his uncle.

If this Saturday stayed calm, they could brainstorm for a couple hours this evening and make real progress toward how they wanted to implement the ideas they had been passing back and forth on communion as well. Once he and Walter had a plan, he'd then speak to Jeff and with three they would have enough to run a small scale test either in the ER or in the ICU. Ryan knew they were still in team formation, pre-season planning, but game day was coming when they would have actual new protocols in place for the hospital. Those metrics his office tracked daily would finally begin recording an engaged fight designed to drive the numbers down. He was eager for that day to arrive.

Ryan headed for the chapel on the second floor, determined to find an hour simply to sit in God's presence and thank him for this last week. He needed to learn something else Connie was showing him with her life. He heard it in her remarks, like the day at the garden park, "Jesus said, 'let's take a walk' and I said 'okay'. We ended up here." She knew God in a comfortable, I know him, relaxed way. Those kinds of remarks were not like his experience.

He was comfortable with God, but she'd shown him how much more was possible. She'd stirred a hunger in him for more of God, more time with him, more interactions, more shared history. He wasn't sure there was a formula you learned for how to do this. But he knew the first step. Go hang out with God without a particular agenda just because you liked his company. It was how any good friendship started. He settled on the back bench in the chapel. He was the only person present for the moment. He draped his arms across the back of the pew ahead of him and let his entire body relax, his mind slow down.

"Hi. This is a really nice Saturday."

He didn't try to come up with more words. That pretty much was the entire reason he was here. He lowered his chin to rest on the back of his hand and he let his smile be the rest of the conversation. God had been speaking since creation, he could handle figuring out how to speak to his adopted son in a way he would clearly hear his voice. Ryan could feel God's pleasure just in the peace that settled in his heart.

****

Ryan spent an enjoyable hour and a half brainstorming with his uncle then drove home. He planned to pick up Melinda tomorrow after church and make the two hour drive north to meet her brother. Spending the Sunday afternoon out on a charter fishing boat would be a new experience. He was looking forward to it, not only because Melinda had asked him to go, but because it was yet another move outside his comfort zone and those had been piling up lately, teaching him some much needed flexibility.

He liked Melinda. He wanted to like Melinda's brother. And tomorrow would reveal a lot of information. It was going to be interesting to see if her nice personality held up under the pressure of a wet, cold and tiring excursion. And sometime during the two hour drive each way, he wanted to find out what Melinda thought in a general way about praying for the sick. He didn't need her as curious about this subject as he was, but he needed her to be at least a rung above merely polite. If this was where his future was heading, he'd be talking about the subject regularly over the next few years. Having a date who fundamentally didn't agree with him on the subject would get old very quickly. He wanted tomorrow to be the kind of success that made it easy to ask if she'd like to go on a third date.

And if he were wise, he'd let that topic rest until tomorrow. It had been a few years since the last truly serious girlfriend. While he was ready to take that step again, he was borrowing trouble anticipating how things would play out with Melinda.

Ryan turned on the radio, heard a talk radio show and remembered Connie had given him a flash drive that morning. He patted his shirt pocket and found with relief it was still there. He pulled into the filing station, set the pump for twenty dollars. While it slowly ticked upward in pumped gas, he used the time to retrieve his laptop and load the audios. One longer audio titled Saturday and four shorter ones. The fill-up dinged complete, he set the pump nozzle back in place and retrieved his credit card receipt. Ryan chose to start the longer of the audios for the remainder of the drive home.

"Let's start with a scripture: And he [Jesus] went about all Galilee, teaching in their synagogues and preaching the gospel of the kingdom and healing every disease and every infirmity among the people. (Matthew 4:23)"

Connie's voice sounded more distant than Ryan was accustomed to, which suggested she had opened her laptop on a counter or table and was speaking while she moved about, but the audio was clear enough he wouldn't have a problem following her as long as he turned the volume up a notch.

"That verse is a good summary of the public years of his ministry. Jesus also invested a great deal of his time privately in teaching a group of disciples, 12 men in particular. Jesus is teaching them with the intention that they become like him. 'A disciple is not above his teacher, but every one when he is fully taught will be like his teacher.' (Luke 6:40) There's a day in particular where that training gets very interesting.

And he [Jesus] called the twelve together and gave them power and authority over all demons and to cure diseases and he sent them out to preach the kingdom of God and to heal. (Luke 9:1-2)

"Jesus says it's time to learn by doing. These guys were mostly fishermen, common guys, who at this point were not born-again, who didn't have the Holy Spirit dwelling in them, for that would come only after the resurrection. They were simply guys who had been with Jesus and had been taught by him.

"Jesus gave them power and authority. How did he do that? Jesus gave them what he had. It's Jesus saying to the twelve, 'I'm sharing my authority as a son of God with you and the Holy Spirit that is with me, I'm sending him out to be with you.' Matthew says Jesus sent out the 12 with the instructions to 'heal the sick, raise the dead, cleanse lepers, cast out demons and preach as you go, saying, `The kingdom of heaven is at hand.''

"The twelve go out and they heal people and cast out demons in Jesus' name. It's a big deal. No one in the history of scripture has ever acted like this group of guys. For the rest of their lives you see people bringing those who are sick to these men expecting them to heal the sick like Jesus does. Jesus has successfully made disciples who do what he does. He's managed to take guys, fishermen mostly, who aren't well-versed in the word of God and turn them into evangelists who can heal people and do it in less than three years. Jesus is a very skilled teacher. What the 12 needed was training, delegated authority and the Holy Spirit and they were able to do miracles. But Jesus isn't finished.

After this the Lord appointed seventy others and sent them on ahead of him, two by two, into every town and place where he himself was about to come. And he said to them, "The harvest is plentiful, but the laborers are few; pray therefore the Lord of the harvest to send out laborers into his harvest. Whenever you enter a town and they receive you, eat what is set before you; heal the sick in it and say to them, `The kingdom of God has come near to you.' (Luke 10:1-2,8-9)

"Jesus sends out 70 more disciples, those who haven't been with him as tightly as the 12 have; he sends them out to learn by doing, to heal the sick and preach the kingdom of God and he tells them to start praying for more laborers, because Jesus wants to send more than just the 70 into the harvest. Jesus gives them instructions, delegates authority and he sends the Holy Spirit with them. They come back full of joy. They've healed the sick, preached, even cast out demons in Jesus' name. Jesus has successfully taught a group of 70 to be like him. What it took was training, delegated authority, the Holy Spirit and they were enabled to do miracles. There's a pattern developing here.

The seventy returned with joy, saying, "Lord, even the demons are subject to us in your name!" And he said to them, "I saw Satan fall like lightning from heaven. Behold, I have given you authority to tread upon serpents and scorpions and over all the power of the enemy; and nothing shall hurt you. Nevertheless do not rejoice in this, that the spirits are subject to you; but rejoice that your names are written in heaven." In that same hour he rejoiced in the Holy Spirit and said, "I thank thee, Father, Lord of heaven and earth, that thou hast hidden these things from the wise and understanding and revealed them to babes; yea, Father, for such was thy gracious will. (Luke 10:17-21)

"What had just been revealed to the 70 disciples that has Jesus bursting with joy? It's that, in the kingdom of God, ordinary men would again rule the earth with the power of God, having authority over the devil and demons, over disease and sickness, by the Holy Spirit being with them. The dominion over the earth, given to mankind by God in the garden of Eden, is being returned to mankind by

Jesus. Jesus is training his disciples how they will rule over sickness and disease, over demons and all the power of satan, in his name.

"After his resurrection, before Jesus returns to heaven, he spends 40 days talking to his disciples about the kingdom of God and giving them instructions. There's a particular conversation Matthew records that is worth considering in detail.

> Now the eleven disciples went to Galilee, to the mountain to which Jesus had directed them. And when they saw him they worshiped him; but some doubted. And Jesus came and said to them, "All authority in heaven and on earth has been given to me. Go therefore and make disciples of all nations, baptizing them in the name of the Father and of the Son and of the Holy Spirit, teaching them to observe all that I have commanded you; and lo, I am with you always, to the close of the age." (Matthew 28:16-20)

"Jesus is talking to the 12 disciples (less Judas) and he's basically saying, the teaching and training I put you guys through, put your disciples through that same training course.

"Observe means to do. Teach them, give instruction, so they know what to do; to observe, to do in like manner, all I have commanded you. What had Jesus commanded the 12 to do? Heal the sick, raise the dead, cleanse lepers, cast out demons and preach the kingdom of God has come.

"The 12 disciples were to teach others, show them how to do stuff, just like Jesus had done with them, until the new disciples looked like the original ones who were teaching them. It's Peter and Paul's instruction to the believers, 'Imitate me as I imitate Christ.'

"The 12 and then the 70 are the early pictures, the examples, of what Jesus was going to bring to life on a larger scale with the church. In Jesus' name, disciples would go throughout the earth healing the sick, preaching the kingdom of God and making more disciples. After the cross, instead of just 70 disciples to send into the harvest, 3,000 would come into the church in a single day, to be trained to be disciples and then sent out into the harvest.

"Jesus' method of making a disciple has not changed in the last 2,000 years, nor has the mission changed. He's going to take ordinary people, he's going to ask them to hang around with him and learn from him, he's going to give them the Holy Spirit and the delegated authority of using his name and then send them out to go heal the sick and proclaim the kingdom of God.

"Jesus is the King of a kingdom. It's the reason why we reign. It's nice to know how he restored the kingdom and defeated satan, but it's not knowledge that you nod at, say 'that's a relief' and then just sit there. It's knowledge that leads you to go do something with Jesus to bring his kingdom all around the earth. We are to use his authority to shut down and stop what satan is doing, just like Jesus did while he was on earth, modeling for us what a son of God does.

> You are my friends if you do what I command you. No longer do I call you servants, for the servant does not know what his master is doing; but I have called you friends, for all that I have heard from my Father I have made known to you. You did not choose me, but I chose you and appointed you that you should go and bear fruit and that your fruit should abide; so that whatever you ask the Father in my name, he may give it to you. (John 15:14-16)

"Jesus expected us to be like him, to go and bear fruit. This isn't the fruit of character which Paul talks about, this is the fruit of works that we do in Jesus' name. Jesus spent his entire life doing his Father's will. So if you want to safely be doing the Father's will, simply do what Jesus did. Multiply bread to feed the hungry. Still the storms. Heal the sick. Raise the dead. Open the eyes of the blind. Make the lame walk.

"That's what Peter did; he started doing what Jesus did. He healed the lame man. He healed the sick. He raised the dead. It got to be that he was so aware of the Holy Spirit being with him, that as he walked by, his shadow would heal people. The guy was a gushing river of living water spilling out on anyone near him. Peter was doing the will of God. You want to know what a disciple looks like, Peter is a good place to start.

"Stephen. Full of the Holy Spirit, grace and power. He did great signs and wonders among the people. Philip. He healed people and the entire town rejoiced. Paul gets shipwrecked and then healed everyone on the island who was sick. We need to be less timid about being who we are. We are Jesus' followers. And when we are well trained by the word, we look and act like the other disciples he trained.

"John says we are to walk as Jesus walked. Paul says imitate me, as I imitate Jesus. That is a serious charge to Christians from two of the major leaders in all of church history, not to mention Jesus' own instructions. We've forgotten that, through the Holy Spirit, they are also speaking to us.

"Jesus has never played favorites. If you want to heal people like Peter did, the Holy Spirit will teach you how. We think this generation can't do what the first century churches did. Who told us that? Satan. We bought a lie, so we sit here with knowledge, but no works. Satan is terrified of us. A Christian who understands his 'in the name of Jesus' authority is the one who can plow through the enemy's camp, stop evil, restore justice and confront head on with what is wrong `in the world. Jesus is Victor. We're the generals on a conquered battlefield. It only looks a mess because we haven't stepped in issuing orders to set it right.

"A local church in this generation has the potential to be the most Christ-like group of disciples in any generation, to be the top church as judged by Jesus to have ever existed. The Holy Spirit does not train to a lesser standard today than he did Christians in the first century. Jesus does not lead the church to a lesser standard today than he did in the first century. How much do we as a local church body want to look like Jesus? He's willing to take us there. God wants to do more than we can ever ask or think. It is impossible to set a bar too high.

"Most churches are content to be good according to their generation's standards. Jesus would love a church to say, 'We want to be your best disciples ever. What do we need to do?' And then listen and follow. It's not that Jesus doesn't want to lead everyone to that place, it's that we've become mostly sheep whose love has grown cold, who are content with what we see, comparing ourselves to others around us. No wonder Jesus offered the question—when the Son of man comes, will He find faith on earth?

"Jesus calls us to be his disciples, to never stop pressing forward. You are a light. Choose to shine brightly, which is your reasonable service to God who loves you. Imitate Christ and make disciples around you who also imitate Christ. That's your mission and the mission of the church, until Jesus comes again."

The recording ended there. Connie was bringing the truth from every direction and if there was a hard place left in his heart, it was becoming ever smaller. Her passion for what the local church could be was ringing in her words. Arriving home, Ryan heated up the chili his mom had sent as leftovers, then headed to his home office to study. It had become an adventure to see where the Holy Spirit would lead him on these nightly journeys.

Ryan Notes / conversation seven / additional references

A disciple is not above his teacher, nor a servant above his master; it is enough for the disciple to be like his teacher and the servant like his master. (Matthew 10:24-25a)

And Jesus went about all the cities and villages, teaching in their synagogues and preaching the gospel of the kingdom and healing every disease and every infirmity. When he saw the crowds, he had compassion for them, because they were harassed and helpless, like sheep without a shepherd. Then he said to his disciples, “The harvest is plentiful, but the laborers are few; pray therefore the Lord of the harvest to send out laborers into his harvest.” And he called to him his twelve disciples and gave them authority over unclean spirits, to cast them out and to heal every disease and every infirmity. These twelve Jesus sent out, charging them, “Go nowhere among the Gentiles and enter no town of the Samaritans, but go rather to the lost sheep of the house of Israel. And preach as you go, saying, `The kingdom of heaven is at hand.' Heal the sick, raise the dead, cleanse lepers, cast out demons. You received without paying, give without pay. Take no gold, nor silver, nor copper in your belts, no bag for your journey, nor two tunics, nor sandals, nor a staff; for the laborer deserves his food. And whatever town or village you enter, find out who is worthy in it and stay with him until you depart. As you enter the house, salute it. And if the house is worthy, let your peace come upon it; but if it is not worthy, let your peace return to you. And if any one will not receive you or listen to your words, shake off the dust from your feet as you leave that house or town. Truly, I say to you, it shall be more tolerable on the day of judgment for the land of Sodom and Gomor'rah than for that town. (Matthew 9:35-38, 10:1, 10:5-15)

After this the Lord appointed seventy others and sent them on ahead of him, two by two, into every town and place where he himself was about to come. And he said to them, “The harvest is plentiful, but the laborers are few; pray therefore the Lord of the harvest to send out laborers into his harvest. Go your way; behold, I send you out as lambs in the midst of wolves. Carry no purse, no bag, no sandals; and salute no one on the road. Whatever house you enter, first say, `Peace be to this house!' And if a son of peace is there, your peace shall rest upon him; but if not, it shall return to you. And remain in the same house, eating and drinking what they provide, for the laborer deserves his wages; do not go from house to house. Whenever you enter a town and they receive you, eat what is set before you; heal the sick in it and say to them, `The kingdom of God has come near to you.' But whenever you enter a town and they do not receive you, go into its streets and say, `Even the dust of your town that clings to our feet, we wipe off against you; nevertheless know this, that the kingdom of God has come near.' I tell you, it shall be more tolerable on that day for Sodom than for that town. (Luke 10:1-12)

The seventy returned with joy, saying, "Lord, even the demons are subject to us in your name!" And he [Jesus] said to them, "I saw Satan fall like lightning from heaven. Behold, I have given you authority to tread upon serpents and scorpions and over all the power of the enemy; and nothing shall hurt you. Nevertheless do not rejoice in this, that the spirits are subject to you; but rejoice that your names are written in heaven." (Luke 10:17-20)

Be imitators of me [Paul], as I am of Christ. (1 Corinthians 11:1)

he who says he abides in him [Jesus] ought to walk in the same way in which he walked. (1 John 2:6)

What you have learned and received and heard and seen in me [Paul], do; and the God of peace will be with you. (Philippians 4:9)

Remember your leaders, those who spoke to you the word of God; consider the outcome of their life and imitate their faith. (Hebrews 13:7)

For I [Paul] will not venture to speak of anything except what Christ has wrought through me to win obedience from the Gentiles, by word and deed, by the power of signs and wonders, by the power of the Holy Spirit, so that from Jerusalem and as far round as Illyr'icum I have fully preached the gospel of Christ, (Romans 15:18-19)

****

It had been the best Saturday of his life and Ryan didn't want it to end. He stepped outside to pick up the Sunday morning paper which a courier delivered around midnight. He let himself linger enjoying the stillness of the night and the bright full moon. "Dad, I'm so looking forward to this next season with you. I asked for breakthrough and you answered my prayer. My basic knowledge of my own faith has risen to the point I even know how to pray to raise people from the dead." He smiled at a thought. "I want more, God, more of you and more of what Connie understands regarding implementation of these things. Thank you God, in advance, for your incredible goodness to me. It really is nice, living life with you."

14

There were a handful of shorter audios on the flash drive Connie had given him. Ryan listened to the first one as he walked to the coffee shop Monday morning. The walk was helpful, as his body had stiffened up overnight. Sunday's boating excursion with Melinda and her brother had exercised muscles his desk job did not normally require.

Melinda's brother had been checking him out Sunday to see if he was a wimp. Ryan had been checking her brother out to see if he could handle holiday meals with him for thirty years. Ryan thought they'd both come away from the initial meeting relieved.

He was simply glad he hadn't suffered being seasick given the water had been choppy and the fish caught were not the trout size ones he was accustomed to catching on the occasional vacation. They were seventy pound walleye, at least he thought they were walleye, he'd heard and forgotten what they were fishing for, and he hadn't wanted to ask the question again and appear as much a novice as he was.

He felt wind burned rather than sun burned and the nice tired of having been active. It had been a good break from his normal life. He'd not hesitated to ask Melinda if she wanted to go on a third date. They'd spend Wednesday evening taking in a show downtown and dessert somewhere fancy with a view. He'd enjoy the upcoming evening with her, but suspected he'd actually find their date having gone fishing to have been the more useful of the two. She was a nice lady even when cold, wet and tired, and still able to laugh at life. Everything he had hoped to see. It had been a totally good day. Even his personal life had taken a good turn in the last couple weeks.

"Ryan, we'll call this short audio A, because it is less than a minute and it's three quick observations.

"The most powerful prayer I know? 'God, show me the unbelief in me so I can toss it in the trash! Amen.'

"Number two: Jesus himself was never sick. Jesus never made anyone sick. Jesus never said to someone, 'it's not the Father's will to heal you.' They are three basic reminders sickness isn't from God. They are from satan and death.

"Third one: Jesus trusted God. Even the Pharisees mocking Jesus as he died on the cross understood that about him. 'He trusts in God, let God deliver him now,' not realizing Jesus was showing them he was the savior of the world by the fact he didn't come down from the cross. At the core of this, healing comes from trusting God and acting on that trust. This isn't hard. Just follow Jesus. Let it really sink in that Jesus knew the Father's will about sickness when he went around destroying it, then go do the same. Trust God and do stuff."

Ryan tagged the audio as one he'd listened to. "God, I like that first prayer she mentioned. Would you do that for me, show me the unbelief in me so I can toss it in the trash? Thank you." He scrolled the list to find another of the short audios, thoroughly enjoying this first sample.

Ryan started the second short audio from Connie, judging he would have just enough time to finish it before he reached the coffee shop.

"Ryan, a brief note on prayer. If you feel like you're having to convince God to answer your prayer, go back to the bible and look to see if what you are asking is what God wants. Ask God, is this your will? First pray until you are clear on what God wants, then pray with confidence knowing God is the one who deeply desires to answer your prayer. God wants to do his own will. He's just been waiting for someone to pray so he can answer. We try to lump the two stages together, to pray with confidence something we're not sure is God's will. Our words don't have much faith and when the prayer isn't answered, we are uncertain why it failed. We didn't have enough faith? It wasn't God's will? And we create all kinds of errors in our thinking, because whatever conclusions we draw, odds are good we will misjudge what actually happened. We create more wrong doctrine out of our experience than any other source.

"Most of the time we perish for lack of knowledge. We didn't know God's heart, thus couldn't figure out his will and then failed at a prayer. It becomes a mess. That's why prayer was designed never to fail. We weren't intended to spend our lives down in the weeds figuring out problems like unanswered prayer. It's an oxymoron, a failed prayer. All the promises of God find their yes in Christ. We need to be better taught who God is, his goodness and how prayer works. We receive what we say with faith. We talk to God. Then we speak to the problem in front of us and tell it in Jesus' name what to do. That combination gets results.

"Look at Jesus. He talked about everything from how to handle your money to what happens when you die, said 'all that I have heard from my Father I have made known to you.' What did Jesus never mention? How to deal with failed prayers. They didn't happen in his life and they aren't intended to happen in the lives of his disciples, either. What Jesus said happened. That's our standard, too."

The advice was timely. Ryan could testify to a life wrestling with prayers that had seemed to fail. He loved the certainty of her statement that a failed prayer was an oxymoron. He pocketed his phone as the coffee shop came into view and tugged out his wallet to get the eight dollars he spent on their combined coffees and breakfast.

Ryan chose a tall table near the window and nursed his large coffee as he watched the crowd, able now to nod a greeting to the other regulars. Connie walked in right at 7:45 a.m. clearly showing a need for more sleep. Ryan handed her a large coffee and a sweet roll and gave her a minute to savor the hot caffeine before they set out on the walk. "On a day like this, I'm more aware than ever the gift it is that you're sharing your time of a morning."

Connie gave him a tired smile. "If I didn't enjoy the conversations, you can be sure I would have found a way to scale them back by now."

He held open the door for her.

"These are nice days for me, Ryan. No one is shooting at me, for one. I get to talk about God, walk to a pizza shop I own, spend a few hours making pizza's and feeding people and call that work. This is close to heaven on earth, with the minor point I need some more sleep given how full my evenings have been running lately." She tipped her coffee toward him. "I appreciate the coffee and the breakfast."

"An easy thank you."

"Today, I just want to make an observation about God."

Ryan, curious where this topic would go, nodded and set his phone to record the conversation as they walked.

"People talk a lot. We're sharing information, sharing perspectives and opinions, we're well meaning about most things we say, but most of what we say and hear, we forget.

"God is different. God does not speak a careless word. He remembers everything he says. Once he's spoken, that's what is. There's a story in the Old Testament that is particularly useful in helping us see this side of God and understand it.

"In Daniel's time, it was a law of the Medes and Persians that no interdict or ordinance of the king could be changed. Even the king couldn't change a decree once he made it.

"King Darius gets talked into signing an interdict, only to find out the order was a trap, designed to send Daniel to the lion's den. The King, in much distress, sets his mind to deliver Daniel; he labors till the sun goes down to rescue him, but can't. He has no choice but to order Daniel thrown into the lion's den.

"God sends his angel to shut the lions' mouths and rescued Daniel. It's a familiar true story, but we often overlook one of the reasons the Holy Spirit had the event written down. God had mercy not just on Daniel, but on King Darius. God reversed the unwise word of a king who could not change his word once it was given.

"God was showing us an example of the problems that could be caused if the king was not perfect in wisdom and knowledge. He'd speak a word that couldn't be changed only to find he really wished he could change it.

"God was giving us an illustration of himself, saying in effect, 'Aren't you glad I'm not like King Darius? Well-meaning, but I get it wrong occasionally?'

"God is a King whose word, once spoken, will never be changed. Even God cannot change the word he speaks. His words are creating and doing what he has spoken. They can't be called back and unspoken.

"I think God knew how powerful that word picture would be once men grasped it. It is a tangible living way to see God's perfection. God is perfect. God never makes a statement that he will labor all night wishing he could change. The words he speaks will last forever. And they are all perfect words.

"Jesus never spoke a careless word. He understood speech as God understands it. Jesus understood he was the son of God and that his words would also be creating and doing things.

"Now consider us Christians. We've been accustomed to speaking whatever we wanted to say and it never had much impact; in fact, our words had so little impact we forgot most of them. But God just changed our nature. God just adopted us as sons. Our words suddenly do have creative power and do accomplish things.

"The most dangerous thing for a Christian to do is talk without realizing there's suddenly a permanent amplifying microphone in front of him and it's both the invisible world and the material tangible world around him which is listening. We say 'its flu season and with my luck I'm going to be one of the first to get it this year' and we wonder how come we get the flu.

"God never speaks a careless word because he understands what his words do in the invisible and visible realms. His words are creating and doing things, they have consequences.

"That reality goes for the sons of God, too. God doesn't say, 'oh she doesn't mean it' and wipe out the effect of my words. When God says there is life and death in the tongue, he is not exaggerating. What we say is what we get, both good and bad. We have a responsibility to understand the power in our words and to stop speaking carelessly. The words of an adopted son of God are creative in their very nature, whether we intend them to be or not. They create darkness as well as light. There is life and death in what we say.

"God does not treat Jesus one way and us another. We are sons of God. Jesus is the first-born and we are adopted, but we are all true sons. That is why Jesus said 'nothing will be impossible to you.' God's creation, this visible world, responds to the words of his sons, just as it does to His words. We need to speak with the wisdom of knowing that what we say can't be called back and changed. It's become active by the fact we spoke it."

She stopped there and Ryan loved the observation. "Thanks, Connie."

"I'm tired. I don't have much profound to offer today."

Ryan laughed. "I enjoyed this one." They still have a few minutes to walk before they reached the hospital. "Would you tell me about how you chose to become a medic? I've been curious about that for a long time."

She nodded and did so as they finished their walk. It felt good, simply knowing he was getting far enough through the subjects she wasn't opening brand new topics every day, but helping him better see prior ones.

****

Ryan located his brother Jeff in the stairwell behind the ER Monday night, timing his search to his brother's first schedule break, not surprised to find him sharing a step with his wife. The sandwich on the plate beside them looked like roast beef on rye. Ryan stopped on the steps below them so he could be eyes level. "Good evening, you two."

Jeff reluctantly broke a brief kiss with his wife though he left his arm around her. "We're going to have to find a new location not to be seen."

Ryan couldn't help but laugh. "Jeff, one of your staff slaps a large heart on the stairwell door with the words *lovebirds present* to warn others not to enter every time you two are spotted heading this direction. The floors above and below go with 'open this and face ER staff wrath' stop signs. You two are like the hospital protected soap opera, have been ever since you started dating."

"I'm getting a sense we're being well watched and well protected. I rather like my staff," Jeff decided.

"Same here," Lisa concurred with a smile.

Jeff reluctantly gave Ryan his attention. "It's important or you wouldn't be here. Got that. What's up?"

"New protocols for the ER. No one is pronounced DOA or given time of death until Walter and I have been called in and been by. We're a religious hospital. We will pray for you when you're sick and pray for you after we've lost a heartbeat. We don't give up on any patient until God signs off that we're done. Walter and I will take the heat for that new policy for now."

Jeff simply nodded. "It's fine with me. I heard the audio and thought 'well, why not?' My staff are a hardy group, they can roll with a successful resurrection. They'll call it a day at the office and give some hand slaps in the break room to celebrate."

Ryan laughed at Jeff's assessment and thought he was probably right.

Jeff mentioned, "You might have some problems though, explaining matters when its one of those obvious cases. To avoid a mob scene when it's a young person, it's not uncommon for paramedics to transport knowing it's simply for us to call the DOA rather than the cops at the scene."

"Those are exactly the cases where we want to intervene. We get a heart beat, they start breathing, I plan to simply glance at the cop or paramedic present and casually mention, 'aren't you glad you didn't decide DOA?' We need to spread the word in fact, to paramedics and cops, that we'd prefer that transport to us over them calling it at the scene."

"I'll casually do so," Jeff offered. "All its going to take is one recovered heart beat on a deceased gunshot victim and word will spread through cops and paramedics to always transport regardless of appearance."

"I haven't lost anyone in the ICU since Walter started visiting with new boldness, telling death to go away," Lisa said. "You're welcome to extend the policy to the ICU as well. It's rather nice knowing we're never out of options anymore."

"Thanks, Lisa."

"There's a lot of curiosity about the audios going around, you admit you've heard one of them you're getting tagged with questions," she added.

Ryan appreciated hearing the grapevine was involved now. "I'm in a quandary with them. It's dangerous to piecemeal them. Listen to only a few, then make an early decision on the whole. Connie's building a foundation across several hours. The overall content is something I think it would be useful for everyone on staff to hear who desires to do so. But if we listen in groups, so we can discuss it, people will really start whispering about what is on those audios before others hear for themselves."

"If an explosion is going to go off, I've always considered it better to have one than multiple smaller ones," Jeff recommended. "Put up all the audios as a group on the hospital net, make those notes you've been writing available and we're going to know rather quickly who is comfortable with the material. The CEO buying into the audios gives cover for those who have an interest. Let staff volunteer who want to participate with new metrics and we'll start tracking who gets prayed for in this fashion. We've always said we're results driven. So let's track the spiritual fight."

"You're okay with that?"

"Sure. I'm talking two check box squares on the electronic chart, prayed against sickness, prayed against death, not more than that. It's easier than the problem you're going to have introducing communion to patients who have never heard it described before as the way God imparts life to us."

"That one is going to be trial and error to figure out what works," Ryan agreed. "Walter is working on something in writing that volunteers can use so everyone is reading the same scriptures and explanation as communion is served—our volunteers pray for you and they bring communion if you'd like to partake. But it's better if we take the next step beyond that as soon as I can get it logistically in place.

"I want communion to be a check box on the meal slips patients fill out. I'm thinking Walter does a chapel video for patients that we put on the internal hospital station as a selection option. A patient can listen to Walter lead them through communion after every meal if they so desire. The bread and juice come with written verses and a text you can read, or you can listen as Walter leads you through the communion service using that same reading."

"Ambitious, practical and highly valuable for metrics," Jeff decided. "It lets you track not only who is receiving communion, but who take the extra step to watch the video as Walter leads communion."

"Anyway, that's what I'm thinking."

"I like everything you're thinking. I understand why you made it private stairway conversation. Now go away. You've had enough of our break time."

Ryan laughed. "Leaving now, lovebirds."

15

Tuesday morning arrived with a strong southerly wind bringing in a mild spring day. Ryan decided to ignore the wind and went with an iced coffee again to celebrate. They lingered at the coffee shop until the donut holes were finished, then set out on their walk.

"So what's the topic for today?" Ryan asked, curious.

Connie laughed. "I'll be making up for yesterday being a light day by going to the other end of the spectrum. Today is a touchy subject. You'll give me grace on this one and hear me out. The Holy Spirit is going to have to show you I'm right. This one is particularly difficult to get across so I'm understood. If there wasn't a point within this you need to see now, I'd skip this one until you've hung around me for a year."

"I'm intrigued already," Ryan replied, starting a recording. "Try me, Connie. You'll probably be surprised."

"We're about to see." She thought a moment, nodded to herself, then went straight to her point. "My body doesn't go from sick to healed because of my works, any more than my sin nature changed to righteousness because of my effort. People make a mistake when they approach forgiveness of sins as a matter of faith, but the healing of their bodies as a matter of their own works. 'Eat right, exercise properly, see this doctor, take this medication.' They plan their own health regime and govern their lives by those rules they've crafted about how to live. Mostly out of ignorance, they've unintentionally substituted works for faith and as a consequence nullified what Jesus did for them. And then they wonder why they constantly get sick despite what they know about the word of God."

She paused there and Ryan couldn't help but laugh in reply. "Okay, wow. I see why it's a difficult topic to get across so it's understood."

She smiled as she continued, "You're going to have to ask the Holy Spirit to bring this one into sharp clarity so you see its core truth, Ryan. The forgiveness of our sins and the healing of our bodies are both grace gifts. Jesus paid the price for both of them on our behalf. They are his finished works and his gifts to us. Because of that fact, they can be received only by faith. That really stuns people to hear, to realize what is being said in the scriptures.

"Separate the two gifts for a minute. Look at righteousness first, the forgiveness of our sins, which we are more accustomed to thinking about. Israel grew up under the law, trying to keep the rules and they figured out over 1,500 years that no matter how hard they tried they couldn't do it. God wanted his people to realize they were helpless to address sin by their own efforts. He let that period last to the point they were clear on the fact sin had them by the throat and they weren't getting free by their own efforts. Then Jesus came, kept the law and gave them righteousness by grace. He offered an exchange, his righteousness for their sins.

the righteousness based on faith says…the word is near you, on your lips and in your heart…; because, if you confess with your lips that Jesus is Lord and believe in your heart that God raised him from the dead, you will be saved. For man believes with his heart and so is justified and he confesses with his lips and so is saved. The scripture says, "No one who believes in him will be put to shame." For there is no distinction between Jew and Greek; the same Lord is Lord of all and bestows his riches upon all who call upon him. For, "every one who calls upon the name of the Lord will be saved." (Romans 10:6a,8b,9-13)

"The only way to be righteous before God is to accept what Jesus did for you by faith. If you continue to try to add your works to the equation, make it Jesus plus you, it nullifies what Jesus did for you and you don't receive the very righteousness you seek. Israel tripped over this point as they kept trying to add back in the law, their good conduct keeping the rules, to what Jesus only gives by grace. If you believe Jesus and what he did for you as your substitute, you're made righteous. If you keep working to be righteous, you die in your sins. The fact that works and grace don't mix is stark in scriptures:

> Gentiles who did not pursue righteousness have attained it, that is, righteousness through faith; but that Israel who pursued the righteousness which is based on law did not succeed in fulfilling that law. Why? Because they did not pursue it through faith, but as if it were based on works. I bear them witness that they have a zeal for God, but it is not enlightened. For, being ignorant of the righteousness that comes from God and seeking to establish their own, they did not submit to God's righteousness. For Christ is the end of the law, that every one who has faith may be justified. (Romans 9:30b-32a, 10:2-4)

"Salvation by faith alone is a well understood fact since the protestant reformation in the 1,500's, when the church returned to the first century understanding of grace. We believe in Jesus and we are made righteous. Salvation is by faith alone, not by our works. So the question arises – do our works change after we believe? Of course. We no longer lie, cheat, steal, murder. Not because we are trying by our works to be righteous, but because we now *are* righteous. Our works change because we are now different people. We have been born again by God and are literally a new creation, a new person.

"A new nature is flowing from the inside, outward. The Holy Spirit is leading us to express who we now are. God crucified our old nature and buried it. Our new nature is like Jesus. We are alive with Christ and we are putting on Christ. Our works (our actions) and our fruit (our character) are both transforming as we walk with the Holy Spirit. God has done this for us by grace. We can never earn righteousness by trying to live right, for all have sinned.

Instead, God replaces our failing works, with Jesus' perfect work on our behalf. God gives us righteousness as a gift of grace, through our faith in the payment Jesus made on our behalf."

Connie paused there to let him think about it and Ryan thoughtfully said, "I can already see the parallels you're about to lay out regarding health. There's something rich here."

She smiled as she nodded and quoted, "'By his wounds you have been healed.' Past tense. Jesus did it for us. It's a finished work which is just as complete as the righteousness he gives. Healing is a grace gift that can only be received by faith. Healing is the same as righteousness. If you try to be healed by your own works, you are trying to add to Jesus' works on your behalf and you end up missing out on the very healing that Jesus paid a very high price to be able to give you as a free gift.

"It's so hard to get this point across with the weight it needs to be said and still be fully understood. You have to really hear it and see what the scriptures are presenting, the truth God is laying out that healing is a finished grace gift only received by faith."

Connie paused and shifted focus a bit. "What I'm not saying is that there is something wrong with exercise and eating by thought-out meal plans and the other things we might classify as works related to healing and health.

"When we believe Jesus for righteousness, our new righteous nature changes our character and our actions—where we once were a liar, now we're telling the truth; once filled with pride, we're now humble; the list of changes is endless. Healing is similar. When you receive the grace gift of healing by faith, you're different inside. So how you live life is likely going to be different. The Holy Spirit may have you sleeping more, living with less stress, doing more activities. But it's not those changes that produce our healing. Your Holy Spirit led life is expressing the fact you *are* healed. That's the core truth nearly every Christian misses.

"We see a disease, infirmity, or sickness and start a works program: doctors and pills, a diet and exercise schedule, add a desperate prayer of 'God, heal me!' and rush off to deal with the problem, thinking God will be pleased with our efforts to get healed and live healthy. What God actually wants is for us to lay down our works program and accept grace from his son. Jesus has *already* healed us. It's already done for us. We need to see it in the word and let Jesus give us healing as the gift of grace it is. Our 'good works' of living healthy do not qualify us to be healed. They can in fact be a detriment if we see healing as coming to us because of our works. We are healed by grace alone, by faith in what Jesus did for us.

"A Christian under grace, knowing they are healed as a gift, goes to the doctor and takes the prescribed pills, takes a walk every evening and does both out of obedience to what the Holy Spirit has directed them to do.

"The Christian beside them in the doctor's waiting room has a gym membership, exercises regularly, faithfully takes the pills prescribed, knows God loves them and prays 'Lord, heal me!'

"Only the one living under grace will enjoy God's gift of health. God wants to give it to both of them, but only one is reaching out to take the grace offered.

"It's important to realize that God doesn't answer us based on our need, he answers us based on our faith. It's love on his part to say have faith, for that's how he can impart all the gifts Jesus gave us. Scripture repeatedly says 'we are saved by grace through faith'. It's the one condition God places upon us for how we live as a Christian. I mentioned before that the word saved in the Greek is huge in its meaning—forgiven, delivered, healed, made whole—saved is being restored fully to life. God will let us remain sick until we seek Jesus' grace to be healed and take it. It's mercy on his part. If God left us thinking that works get us healed, we would never get off the treadmill of trying to do for ourselves what he will give us only as a gift.

"There's a parallel happening. Israel lived under the law for 1,500 years trying by works to earn righteousness. God said stop trying and accept what my son did for you by faith. Most of Israel couldn't do it, couldn't leave the law and accept grace and so they missed receiving that righteousness God freely offered. We're doing the same thing regarding being healed. God says stop trying by our own efforts and accept what my son did for you by faith. Yet we rush on with our own works and miss what God is offering. It takes a humble heart to stop our independent actions and say 'God, you're right. Jesus did this for me. Holy Spirit, show me how to be obedient and receive from you being healed.'"

Connie nodded toward the garden park, offering to extend their walk another six minutes and Ryan nodded his thanks, turning that direction.

"We construct these models from the world about health and how you are to eat, exercise, take pills, add vitamins and all the rest, to control and hold off disease. As if we are still mortal men, ignoring God's word that we are a new creation. His word 'by his wounds you have been healed'. And the practical instructions to 'put on Christ' who was never sick a day in his life and who is our model of what it is like to live a spirit-filled life. Galatians 2:20b says 'the life I live in the flesh I live by faith of the son of God, who loved me and gave himself for me.'

"It's become the Christian book aisle—how to diet for God and live by this plan and please God. In ignorance, we accept a Christian version of the world's plan and wonder why it doesn't take us where we want to go.

"The word of God on the topic of health is different than most Christians understand. Once we become Christians, we actually are different people than everyone else walking around this earth. We are very much a new creation. Jesus said if a believer happened to drink something deadly, it would not hurt them. Where is that in the world's scientific literature? Paul got bit by a poisonous snake, shook it off and had no effects. The people who saw it decided he must be a god. They were close in their reasoning, as he was an adopted son of God walking in God given health.

"We live by the world's ideas when it comes to health and live by our own efforts and we wonder why we live sick and aging lives. We expect to have aging bodies because everyone around us does. Have we never read God's word to us, his different thoughts on the matter? God not only says he heals all of our diseases, he also says one of his benefits is that he will renew my youth so I mount up like wings of eagles. We'll be eighty and look forty.

"Most people hear this topic and think, what's the big deal? Okay, I'll pray, aware Jesus paid a price to heal me and take communion with better understanding, I'll go exercise and see the doctor and take the pills prescribed and somewhere in that set of actions I'll get healed. They try to be realistic and just do everything that might work to get the healing they need. Without seeking the Holy Spirit's directions, they decide a course of action and go for what they think needs done. Only that approach is the definition of being double-minded. They try to listen with one ear to the scriptures and with the other ear to what the world has to say about how to deal with this particular disease or illness and do both. They become double-minded, thinking that's a realistic way to handle matters. But works and grace don't overlap.

"What they don't realize is if you revert back to works, trying to earn what God wants to give you as a free gift, you leave grace and you step back into the law and expose yourself again to sin's dominion and with it sickness, disease and death. When you move back to living by your works, Jesus' grace has no effect for you. The very things Jesus defeated for you are ruling you again because of your decision to work for something Jesus finished. Listen to it in scripture:

You are severed from Christ, you who would be justified by the law; you have fallen away from grace. (Galatians 5:4)

For all who rely on works of the law are under a curse; for it is written, "Cursed be every one who does not abide by all things written in the book of the law and do them." (Galatians 3:10)

if it is by grace, it is no longer on the basis of works; otherwise grace would no longer be grace. (Romans 11:6b)

So again I ask, does God give you his Spirit and work miracles among you by the works of the law, or by your believing what you heard? (Galatians 3:5 NIV)

"We nullify the grace of Jesus regarding healing by living like the world does, in a maze of our own effort and works, as if our efforts can heal our bodies any more than our efforts to live moral lives could make us righteous. With Jesus we have forgiveness of sins and healing of every disease. Without him, we spin our wheels and throw an ever increasing amount of time and money at a string of health problems we will never solve. You will just bounce from one manifestation of disease or sickness to the next.

"There is one way to live healed—have faith in God's word and follow the directions of the Holy Spirit, who is God with you, guiding you directly to what God wants you to do in this situation. Everything else is satan's counterfeit, trying to sell the idea that we don't need God.

"The beautiful thing about God's way – it's a free gift. Having given us his precious son, 'will he not with him freely give us all things?' God is lavishly good. And yet we run around sick, looking to the world for our answers. And worse, saying God's will is for me to be sick or have this injury. We assign to God the darkness the devil created. May God forgive us that error!

"It is God's will for all of us to be healed. Jesus purchased that healing for us and paid a brutally high price to do so. God wants to give it to us. The road to having it runs right through his word. If we come to Jesus with faith and say 'yes, I want it and I'll take it as the free gift it is, not of my own efforts to obtain it,' we are healed. Yet we're scared to accept the gift, for it seems too good to be true; it seems easier and safer to pursue healing by our own efforts. God is grieved by our lack of belief and with reason. God forgives all our sins, heals all our diseases and we don't take the gifts. We'd rather doubt God is that good and continue wandering around sick and infirmed and dying early. It's easier to believe satan's lie, than it is to accept our God is good and his word is true."

They were coming back to the hospital and Connie chose to stop there.

"Okay, that was intense. That second half was like getting blistered by a blast furnace." She had taken him right back to lesson one. God doesn't lie. Yet another major topic was laid on the table and they were out of time. "Thank you, Connie."

"Really?" her skepticism was clear.

Ryan smiled as he closed the recording. "You nailed one truth beautifully. God has a plan for how health and healing is ours. Everything else is satan's counterfeit trying to sell the idea that we don't need God. I'll think about the implications of the rest of what you said, given I do fully understand that."

"I didn't give you enough credit; my apologies for that. If I do have a soapbox, you probably just heard it."

Ryan grinned. "Apology accepted." He held up the phone. "I guarantee I'll have listened to you on this point at least twice more before you see me again."

She laughed, waved goodbye and headed on to work.

****

Ryan was leaning against the brick building waiting for Connie that afternoon when she stepped out of Connie's Pizza and turned to lock the door. He couldn't wait for the next morning to hear the rest of this conversation. "Tell me more. Talk to me about the fact we are healthy because we are a new creation."

"Ryan."

"It's too important a thought to have to endure waiting until tomorrow to hear the rest of what you have to say. I know this morning was only a fraction of it. You've obviously taken a lot of flack on this topic and not been believed. I'm listening. So is my phone. I want the rest of the conversation. I may not understand it yet, but I'm not deciding what I think and saying you're wrong until I have heard you and the Holy Spirit has helped me understand what you said. After that I might have an opinion, but I don't have one yet. I'm listening. I'll buy you dinner, run errands for you, whatever buys me some more time today."

She weighed his words and nodded. "Walk me home."

"Thank you." He promptly fell into step beside her.

Connie thought for a moment, then said, "The scripture says forget not all his benefits, the first two being 'who forgives all your sins and heals all your diseases.' They are linked and come to us through the cross. When we live thinking we receive forgiveness by grace and health by works, we end up with forgiveness, but not health and then rather than fix our thinking by renewing our mind with what the scriptures say, we instead start creating our own doctrine to explain why I'm still sick.

"We were never intended to live working to be healthy. We *are* healthy. We are the workmanship of God. We are a new creation. I have come to fullness of life in Christ. The old has passed away, the new has come. Listen to Colossians:

As therefore you received Christ Jesus the Lord, so live in him, rooted and built up in him and established in the faith, just as you were taught, abounding in thanksgiving. For in him the whole fulness of deity dwells bodily and you have come to fulness of life in him, who is the head of all rule and authority. (Colossians 2:6-7,9-10)

"I have come to fullness of life in Christ. There's no sickness in my new nature. And it is God who does this for me. Listen to it in the scriptures:

I have been crucified with Christ; it is no longer I who live, but Christ who lives in me; and the life I now live in the flesh I live by the faith of the Son of God, who loved me and gave himself for me. (Galatians 2:20)

May the God of peace himself sanctify you wholly; and may your spirit and soul and body be kept sound and blameless at the coming of our Lord Jesus Christ. He who calls you is faithful and he will do it. (1 Thessalonians 5:23-24)

"To spend our time and money working to have health, become healthy, stay healthy is to live as the world does, ignoring our new nature, ignoring the fullness of life we have in Christ and the word of God on the subject that says 'by his wounds you have been healed', past tense, it's finished.

"Sin was in our soul—our mind, will and emotions. Sickness was in our bodies, because when sin entered the world and attacked our soul, death came with it and attacked our bodies. The process of death is sickness and disease. For God to deal with sin, but leave untouched sickness and disease, ignores his holiness, his righteousness. Because God has made us righteous, removed our sin, his own righteousness requires him to remove sickness and disease from us at the same time. And we see in the scriptures Jesus did just that at the cross. When he removed our sins, he also healed us.

"Jesus bore our sins on the cross, not only ours, he bore the sins of the whole world. He took our sickness and bore our diseases, not only ours, but those of the whole world. That's the gospel of grace which Isaiah 53 talks about in detail in the Old Testament. It's what Jesus lived. Paul spends his life preaching and writing about that grace. And Peter summarizes it in the New Testament in 1 Peter 2:24. Two things happened on that Friday when Jesus died for us. 'He himself bore our sins in his body on the tree' and 'By his wounds you have been healed.' Both are past tense statements. Both are inclusive of all of mankind. We accept Jesus died for the sins of the whole world, so why is it so hard for us to keep reading the rest of the verse, to see and believe in God's full grace toward us, that he has also healed us? 'By his wounds you have been healed' is a statement of fact that encompasses every person in every generation. Oh, that we would believe God and live healed!

"Every person in this world has been saved; every person in this world has been healed. They may not have accepted the gifts, but God has finished both in advance for everyone. How many people have heard what the word of God says and understand that? Healing is like the lost blessing. We've forgotten what God did for us.

"God won't let you work and obtain by your efforts what he will only give you by a free gift of his grace. Health is not by works, lest any man should boast, the same as forgiveness is not by works, lest any man should boast. Satan convinced us of the lie that health and healing is by our own works and managed to nullify in the church the second of the great blessings Jesus purchased for us. Satan is the deceiver and liar who is robbing us at every turn because we're letting him. The Holy Spirit and the word of God is the route to our freedom. We just have to walk with Him, learning the truth, so Jesus can set us free.

"Jesus was never sick on earth and he's certainly not sick now. We are his body. He is our life. We are not mortal men of dust like everyone else walking around. We are spirit-filled new creations. Our mortal bodies are being constantly filled with life by the Holy Spirit. But if we don't let God's grace work in us, we end up living like unbelievers.

If the Spirit of him who raised Jesus from the dead dwells in you, he who raised Christ Jesus from the dead will give life to your mortal bodies also through his Spirit which dwells in you. (Romans 8:11)

"People will choose the road that leads to destruction by never accepting Jesus, never being saved. Likewise, there are Christians that get forgiveness figured out, who either haven't heard about, or haven't chosen to accept, that Jesus also healed them by grace and so they don't walk in that second blessing of health.

"A different example. We can battle with the sin of pride all we like and it will win every time. Or we can see the reality of our new nature, put on Christ and the next time a thought of pride shows up we respond to it by faith standing on the truth. 'Pride, you were crucified at the cross. God buried my old nature. I don't think that way anymore. I have the mind of Christ. In Jesus name, leave,' and pride, defeated, stops trying to take us out. What we let conquer us will keep coming at us until we put it away as dead, replacing it with the truth. The old nature is gone. The new nature is mine. And that new nature does not have a pride problem. When I believe that, know that and walk in the new nature, I walk in the victory over pride that Jesus won for me.

"It flows that easily, the new nature. I recognize a prideful thought in my mind. I identify the problem by name. 'Oh. Pride. That's you. You died. Goodbye.' And I let the Holy Spirit back up that goodbye with the power of God. I don't change me. God does. The Holy Spirit is helping me notice the old man so I can agree with God he's dead. My part is to consider the old nature dead and buried. I bury it with my words that the Holy Spirit then enforces. I simply agree with the Holy Spirit and yield; I let go of the old man, so the Holy Spirit can enforce its death. Envy.

Pride. Impatience. Judging one another. Whatever of the old man wants to show up. The truth works for anything in me that needs to change from the old nature to the new nature.

"My best efforts will not make me less prideful. In fact, by trying to be less prideful, I will become more and more conscious of how prideful I am. You can not get transformation by your own effort. But you can easily transform by simply yielding to what the Holy Spirit wants to do."

She slowed their walk as they turned onto her block.

"It's the same with disease. Disease is part of the old nature. You were under the law of sin and death. You no longer are. Your new nature is under grace. There is no disease in your new nature. The kingdom of God rules your life when you are in Christ.

For sin will have no dominion over you, since you are not under law but under grace. (Romans 6:14)

For the law of the Spirit of life in Christ Jesus has set me free from the law of sin and death. (Romans 8:2)

"We have been *set free* from the law of sin and death. That is the good news we need to hear. So you confront disease. 'Disease, death, you were dealt with at the cross. I am a new creation. I am fully alive in Christ. I am healed. I have God's word on it. God now deals with you and vindicates me. In Jesus' name, get out.' We have a responsibility to know the truth, stand on it, say it to our enemy and yield to the Holy Spirit who enforces that truth. We aren't passive in this matter, but we are trusting children who are to hear what God says, think about it, reach the conclusion 'if God says it's so, it's so,' and rest in that confidence, that faith. And we have to quit acting like it's our job to do his job. Victory is Jesus' role, shattering disease. Our part is knowledge of that victory, a thankful heart.

"We can't be ignorant of the truth and expect to receive what is offered, neither can we, by doing with our own efforts, ever receive it. The reason is a practical one – we can't create healing by our efforts because healing is something which is already done. Healing is a finished work. It was completed in A.D. 33 by Jesus specifically for you. Your healing is like a cake. The cake is baked and out of the oven. If you want it, you ask for it and it is yours. What you don't do is start mixing the batter trying to make the cake over again. Healing is as finished for you as the forgiveness of sins and the gift of righteousness, you simply accept the gifts by faith. Our works and self effort take us the wrong direction, away from receiving God's grace. This is why Paul is constantly asking variations of the question: 'Why do you live as if you still belonged to the world?'

"Listen to the full passage." Connie dug a New Testament out of her back pocket, thumbed through it and stopped to read from Colossians 2:

As therefore you received Christ Jesus the Lord, so live in him, rooted and built up in him and established in the faith, just as you were taught, abounding in thanksgiving. See to it that no one makes a prey of you by philosophy and empty deceit, according to human tradition, according to the elemental spirits of the universe and not according to Christ. For in him the whole fulness of deity dwells bodily and you have come to fulness of life in him, who is the head of all rule and authority. In him also you were circumcised with a circumcision made without hands, by putting off the body of flesh in the circumcision of Christ; and you were buried with him in baptism, in which you were also raised with him through faith in the working of God, who raised him from the dead. And you, who were dead in trespasses and the uncircumcision of your flesh, God made alive together with him, having forgiven us all our trespasses, having canceled the bond which stood against us with its legal demands; this he set aside, nailing it to the cross. He disarmed the principalities and powers and made a public example of them, triumphing over them in him. Therefore let no one pass judgment on you in questions of food and drink or with regard to a festival or a new moon or a sabbath. These are only a shadow of what is to come; but the substance belongs to Christ. Let no one disqualify you, insisting on self-abasement and worship of angels, taking his stand on visions, puffed up without reason by his sensuous mind and not holding fast to the Head, from whom the whole body, nourished and knit together through its joints and ligaments, grows with a growth that is from God. If with Christ you died to the elemental spirits of the universe, why do you live as if you still belonged to the world? Why do you submit to regulations, "Do not handle, Do not taste, Do not touch" (referring to things which all perish as they are used), according to human precepts and doctrines? These have indeed an appearance of wisdom in promoting rigor of devotion and self-abasement and severity to the body, but they are of no value in checking the indulgence of the flesh. (Colossians 2:6-23)

"We either live as who we are, as new creations in Christ and yield to God as he transforms us—I am the workmanship of God—or we live this mishmash of part faith and part works trying to make our lives work by our own efforts. That is the recipe for sickness, discouragement, confusion about God and disappointment with our own efforts to live a Christian life. The real Christian life is what most people miss; it is Christ living in us. Anything that shows up that doesn't match up with Christ, it's the old nature. We just haven't told people 'when the old nature shows up, consider it dead, because it is, toss it in the trash and don't live that way. Instead rejoice that your new nature is like Jesus' and you'll start looking a lot like that new nature.' You put on Christ. He wasn't sick, he never got anxious, was never afraid, he didn't worry about life, he just trusted God and did stuff pleasing to his Father. The Holy Spirit was very comfortable resting upon Jesus. We should be able to say the same about ourselves."

They were at her home. Connie finished the thought as she stopped at the walkway to her front door. "1 Timothy 2:4 says God desires all men to be saved and to come to the knowledge of the truth. We tend to forget that second half of God's desire. We receive forgiveness and stop. For Christians, God's desire is that we come to the knowledge of the truth, that we mature as the Holy Spirit teaches us from the word of God.

"We are content to live with our own ideas and theories. We create our own doctrine out of our experience and shape our religion to be something we approve of and agree with, rather than come to the full knowledge of the truth. Never mind that most of our experience is a mismatch of our old nature we let hang around, fragments of scripture we haven't actually read in context, stuff we think is in the bible that isn't and just plain deceptive conclusions planted by satan who loves to add the word 'if' to what God said. The word of God is uncomfortably different from what most Christians think it is. And it sounds overly harsh when I listen to my own words. I love the church, I love those who are young in Christ and learning, but my spirit stresses when I see us stop short of everything Christ paid such a high price to give us. I want Jesus to get what he paid for and that's people who love him and receive all the gifts he has to offer—all five benefits in their fullness. The church isn't there yet and at times it seems to be asleep. Healing is a huge missed blessing and we seem to be content staying sick, chronically sick and dying early. We have to wake up and at least show the next generation how not to live this way."

She chose to stop there.

"Okay." Ryan let that last point sink in and slowly nodded. "Thanks, Connie."

"I can tell, this one was sort of half way believed and half way wasn't."

"No, it just rattled my thinking quite a bit. That's good. I do get the fact you can't have both 'by his wounds you have been healed', past tense, its finished and a life of present works trying to accomplish the same thing."

"Having a conversation on the way home is not my most eloquent hour. I'll see if I can give you a couple of audios that may help put it in better order, or at least approach it another way."

" I'd appreciate that."

"Ryan, remember this, it will help. Disease, sickness, sin that rears its head repeatedly—you're actually looking at an after-image of what was dealt with and done away with by Jesus. It only appears to have power to stick around in the visible world and harass us because we don't know how to see it for what it is and simply dismiss it. We're sons of God and satan loves to blow smoke in our eyes. Only if we recognize something is dead does it lose its power over us. Our new nature has no sin problem, no sickness, no disease, it's not irritable nor easily shaken; it's got a bent to love that is as intense as Jesus' own heart. That's who we become as the Holy Spirit makes us one with Christ. It's our choice to let the new nature flourish, to leave the old nature in the grave where God put it.

"Jesus loves his church. Jesus gave his life for the church. Jesus nourishes and cherishes the church. Jesus will save us completely. We just have to trust his heart and let him. We're like sheep who constantly go astray. If we can just lay down control and say with an honest heart, 'I will listen to your voice and obey', we're going to be fine. How we live in practice will be part of what the Holy Spirit changes. Because God won't stop his work in us until we look like Jesus. We just have to be willing to be his church." She flipped pages in her new testament. "Listen to the scriptures that talk about what Jesus is doing today. He's intensely focused on us:

Christ is the head of the church, his body and is himself its Savior. (Ephesians 5:23b)

> Christ loved the church and gave himself up for her, that he might sanctify her, having cleansed her by the washing of water with the word, that he might present the church to himself in splendor, without spot or wrinkle or any such thing, that she might be holy and without blemish. (Ephesians 5:25b-27)

"'Present her to himself in splendor' is a beautiful description of what Jesus is doing for us. The Holy Spirit wants to set us fully free by the word of God from everything which satan is distorting. We need to listen to the word with the Holy Spirit teaching us its breadth. We perish for lack of knowledge and don't walk in all the benefits God has given us. And since I'm tired and willing to ask the question and risk being disappointed, please tell me you can quote all five."

Ryan smiled. "Pop quiz, Connie?" He had the words etched into his heart now and easily quoted it:

> Bless the LORD, O my soul;
> and all that is within me, bless his holy name!
> Bless the LORD, O my soul,
> and forget not all his benefits,
> who forgives all your iniquity,
> who heals all your diseases,
> who redeems your life from the Pit,
> who crowns you with steadfast love and mercy,
> who satisfies you with good as long as you live
> so that your youth is renewed like the eagle's.
> (Psalms 103:1-5)

"And to repeat lesson one, God does not lie."

Connie smiled. "Thanks. That's why I gave you the time, Ryan. God nudged and said 'he'll listen'. Thanks for that—the listening. I can't understand this material for you, that's God's work unpacking scripture and helping you sort out where what I've offered is right. But it has been kind that you've listened without interrupting or protesting where I want to go when it is an unexpected direction like this."

"That would just be rude. I'll repeat again, Connie, there are times you seem to be circling a foreign universe to me, but I'm a smart man who recognizes when truth thumps me. I'll listen and learn and if I would have said something differently, or nuanced it another way, that's simply the Holy Spirit helping me understand the truth he walked you through earlier. You're responsible to teach, as best you know the material. It's my job to be the student, weighing what you say, given the scriptures. A smart man accepts the responsibility to be a good student." He smiled, for Connie feeling off her game was unusual to witness and it told him her fatigue was running deep. "You're free of me now for a time. I'll see you in the morning for coffee."

"Deal," Connie agreed with a smile. She unlocked her front door, stepped inside with a wave goodbye and Ryan turned back to the hospital. He was grateful for the conversation. She had filled out a lot of what she was thinking, even if it wasn't as eloquent as on some days. He listened again to the two conversations on the topic on the walk back to the hospital, fascinated by the subject itself. Walter and Jeff were both going to have interesting things to say when they heard this and he looked forward to that discussion with them.

16

"Connie." Ryan caught her attention as she entered the coffee shop Wednesday morning, for he was at a back table rather than his usual front one. He had her coffee and sweet roll for her and as she joined him, he set a gold chocolate star beside them. "For wading into a topic you knew would cause a particularly intense reaction."

She smiled, picked up the chocolate, split it in half and then unwrapped the foil. "For listening."

He accepted half with an answering smile. "I spent a fascinating few hours last night thinking about what you said, with Jeff and Walter occasionally joining me for a conversation as their own time permitted. We loved these audios, even as we're still wrestling through their implications."

"I'm glad; because I made you two short audios that might help clarify what I wasn't explaining that well yesterday."

He laughed and accepted the flash drive. "All audios gladly accepted. I followed you well enough, Connie, the second and third time through listening to your remarks. It seems strange, how much the world invests in staying healthy and you basically dismissed it all with a wave of your hand as a waste of time. Walk with the spirit, do what he says, take communion with understanding and you'll live healed and healthy and have an abundant life until your final breath on earth," he said, summing up his own conclusion of what she had said.

She nodded. "The gospel is that simple. We just haven't heard it. We've heard satan's work program and bought it, nullifying Jesus' grace gifts to us in the process."

She picked up the coffee and sweet roll and let him hold the door as they stepped outside to begin their walk. "I did have one thought on the way here that might help. So let me try one more way of explaining this."

He nodded and started a recording.

"God has saved you, but until you trust that word, that salvation hasn't become yours. You have to decide Jesus died for your sins and trust him as your Lord. God wants you to be saved. He wants you to believe in Jesus. But God will let you go to hell. It's your decision. God won't override your decision even though he knows you will deeply regret making the one you did if you reject his son. He warns you that once you die, your decision is permanent and you won't be able to change it (although someone else still alive could change your death back to life for you if they bring a resurrection prayer to bear.)

"God has healed you, but until you trust that word, that healing hasn't become yours. You have to decide God's word is true and trust that you are healed. You trust God and then you let him be Lord. God will heal your body because the word of his power accomplishes what it says. The Holy Spirit wrote 'By his wounds, you have been healed' because you have been. Believe that, trust that word and God brings that word to pass, that word has effect in our body.

"When someone asks you how are you, you answer truthfully, 'I've been kind of achy, but God has it handled. He's healed me.' You consider his word over your symptoms. These are the facts, but the facts change. Abraham considered not his body but rather considered God powerfully able to do what he had promised. So you lift your voice and praise God. You thank him for his word. You express an active faith. God's word is settled forever, you can rely upon it.

"You cooperate with the Holy Spirit so your faith remains active and alive; what he tells you to do, that is what you do. What the Holy Spirit asks from someone who first believes in Jesus for salvation is that they express that faith by baptism. With healing, there isn't a one size fits all action the bible gives that expresses our faith. The Holy

Spirit will direct what he wants you to do in specific situations. Most of the time it is simply to show your active faith by offering thanksgiving and praise.

"Praise is the fastest way I know for healing to show up. You cannot worship God, come into his presence, stay there for long and not get changed by the encounter. The light of God's presence and darkness, are incompatible.

"You are righteous because God made you righteous, then you live out that righteousness; your character and your actions show your new nature. The old nature is in the grave where God put it; your new nature changes who you are as you cooperate with the Holy Spirit and walk with him.

"You are healed because God has healed you, then you live out being healthy for the rest of your life as you obey the Holy Spirit who is flowing that new life into your mortal body. Sickness and disease are your old nature which God has removed from you. You are healthy. There is only one rule again: live in God's grace, walking with the Holy Spirit.

"A fallen man's body has no life source in it and is dying no matter what effort a man makes to stop that process. Death has its grip and is never letting go of a fallen man.

"A Christian has a new life source, the Holy Spirit and a body that is healed, free of death, which will live healthy until the day we take our last breath on earth and next in heaven. Disease does not kill us. God says today is the day you make the transition from one place to another. And even that date is under our considerable influence and choice by prayer.

"We haven't understood God's benefits, so we haven't walked in them. They seem strange; how foreign and beautiful they are, only because we haven't seen them modeled for us by our grandparents, our parents, the church around us, for generations. Had the church of the first century been flourishing for two thousand years, Christians would be astonished today if anyone showed up in their gatherings with even a cold and the person certainly wouldn't leave church still having it. We've forgotten what healing and health look like in God's design for a Christian life. We are a new creation now on earth; it's not something coming to us in heaven after we die. We have been healed and we are healthy; that is our new nature. We don't have that by works. It is a free gift of God's grace, to be fully enjoyed and experienced now.

"We let satan blind us, we bought into his self-works program and now we run around trying to obtain through our works what God has arranged to freely give us only by grace. Our works will not make us or keep us healed and healthy. God's grace will freely do both. We are the losers if we try a life by works. Satan has convinced us that God will not give healing and health as a free gift. And we swallowed that lie. We desperately need a new reformation in the church to slash through the smoke satan has been blowing in our eyes. Jesus lavished healing and life upon us at the cross. We receive that grace gift by faith, not by our works.

"Our new nature is healed, healthy and remains that way as long we obey the voice of the Holy Spirit. Don't let your soul decide your life, what you will eat, drink and do. Ask the Holy Spirit. Then eat, drink and do the activities you desire within his lines. The Holy Spirit is the most practical person I know. He's God. He's perfect. Listen to him, not your mind's idea of how to live life. You're clueless to the real picture most of the time. God is not. And the delightful thing is God makes us healed and healthy primarily so we can enjoy an abundant life full of stuff we like without needing tons of rules on do's and don'ts. There is one rule: 'live in my grace and obey my voice'. From that place go enjoy the life God made for you."

She stopped there and Ryan thoughtfully nodded. She was opening up solid new ground on what it meant to actually live with God abiding in you, keeping you healed and healthy. "Thanks, Connie."

"I'm sorry I'm not finding the right words, Ryan. I understand this topic, but can't do a good job teaching it yet."

"You're doing better than you realize. I can see it. I might not understand it yet, but it's still new ground for me." They were nearing the hospital and Ryan decided wisdom wasn't to hold her up with questions now; he'd have better ones after he'd had more time thinking about this subject. "Same time tomorrow?"

"I'll be there." She turned toward Connie's Pizza with a wave goodbye and headed to work.

****

The day was going to be busy, but Ryan didn't mind. He picked up the paperwork he needed for a morning meeting with the architect working to reconfigure one of the hospital clinic buildings into an urgent care 24/7 center, confirmed with Janet there was nothing critical happening he needed to deal with before he left, loaded Connie's audios to his laptop so he could listen to them on the drive across town and grabbed a soda from the vending machine on the way over to the parking garage. As he left the hospital grounds, he activated Connie's audios to play in sequence.

"Let me try this topic: you can't be healed by your own works, again. Let's start with a core scripture:

For sin will have no dominion over you, since you are not under law but under grace. (Romans 6:14)

"Healing is a finished work of the cross. I am to consider God faithful. My faith lets God manifest my healing and bring it to pass. God can't operate in your life unless you believe his word to you is true. Abraham had to believe God for Isaac to be born. God has given you free will. You have to bring your faith to the equation, but not your works. Healing is received by faith alone.

"God has saved you. You still have to accept salvation by trusting in Jesus' name. God has healed you. You still have to accept his word on that matter is true. Because in his word on that matter is the power to manifest you healed. By his stripes you are healed. Believe that word and that word accomplishes that in your body. Don't believe it's written to you, don't believe it's for you and you won't let the word change your body. God will let you say no. Your doubt can kill God's word and make it null and void to you.

"When this body needs healed, I ask the Holy Spirit how he wants me to express my faith so that I manifest the fact I'm healed. I cooperate with God however he leads. I obey the written word. I take communion and proclaim Jesus death is *for me*, 'by his wounds I am healed', I partake knowing his body was given for my healing and his blood brings me life. I express my authority as a child of God and speak to the symptom and tell it to leave. If the Holy Spirit says, 'make an appointment with the doctor', I make the call. If the Holy Spirit says, 'I've got this covered', I go about my life and the symptoms disappear. I am God's workmanship. I let him do the work and I cooperate with what he's doing.

"Sometimes healing comes by simply going back to the foundational truths and speaking aloud what you know in your heart. 'I'm bought with a price, I belong to Jesus, I present my body as a living sacrifice and all my members I yield to righteousness. God, sanctify me by your word. By Jesus' wounds I have been healed. Thank you Holy Spirit for bringing abundant life into my mortal body. Amen.' In the light of that truth, the symptoms disappear. Disease is darkness and it can't remain in the light. When you turn on a light in a room, it's not like pockets of darkness can take their time leaving. Darkness and light are incompatible and light is much more powerful than darkness.

"God is more powerful than disease. We often make the mistake of thinking unconsciously that the disease we see is more powerful than the God we don't see. The fact God is with us, invisible to our physical eyes, is his gift to us, as he's so bright our physical eyes would be blinded by his presence. God's the powerful one, remember that when you look at a symptom of disease. Tossing disease out of our body is like blowing a bit of lint off his sleeve for God. He is all powerful. Nothing in the universe anywhere is more powerful than God. Seeing his greatness increases our faith which is a good place to begin. Then we speak to the symptom. 'In Jesus' name, I am healed. Get out.' It's amazing what our authority accomplishes when it's the Holy Spirit enforcing what we say by his power."

The first audio finished and the second one started with the sound of a faint radio station playing music in the background as Connie began the recording.

"That first attempt was decent, but I don't think I hit the mark, so here is attempt number two. When we try to live by the law and not sin, thinking that we can earn righteousness by our good works, we become like the Pharisees who failed to obtain what they were trying to earn. We nullify the grace of Jesus in our lives by not stopping our works and coming in simple faith to receive grace.

"When we do the same with health, when we try to live by the law (eat this and not that, exercise, take this medicine, that vitamin) thinking by our works we can make ourselves be healthy, we fail to obtain the very thing we are trying to earn. When we look to our own works first, we nullify the grace of Jesus in our lives. We never receive the free gift Jesus holds out to us—he took away all our sicknesses and diseases and healed us. When we try to be righteous by works, we fail. When we try to be healthy by works, we also fail.

"One person accepts healing as a gift and goes running because they enjoy running. The person running beside them thinks that by running, they will be healthy and wonders why they never are. Two people, same action, only one is receiving health from God. The righteous shall live by faith. We are healed by a gift of grace received by faith.

"If God says 'let's take a walk' I go take a walk and enjoy the time with him. I don't sweat trying to keep track of how many steps I take as if that will make me healthy. God can take care of the details. God whispers 'why don't you go take a nap?' I'm smart enough to say 'okay'. Maturity is letting God with you, the Holy Spirit, the one who knows you best, direct your life. Quit working to be healthy. Accept Jesus' grace and *be* healthy. It's a whole lot easier on your time and money and you actually get what you desire with God's plan. On your own, by your own works, you're going to fail every time.

"I can live righteously without sinning because I have been made righteous as a free gift of God. I can live healed because I have been made healthy as a free gift of God. I have a mind which is at peace, I'm not anxious about anything, because Jesus gives me rest. Life is good. I didn't earn that good life by my works, I received that good life as a gift from God and thus enjoy living it. God's gifts first, then our actions which arise out of his gifts to us.

"We still have mortal bodies, made of dust. God says death is the last enemy to be removed, but for now it has no more sting, it has no ability to bring sickness or disease to us. We are enabled to be fully alive in these mortal bodies. At the moment of death we simply take a last breath on earth and the next breath in heaven, alive in the presence of God. When Jesus comes back, our bodies will cease to be of dust; we will have bodies like Jesus now has, a heavenly body.

"We don't need to get sick in order to die. Look at Moses as the example. Perfect health, climbed a mountain the day he died; he took his last breath on earth and then he was in heaven. God told him that morning today you'll die and be with me. That's the way our last day is supposed to be. It's all good for us who believe.

"There is a difference between being healthy and being sick. There is a difference between bodily training and a healthy body. Muscles respond to use. A guy with a manual labor job is going to have stronger muscles than a guy who works behind a desk and on weekends works around the yard. But a man with normal muscle strength without disease is in line with God's design.

"Work out if you enjoy it. Don't work out to be healthy. You *are* healthy. Enjoy working weights if you like it; otherwise, go pick up your toddler occasionally, carry in groceries, do some yard work – your muscles will get all the activity they need while you live your life. The Holy Spirit can keep your body as God designed it to be, healthy and functioning fine all the days of your life, without you adding your thoughts to how to do it. Simply obey the Holy Spirit's voice and all that you need is covered.

"Jesus got tired after a long day of travel and needed to rest. That is how a healthy body functions because we are designed to rest. Jesus got thirsty, that is also normal health. See with discernment what you are doing and why you are doing it.

"If the Holy Spirit says take a walk, do so. If the Holy Spirit says don't do something, whatever it is, the right answer is to obey that voice. But it is very much the wrong thing to do to decide 'I think the Holy Spirit would like me never to eat sugar' and do that thinking you are pleasing God when he has never mentioned the subject. You can live a life of obedience, or you can live a life making up your own rules. You can't do both. God is perfectly able to get his directions for you to you clearly. He may, in fact, give you some rules and until he changes what he says, stay within them. I personally have learned God rarely has a rule about my body and my health; he instead has a day by day voice.

"Jesus said don't worry about food and drink and clothing. Let God solve those questions. Just hang out with him. If someone shows up with pie, enjoy a slice a pie. If someone asks you to join them for dinner, go enjoy what they've fixed. If you're standing in front of the refrigerator, ask God, is there anything here I should not eat? If you should not have something, he'll tell you. Then within that answer, eat what you enjoy. God is involved in what your days are going to be and knows how they will unfold. Let him handle food and drink and stop stressing about doing it for yourself.

"There will be days you get up and before your feet hit the floor, you'll hear the whisper, 'let's fast today'. The right answer is to say 'okay' and you'll find in that agreement with his word the reality you won't be particularly interested in food that day. Another day, you'll be getting hungry and think 'a hamburger sounds really good right now' and without you planning it you'll find yourself sitting down to a hamburger and fries that night because friends invited you to join them for a casual meal.

"God is a very present interactive God who enjoys living life with us. God made food to be enjoyed. He made doing things to be enjoyed. Don't turn the life God designed to be enjoyed into a works program you have to monitor to decide if you're following the right rules closely enough. One is life walking with the spirit, the other is a self-works program designed to make us think we don't need God.

"The simple fact is God loves us. He healed our bodies and keeps them healthy for us as a gift so we don't have to worry and stress and plan fitness routines and health plans and spend our lives obsessing about how to get healed and be healthy. God gives you both as free gifts, gave them to you in advance, so that picture of trying to do it for yourself wouldn't be your life. He loves us too much to create us as living beings in his image then watch us spend every day of that life trying to stay alive. Life is a gift from God. It's a good life. Our bodies are gifts which he heals and keeps healthy for us so we can go enjoy this life and planet he gave us. He'd love for us to read Psalm

103 and his benefits to us, laugh with joy and with gladness go enjoy all five.

"When you live like the world does, that should be a flashing red danger sign that you have missed what God offered you when he said come follow my son Jesus. The Christian life looks nothing like the world. So look at your life and let it be the mirror. Which are you living in? If it's not the kingdom of God, its time to run back home."

The audio finished. Connie was eloquently dismissing what most people did as being a waste of time. The time and effort spent controlling food and exercise and trying to manage the body was simply a self-effort works program that didn't need God and would inevitably fail, for at its core it was based on a lie satan had sown that had killed the free benefit God was offering.

Ryan thoughtfully closed the audio files. Connie was trying so hard to convey a profound idea. He could hear her struggling to find the eloquence to make it simple to grasp. A week ago the entire topic of healing and health being received as grace gifts had been foreign to him. Now he understood some of the subjects well enough to pick out nuances in how she was presenting the information. That was real progress.

Ryan thought about it and then smiled. He wanted relationship and this was the heart of it, figuring out stuff together. Asking his Father to help him understand a topic, work it though with him, show him the truth, would be enjoyable hours spent together. God does not lie. Lesson one. Even if Connie wasn't finding her usual eloquence, God knew the right answers. He'd figured this topic out with God's help.

"Thanks, God, for considering me ready to think about all of this, both healing and health, the total picture. This is one incredibly mountain we are exploring. Teach me, God. There is no teacher like you, perfect in every respect. You understand where Connie has this right and where her explanations are incomplete. You understand where I'm on the right track, where I'm in the ditch, where I'm floundering. Get me squared away with the full truth, with no shadow of lies left distorting what you want me to understand. That would be a really nice outcome of this present learning curve. I'm closing this prayer now because I'm at my meeting location, but the conversation between us on this topic is just beginning and I'm really grateful for that fact. It's been an incredible drive. Thanks for that."

Ryan pulled into the parking lot of the architect firm. Connie challenged him to think, that was the best gift of all of them that she'd brought him. To think he could have missed this by not taking to heart her initial comment, 'did someone pray to raise them from the dead?' as being truth he needed to hear. He'd received a gift, an answer to his prayer for help to understand healing and with it had come a vast mountain of treasures around that one question.

****

Ryan listened to the last audio he had from Connie on the drive back to the hospital.

"Ryan, I have two comments for this audio. Not related, but both I think useful to you. Let's start with scripture. There are four wisdom scriptures in particular you should know.

> My son, be attentive to my words;
> incline your ear to my sayings.
> Let them not escape from your sight;
> keep them within your heart.
> For they are life to him who finds them,
> and healing to all his flesh.
> (Proverbs 4:20-22)

"The Hebrew word translated 'healing' also translates 'medicine'. The medicine we need to heal our flesh is in the word of God. A thousand years before Jesus, God is already saying look to my word for the life and healing you need. He hasn't changed.

A tranquil mind gives life to the flesh (Proverbs 14:30a)

Pleasant words are like a honeycomb, sweetness to the soul and health to the body. (Proverbs 16:24)

A cheerful heart is a good medicine (Proverbs 17:22a)

"We are a spirit, we have a soul and we inhabit a body. Our heart is like the innermost part of who we are as a person. While our spirit is very different than our body, we live as one being. It's hard to have joy in your spirit and depression in your body. It's hard to have a war going on in your mind and have your body be at rest.

"Life flows from your spirit to your heart, then soul and body. When you focus on removing anxiety in your heart by reading assurances from God in his word, you suddenly realize your mind went calm and your body is relaxed. You weren't focusing there, but the benefits flowed to there. It is easier to calm your spirit and let it flow out to the rest of you, than it is to calm your body hoping to get your spirit to stop being troubled. That's God's intended design. We live from the spirit, outward. Not from outward experience, in.

"My second thought for tonight – God desires us to come to the knowledge of the truth. Not some of the truth, but all of it. To walk in the freedom that comes through his word to us, through Jesus who sets us free.

"A simple example. There are those who say don't eat meat because it isn't healthy for you. In the garden of Eden, Adam and Eve ate fruit from the trees, the animals ate the plants of the field. So since they didn't eat meat, neither should we. It sounds biblical.

"Only they've missed the rest of the story. God told Noah in Genesis 9, 'Every moving thing that lives shall be food for you; and as I gave you the green plants, I give you everything.'

"Can God give his children something harmful? God wasn't talking to mankind in general when he gave this gift, he was talking to Noah, the only righteous man, the only person saved, when God destroyed everyone else on the earth in the flood. The Holy Spirit begins the chapter text by saying 'And God blessed Noah and his sons'. By definition, to give Noah and his family something harmful would be to violate God's goodness and would be cursing them rather than blessing them.

> And God blessed Noah and his sons and said to them, "Be fruitful and multiply and fill the earth. The fear of you and the dread of you shall be upon every beast of the earth and upon every bird of the air, upon everything that creeps on the ground and all the fish of the sea; into your hand they are delivered. Every moving thing that lives shall be food for you; and as I gave you the green plants, I give you everything. Only you shall not eat flesh with its life, that is, its blood. (Genesis 9:1-4)

> By faith Noah, being warned by God concerning events as yet unseen, took heed and constructed an ark for the saving of his household; by this he condemned the world and became an heir of the righteousness which comes by faith. (Hebrews 11:7)

"Eating meat is fine with God. He gave it to us as a gift to enjoy. You are not healthier if you do not eat meat, nor better off if you do. Enjoy what tastes good to you. All foods are good for you when they are received by prayer with thanksgiving. If your preference is to be a vegetarian, enjoy it and do so giving God glory; if you enjoy eating meat, God is equally blessing you.

"(Paul's discussion in his letters concerning do you or do you not eat meat was dealing with it as a matter of conscience because in first century Roman society the majority of the meat sold in the marketplace had first been offered to idols in the temples of the Roman gods. Christians were concerned not about the health implications of meat, but whether it was okay in God's eyes to eat what had once been offered by others to an idol. Paul said it's fine, you know there is only one true God, but if your brother is weaker in faith and is troubled by it, for his sake, don't eat meat when you're with him.)

"Ryan, the more time I spend with God, the more it seems like the world's wisdom is mostly satan turning on end truth in the bible, trying to get us to go the opposite direction. The actual truth in scriptures reflecting God and his heart toward us is fascinating in its breadth and goodness. We need to listen to God first, so he can show us where the world's ideas are distorting how we think about him and life. There's so much more freedom and answers in what God is offering than we've grasped. We're healed. It's a pure gift. How cool is that? I deeply look forward to the day every Christian knows and shows who they are."

The audio concluded. Ryan thoughtfully marked the audio as one he'd listened to and scanned the collection one last time. He'd finally caught up with Connie and heard everything she had recorded for him. And he was so mentally tired he was sincerely looking forward to the date with Melinda tonight where the conversation would be interesting and informative and yet nothing at all on this level. He half laughed. "God, I don't want to say I'm saturated, but I can feel the change, that my mind has begun to say enough for now. Without changing my heart's desire that you keep bringing it on, God, keep teaching me, I'm ready for a night of rest and enjoyment of another kind this evening spending it with Melinda. Thanks for that in advance." Ryan could literally feel God's blessing on him recently and joy was becoming a steady companion. It was a nice way to live.

17

CONNIE AUGUST

Connie looked up as the door chimes rang, signaling an arriving customer. She registered the uniform, the stature, the confidence of the man in a single glance and turned her attention back to the green pepper slices in her hand, not giving the welcome intro for a new customer because she knew before he reached the counter this wasn't a customer who had arrived simply looking for good pizza for lunch. She quietly asked God a question, heard the Holy Spirit's answer and settled how to handle matters. She finished the pizza she was creating and gave him her attention, offering a smile as he joined her at the long counter. "Commander, I'm Connie August. How can I help you today?"

"I'm hoping you and I might have a conversation about some matters the Secretary of the Army asked me to look into."

An interesting way on his part to broach the subject, given he wasn't army, but navy. She smiled at the realization they had crossed branches of the service trying to figure out how to handle the situation. "I wondered when someone like you would walk through the door. It will need to be this evening, Commander. I run this shop on my own and immediately after work isn't my best time of day."

"I can offer a small conference room at my hotel if that would suit you."

"That would be fine. I could join you, say 6 p.m.?"

"That time would work. Thank you." He set one of the hotel business cards on the counter and his business card with contact information.

Connie recognized more of the ribbons on the dress uniform now that he was close enough she could place them. He wasn't showing off, she knew he was in official dress uniform only because he was on official pentagon business. He'd been in the service since George H.W. Bush liberated Kuwait. "Pizza is on the house if you're interested in lunch. Any military uniform gets the courtesy, it's not just that silver star you're wearing, though that would create an instant policy of its own."

He smiled. "I'm always willing to enjoy a slice of Chicago pizza."

"The far end is bacon cheeseburger, middle is supreme, toward this end is a four cheese. There's also a pepperoni and a sausage mushroom. I'm making to order if you've another particular favorite. They rotate out in about fifteen minutes."

"I'll be good with what's on the pizza bar."

Connie spun out another ball of crust into a pan. "May I ask one question?"

"Sure."

"Have you spoken to George Whittier yet?"

"He'll be the last after you. I've spoken to 76 individuals, mostly retired army. Harrison Davy, in particular, asked me to convey his hello."

She grinned and simply nodded. The man had done his homework. "Enjoy your lunch, Commander Baker."

She pocketed the two business cards. She had a few hours reprieve and was grateful for the time. She rarely got nervous, but this would be an exceptional test of how calm she truly was, when asked about what she had seen as a combat medic. The Holy Spirit would have to give her the right words to say as the conversation evolved, for she didn't have them yet.

****

Connie caught a ride to the hotel, one of the discrete smaller hotels in Chicago which would be full if there were thirty guests, where the ambiance was from a time when the doorman wore white gloves and three staff handled your luggage, confirmed your room was satisfactory in every respect and called you by name should they ever be able to serve you again in the next twenty years. She wasn't disappointed. She paid for her ride, stepped out on the sidewalk in front of a discrete canopy which simply had a cursive HH in white and the doorman moved to open the front door for her. "Sergeant August, welcome this evening."

"Thank you. It's nice to know I'm expected."

She stepped inside the hotel and it was a tie between the bellman and the woman at an antique elegant writing table who rose to greet her. The woman managed to speak first. "It's a pleasure to have you as our guest this evening, Sergeant August. If you would allow me to escort you, you'll find the state room seating comfortable and we took the liberty of bringing some refreshments out."

She'd lived through years of combat, she was accustomed to nothing being what she expected and so rolled with the change in plans. "Sure, thank you." The woman escorted her with the bellman protectively moving ahead to make sure all was arranged. Connie found the entire experience surreal.

"Commander Baker asked us to give you a few minutes before we showed you to the conference room. His wife is traveling with him for this trip and she discretely asked if you would be willing to consider an autograph for her wall of heroes. She didn't wish to impose to ask herself. The Commander's wife is Kelly Baker and the blue photo book is hers. She thought you might appreciate knowing some of the Commander's background, as he has become familiar with yours."

Connie took a seat on the couch in a conversation grouping of chairs and facing sofa. The book mentioned was on the table, beside a tray of refreshments and pot of coffee. "This looks lovely, thank you."

"We'll give you twenty minutes. There is a powder room down the hall to your left should you desire to freshen up. The conference room is just upstairs."

Connie nodded her thanks. She poured herself a cup of coffee, surprised she was able to do that for herself and selected one of the sandwich squares. The hotel had been a wise decision for where to meet, as the surroundings provided a wealth of elegant comfort.

She picked up the photo book to see what the Commander's wife had thought she should know. Six pages into a photo journal put together by a loving wife she'd figured out part of it. The Commander had been a Navy SEAL in his early years and if she wasn't mistaken, that was her brother standing in a group picture of twenty men. She continued to turn pages, the Commander's military history mostly inferred through the numerous foreign countries his wife had documented as they traveled between various military bases for at least part of their lives together. Connie paused at the official photo in the back, able to read easier now the line of military ribbons and see the repeated V's. He had seen far more combat than she ever had.

She picked up the rich cream cardstock and expensive pen and signed a bold Connie August, added her Whiskery 68 call sign initials behind it, for she knew why the question had been asked. She would likely never wear the Silver Star, the Distinguished Cross, or the Medal of Honor, but she understood the acts of valor and heroism that earned those military honors.

The bellman had been discretely watching the time. He stepped in with a smile and an offer to escort her to see the Commander.

The conference room upstairs, rather than being a long table surrounded by many chairs, was a comfortably sized room with six captain chairs and a long wall-side table within reach for paperwork. The Commander was reading a book when the bellman lightly knocked and showed her in. He was in civilian clothes tonight, jeans and a jacket over a light blue shirt.

"Welcome, Sergeant. Please have a seat."

She found her palms were sweaty, a rare reaction for her. She shook hands anyway. "Good evening, Sir." She accepted a seat and nodded as he offered coffee from the pot on the side table.

"You've had a very interesting career, Connie."

"Thank you, Sir."

"Joe is fine." He relaxed in the seat he'd chosen, nodded to the folders on the table. "A fraction of what I asked archives to pull as I've been reading through your history."

She glanced at the stack, wondering what year he had reached. "The name Harrison Davy clued me in."

"You are very well liked by all those who know you."

"That's kind to hear."

"August is an unusual last name. I realized after this began that I knew your brother through the language school. He taught the regional dialects that pocketed Afghanistan and Pakistan and did so with remarkable skill."

"He had a flair for languages, loved their variety even as a child."

"He was killed in a car crash in San Diego during your fourth overseas deployment if I have the timeline correct."

"You do."

"I'm sorry for your loss."

"Thank you, Sir." She noted his amusement. "Joe would be my cousin and respect for the uniform would still make you Sir."

He chuckled. "I'm feeling my age. The Secretary of the Army has been kept abreast of the award nominations moving through channels regarding the events of March 19th, 2016. When a field commander recommends two Medals of Honor, six Silver Stars and an assortment of lesser awards, the entire Pentagon notices."

"I can imagine, Sir. The fight was intense and did not ease off that intensity for some hours." She refused to go back mentally to that convoy ride as they drove into that firefight. She had been there and she knew the man seated across from her would have seen the battlefield reports, read the after-action reports, probably watched every minute of its duration via drone footage in both infrared and visual. He knew far more about what had happened that day on the battlefield than she did.

"You're aware you have been nominated for a Silver Star."

"I am."

"I'm not here to add to the evidence the award board of review will consider in rendering their recommendation. It's my understanding their decisions regarding this particular battle are going to be presented as a group to the SA and he will make a verdict and public announcement toward the end of the year.

"There are some… irregularities in that day which have been noticed and need explained. The Secretary of the Army chose to have the Navy look into the matter, retired Navy at that, so as to minimize how much Army traditions and loyalties would impact an independent assessment. I've been asked specifically to look into your actions that day and those of Chaplain Whittier and provide the SA with an independent recommendation if those actions warrant a Silver Star for one or both of you."

Connie felt a glimmer of hope that there was a way to bury what had happened that day back into the personal history of a few men and leave it there. "I can appreciate the SA might have some questions, Commander."

He gave a brief smile at her understatement. "You've spoken with the award investigators and given your statement regarding March 19th."

"Yes."

"Is there anything you wish to add to that statement?"

She considered that question and then shook her head. They had asked about the battle and she'd given them accurate and detailed answers through the conclusion of the fighting.

"I know your skills as a combat medic. I like to start at the beginning of a question, so I've been following your career since you enlisted, talking with people who have intersected with you. You excelled at your job long before the events of this particular day."

He picked up a remote and played the video he had cued up. The picture was infrared, the burning vehicles white with intense heat, the people in motion visible as light red heat body shapes moving against the gray of cool earth and stone buildings. He tapped a moving image running across the road. "You're fast, Sergeant. This is within the last forty minutes of the fighting, you've been in this for hours and you're still making that run. The analyst on this footage tells me under more ideal conditions you'd likely medal in the hundred yard dash."

"I had an incentive to be fast that day."

He smiled at her remark and shut off the video. "I've watched your actions of March 19th to the point I likely have a better memory of them than you yourself for what was accomplished. I watched you repeatedly risk your life getting to injured soldiers, render aid and move to the next group, for over a period of four hours. The fact the chaplain was hustling around just as much as you were in no way lowers the valor you yourself displayed. I thought personally at times you both were nuts, watching the dashes you would make across that road that had become a zeroed in mortar drop zone. The flying shrapnel was going to kill you if a bullet didn't."

Connie offered a glimmer of a relaxed smile. "Respectfully, Sir, they were in a load and launch routine, we had the timing down. Even if they wanted to drop one faster, they had too hot a tube. And I can outrun most shrapnel when the maze of destroyed vehicles becomes your absorbing blast walls. It was intense, but it wasn't reckless. We knew how to do what needed done."

The Commander chuckled. "I am going to enjoy hearing George try to tell me that too, as the man is fifteen years your senior."

"He was mostly… his Irish was up, Sir, he was full on mad. He was getting to the guys that he knew, who needed him and he didn't care who shot at him in the process. I mostly ran first because no one can sight on me at a sprint so I was only dealing with the random quick trigger fire that was as likely to fly ten feet over my head and into the dirt, as come anywhere near me. I didn't mind those odds. I had a job to do and it was constantly on the other side of the road. We learned how to make that dash to where we needed to be. It was necessary, Sir. And in a fight, you do what's necessary."

"They called you the road runner for most of your eight years."

"The Disney character, yes, Sir. They'd buy me the patch for my jacket, print out cartoons, mostly because they forgot my name, but road runner they could remember. I traveled with whatever convoy needed a medic, or traveled with the chaplains, doing routine medical house calls. I wasn't in a front line combat unit as those were limited to men with my training until the fourth deployment when those assignments opened to women. I saw combat only because the war wasn't respecting any particular front line."

He listened and thoughtfully nodded. "For the actions you took that day, it's my opinion they represent valor due at least a Bronze Star. I'd personally elevate it to the Silver Star simply for the sheer number of runs you made after you took two shots to the vest and got slammed down in the middle of the road, crawled across, then went out again and caught a third round in the back of the vest before you made it across that time. That was at hour two. This footage is closer to hour four. That's raw courage or it's sheer stubbornness, but put it together, it is above what any army medic could reasonably call the job description."

"Getting shot is not heroic, Commander. You've been shot yourself, I would guess; it's the hazard of the job. You get up and keep going because when you're not bleeding it was a good day and there is still work to do. I took some bruises and my ankles hated me for a few weeks because I was running in boots, but that day was mostly long and hot and you were just doing what was necessary until it was over. No particular dash was unusual. Nor any injury I treated unexpected. The only reason we're here is the duration of the fight. Within any twenty minute stretch of it, the events were reasonably close to what I had experienced many times across many tours of duty. It wasn't anywhere close to what I think of as the most dangerous situations I had been in."

"The school double blast in April of '15," he offered as a guess.

She nodded. "And the plane crash in July of '15. We had casualties over a half a mile of terrain and every enemy combatant within five miles trying to get there first." She took a moment to drink the coffee. "Respectfully, Sir, I appreciate what the award means, it's an honor to be considered, but it was the job. I didn't sign up to do an average job. I did it with excellence that day, I'm proud of that. No one died. But it was in fact simply me doing the job the Army hired me to do."

"Was it Connie?"

He picked up the remote again and showed a second set of footage, let the edited together segments play through. Connie watched video of what she had only suspected was in the record, having not seen this before. The clarity was what she had feared might be the case.

"That's drone footage of a vehicle explosion and four body bags later being carried to the mortuary truck. That's four soldiers whom I spoke to last week who are obviously very much alive."

She didn't say anything.

"The SA selected me because I'm a religious man and not afraid to say so in a profession that rarely makes room for statements like love your enemy. I'll remind you of what you already know.

So also good deeds are conspicuous; and even when they are not, they cannot remain hidden. (1 Timothy 5:25)

"Your deeds have become known, Connie." He leaned back in his chair and just let the paused video be the conversation.

Those were soldiers in body bags who were now alive. To talk about what happened after that truck left the field of battle would be going somewhere she had never officially gone before. It was one thing for the person involved to be aware of irregularities, another to make a statement to an investigator. There was really only one answer, for she neither lied, nor discussed a matter like this. "I don't talk about what I've seen on a battlefield, Commander."

"We'll go off the record for a moment." He tugged out his phone and made a call. "I'm with Connie August now. Would you mind making an introduction? Thanks."

He held out the phone.

She did not want to accept that phone, because it was going to be someone of serious enough rank she'd feel like standing just to take the call, or it would be someone from her past, her brother's past, whom she deeply respected and owed a favor. She took the phone and said, "Hello."

"Don't tell him anything, Connie."

She closed her eyes as Paul Falcon's reassuring voice was on the other end of the line. "Though if you were to talk about whatever this is, my wife knows him well enough to have written the story of how he met his wife. I'll loan you a copy of the book if you're interested. You can trust this man knows how to keep a secret, his word is as solid as they come. You want to come over for a wind-down hour when this meeting is over? I've got a dog looking for a belly rub and I still make a mountain-size milkshake."

"Yes, I think I might appreciate that Paul."

"You know the address. Just text and come. It will be nice to see you."

She returned the phone.

"Thank you, Paul." The Commander hung up the call and pocketed the phone. "What do you want to do, Connie? Off the record, would you talk to me about how it goes from that," he nodded to the paused video, "to me having a conversation with the four of them last week?"

She didn't want to take that step.

"The guys remember the explosion and their vehicle rolling. They said after the casualties had been handled, they were directed to a truck to return to base, which made sense, as their ride was totaled. They rode back with the chaplain and you. Once back at Charlie base, they decided to go play darts and catch up on news of how the injured were doing from the field hospital staff coming off duty. They don't remember a heavenly light, an out-of-body experience, being anywhere other than the scene of the fighting."

She simply nodded at that information.

"What really happened in that truck, Connie? Four body bags are loaded in the truck, you get in, George gets in, there is a drive to Charlie base and when the truck arrives the men climb out alive. I know what happened, I can name it, as hard as it is for my eyes to accept what I'm seeing on that video and when I talked with them last week. But what I need to know is what happened in that truck."

"Why do you need to know?"

"Because I've been chasing rumors that follow you and George for years that suggest it was neither a one off occurrence, nor the most interesting miracle which has happened in the vicinity of you two. The battlefield injuries healed appear to range from traumatic brain injuries, blown off limbs and third degree burns, to straight fatal gunshots. To walk away and say this looks like a miracle and not ask the basic question of what happened would be doing a disservice to the man who asked me to give him an opinion. I'd like a sense of the mountain I'm dealing with."

"I'd like something in return."

"Okay. I'm listening."

"I don't talk about what I've seen on a battlefield. Neither will you, if I answer your question. Tell the SA whatever you wish drawn from evidence outside this conversation. Our conversation, this part of it, stays in this room."

He considered that request and nodded. "Agreed."

Connie took Paul's word on his character and let herself relax a fraction more. "I won't disagree with what you can plainly see. They died and they are no longer dead. It would classify as a miracle in that God acted that day to bring about what happened. I would suggest however, that it was neither unusual nor particularly noteworthy. George is a good chaplain, he knows God and the scriptures and he's a good teacher. He taught me what he knows. And I listened."

She thought about how to say this. "Sometimes death is present, but the outcome is still open to variation depending on what someone else does to help you. We think in terms of a doctor jolting a heart to get it beating again. Or someone who drowns in cold water being warmed slowly to get a heart beat back. In the same class of intervention as a doctor getting a heart to beat again, I would put someone praying a resurrection prayer, telling death to get his hands off you and for you to wake up in Jesus' name. You can be dead, but someone else can intervene and change the end of the story."

The Commander leaned forward, intrigued. "Really. That's what George did, or you did, some hours after they had initially died in the vehicle blast."

"Yes."

She thought it better to simply paint the picture and let him adjust than explain the theology. George could answer his questions on that topic so much better than she could.

"I think of it this way, Commander. When you die, it is not a finished final death until the outcome of what the people around you will do has been factored in. If you die on the operating table, no heart beat, no breath, but the surgeon works to revive you, are you dead or are you alive? If the surgeon stops trying to revive you, it's done, you're permanently dead. If he keeps trying, gets back a heart beat, you're still alive. Death can be considered to be not absolutely final if there is someone there who might intervene and bring you back to life.

"We think in terms of doctors reviving someone in the minutes after they die before too much brain injury has set in from lack of oxygen. God's time frame is wider than man's. Jesus prayed for Lazarus four days after he was in the grave and he came out of the grave perfectly healthy.

"Jesus says when you die you'll be with me, but I think sometimes Jesus just joins us on earth or has an angel waiting with us while other people are still influencing the final outcome of the situation.

"George taught me the resurrection prayer late in my second tour. In this situation both George and I were available to intervene and the Holy Spirit arranged for us to be able to pray for them on the drive back to Charlie base. God granted all four men life. We simply asked God to do so. To look at George or myself as special is to miss the obvious. God acted. We would rather not be noticed, frankly."

He gave a quick grin. "I can anticipate why. Would you walk me through that trip, Connie and explain what you can? My word it will not leave this room."

"It's not as complex as you would think, Commander. The battle was over, the casualties had been transported, I was winding down my own work. I heard the Holy Spirit say you need to go back with the deceased. George had the same impression, which in situations like this is confirmation of what God is arranging for us to pray. We don't want spectators to see us praying over the dead, but we don't work out the details of how to arrange to do this quietly. God arranges it and we step into what he's got worked out. We use that as another confirmation of what God has in mind for us to do. Riding back to base with the bodies is perfect.

"We got in the truck when it was ready to leave. Once we were underway we opened the body bags and inverted the edges back under the cots like you would do a fitted sheet, so the men are lying on them rather than in them.

George then anointed the four men with oil and prayed for Jesus to display the power of his resurrection on their behalf. I followed behind George, speaking to each man individually. I told death to get his hands off them in Jesus' name, I told their bodies to heal and I told them to wake up and open their eyes.

"They did.

"It's mostly head injuries which had killed them. One had a broken neck. All had some degree of burns either on an arm or their chest, their face. Their bodies healed, the burns faded as if they had simply gone through a normal healing cycle in a compressed amount of time, the blood on their uniforms faded as though washed out and I found it fascinating even the burned fabric reversed; then they opened their eyes."

"You saw four people come from death back to life."

"In the space of about four minutes, yes."

"Wow."

Connie smiled. "I'll agree with that. The guys weren't aware they had been dead. They glanced around the truck and relaxed as they realized their buddies were with them.

"It's happened so many times I just offered my standard version of hi by saying, 'Hey, guys, sorry for the jolt awake, this road is particularly bumpy. I'm Connie, the medic that was traveling further back with the convoy. You got shaken up pretty good with that vehicle blast, but you aren't hurt enough to warrant anything more than my company for the ride back to Charlie base. Don't worry about any sense of lost minutes of time, a bit of disorientation, it's the fading adrenaline and sleep playing havoc with your brains. We'll be back on base in about ten minutes. If you feel anything more than the occasional twinge of a bruise once you're walking around, any blurred vision, headache, ears ringing, your bones ache, you have any new sense of lost minutes, or you just feel off, like something isn't right, the doctors want to check you out again now, otherwise you can make that call when you want to walk over and have them medically clear you, if you go tonight or in the morning.' And then George and I simply start chatting with each other about other things.

"In the ten minutes until we reach the base, you can see the guys feeling better with each passing minute until they're not just feeling well, healed, but feeling really good like you do after a great night's sleep at the end of a vacation. They're chatting among themselves about the days events and its normal conversation, 'Kyle took a bullet in the shoulder', 'I saw Kevin broke his leg', 'I'm glad we weren't in the front of the convoy rolling into that firefight', its normal chatter among unit guys.

"We arrive on base and they decide to head over to the after-hours club and play darts, get the scoop on how the fight had looked from the vantage point of drone overhead and get the latest updates on the injured from the medical staff coming off duty. They are, all four, feeling fine.

"We folded up the body bags and returned them to the stack in the mortuary supply room then went to get coffee. We mostly stuck around because we know what's coming and it's easier if the guys with the questions can find us.

"It takes about ten minutes before we get the question. It's not hard to avoid lying. Just don't say a lie. Asked, 'didn't you ride back with 4 KIA?' You don't answer the question. Instead, you say the current truth. 'The guys I came back to Charlie base with are over at the after-hours club, very much alive. You have names for the KIA?'"

"Given the names, you nod. 'That's them. Try the after-hours club.'

"You don't explain. No one is going to say, 'you must have raised them from the dead.' Let people come up with whatever explanation they like, from battlefield fog of war, to paperwork error, to some kind of not-so-funny macabre practical joke. People will go with what their eyes are telling them.

"You would think the hardest thing with a resurrection is handling that confusion, those who are certain they saw the person die, the one who moved him to a body bag and yet he's standing over there alive and well. That actually can be managed if you choose carefully where and when you pray for the person to wake up and can have some time elapse before the person who knows something takes that jolt.

"George would have a quiet conversation with them, 'he's alive and fine and for his sake let it go how, confusion on the battlefield, a judgment error by a medic. Can you do that?' If that conversation wasn't going to work, I'd admit I prayed for him and the guy woke up, but we're simply leaving it that it happened. Maybe his mom back home had sensed a need to pray for him and that prayer got answered. We talk them around into keeping quiet and letting it go.

"The hardest thing with a resurrection is how they explain problems that are no longer problems. In my experience, resurrection life tends to reverse anything that had been bothering you before you died, from the bones, outward, so the backache is gone because the vertebra are no longer worn, the aching shoulder doesn't hurt anymore because the building arthritis is no longer there. Sometimes resurrection life flows so strong they don't need glasses the next day.

"Occasionally a conscientious doctor will write up the mystery of a spontaneous healing and a few people will ask the soldier what happened and the guy will shrug, with no idea what happened or when. He's just glad he doesn't need to see a doctor for anything anymore.

"Most guys don't remember being resurrected as an event itself. Some remember waking up with a medic patting their shoulder, saying 'you're going to be fine, soldier. It looks like you got knocked out cold but you're not bleeding and nothing is broken. Just lay there a minute until you get your bearings. I've got a buddy of yours to check out who is hurt worse than you are. I'll be back.'

"This happens on the battlefield a lot more than anyone realizes, Commander. A decently trained chaplain or medic is going to say a resurrection prayer before assuming your death is final. Especially anyone who has been around George for any period of time and he's trained most of the chaplain corps now. You tell death to get his hands off the soldier and then order the soldier in Jesus' name to wake up. It's easier with soldiers than civilians, as the guys are accustomed to taking orders."

Joe chuckled at that remark. "Oh, I can imagine that comes as one intense order. George taught you."

Connie nodded. "Toward the end of my second tour. It's a basic prayer. It simply assumes correctly that this man died before God wished him to die and you ask God to give him back his life. Who most wants to do God's will? God. If God wants the man alive and you ask him, the guy opens his eyes. The rest of this is mostly figuring out how to do it and not get noticed."

"You've been doing a lot of this."

"Sure." Connie struggled to explain why it really wasn't that big of a deal. "Death isn't final, Commander. Society has assumed it is, but I think Jesus was right in his language when he said the 12-year-old girl who had died was sleeping, when he said Lazarus, who had died, was sleeping.

"You yourself are dead; you can't influence your situation any more, but if someone is there to pray for you, they can influence what happens. It's not a finished final death until the outcome of what the people around you will do has been factored in. If you die anywhere near me, I'm going to tell you in Jesus' name to wake up. And most dead people do. It's neither a hard prayer, nor a particularly surprising event. I think God would like most people to live to be close to 120 years old. If God doesn't answer my prayer, okay, that one is a mystery. I've got faith enough to ask it for anyone who dies around me."

"You've gotten comfortable doing this and seeing results."

"I'm more surprised now when someone doesn't open their eyes, Commander."

He laughed.

Connie smiled and made a final observation. "What the four guys described as their experience makes sense to me. We are a spirit, we have a soul and we inhabit a body. When you die, your spirit and soul separate from your body. I don't believe people's spirits linger around like ghosts once the outcome of their death is finished, but I think the spirits of the recently dead can be nearby waiting for the outcome of what others do who might help them. In this case, I don't think the spirits of the four guys had gone very far. I say that because of what they describe of the events that they remember.

"They were still as a group and together on the battlefield. They were aware of what their buddies were doing to help the other casualties. They don't remember themselves or their buddies as being injured. I think they were shielded from seeing their own bodies being moved to mortuary bags and loaded on the truck.

"I suspect an angel presented himself to them as an army officer. The angel directed them to the truck to travel with their bodies. As far as they were concerned they were simply following orders. I think an angel was shepherding their spirits from the time of the explosion on, while the outcome of their death was being determined by the actions of others, namely George and myself. That would align with scripture:

> Are they [angels] not all ministering spirits sent forth to serve, for the sake of those who are to obtain salvation? (Hebrews 1:14)

> Do not neglect to show hospitality to strangers, for thereby some have entertained angels unawares. (Hebrews 13:2)

"When we prayed, their spirits returned to their bodies and they woke up. It doesn't seem particularly hard for them either, this resurrection process; it's like stepping back into your own home. Your spirit is comfortable with your body. They were simply dependent on the actions of others to help them after they died; they needed someone to ask God to give them back their lives."

"I follow that. They had memories of between the blast which killed them and waking up in the truck."

"Yes, Sir.

"There's a reason we don't talk about what we've seen, Commander. One, its easier on the guy if he doesn't realize he died and someone brought him back to life. For the rest of his life he's wondering when I die the next time, does someone know how to pray for me not to be dead? Will they do that for me? That's a complicated way to live. Second, it's easier to do this work if no one knows you're doing it. God sends me to where he wants me to be and I treat the person in front of me. If people were deciding where I should go and who I should pray for it would be literally chaos. I listen to the Holy Spirit regarding the injured and dead in front of me and that's my field of ministry. George does the same."

He thoughtfully nodded. "What have you seen regarding healings?"

Connie flashed him a smile. "Respectfully, Sir, what's on that video is enough for this conversation. I'll admit we pray for every injured person to be fully healed. And I'll mention that healings are more difficult than resurrections, in part because the person you are trying to help has a free will and what happens is often in part what they are deciding. You pray to stop the bleeding, the infection, the pain and then the person is on their way to the field hospital. Healing is a different vein of ministry that often needs more time.

"I've seen George pray and watched creative miracles happen, eyes see again, brain trauma clear, injured limbs heal as new. George has had bullets come back to the surface and out into the palm of his hand, as the injury heals from the inside out. I'm learning to pray for the living like George does. It is simply easier to pray for the dead than the sick or injured. The pressure on you of what other people think is a lot lower when it's you, a dead person and God and no one else is present."

The Commander considered that answer and nodded, rested back in his chair, signaling he'd accept the conversation was mostly over now. "What do you want to have happen in this case, Connie?"

She thought about it and shrugged. "All I did, Commander, was pray. I told them to wake up. I delivered the good news that God didn't want them dead. That's like a postman delivering a party invitation. You're very glad the postman did his job, but the person who is giving the party is the one you call and thank. I did my part with excellence, I told four dead people to wake up with confident faith God would give me what I asked. God was the one who gave them back their lives. To give me an award for that would be to show honor to the wrong person. Let the… irregularities be just that. I would prefer there be no award, so this battle doesn't follow me around all my life, my name listed in the history books. I would be, what, the third female Silver Star recipient in this generation? I can do without that earned fame. The less conversation and questions there are about March 19th, the better it is for me."

"Alright. I'll convey your desire to the SA. I can't predict what he may decide, or what he might list on the citation if it is given."

"That conversation itself is useful to me, thank you. Is there anything else you need tonight, Commander?"

"I have what I need for now. After I talk with George, I may be back for another conversation. I'd like to understand better what George taught you."

"There are some audios floating around, from a conversation with someone else who recently asked a similar question. I'll see about arranging a set for you if you like."

"That would be useful, Sergeant. Thank you."

Connie stood as he did, shook hands with the man and stepped out of the conference room, took a deep breath and let it out, more relieved to be done with that meeting than nearly any in her lifetime.

The bellman met her at the base of the stairs. "Sergeant August, would you like to spend a few moments to unwind, enjoy coffee, refreshments, as our guest tonight?"

"I've another appointment this evening, but I appreciate the offer."

"Then please, let me arrange transportation. The hotel chauffer is available to take you wherever you would like to go this evening."

"That would be very helpful, thank you."

Four minutes later, Connie gave Paul's address to the hotel driver and settled back for the short ride to Paul and Ann Falcon's home.

She was tired, the kind of wrung out tired that said she had reached the point of being overloaded mentally. She needed time to enjoy a dog, drink a very large milkshake and maybe ask Ann some questions about the Commander and his wife Kelly. That would help. Just a break from the weight of the topic under discussion would help. The thought of another conversation with Ryan in about nine hours on a similar subject as tonight was beyond her at the moment. But it would be rude to cancel meeting for a walk when she would be heading to work walking in that direction.

"How'd I do, Holy Spirit?"

She whispered the question and it was like a blanket of love dropped around her shoulders, lightweight and soft and a light lovely blue, which she'd come to realize was one of Jesus' favorite colors. She let herself relax deeply into the impression of it. She was so tired the Holy Spirit wasn't even trying to answer her in words tonight, he was simply replying with a touch.

She was aware, more than most, of the number of people who would die in Chicago tonight. And was aware she was consciously deciding she wouldn't help any of them, not tonight and probably not tomorrow either. If it was critical maybe God sent her tomorrow night to wake up someone who had died tonight, but that would be highly unusual for him to do in a civilian setting right now. She was still mostly operating below the radar and after 24 hours dead, it would get press attention.

It would help, having Ryan trained and those who worked at Mercy Hospital involved. So she'd be there for coffee in the morning, if only because that training curve was where the multiplication rested which lifted this weight off her. George had taught her and most of the chaplain corp, she'd teach Ryan and the group of seven, Ryan would probably train thirty to fifty in the next couple years given how quickly he was absorbing the lessons. Heal the sick, raise the dead, preach the good news of the gospel – being a Christian was a full-time life.

The car arrived at the Falcon's home and Connie thanked the driver, offered a tip that was graciously declined, accepted a sincere thanks for her service in the military which he offered her in return and then she turned toward the building lobby. The doorman met her with a smile, the news she was expected and the elevator whisked her up to the fourth floor.

Paul met her, the dog maneuvering in front of him, tail wagging with a force that could knock over furniture. Paul smiled. "I'm going to guess the Silver Star conversation just took an interesting direction."

She laughed and simply nodded. She knelt and rubbed her hands through thick black fur greeting the dog. Black joyfully leaned into her, then darted away and came dashing back with a well worn bear that squeaked when he bit down hard. She laughed for the joy the dog conveyed and tugged the bear's foot to show her appreciation of being shown his favorite toy.

"I'll fix milkshakes," Paul offered, "you can toss that dog his favorite pair of balled up socks and we'll find something like art or sports to talk about to put this night on a lighter footing. Ann's finishing up a call with my mother; she's going to need a milkshake, too, when that call ends."

Connie laughed. “Deal.” This had been the right choice for how to end her evening. The Holy Spirit had known what he was doing when he arranged for Paul to be the one the Commander called. Connie let herself relax and step into the flow of what was here for her, a friendship she could trust, with both Paul and Ann and entertainment in the form of their dog she was coming to adore.

18

RYAN COOPER

On Thursday morning, Ryan bought Connie her preferred breakfast and mirrored hers with a sweet roll and coffee of his own. He noticed the fact her face was drawn and her color off, her smile was tired, though her good morning was her usual upbeat tone. He didn't ask who had died last night, where she had been, what had happened. He was comfortable being nosey with questions, but a wise man offered space when a woman was showing the appearance of a long night.

He held the door of the coffee shop for her and they began a walk that had become routine now for who walked on the left and right, how they handled crossing streets with only a stop sign to slow traffic and who went first when the sidewalk got congested with other pedestrians preventing them from walking side by side.

Connie didn't immediately offer a subject topic as she sometimes did. She nursed her coffee and then mentioned, "I'd like to extend a last minute invitation if you happen to be available. You can join the group this evening if you like, meet the others who have been learning this material. I'm hosting tonight at my home. The group gathers at 8:00 and meets until 9:30. There's confidentiality in both who is present and what is said. You won't discuss it with others, nor record it."

"Understood." Ryan was grateful for the offer. "I'd like to come, Connie, thank you. I've a donor presentation, but I should be done shortly after seven."

"Feel free to come over early and join me for dinner. The meal is going to be casual and not something that needs timed. If you show up, I'll feed you, if not I'll see you at eight."

"That flexibility is appreciated. I'll see how the day unfolds." As she hadn't already offered a topic, Ryan thought it a useful opportunity to offer one of his own questions as he started the recording for the morning. "I ran into a situation with my honorary grandmother which has me wondering how you handle something. When you are with a person, how do you handle their expectations about how you will pray? Do you explain why you're going to pray as you do, before you do so? And a corollary question. How effective is prayer for someone when you are not with them and they don't know you are praying for them?"

"Good questions," Connie mentioned. She gestured with her coffee. "I have two ways of handling the expectations of someone else. The first that I routinely use, I simply say I'm going to pray for God to heal you. Then I explain I'm going to do so with a prayer of command which an army chaplain taught me. The wording will sound different to you, but it sounds like him and he was a man who got a lot of people healed. Then I keep it direct to what I want done. 'In Jesus' name, death, get your hands off her. Disease, get out. Holy Spirit, fill her body with abundant life. Now be in perfect health, as Jesus heals you. Amen.'

"If I feel like that prayer was accepted, I leave an index card with what I prayed written down for them. And because I know children are particularly good at having faith that what they say is what is going to happen, I'll mention, 'Have your grandson pray this for you when he comes to visit. Boys in particular love giving commands.' That kind of suggestion often gets followed. I've found that family members praying with faith are particularly effective.

"The second method is useful when I'm dealing with the expectations of more than just the person who is sick – they have family and friends present, or I'm in a public setting. I personally find it helpful to pray in Italian. I tell them in English I'm going to pray for God to heal you. Then ask, is it okay if I pray in Italian? I learned English, but when I talk with God I'm better in my other language.

Then I pray in Italian. Then I say Amen in English so they can agree with me. I can pray as I would like without them being concerned I didn't pray the way they had been taught. We've agreed I would pray for God to heal them and there is power in that agreement. But they can't disagree with me on the specifics of what I pray and negate my prayer if they don't know how I phrased it."

"That is an elegant way around the problem. I know some French."

"Keep the idea in mind as something useful." Connie drank more of her coffee and then added, "Prayer at a distance works as long as you see them healed and are praying for what they are to become, not praying with sympathy thinking of them as sick. The picture in your mind and your words need to be in agreement when you're praying at a distance. I don't know why, it's just the strongest overlap I've noticed.

"The best outcome is to lay your hand on their arm, or whatever injury is to be healed, pray aloud with authority and receive their echo of your amen. That's checking off every power base you have, the power of agreement, the power of authority, the laying on of hands.

"Laying on hands is particularly effective, because it's showing active faith and is releasing the power in Jesus words recorded in Mark 16, 'these signs will follow those who believe in me, in my name they will lay hands on the sick and they will recover.' Jesus often healed this way, by laying his hands on the sick, so it's an important way God the Holy Spirit likes to work. I don't need to understand why or how to rely on that promise and experience it. My hunch is that something in the sick person is blocking the grace of healing from reaching them, God wants them well and when you lay your hands on them the Holy Spirit can flow grace and healing to them through you. Your touch makes the two of you, in effect, one person. You become like the detour the Holy Spirit can use to get healing to the person in need. Your touch is the contact point God is using to release his power. Similar to when we speak a word of faith, it's God the Holy Spirit releasing power which brings the answer. He just likes to use us, to work through us and with us, so we learn how to bring the kingdom of God to meet needs around us.

"It is reasonable to ask a sick person to move an inch, but not a mile. Starting a conversation about how God heals so they can cooperate with you after someone is sick enough to be in the hospital is like trying to light a candle in a hurricane. So understand where they are and look for a way through the maze to help them. There's a path there somewhere.

"The authority to heal the sick comes from what Jesus did on the cross. That's the good news. The bad news, it's you, it's God and it's a sick person. And a sick person is still thinking, has beliefs, ideas on what is going on, will go on, they have a free will.

"Satan and death have become very skilled at making people sick and keeping them sick. They try to get a patient to want to stay sick, 'my son only visits me because I'm sick, so I guess I'm glad I'm sick', or to make repeated statements of discouragement like 'I'm always sick', 'I'm never going to be well again', 'this body is cursed, everything in it breaks'. That's enough permission for death to flatten a person. They are making agreements that this is who they are. They haven't realized how dark their own language has turned against the idea of them being well again. Those are not throw-away words, they are showing the idea of being permanently sick has settled in their heart and that's what they believe.

"When you desire to heal the sick, you often first have to get a person to agree that they want to be well. It can be expressed in as varied a way as there are individuals, the quip they make, 'I'm ready to never have an aching back again', 'I am going to be so glad to get back home and work out in my flower beds again', to as simple as the remark 'I'm tired of being sick'. But you need that agreement unless they are so sick God will let you simply act in their best interests irrespective of their words.

"You heal the sick by bringing the kingdom of God to bear on the problem, telling sickness to leave in Jesus' name, by telling death to get its hands off this person in Jesus' name. The prayer of faith will heal the sick person. It's the same faith needed to raise someone from the dead. It's standing on the fact God wants this person well and I'm speaking under delegated authority what is going to be done."

Connie nodded toward the garden park and Ryan gladly accepted the additional time for this conversation and turned that direction.

He could see a very practical question to ask given that advice. "I pray for someone whom I have heard is sick. I pray with authority and with faith, in Jesus' name telling death to get his hands off them, for sickness to leave, for their body to be restored to health. While I am praying for them, fifty miles away, they are in the hospital and what they are saying to themselves, their family and friends, is statements like 'I'm going to die', 'this heart condition is killing me', 'I'm never getting out of this hospital'. Who wins?"

Connie nodded, accepting the question, then simply looked at him. "Answer your own question. Who wins?"

"Jesus has healed them at the cross, the health they need is right there waiting for them. I have authority to tell death and sickness to leave in Jesus name. They've decided they are going to die." Ryan winced, seeing the answer. "So they die."

Connie nodded. "Basically. Free will is the trump card every individual plays in this life. God basically says, 'if I won't let my perfect will override a person's free will, I won't let your prayer of faith override it either'. That's the line. But God will use your prayer for the person to send them as many lifelines as necessary to get them to want to be healed and well again, to change their way of thinking.

"Free will moves around, it's malleable, it's not concrete. They can, in the middle of the night, simply get mad at being sick and say to themselves, 'enough of this,

I'm fed up with being sick, I want my life back' and your prayer will immediately slam into them like dynamite going off and have a powerful effect because they've come into agreement with you (whether they realized you were praying for them or not).

"A family member or friend visiting them can encourage them by sharing stories of good days and bringing laughter, can spark something in them, so they want to be well again. They have new hope they'll get better and your prayer will immediately set to work helping them. Their situation can be turned around by their decision to live all the way up to the moment they are dead. When they die, their free will stops resisting you, so you can pray to raise them from the dead. That you can do by your own prayer of faith."

"It's easier to pray for someone who has died, than it is to pray for the sick."

Connie nodded emphatically. "Much easier. It's your prayer of faith, God's desire they be alive and a dead person who doesn't get to vote."

Ryan laughed at the way she said it.

Connie smiled. "Praying for someone who died is incredibly easy. It's simply more complicated logistically, because people don't routinely pray for the dead to wake up, so when it happens, family and friends can freak out, whereas people are always praying for the sick, or at least saying 'I'll pray for you'.

"Praying for the sick has become an act of sympathy and politeness because no one expects anything to happen. The thought that a person in a wheelchair will get out of it, not needing it any more, isn't even in the frame of reference of the person praying most of the time. If you say 'I'm going to heal you', that can cause friction. Saying 'I'm going to pray for you', that's viewed as being nice. Society and the church have lost so much of the truth about healing that our very language shows us the grand canyon-sized problem that has developed. We don't expect people to pray for the sick and actually heal the sick. We expect prayer for the sick to be some comforting words and an affirmation that 'you're enduring this sickness with such a good spirit'; at best it's a 'maybe God will help you' hope.

"Praying for the sick is a challenge because people don't expect anything to happen when you pray. They don't expect a broken bone to heal faster. They don't expect to be healed of the pneumonia right then, or cancer. And that is a real problem. People have grown accustomed to having an expectation of disease and how it will progress. Heart disease, arthritis, cancer, you name the condition. It will progressively worsen until it impairs their lives and they will take more pills, face more surgery, more therapy, trying to manage this thing killing them.

"People label themselves with what the doctors have diagnosed. I am a person with heart disease. I am a person with failing kidneys. That's their free will, in part, deciding this is who they are. We lock ourselves into being sick without realizing it. Those are facts, but not who they are. They are a healthy alive person who temporarily has – name the condition – which needs removed. But they have no expectation and no hope that it can be removed, that they can be freed of sickness and actually be 100 percent healed and healthy.

"A person who is alive into their 80s lives 30,000 days. They die on one day at the end of that. While I'd like to simply say I only pray for the dead because it is so much easier, it would mean letting someone deal with sickness and or chronic disease for going on ten to twenty thousand days for the unfortunate ones, before I help set them free.

"Jesus said 'heal the sick' for a reason. You can't avoid this fight. It would be cruel to let someone be sick all their life because it's simply easier to help them after they die.

"I keep it as simple as I can. I try to get verbal agreement they want to be well and then I pray in Italian so they can't contradict me and when their arthritis is healed and their doctor is amazed a chronic condition left, I simply say ‘God was really kind, you should thank him’ and try to leave it at that.

“Teaching the fact we are healed at the cross, how to live healed, those are separate battles that can’t be done at the bedside of someone who is sick. Heal the sick, then when they are well, tell them the good news of the gospel in a more complete way. That seems to be Jesus’ model. He’d have days healing everyone who needed healing. Then days he’d spend teaching. Or he’d teach awhile, then heal awhile. Teach and raise hope, then heal and bring relief, then repeat the cycle again.”

They had finished a loop of the garden park and were coming back to the hospital. Connie stopped walking, but chose to stay to finish her thought. “Healing the sick is a different battle than raising the dead. It’s more complex. You’re always working on a continuum, what you understand and believe as the person who is praying, what the person who is sick believes, how the sickness has reached this point, if it’s new or chronic, with all the implications of how people have adjusted to live with it.

“Listen to people carefully. Listen for the labels they have given themselves. They will tell you what the fight really is.

“You can heal an atheist who says, ‘I deserve to be healed and healthy for the rest of my life’ – you can drive a freight train through that agreement and kill cancer in them easily. Your belief in Jesus is enough. Then you tell them it was Jesus who just healed you. They’ll be more receptive to hearing the gospel after they are healed.

“You can heal someone who does not believe Jesus heals today if you can get agreement ‘I want to be well’. Your belief in healing is enough. The fact they are healed will change their minds about Jesus healing today.

“You can’t heal someone who says ‘as soon as one thing gets fixed in this body, something else breaks’ until you change their heart. You can heal their present symptoms, but they are already telling you the sickness will simply move to the next problem and it will because their free will lets it. We have to learn to resist what the devil is doing to us, to not accept sickness. If you don't think you have an enemy doing this to you, if you don't think you have authority to resist him, you will keep getting run over by him. If your heart says you're defeated, even though the truth is Jesus gives you total victory, you will still be living defeated.

"Someone who sees themselves as chronically sick always will be. Because at the root, they don't have a sickness and disease problem, they have a heart problem. Their heart is poisoning the idea that they can be healed and healthy. Listen to people, to figure out what you are really fighting. Then you can do some good.

"Words tell you what is in someone's heart. Changing their words does not heal them. God heals them. Changing their words starts changing their heart and their free will, so God can help them. 'I want to be well' is a good place to be. They want something good to happen. They are actually saying I want God, who is the one from whom all good things come. They are opening a door for God and thus for you, to help them. You can find agreement with them in those words and bring a powerful prayer because they are no longer blocking God's help. There's a reason the guy who brags 'I'm as healthy as a horse' rarely sees the doctor. He sees himself healthy. He may have a pride problem, but he doesn't have a sickness problem in his heart.

"God hates sickness with a passion. He's already stripped sickness away from the entire world, that's how much he hates it. But we all have free will. All God can do is say, 'I don't lie, I heal all your diseases' and send people to help you who have faith and are willing to pray for you to be healed.

"God knows people are hurting; he doesn't want this, but God has this ability to respect free will that is foreign to us. We flatten anyone who gets in our way on even a minor thing we want to do. God, who wants to give us only good and perfect gifts, stops when a person says 'no, I don't believe you want to do that for me'. God will let someone stop his goodness on the basis of a lie they have believed rather than overrule their free will. It's weird, the way God loves people. He lets us be free. Even when we make decisions like deciding to stay sick."

Ryan laughed at the way she said it.

Connie smiled. "I've got to go, I'm lingering around talking when there is a prep schedule that doesn't give minutes in leeway. But one last, final thought.

"If people come to you wanting to be healed, you can heal them easily. I think that's why Jesus simply modeled that way of healing through the majority of his life. The fact people came to him, or someone brought them to him, said their heart was ready to receive healing and he could heal them. God respects free will. When you go to someone who is sick, that's an act of love, but they are likely not ready to receive healing when you first walk into their room. You have to move them to want healing before you can give them healing. That's why most prayers for the sick don't have an effect. The person praying doesn't expect anything to happen, the person prayed for doesn't expect anything to happen and God honors free will."

Ryan could literally see her debating the minutes on the clock versus one more sentence. "I love this conversation, but go, Connie, we'll talk more later. You're already going to have to run or else deal with being behind when the sign on the door turns to open."

"You're right. I'm going. See you tonight if you can make it." She turned and this time when she moved into a run, she kicked into a higher gear and ran like the wind. Ryan watched the change, startled. She'd walked, jogged and run before, but that was a sprint. She'd make up those minutes with a few to spare at that pace. He was almost glad she'd made herself that far on the edge of late so he could see her true speed.

"God, why was she so tired this morning? I caught on partway through the conversation that she was talking more because she was tired than because the subject matter required that many words. She's struggled with healing the sick, I could hear that in her words, too. She knows how, but it's two free wills involved, hers and the person who is sick and the healing that she longs to bring doesn't often get there when she knows it should.

"The one thing Connie is not is patient. She is intense driven conviction. The frustration would be intense for someone who longs to heal and can't figure out how to get agreement with the person sick."

Ryan caught the full truth of his own words. "And I realized I also just described you, God. I don't understand your respect for free will at the level you give it. You don't appear to have a few loopholes, 'in this situation, for your own good, I'll ignore your free will.' You love us, you died for us and yet you won't save our life by overriding our free will."

God would let people believe he caused sickness. He would let people believe he let children die young. He'd give people the freedom not to believe him. God had made people free. And even for their own good, God wouldn't remove their freedom.

Ryan was beginning to really see what was ahead of him. He walked on to the hospital, thoughtful now in his conversation. "God, I want to get very good at healing the sick. Connie showed me the challenges of that in stark relief today. It's not just learning how to heal the sick, it's learning how to talk with the sick so they will accept being healed. What works? What gets people willing to let you heal them? Seeing someone healed, so they want the same thing for themselves?"

That idea fit what Jesus had modeled. "God, we need people visibly, publicly, healed in Chicago so sick people will come wanting to be healed. How's that for a first prayer? You've already made arrangements and done what I'm asking, so I will pray it with boldness now. God, give us public, visible healings in Chicago, so people will come wanting to be healed."

Ryan laughed at a realization. He ran a hospital, the definition of someplace people came to be healed. "How do

I get people to accept you as their physician, the same way they accept one of the doctors on staff? They are here because they want to get healed, they just expect it to come through a doctor and a pill, rather than God and a prayer. So how does that shift, God?" That question was yet another puzzle to think about and get solved. The good news was God wanted it solved even more than he did.

"Thank you, for loving me enough to raise the bar and trust me with this subject. Please show me how to faithfully use what you are teaching me to heal the sick. I'm ready for it God, the practical experience that is coming. It's time to start learning by doing. Walter and I will be making rounds together this afternoon. Help me bring healing to patients today, God. I'm hungry to help people by bringing what you have done for them to them. I see where Connie's passion comes from, healing the sick and raising the dead, it's worth spending a lifetime doing. I'm going to love this adventure with you and celebrate the victories. I can see them coming. That is very good news."

19

Ryan remembered Connie's home had a deep olive green front door and a red mailbox and it turned out to be a unique combination. He found and rang the bell. Her voice called through a speaker hidden above him, 'Its open, Ryan. Come on in."

He opened the iron gate, then turned the knob on what looked like a century-old oak-slab door hung perfectly balanced and stepped into her home. He had anticipated long and narrow given it was a converted store front, but that thought didn't do justice to the space. It was as unique as she herself was.

The walls on either side were original old building brick, the lighting dangling from original beams set in ceilings twenty feet tall, the flooring a dark polished pine; it was a canvas waiting for someone to etch in their own personality. Connie had. In the entrance area there were well-used leather packs and combat medic backpacks hung on wall pegs, hats of various types – cowboy, beret, ball cap, military – and the bench where she might sit to put on boots shared its length with a stack of blankets that looked more like saddle blankets than soft throws.

Connie hadn't bothered to break up the space with tall furniture or privacy walls, he could see to the back of her home to the one wall that must separate off the bedroom and bath, in between the kitchen was open, the table area, the section turned into a living room .She was twenty feet away poking at something in the oven.

"If you don't want a burnt dinner, leave me be for the next few minutes, this is turning into more of a thing than I expected. Wander, help yourself to whatever's cold to drink in the refrigerator."

"I can do that."

He dumped his jacket on the bench and set down the binder he had brought on the table. There was a leather couch in a rich burgundy and a good size television screen, a large square hassock in cream fabric currently hosting a stack of six books and some paperwork. White rugs warmed up the floors throughout the space. She had a trio of cushioned rocking chairs set around rather than upholstered chairs.

The long walls were filled with ten foot long shelves, books dominated some shelves, shiny brass tins and pots that gleamed reflected light lined others, four shelves were filled with framed photos in matching matt black frames. "Someone likes taking pictures."

"I'm obnoxious that way," Connie replied easily.

He walked over to check out the images. She favored people, group shots, four or five guys, nearly all of them collections of soldiers decked out in various flavors of gear. Mostly US army, a few Brits, local soldiers, probably Iraqi and Afghans. He could see the chronology. Her hair changed length, her tan deepened, she had transformed over the years into the woman as he'd met her, her face and eyes no longer as innocent as in the early photos. He glanced her way. Reverting to civilian life had softened her appearance, but it hadn't softened her intensity.

He realized there was a long sheet of mirror finish tin with cut out stencil words hung on the back side of the front door nearly to the floor and he wandered back that direction to read it. The stencil quoted several scriptures.

If one loves God, one is known by him.
1 Corinthians 8:3

Love is patient and kind
Love does not insist on its own way
Love rejoices in the right.
Love bears all things, believes all things,
Hopes all things, endures all things.
Love never ends
Faith, hope, love abide
The greatest of these is love.

1 Corinthians 13

Familiar words, yet poignant. He glanced over as she joined him. “You like reading scripture.”

“The world isn’t going to define love that way. I need reminded of its true definition before I walk out the door and deal with that world.”

She handed him the second mug she carried. “An acquired taste. Don’t care for it, hand me back your mug. Like it, there’s more on the stove.”

He took a cautious smell then taste. Not something he could easily put words to, not black coffee, not chocolate, but interesting and not unpleasant. The lingering aftertaste was good, had the sharpness of peppermint. “Thanks.”

“I like hot drinks on a cool day. We’ll eat in about fifteen minutes.” She turned toward the living room area. “Shall we share small talk, how was your day? Or simply consider that a conversation for another time and dive into an interesting topic?”

Ryan followed her with a smile. “Neither one of us particularly cares for small talk, I’d wager. And since I’m probably the most taxing part of your day thus far, we’ll skip that too.”

Connie laughed, but he noticed she didn’t disagree with him. She diverted to the kitchen area and finished setting the table.

He remembered his phone, set it on the ottoman, started a recording. “I’m recording our conversation, but remember your caveat and will put it away before the group arrives tonight.”

“Sure. And thanks for that in advance.”

There was one rather large piece of artwork on the back wall of the living room section of her home, a needlepoint, the rich blue fabric panel hung between inch diameter wood poles at the top and bottom. Made of simple x stitches in white embroidery thread, the tracings for the words still fainting visible beneath the thread, she’d stitched a passage of scripture. The piece looked old enough he would guess she'd probably made it when she was a teenager, for her initials were stitched in the lower corner. Five words were underlined in a rich bright red thread. He took time to read the art.

Let love be genuine;
Hate what is evil, hold fast to what is good;
Love one another with brotherly affection;
Outdo one another in showing honor.
Never flag in zeal, be aglow with the Spirit,
Serve the Lord.
Rejoice in your hope,
Be patient in tribulation,
Be constant in prayer.
Bless those who persecute you;
Bless and do not curse them.
If possible, so far as it depends upon you,
Live peaceably with all.
Do not be overcome by evil,
But overcome evil with good.
from Romans 12:9-21

"An interesting choice of words to highlight, 'be aglow with the Spirit'"

"I made the panel the summer I met the Holy Spirit in a personal way."

"You lean to the charismatic end of Christianity."

"I lean toward relationship, call it what you will." She took a seat on the couch and curled her feet up under her with the ease of long habit. "Be aglow with the spirit happens when you enter into conversation with God and start reflecting who you've been looking at; scripture isn't overstating reality when it says God is a consuming fire. John in Revelation describes the risen Jesus of today as 'his eyes were like a flame of fire, his feet were like burnished bronze, his voice was like the sound of many waters; and his face was like the sun shining in full strength.' John fell on his face as though dead when he saw him and John was the one closest to Jesus during the years he walked on earth. Jesus as he is in his glory isn't a soft Jesus, though he is gentle. His character is good. But his glorified presence is overwhelming. We should pray to be overwhelmed more often. It changes us, seeing him as he is today."

"Yes, it does." Ryan considered her and gave another glance around her home, then chose one of the rocking chairs across from the couch. "Talk to me about whatever is your favorite subject, Connie."

She smiled. "That changes depending upon my mood."

"What would it be tonight?"

"I'm not sure you're ready for me to answer that, given the topic I would choose." She set aside her drink. "Let me make a brief remark instead. Do you realize what God let Daniel see, hundreds of years before Jesus came to earth? Daniel was shown the end of times, just as John was in Revelation, only Daniel saw it before Jesus was born and John saw it after Jesus had returned to heaven. Listen to part of what Daniel saw:

> As I looked,
> thrones were placed
> and one that was ancient of days took his seat;
> his raiment was white as snow,
> and the hair of his head like pure wool;
> his throne was fiery flames,
> its wheels were burning fire.
> A stream of fire issued
> and came forth from before him;
> a thousand thousands served him,
> and ten thousand times ten thousand
> stood before him;
> the court sat in judgment,
> and the books were opened.
> (Daniel 7:9-10)
>
> I saw in the night visions,

and behold, with the clouds of heaven
there came one like a son of man,
and he came to the Ancient of Days
and was presented before him.
And to him was given dominion
and glory and kingdom,
that all peoples, nations and languages
should serve him;
his dominion is an everlasting dominion,
which shall not pass away,
and his kingdom one
that shall not be destroyed.
(Daniel 7:13-14)

"That glimpse into what happens at the end, it's not just a vision he saw, Daniel was seeing a real event. Daniel is describing the same event John does. God has already experienced what we think of as the future. We bustle about on earth, occasionally thinking of God, while He is writing down images like that using two different people hundreds of years apart allowed to see the same event, so God can grab our attention and warn us, so we won't get so caught up with happenings here on earth, that we forget to pursue God's kingdom first.

"Jesus is coming back much sooner than most Christians realize. All peoples, nations and languages are standing before Jesus now. When the fullness of their numbers are reached, this world ends. The final day waits only the Father's announcement, its today.

"Jesus prophesied before the cross that he would be dead three days then rise. When he rose from the dead on the third day, he did so at dawn, he didn't dawdle around until four in the afternoon. Jesus prophesied that his return was coming soon. He doesn't know the exact date, only the Father does. But I think the Father is much like his son, not one to delay when the day comes. God says a thousand years is like a day to him. If the Father also thinks three days, for he likes symmetry and sends Jesus back at the dawn of the third day, that puts it right around 2,033. Or if the Father is counting from the birth of his son, *right now*. I personally think we're in the closing days of human history. I think his return comes in my lifetime.

"The biggest mistake we can make is thinking 'coming soon' means anything other than what it says. Like everything else in scripture, there will be many surprised at the day He returns and we will be judged by the word as having no excuse, for all were told Jesus was coming soon. God doesn't lie."

Ryan smiled. "Lesson one."

Connie nodded as she smiled in reply. "I like coming back to the beginning of things, too."

The fact she thought about this topic in part explained why she lived so intensely focused on God. She didn't want to waste any of her days. Ryan found he wasn't inclined to do so, either. "What subject did you just skip a few minutes ago?"

"Ryan. You have plenty on your plate right now."

"Humor me."

She thought for a moment and then gave him a brief answer. "Christians are new creations, adopted sons of God. We only look like other men, inside we have a new nature and God himself, the Holy Spirit, dwells in us. It means we are both under authority and with authority now. Our words make things happen. In Jesus' name, we can do miracles, heal the sick and raise the dead. We are citizens of heaven now, living on earth as aliens. Our conversations have been working through those new realities. But those aren't the only ways we are different from fallen men around us. That was the topic I chose to skip, Ryan."

Ryan thought about how else a Christian was different than other men around them. "You're talking about the rest of the gifts of the spirit. That's what you chose to skip."

"Yes." Connie shifted on the sofa to reach for a throw pillow. "Controversy comes with the subject of healing the sick and raising the dead, so it helps that I am neither religiously nor politically correct, nor do I try to be. But I don't stir up controversy for the sake of doing so. If I need to move into a subject to help you, then I will go there."

Ryan ignored her caveat and thought about what the scriptures listed as the gifts the Holy Spirit gave Christians. "The gift of faith is mentioned, miracles, gifts of healing, prophecy. None of those surprise me given where you have already gone. So you avoided, what? Speaking in tongues?" He smiled at her. "I have to say, given everything you have already talked about, that one seems like a mild topic to avoid."

He filled in part of it, comfortable with the subject. "When the disciples initially received the outpouring of the Holy Spirit and were filled with his presence, Acts records that they started speaking languages they hadn't learned as the Holy Spirit gave them utterance, so that everyone in Jerusalem heard the news about Jesus in their own language. Our tongue was the part of our nature most fallen and the first member of our bodies that gave evidence of being redeemed. Our words had been returned to having power and purpose again. It was nice symmetry on God's part. So talk to me about talking, Connie. You've convinced me I can raise the dead if necessary. Yet rather than that topic, you'd choose this one as your favorite subject? Why?"

"Relationship." She nodded to the fabric tapestry. "We are designed in God's image. God created us to talk, to chat, to share ideas and experiences. It's how we get to know one another. Words, language, that's how we share our lives with one another. We get to know God the same way. We talk with him. Prayer—a conversation with God—is the primary purpose God gives for his own house. 'My house shall be called a house of prayer for all people.' Given the importance of language to relationship, it fascinates me that God chose to give us a gift specifically related to language when he adopted us as his sons."

"I'd agreed with that and I can see why you consider this particular gift special," Ryan replied. "Tell me about what you've discovered. All of it Connie, not the safe surface reply."

Connie chuckled at his way of phrasing the request. "I don't mind the subject, Ryan, I simply don't volunteer it.

"God is fluent in every language on earth. The Holy Spirit wants to talk to everyone in Jerusalem about Jesus on the day of Pentecost, he nudges the disciples, 'hey, open your mouth and start speaking and I'll give you the words' and they are suddenly talking fluently in languages they had never learned. I love that image. That is a communicating God. That's God choosing to use a gift from his Spirit to help us talk with other people on earth. God also uses that same gift from the Spirit to help us talk with him.

"We find when we read the bible that Greek and Hebrew are much richer languages than English, so that we have to translate one word in Greek into five or six English ones to get the nuances of what was said in scripture. When we talk to God we are also running into the same problem and he with us. Our language is often inadequate for what we want to express, it lacks the precise nuance we need to capture a thought or emotion we have that we want to share with God and He with us.

"So God decided, rather than try to fit what he wanted to say to us, his newly adopted sons, into the limits of English, or French, or Spanish, whichever language our mind speaks fluently, that he would give us a gift of a language that had the richness of heaven. A 'welcome to the family' kind of gift, he would give us his own language, a prayer language, with all its beauty and perfection. Just as the Holy Spirit can give us words to speak in an earthly language which we did not learn, he can also give us words to speak which are in a heavenly language.

"I am a spirit. That's the true me. I have a soul. I inhabit, dwell in, a body. My spirit has been made alive again, it's perfect and it's comfortable both in my body and in the heavenly realms. My soul (mind, will, emotions) is my personality, my person, tied to my experiences on earth.

Both my spirit and my soul are language and word based in how they express themselves. But their languages are different. My mind speaks languages of earth, English and some Italian, my spirit speaks a heavenly language.

"When I pray with my mind, the English words I speak are sincere, it's the best prayer I can make, given what my understanding is of God's plan and the needs around me, but it's probably got a lot of my own ideas within it, making it partly good and partly not.

"My spirit is hanging out with the Holy Spirit. When my spirit talks to God it does so with perfect understanding of God's will. All my spirit's prayer is good. And my spirit has perfect faith. So I let my spirit talk with God. 'I yield to my spirit, if you'd like to say anything to God,' and I just start talking and it's a language I don't know. It's a beautiful language.

"I'm a new creation. I now have a spirit and a soul who both use words and language as their primary ways of expressing themselves. They simply speak different languages. As fluently as my mind speaks English, it's still a limited language compared to the heavenly language my spirit speaks. People think it's spooky. But its not. I'm just talking to God in his language rather than mine. It's a lot less spooky then looking at a dead person and saying 'in Jesus' name, wake up' and knowing that they will.

"I love talking to God, having a private conversation with him in his own language. I love listening to my spirit and God talk to one another. I'll ask later 'what was my spirit talking to you about God?' And God will tell me. I'll receive an interpretation in English my mind understands.

"We've been living only out of our souls before we were Christians, using our logic to make decisions and plan our lives. We're accustomed to trying to figure things out for ourselves. Letting my spirit talk to God is very valuable to me. That's my born-again me having an incredibly rich conversation with God.

"The best thing by far I can do for myself in any situation is let my spirit have a heart-to-heart conversation with God. My soul gets to listen to them talk in their own language and will then receive divine wisdom on what to do. My mind will receive from my spirit the benefit of what has been discussed.

"Fallen man lives out of his soul, doing for himself, a Christian is designed to live from his spirit first. By making it a new language our mind doesn't understand, we don't fall into the habit of trying to live by our soul first. Our spirit talks to God and then reveals to our mind what we are to do. Our mind directs our body and we do what God wants done. We have returned to the correct order of living, spirit first, directing our soul (mind, emotions, will), which in turn directs our body.

"Paul said 'I thank God that I speak in tongues more than you all'. It was a very valuable gift to him. Scripture says 'One who speaks in tongues edifies himself.' Edify is to build up, make stronger, make capable of handling more. One who speaks in a tongue speaks to God, not to men. Scripture says you speak mysteries—your spirit is talking to God about things your mind doesn't yet know or understand.

"Letting your spirit pray is a very valuable gift from God but not well understood. It's why Paul also told the Corinthian church 'do not forbid speaking in tongues.' People in general will accept miracles easier than when I mention I speak in a heavenly language. They don't understand how words can be anything but gibberish if my mind doesn't know the language. Not understanding that the heavenly language my spirit speaks is far more valuable to my life than having the faith to do miracles. My spirit is the source of my faith, my understanding and the more my spirit converses with God the better off I am.

"It's a choice just like every other facet of the Christian life. My mind can shut down the faith that is in my heart, prevent it from moving and doing stuff, because the impulse faith is prompting—to invite someone to church, to sign up to be a youth group leader, to give to a missionary in Chile—doesn't seem like a safe thing to do.

In like manner, my mind can also shut down my spirit simply by refusing to yield and let my spirit speak to God. I have to let my spirit lead. 'I yield to my spirit, if you'd like to say anything to God' and I start talking and it's a language that is from my spirit not my mind.

"Most Christians don't realize they are pushing down their spirit when they desire to always stay in control, when they insist on always understanding what is being said. They are elevating their mind over their spirit when they don't let their spirit pray, just as they are suppressing the faith in their heart when they choose to live only what feels like a safe Christian life. They miss out on a very good gift from God.

"God literally can't give a bad gift and this gift of language was His first gift to us for a reason, for from this one comes the capacity to have the intimate relationship with God which we all so deeply desire. God is spirit. Talking with your spirit to God is you having a face-to-face conversation with Him in the deepest sense of intimacy. The results of those conversations are amazing. Your heart comes alive."

Connie paused there and Ryan nodded thoughtfully. He didn't come from the background she did, where the dynamic gifts the Holy Spirit were discussed as freely as scriptures were shared, but the reason she found this gift so valuable made sense as she explained it.

Connie smiled as she watched him think. "People don't realize, or they've forgotten, that the Holy Spirit also has perfect knowledge of everything. He's Google on steroids with no 'fake news'. And He likes me. The fastest way for me to figure out something is to ask the Holy Spirit my question, then let my spirit talk with God and I find a thought comes to mind revealing the answer I need.

"The Holy Spirit has perfect knowledge of scripture, general facts, history, science, what is going on right now in the prime minister's office in Tanzania. If I need to know something, am curious about something, wonder about something, I ask God. He delights in explaining everything from designs to how-to directions. The key I've learned is I have to ask.

"There's something really interesting about God. The Holy Spirit is a gentleman in every respect of that word. God isn't pushy. God's way is to tell us about himself, to write it down in scripture so it's clear and then let us use that knowledge to enjoy a relationship with him. God respects our free will. God tells us something to the point we understand it, then he backs off and gives us the dignity of deciding what we want to do with that knowledge. Scripture is full of God's loving heart toward us. 'I know everything, ask me', 'I heal all your diseases, let me', 'I don't lie, trust me'.

"God deeply values free will. We've never really grasped that. We don't value free will like he does, we're rather pushy people. 'You do it like this, here, let me show you'. 'You want to take Jefferson Street at this time of day, its got less traffic'. 'You shouldn't take that job, you'll be stuck behind a desk and hate it'. We have knowledge and opinions and can't wait to share them. God is different. God waits to be asked. If we would finally get our hearts and minds around the truth that God values our free will to the point he will not insert himself across that line, much of our friction with God would disappear and we would be living in a much richer relationship.

"My spirit knows who God is, 'gets him' and talks to Him with perfect understanding of God's ways. My spirit has no friction clouding its relationship with God. My spirit can help my mind understand God better, recognize his ways, remove misunderstandings. My spirit can 'show me' God, can help me catch things like 'oh, he values free will. I have to ask him if I want him to tell me something.' So I switch over to a life that has a lot of 'Hey, God, what's the answer to this?' dialog going on. Life improves as I move in sync with God. And both God and I (the soul part of me) are now enjoying the give and take.

"God created and gave me both my spirit and my soul, he likes and enjoys both, but they have different functions.

My spirit is designed for heaven, my soul interacts with earth through my body. At my best, my spirit and soul are in cooperation, not competition. I am a new creation, I am designed to live first out of my spirit, giving direction to my soul. I am designed to walk by my spirit being with the Holy Spirit, giving direction to my mind. It is fallen men who live first out of their souls, thinking their mind knows best what decision to make and how to live. Fallen men are self-directing their lives without God's input. Christians are to live with better input and praying in the spirit is the 'fast download' way that happens."

Ryan realized abruptly what she had really been telling him as this conversation unfolded. He hadn't missed it this time. He leaned forward in his chair, and broke in: "This is how you learned what we have been talking about the last couple weeks. George walked you through the scriptures, but it was the Holy Spirit which explained them to you."

Connie smiled. "Yes."

"And this is how he did it."

"It is. I let the Holy Spirit teach me. What I don't understand, I ask God to explain. He does. When I pray in the spirit understanding happens much faster than when I try to learn by just my mind reasoning out the scriptures. My spirit talks to God. My spirit is speaking mysteries, talking to God about subjects and details my mind doesn't yet know or hasn't understood yet. My spirit quickly receives and understands answers. What my spirit talks to God about then comes as thoughts into my mind and I see what I didn't understand before. Most often its scriptures which link together gracefully showing an idea I hadn't grasped before. The picture comes together in a new or fresh way. It makes sense where before I hadn't seen it. My mind receives both knowledge and understanding. And it is happening because I'm letting my spirit talk with God."

"That just happens. It's easy to figure out complicated subjects."

"It's that easy," Connie confirmed. "Subjects are only complicated to us because we haven't understood them yet. The Holy Spirit fully understands everything. So I ask a question. Then I let my spirit talk to God in his language and my spirit then reveals the answer to my mind in English. I let my spirit pray, then I trust the answer is going to show up and it does. I'll have a thought that puts the puzzle together, or read something that has the exact answer, or see a scripture with more understanding.

"You know you've heard correctly by letting the peace of God rule in your heart. That peace of God is a confirmation note. The Holy Spirit is called the Spirit of Peace. When your heart is unsettled, it's the Holy Spirit telling you something is amiss. You've reasoned something out incorrectly. Or the decision you're considering making is the wrong way to go. When there is peace in your heart on a subject or decision, it's the Holy Spirit's assurance, 'you've got it right', 'you've heard and understood what I said correctly.'

"It's a basic truth that when we come to God wanting help, God is good and helps us. He gives wisdom to anyone who asks. Letting your spirit pray is a faster way and clearer way to get help than just relying on what your mind can reason out, what your mind can pray, but it's always a choice. God is going to give you the same answer, the same truth, in reply. It's just your capacity to receive his answer differs based on how you pray. Paul said I'll pray with my spirit and I'll also pray with my understanding, my mind. The Holy Spirit listens to both my spirit praying and my mind praying. My mind is simply slower to grasp what the Holy Spirit shares in reply than my spirit. It's like having a high-def, high-bandwidth channel and slower frequency. God lets us choose how we come to him and he will meet us there with the same good will and same good answer to what we've asked. God is always for us.

"The trouble comes when we try to figure out a matter without asking God for any help. He'll let us flounder around getting wrong answers and think we've understood a topic, when what we've really demonstrated is our independence of God and the fact we've found what satisfies us rather what is probably the truth. The free will God gave to man gets us into enormous trouble if we aren't careful to keep ourselves yielded to God. Be humble enough to ask God for help and then stay in his presence until the peace in our heart assures us we have understood God's answer."

The oven timer began to ding. "And there's the cue dinner is ready to serve." Connie got up to see to their meal.

"Thank you, Connie, for yet another fascinating conversation."

"I appreciate you listening." She pulled the roasting pan from the oven and set it on the stove top, lifted the lid with care to avoid the steam. "This looks promising." She pulled a serving platter out of a cabinet and transferred the meat and vegetables, using a ladle to move gravy to a serving dish.

Ryan moved over to the table for their meal.

"That sense of intuition you sometimes have?" Connie mentioned. "It's often your spirit, knowing what is coming, nudging your mind with a sense of what is about to happen, with which direction an outcome is going to go."

"Really?"

"How do you think I avoided getting shot for much of my career? 'Lean left' is a nice thought to have when someone is about to pull a trigger."

She brought the serving platter over to the table. "We're having what is generally called roasted lamb chops with herbs, carrots and cabbage. This recipe is from a lady who slow cooks kettle meals over a fire pit. I can't locate a fraction of her secret ingredients even with the richness of Chicago's ethnic neighborhoods. The potatoes I added for your benefit as the cabbage is an acquired taste. It would be more accurate to call my variation of her meal 'roast lamb stew'."

"It smells delicious."

"Dip up a sample and see what you think. You won't offend me with 'where can I find the peanut butter and jelly?' You can trust the bread is safe as it comes from the bakery we pass every morning."

Ryan laughed, willing to try anything.

Connie came back with a hot foil wrapped loaf of bread, pre-sliced. She took her seat and her prayer for the meal was simple. "God, thank you for the good food and a guest to share it with. Amen."

Ryan selected a bit of everything on the platter, added the gravy, tried a sample of the meal and smiled. "I should have expected you were underplaying reality. This is delicious."

"A recipe that calls for cinnamon and ginger and molasses is going to be promising." She buttered a slice of bread for herself. "Let me tell you some about tonight's group while we eat."

Ryan obligingly reached over and shut off the recording.

Connie nodded her thanks. "There are seven in the group. Three will be new faces to you. A brief sketch of them, without names for now. The two paramedics joining us are with Fire Department Company 52. They'll be just coming off duty, so may arrive late depending on the final call out particulars. They are familiar with Mercy Hospital and know your brother Jeff well enough to be comfortable ragging on him about his basketball tournament picks. Good ice breakers with them are anything fire related as they were smoke eaters before adding paramedic level training. They both play hockey and have teenage sons. The taller man is happily married. The older one has been divorced for about six years.

"The third man I don't think you will know. He's a chaplain in his 30s who works with the Veterans Rehab facility in Oakbrook. He has apparently played wheelchair basketball against your uncle's squad frequently enough to know Walter likes to pass the ball more than shoot it and shoot it more than move. There's some friendly wagering of steaks when they compete, which is apparently much enjoyed no matter who is picking up the check. My sense is he admires Walter and has a fairly accurate view of Mercy Hospital. Good ice breakers with him are his wife, two daughters, and anything relating to the rehab center. He's also got an encyclopedic knowledge of butterflies. I love the photos on his phone as he collects butterfly pictures from all around the world.

'The two doctors, surgeon and nurse, which round out the group are either people you know or are acquainted with."

"I'm surprised to hear how small a world it is in Chicago, if seven people chosen from the medical profession turn out to all be acquainted with either me or my hospital."

"Part of that is geography. To be able to have all seven at every meeting meant I was looking for people primarily within a specific distance of each other."

He picked up the three-ring binder he had brought with him and offered it to her. "My accumulating notes," he explained.

She paged through it, curious. "You've been studying."

He heard the pleasure in her voice and was pleased by it. "Working on it. I have copies of our audio files for everyone and those scripture notes are also on the flash drives."

"They'll find both helpful. I appreciate this. Remind me to give you a flash drive as well before you leave. I have a couple small audios for you."

He nodded. "I'll remember."

He was looking forward to this evening and the conversation with people from the medical profession on these topics, curious to hear their perspectives.

****

The group began to arrive minutes before eight p.m. Ryan realized no introductions were going to be needed for the first of the arrivals. Two were doctors he knew personally. The surgeon he had met through mutual friends. He rose to shake hands as they came to the table. The man he had not met before, Connie introduced as the chaplain she had mentioned.

The last three in the group arrived together and Ryan felt a deep surprise ripple inside. He knew the lady who entered with the two paramedics. Marcie French. She was one of his. Mercy Hospital's chief neonatal nurse was one of Connie's group. He thought about the wall of stats in his office. There had been no pink on the death chart for over ninety days. No deaths in the one-day to three-year age group. He offered his hand with a grin. "Oh, very well done, Marcie. You've been flying very much under the radar but I've got your fingerprints on my office wall. I know what you've been doing and you've been doing an excellent job."

She shared his smile. "Thank you, Ryan."

They pulled around chairs and assembled in the living room area. Connie began the group meeting right at eight, with a nod his direction. "I'd like to introduce Ryan Cooper, the CEO of Mercy Hospital. He's joining us tonight because he's been on a parallel path to this group and the conversation tonight will be helpful to him. He understands the confidentiality of the room and will respect it.

"We're going to spend the majority of tonight talking through specific situations we are dealing with. What's working with individuals. Where things are stuck. Diagnosing what might be going on and how to overcome the problem. But before we get to that discussion and the brief comments I have, we've been individually telling our personal stories and tonight to close us out, I've asked Tom to share his. How we reach the point we chose to pick up the challenge of a group like this is as varied as our professional lives and every story shapes the focus of the ministry which Jesus will call us into from here." She looked to the man comfortably seated in the chair to her left. "Tom."

"Thanks, Connie. For Ryan's benefit, I'm Tom Peterson, a surgeon at Philip Crest. My story that leads to this group starts a number of years ago. My wife Jennifer died of cancer after the best fight we knew how to mount to save her. Best doctors, best available treatments, she was confident throughout the journey that Jesus would heal her. She died young. I lost the 50 years I had planned to spend with her.

"I was in Texas at the time I met her, a successful surgeon, involved in my church, my family was in the area. I led Jennifer to Christ, asked her to marry me, then cancer was discovered; our wedding was squeezed in between hospital stays. She led five of those closest to her to Christ, the sixth she was working on came to believe in the year after her funeral. She led a victorious life, in all respects but one. The health question we didn't understand.

"If I had known then, what I now understand, I wouldn't have lost her. She already had the faith to know Jesus would heal her, we just didn't know how to bring that healing into flourishing effect. That's on me. I was the oldest Christian in the group, surrounded by baby Christians who had great faith in their new God, but only the beginnings of scripture knowledge. I should have known this subject like the back of my hand. But I didn't understand how Jesus had healed us at the cross, or how to bring that healing to my wife.

"Jennifer could have been healed of the undiscovered cancer at her baptism had we understood the full exchange made at the cross so that she had faith in all the benefits that were hers by Jesus' death. That healing would have come as a gift along with her new life.

"The fact my faith, that of those closest to her, survived despite losing Jennifer is a testimony to the fact we all knew what happened wasn't right. Her death wasn't right, it wasn't God's outcome. We had just missed the truth we needed to know at the time to stop it. She died in my arms, but it didn't even cross my mind to whisper, 'in Jesus' name, wake up'." Tom paused, struggling with the overwhelming emotion still in that memory. "And that lack of knowledge is also on me. My unforced error. God would have answered that prayer had I known to offer it. I know that outcome would have suited him just fine. The disease that harmed her wasn't his will nor was her early death.

"God wasn't hiding the answers we needed. We just missed the signs pointing toward those answers. In the stress of that season of life, watching the cancer take her life, the ability to hear God's voice got difficult and at times muted. I didn't have the capacity to learn during that season what I needed to know to change what was happening.

"Jennifer both loved me and taught me and changed me. It's simply part of what she taught me, she taught me by my failure to save her. What I understood about God wasn't enough to save her and I needed to figure out why, what I didn't know, what had gone wrong.

"Receiving your invitation, Connie, that first dinner, as you moderated the discussion and I realized I was sitting down the table from someone who could have changed my story had I met you years earlier—I nearly didn't come to these group conversations, the pain of that realization was so deep. I'm glad God, through Ann, whispered go, to that first dinner and to the group conversations which have followed. I'm glad I endured facing what I hadn't understood before.

"I can both empathize with my patients having experienced cancer and loss, bring them help through what I know as a surgeon, but also now finally minister healing from the hands of the physician Jesus who can get the full job done. I no longer view any patient as beyond full recovery. That's the gift these conversations have brought. Hope. How-to answers. God turned that loss into the drive to understand what went wrong. Jennifer would have enjoyed this group immensely. She was a doctor who loved kids, spent her life helping them with what she knew and would have taken to this subject as though God had designed it specifically for her."

His words ended. It hadn't been easy on him, that story and the room was quiet in reply.

"Thank you, Tom," Marcie offered.

Connie nodded her agreement and didn't break the silence that followed for nearly a minute. "Tom's a surgeon, not a cancer doctor, but healings are showing up in pronounced ways within his subset of cancer patients. Tom is following the rule you don't speak about what you've seen on the battlefield but two of his patients who were in hospice are now home doing very well with normal blood work. Four others are looking at shrinking tumors."

"Wow."

The group laughed at Ryan's startled reaction.

"Why is that happening, Tom? Do you have a sense of it?" Connie asked.

"I've been mad about what happened with Jennifer for a long time. My prayers have pounded into heaven against cancer for years. I just didn't know how to turn that intensity from being directed at heaven, to instead turn and pin death to the wall and wipe the floor with him. I have that authority in Jesus' name to toss death off the playing field, I simply didn't know how to do it before. I'm seeing victory over cancer because I've been asking for just that for years. When the understanding arrived for how to enforce Jesus' victory, cancer fell first, because I've already been given that ground."

Connie nodded. "The shift to using authority. Instead of praying to heaven for victory over cancer, you look at the patient and use Jesus' authority and victory over death and toss out cancer. You bring the victory of healing."

"Yes. That's been a substantial part of the breakthrough and the faith that these conversations have created. I know that authority now and have the faith to use it."

Connie scanned the group. “Anyone else this evening, have a particular trend starting to develop? Marcie’s is still going strong. Jesus has reversed every close call in the neonatal and pediatrics unit.” She caught a nod. “Yes, Gary.”

“I’m looking at PTSD that seems to be falling in a regular fashion. It’s beginning to look like a trend.” He tugged a folded piece of paper from his pocket to read what he had written down. “I’m seeing good success with this prayer: ‘I give you the peace of Jesus. I command this painful memory to fully process with Jesus’ help until all trauma is resolved. You will walk free of this event, without burden mentally or emotionally. I speak to your body, soul and spirit—be healed, in Jesus’ name. Amen.’”

Connie smiled. “I can see why it’s effective; that is really good. Why is that prayer working, can anyone break it down for me?”

The doctor to Ryan’s left picked up that question. “Jesus has given us his peace and since it is ours now, we can do what we want with it, we can give it on to others. Giving a gift is always a blessing. Peace is what the person doesn’t have and most needs. The prayer is speaking to the memory, as well as speaking to the person. You already know God wants this person healed. You’re describing what healing looks like and bringing it to pass by your prayer of faith.”

Connie nodded. “A good analysis.” She looked around the group. “Anyone else?” She gave it a moment and moved on. “Alright. I have one brief remark to offer before we dive into the work of this evening.” She opened a notebook and scanned her entry to refresh her memory, then closed the notebook. “It’s a simple one tonight, but rather important.

“Truth is from God. We understand that, but it helps to step back and just reflect on the implications of it. God has no secular and spiritual line with truth. He will talk to a man who doesn’t know him about how gravity works and give the Christian and the non-Christian the same answer.

He may be able to explain it at a deeper level to a Christian, but the truth is what God shares with both.

"We use medical knowledge and the best protocols man understands because we recognize knowledge about the body and how it works is from God. That doesn't mean God doesn't have a better way to heal someone than man currently understands. God would rather use a prayer of faith to heal someone than a medication that has toxic side effects. He'd rather have the person helped with a medication that has side effects, than suffer worse agony for several years because no one understands how to pray with faith and remove the disease.

"God is love and has given us the full answer we need – we're healed by Jesus. When we aren't receiving that gift, God still helps us as much as we will allow him to do so by teaching us truth about the body so we can get relief from disease – think of it as his fallback plan B. Mankind has been living primarily under plan B because we didn't understand how God gives us 'by his wounds, you have been healed'. As a group we are on a journey to bring healing to people by bringing to bear everything God has taught us about how he works. We are beginning to heal not only by what our training has taught us, but to also heal by faith and restore full health with God's plan A.

"It's a credit to our profession that when people start getting healed who looked beyond hope, other doctors notice and start asking 'what's going on? what have you discovered? I want that for my patients, too.' We are in an ideal profession to share God's truth with the world because we are a profession which is results driven. Given that, I want to end my remarks by making a practical point.

"By a show of hands, how many have now raised the dead?"

Ryan caught his breath when he saw the hands that lifted.

"By a show of hands, how many have seen a near death patient make a u-turn and rapidly recover?

"By a show of hands, how many are dealing with a situation with a patient where there seems to be no progress being made?"

Connie nodded. "The same people raised their hand for all three questions. Including me. That tells me the learning curve is working. This is a journey filled with its mysteries and its celebrations." She glanced his way and chuckled. "Breathe, Ryan. We've been doing this for a few more months than you have."

He realized he needed to do just that. "The beauty of what I just saw in those answers—thank you. I've been listening to Connie and knew this was what could happen. Knowing it's going on, seeing it, that's amazing."

"You'll join us with those same answers in the year ahead," Connie predicted. She looked to the group. "Let's see what we can diagnose together so we get more celebrations. What situations are giving you trouble?"

Ryan listened and learned for the next hour as heart disease and blindness and paralysis were discussed. Connie drew the discussion to a close at 9:25 p.m. "I have a request from Jason Lasting for the group. Lake Christian Church would like to offer prayer for those who wish to come forward at the end of the second service and is asking if any or all of us would like to participate. There is value in anonymity, so I have no particular opinion either way.

"This would be the most low key way to move into a public setting that there probably is. A church which has been teaching on healing for some months is the most likely place to see a public breakthrough where we get the lame to walk, or the blind to see and it's an opportunity to pray for a wider variety of conditions than we individually encounter. That said, this doesn't need to be a step all of us take, four out of seven would let us work in teams and be part of a group, people won't see individuals as much as a member of the group if that's the language we use."

The doctor to Ryan's right lifted his hand. "I'm in, Connie. We know what we can do, have been doing it in individual ways, its time to find out what happens when a crowd of needs meets a few people willing to say with faith, 'yes, God will heal that.' I'm ready to take that step and see what happens."

"Alright. Anyone else?" Connie smiled as all the members of the group raised their hands. "You guys no longer surprise me with your willingness to dive in. Thanks. We'll consider this coming Sunday a trial run, be on hand to pray for people who want to come forward after the second service, then gather to debrief what happened and what we would change, when we next meet as group. Lake's second service starts at 10:30 so the earliest they would ask people to come forward to receive prayer would be 11:20 a.m. Those who wish to attend their regular church service and then drive over to Lake to pray for people should have time to do both."

Connie closed the meeting and the group began to disband. Ryan made a deliberate choice to say a brief goodnight to each one, give out flash drives with the audios and notes he's brought, but not to linger, so they could discuss his presence or any other concerns they had with Connie, without feeling like he was intruding into their time. With Connie, he simply smiled, said he'd see her for coffee in the morning and accepted the flash drive she handed him. More homework. He was coming to expect it from her and grinned as he said thanks.

****

It was a night with so much to consider that Ryan drove home in silence, not trying to pray, nor sort out what he had learned, he simply let the memory of the evening unfold again, listening to the conversations play out, letting himself feel the surprise when he saw Marcie, the emotions when he heard Tom's story. He had needed tonight more than he realized, the awareness of the group and the different people exploring this subject. Healings and miracles were happening around Chicago. And he was on the verge of stepping into that experience too.

As had become his habit, he studied when he arrived home, taking an hour to add to his notes, paying special attention to the verses the Holy Spirit highlighted as he read. "I love this material, Holy Spirit. I might not understand it as well as I would like, but I see why Connie loves the relationship focus of her life with you. It was nice to simply hear her explanations." Ryan felt like he was holding an uncut diamond with tonight, having discovered something precious, yet not sure how to bring out the beauty he could see was present. "Thank you, Holy Spirit. I am so grateful that you are with me and that I'm not trying to figure this out on my own. The one who understands all this best is you. I'm asking tonight, explain this to me, God. I want to learn."

Ryan Notes / conversation eight / additional references

For as in one body we have many members and all the members do not have the same function, so we, though many, are one body in Christ and individually members one of another. Having gifts that differ according to the grace given to us, let us use them: if prophecy, in proportion to our faith; if service, in our serving; he who teaches, in his teaching; he who exhorts, in his exhortation; he who contributes, in liberality; he who gives aid, with zeal; he who does acts of mercy, with cheerfulness. (Romans 12:4-8)

To each is given the manifestation of the Spirit for the common good. To one is given through the Spirit the utterance of wisdom and to another the utterance of knowledge according to the same Spirit, to another faith by the same Spirit, to another gifts of healing by the one Spirit, to another the working of miracles, to another prophecy, to another the ability to distinguish between spirits, to another various kinds of tongues, to another the interpretation of tongues. (1 Corinthians 12:7-10)

Make love your aim and earnestly desire the spiritual gifts, especially that you may prophesy. (1 Corinthians 14:1)

the one who prophesies speaks to people for their strengthening, encouraging and comfort. (1 Corinthians 14:3b NIV)

Anyone who speaks in a tongue edifies themselves, but the one who prophesies edifies the church. (1 Corinthians 14:4 NIV)

For one who speaks in a tongue speaks not to men but to God; for no one understands him, but he utters mysteries in the Spirit. (1 Corinthians 14:2)

Now I want you all to speak in tongues, but even more to prophesy. (1 Corinthians 14:5a)

since you are eager for manifestations of the Spirit, strive to excel in building up the church. (1 Corinthians 14:12b)

For if I pray in a tongue, my spirit prays but my mind is unfruitful. What am I to do? I will pray with the spirit and I will pray with the mind also; I will sing with the spirit and I will sing with the mind also. (1 Corinthians 14:14-15)

Likewise the Spirit helps us in our weakness; for we do not know how to pray as we ought, but the Spirit himself intercedes for us with sighs too deep for words. And he who searches the hearts of men knows what is the mind of the Spirit, because the Spirit intercedes for the saints according to the will of God. (Romans 8:26-27)

I [Paul] thank God that I speak in tongues more than you all; (1 Corinthians 14:18)

Do not forbid speaking in tongues (1 Corinthians 14:39b)

But you, beloved, build yourselves up on your most holy faith; pray in the Holy Spirit; keep yourselves in the love of God; wait for the mercy of our Lord Jesus Christ unto eternal life. (Jude 1:20-21)

20

Ryan listened to the short audio Connie had given him as he walked to the coffee shop to meet her Friday morning.

"Our biggest problem is we take our experience and make doctrine out of it. Someone we care about doesn't get well, they die, so it must have been God's will not to heal them. We've now got this nagging layer of our own truth that says God isn't always as good as I would be in his place and that flows along for the rest of our lives as the undercurrent of what we believe about God. If we were God, we would have healed that person. We kill our faith with false beliefs. We nullify the word of God by our doubts and false conclusions.

"If we would quit doing that one thing – letting our experience determine what we believe – we would be able to push through problems with God's help, get them solved and get the results we desired. God's will regarding healing is clearly written in his word. Jesus healed every person who came to him of every disease, showing us the Father's will in action. Jesus paid the price at the cross to heal everyone. We now bring that healing to people by faith.

"When someone isn't healed, something went wrong. We should face that fact, sort out with God what happened and learn from it so it doesn't happen again.

"Faith and doubt exist in every person to some degree. When you want to have a stronger faith, work on removing your doubts. Faith the size of a grain of mustard seed, without doubt overwhelming it, can move a mountain."

It felt very much like a summary audio, Ryan realized. The material was becoming familiar to him. That was a remarkable fact, given where his knowledge base had been two weeks ago when this began. "Thank you, God." It felt really good to be at this place in the learning curve.

****

Connie was a couple minutes early, but he'd still managed to arrive first. Ryan handed Connie her coffee and picked up his own. "I appreciate you having me over last night. It was an incredible conversation and group."

"We enjoyed having you," Connie offered as they left the coffee shop. "The feedback after you left was positive. You did beautifully, how you handled seeing Marcie there."

His smile widened. "I was overjoyed to realize I already had one metric of how effective this is. There hasn't been pink edged deaths on my metric wall in the last 90 days. That is a huge gift and it was Marcie. I can't wait until I've got ten like her, twenty, spread throughout the hospital. It's going to be very exciting to see what God does with that."

Connie laughed at his enthusiasm. "You'll likely be there this year."

"I'm certainly planning to be."

She started on her sweet roll as they walked. "I don't know if you realize this," she mentioned, "But Tom's wife Jennifer and Ann Falcon were very close friends. After Jennifer died, Ann wrote a series of books about that last year of Jennifer's life, how she met Tom, their wedding, those Jennifer introduced to Jesus."

"The O'Malley series," Ryan replied with a nod. "I put the pieces together when Tom said he was working as a surgeon in Texas when he met Jennifer. Ann's been listening to these audios, Connie and has, from the brief conversations we've had on their content, been receptive to what you are saying. I'm surprised she is handling these subjects as well as she is, that Tom is able to handle the discussion. Losing a wife, a friend, to cancer, realizing now it could still have been turned around even after she died, that's not just deep waters, its ocean bottom deep kind of waters. That is a lot of turmoil to stir up in someone, not just in a widowed husband, but in a best friend."

"I know," Connie agreed, eating her sweet roll.

"How do you deal with the fact every person you teach this material to has friends and family they lost to either disease or early death that they now know could have been helped if they knew more, that it didn't have to happen?"

"By simply saying I know."

Connie walked for a while eating her breakfast, watching passing pedestrians and Ryan didn't interrupt. Those hadn't been casual words. Connie glanced over at him, at the phone. He killed the recording.

"Thanks." She drank more of her coffee. "I was in my fourth deployment overseas when my brother was killed in a car crash in San Diego. He was seven years older than me, he'd always been my hero. I'm in a foreign country, I've successfully seen the dead come back to life, but I haven't talked to my brother or my parents about what I'm learning from George. What I've seen. I don't talk about what I've seen on a battlefield.

"My parents have the funeral plans underway when they call to tell me the news. His body is at the ME's office and has been scheduled for an autopsy at the military's request. He was driving an official military vehicle. The other driver had been injured. They need a ruling on cause of death, did something happen medically which led to the crash. I have no idea what the maximum time window is for me to act, the longest death I had seen reversed at that point was two hours. This is about sixteen hours after it happened given the time zone changes and the fact they couldn't get through to me until I was back at base.

"I can try to pray for him from where I am and hope he starts breathing on the ME's table before the autopsy starts, so that his being alive appears to be a mistake by the paramedics at the scene. Without being told the details of what his injuries are, I know they are talking about a closed casket service, that it had been a bad car crash. I have no idea what happens if I tell him 'in Jesus name, wake up' from that distance.

"The autopsy itself doesn't bother me, if God's going to bring him back to life, God's going to already be repairing serious injuries and recreating organs isn't beyond God's actions. It's the location and timing of my brother waking up that are the concern.

"I can wait, go home, get a private moment with my brother and tell him to wake up. If he does, he spends the rest of his life with that resurrection being his life story, he will never get away from the public nature of how it happened. Everyone knows he is dead and he's going to be dead three days before I can get to his side. So my decision becomes the focus of the rest of his life.

"If I come home, tell him to wake up and he does not for whatever reason, the amount of elapsed time, the fact this is my brother and I'm very emotional, the fact no one around me has any faith for a resurrection to agree with me on the matter, what does that do to my faith? I'm saving lives on the battlefield, I've seen dead soldiers come back to life. Does a failure with my brother shake me enough I lose faith and stop seeing miracles as a combat medic?

"My brother had been a solid Christian for decades. I came to know Jesus myself because I watched him and wanted what he had too. I'm thankfully not dealing with wondering if he is with Jesus or not as part of this mix.

"I got off that video call with my parents. I went to the emptiest corner of the base I could find. I sat down on the dry dusty ground and said, 'God, what do I do?' And I got silence, a lot of empathy, God sitting beside me presence, but silence.

"I came home, I buried my brother, and I let him go. I never said to him, 'in Jesus' name, wake up.' I didn't try it from where I was. I didn't try it when I arrived. I simply said goodbye. Because it was the right decision for my parents and my brother, even though I had to carry that loss as an extra weight because I could have said those words and he would have opened his eyes. I knew it. And I looked at the situation and didn't act.

"That's why God didn't say anything when he sat with me. If I had asked, 'will he wake up?' God would have said yes. God wouldn't have lied to me. I had the faith for it. And I didn't want to hear God says that. I also didn't ask God, 'what do you want me to do?' God may have been ready to make all this public years ago using my brother and my prayer for him as the fulcrum to bring it public.

"I knew what would happen if my brother came back to life sixteen hours after a bad car accident on the ME's table or three days later at a funeral home. I was committing his life and mine to be this story for the rest of his life. He wasn't there for me to ask him, do you want this? And I chose not to make the decision for him. I was ambivalent if I wanted that to be my own life. 'I don't talk about what I've seen on a battlefield' had been my way of avoiding this situation. So I buried my brother and said my goodbye.

"It was two days after the funeral that I realized the obvious. I also hadn't asked God, 'does he want me to wake him up?' The thought hadn't crossed my mind to ask the question. My subconscious had decided, 'I don't want to do this' and so the logical question to ask was suppressed, because I didn't want to hear my brother would say yes. I couldn't take the public reality of what it would mean to my life to say the words. I cost my brother fifty more years of life because I didn't want the public pressure of explaining what I had learned and thus done. I grieved that knowledge about me more than I did his death. I was the weak link to what God might want to do. For all the knowledge I had, the soldiers I was helping, I realized I would help if it could be quietly done or I wasn't helping.

"I went back to my job, did another three tours overseas, finished 8 years as a combat medic and told God I'm ready if you want to use this in a civilian world. I had accepted the burden that I hadn't been willing to carry before. These conversations with people have been what unfolded. I've basically been waiting for George to arrive in Chicago and letting God have space to show me what he wants this to look like next. There is wisdom in remaining anonymous. Jesus often told those he helped not to say anything. But sometimes what is required is the courage to be seen and I had to learn that. It was easier to learn to raise the dead than it was to learn how to handle the responsibility. This world doesn't know what to do with Jesus, let alone healing miracles and the fact the dead can be told to wake up."

Ryan had been listening to her story, absorbing the emotions of it and as she finished he remained quiet for a time then simply nodded. "I'm sorry, about your brother," he offered. There weren't any words that suited the rest of what he felt.

"So am I."

He'd be facing his own moment like that if he kept on this journey. She was right about the implications of being publicly known. There would be a point his name was public for something which occurred and he'd never be able to undo the change that would come into his life as a result.

The hospital was up ahead. Connie nodded toward the garden park to continue the walk. "I haven't told that story before, other than to George. I haven't told the group. And I still don't know how to describe the emotions I deal with now as I think about how I got here. The journey my own story has taken me. So for now, why don't we switch to what I was going to discuss this morning and we'll talk about this again another day."

"Alright." Ryan started a new recording on his phone.

Connie visibly relaxed with the change in subject. She handled being in teaching mode easier than she did the personal. That wasn't a surprise to him. As much as she taught using her own experiences as illustrations, it was her own story that had been the deepest personal and private piece of her.

"I want to talk about rest today and how it relates to how we receive gifts from God."

Ryan nodded and settled in to listen, curious to know her thinking about the subject.

"God gives us five benefits as free gifts of his grace through Jesus and they are the definition of good news:

> Bless the LORD, O my soul,
> and forget not all his benefits,
> who forgives all your iniquity,
> who heals all your diseases,
> who redeems your life from the Pit,
> who crowns you with steadfast love and mercy,
> who satisfies you with good as long as you live
> so that your youth is renewed like the eagle's.
> (Psalms 103:2-5)

"God wants us to have these benefits. He does not make the process hard or complicated. But it requires a shift in our mindset. From these being things we labor to have to them being something we accept as free gifts of grace. These five benefits come to us by faith, not by our works. God will not let you add your labor to what Jesus has done for you. We receive by faith and we are richly blessed. If we insist on adding our own works, we will not obtain the very thing we desire.

"You can't work to be healed, because you already *are* healed. 'By his wounds you have been healed', past tense, it's a finished work. What you need is not healing, but to show that you *are* healed, to look like who God says you are now.

"When we enter into the finished works of God – he's forgiven all our sins and healed all our diseases, for example – those benefits become ours. The process of entering into God's finished works is described in Hebrews chapters 3 and 4. Listen to some of the scriptures:

his [God’s] works were finished from the foundation of the world (Hebrews 4:3b)

there remains a sabbath rest for the people of God; for whoever enters God's rest also ceases from his labors as God did from his. (Hebrews 4:9b-10)

...we who have believed enter that rest (Hebrews 4:3a)

And to whom did he swear that they should never enter his rest, but to those who were disobedient? So we see that they were unable to enter because of unbelief. (Hebrews 3:18-19)

For good news came to us just as to them; but the message which they heard did not benefit them, because it did not meet with faith in the hearers. (Hebrews 4:2)

“For 40 years Israel wandered in the wilderness until the adults in the generation that left Egypt died. God loathed that generation, because they had seen his works, heard his good news about the promised land and they didn’t believe him. The good news did not meet with faith, so its benefits couldn’t reach them. God had to wait until they all died in their unbelief, then he could take their children into the promised land. (The only two who didn’t die from that generation were Caleb and Joshua who had believed the good news.)

“We enter into the five benefits when we enter into God’s rest, into God’s finished works and we can only enter God’s rest if we believe him. We hear the good news. That good news meets faith. That faith brings us into God’s rest. We cease our labors as he ceased his. ‘Oh, I’m healed, I see that now’ and that truth causes us to stop our unnecessary works of self-labor to be healed. We realize we *are* healed as a free gift from God’s grace. Our rest is us entering into God’s rest. It is us ceasing from our labors just as God did from his. *The truth causes us to rest.* Our labors are no longer necessary. My faith in God's word brings the benefits in that good news to me.

"God desires us to enter his rest. God desires that we cease from our labors as he has done from his. God arranges for us to hear the good news. When that good news meets faith, the benefits become ours. We *enter into* what God has done for us. God's works are finished, that's the beauty of it. It's not God saying 'I will do that for you'. It's God saying 'I have done that for you'. He is resting having finished his labor. When we believe that good news, we enter his rest and we too cease to labor and now rest. Resting in God's finished work, ceasing our own labor, is evidence of an active faith. You cannot work to receive a grace gift, you must accept it by faith and rest in what God did on your behalf. Your rest is evidence you believe your healing is finished.

"Resting does not mean lack of actions. A living faith is active. You do what God tells you to do. But the actions you do now are coming from obedience to the voice of the Holy Spirit. They are coming from a place of rest. God has healed me. Now I'm stepping into the reality I am healed by obeying God's voice. The resulting actions are not *you* working to be healed. The actions you take are God walking you into what he's done for you.

"It's like following directions to drive to a party. The party is put together by God. You're his guest. You have no work to do for that party as it's in your honor. You simply arrive there and enjoy the party. Your arrival is accomplished by following his directions. You are healed and healthy from an active faith of obedience. You rest and cease your own labors. He directs you into what he's already done for you. Sometimes his direction is 'the party is coming to you, open the door'. You're healed right where you stand when you hear the good news. Sometimes it is an action he wants you to take in faith – 'go tell your friend I healed you'. You obey and your healing appears. Jesus would tell the lepers, 'go show yourself to the priest,' and as they went, they were healed. Jesus would tell a blind man to go wash his eyes in a particular pool and he would come back seeing. Elijah told Nathan the leper, 'go dip in the river Jordan seven times and you'll be healed'. When he did, his leprosy disappeared. Their actions were showing their faith. They followed what God told them and the healing he had given them appeared.

"Actions show your heart. If you have heard the good news, believed it and ceased working to obtain by your own efforts what God has given you, you are resting. Your actions, based on God's directions to you, are coming out of that rest. Rest is not a lack of activity. It is a lack of labor. You are not trying to work to obtain healing, you *are* healed. You are rather walking into the healing which is already done for you. Your actions are your arriving via his directions.

"Or your actions which show your heart will show the converse, they will show your unbelief, as you labor to heal yourself and keep yourself healthy. We hear the good news, we hear the five benefits God gives everyone by grace, but we don't believe it. This is too good news to be true. There's got to be strings attached. It surely must be my efforts involved to be healed. We decide his word must not be true as written. We try to add our works, or add caveats, to qualify it must be people who deserve to be healed of their disease. Those who didn't bring it upon themselves. Those who are living healthy lifestyles now. Take your favorite line of thought. We change what is written to suit our viewpoint. The result is that the good news does not meet with faith and so we don't receive the benefits. The benefits are blocked by our unbelief from reaching us.

"We do not enter into the benefits when we add our own works. Nor do we enter into the benefits when we meet the good news with unbelief. It takes the good news being met with faith to receive the benefits. Otherwise our unbelief blocks the benefits from becoming ours. A corollary to the fact we get what we say is the fact we get what we believe. The benefits are there, the good news is true, but they aren't reaching us because they aren't being met with faith. Faith is like the transport and our unbelief is blowing up the bridge that brings the benefits from the invisible world to the visible one.

"We must enter into God's rest if we wish to walk in the five benefits God has done for us. We must hear the good news and have faith in it. God does not make this hard, but he insists we believe him and his word. These benefits are sitting out there with our name on them, waiting for us. God wants to give us these fabulous free gifts. It's time we realized they are ours only as free gifts of his grace, to be received by faith and follow the simple instructions in Hebrews 3 and 4 so we can walk in these benefits. It's time we let God be this good to us. Our unbelief arises mostly because we can't believe God would be so lavishly good to us. Without effort and without working to earn it, I'm forgiven, I'm healed, I'm redeemed, I'm crowned with love – the five benefits are astonishingly joyful acts of a very good God who loves us.

"Jesus has already purchased these benefits for us at great personal cost. Get rid of unbelief, hardness of heart and our own labors, the problems Hebrews chapters 3 and 4 focused on and we would find ourselves walking freely in all five benefits.

"The five benefits are not ours by works, they are ours by faith. We hear the good news. That good news meets faith. We enter into what God has done for us. As we enter his finished works, we rest, too, we *cease* from our labors to work to earn the benefits and instead we *have* the benefits.

"It really is that simple and that's the problem. People expect the process to be hard. Expect they have to earn what they are being given. Expect they have to perform to deserve what they are being given. God says freely receive from Jesus, that is how you walk in an abundant life. God won't let us work to try to earn these benefits and that drives us crazy. For everyone in our entire life, from family, friends, coworkers, bosses, neighbors, have expected performance from us. God has a different standard. Belief is the action God wants from us for these free gifts of grace, not our labor.

"We need forgiven. We need healed and to be healthy all our lives. We need redeemed. We need loved. We need our youth restored. We should be eager to take God at his word. And yet the very fact God holds out the things we need and says 'please freely accept them from my grace' makes us leery to believe him. We don't believe God is that good. Satan has convinced us his lies about God are more true than God's own word to us. We think healing and ongoing health are by our own efforts. Who taught us that? Satan. You want to see how deep that lie has gone? Check your own reaction when you read the five benefits. We're still more comfortable thinking wrongly—that healing and health are by our own efforts—even after we read God's word on his benefits to us. We are more comfortable living in the world and believing satan's lies, than we are living in the kingdom of God and believing God's word. And we wonder why we are sick and living stressed lives. The church has a heart problem. We don't believe our own God. And we suffer greatly for it."

It was a fascinating conversation. To work at being healed was to labor to do what Jesus had already done. Healing could not be obtained by works, but could only be received by resting in what Jesus had already done. "Thanks, Connie."

"I keep trying to find the right way to bring the 'how' into focus. I can feel the pull in this material, but I haven't presented it effectively yet."

"I'm finding every attempt useful, it's adding to my thinking and I appreciate that," Ryan reassured.

They were back at the hospital and Connie diverted toward work with a goodbye smile.

Ryan pulled up Hebrews chapters 3 and 4 on his phone and read the passage as he walked on to the hospital.

The effort was to focus on Christ, see his finished work and when that truth came clear you automatically rested and ceased from your own labors. See it done and you entered into the fact it *was* done, your body showed you were healed.

Ryan felt the shift inside as he grasped it. Connie was standing on the right ground. He was feeling the same certainty now too. Grace was found in rest.

When Ryan got back to his office, he added the audio to his collection of them and he copied the scripture into his notes.

Ryan Notes / conversation nine / additional references

See to it, brothers and sisters, that none of you has a sinful, unbelieving heart that turns away from the living God. But encourage one another daily, as long as it is called "Today," so that none of you may be hardened by sin's deceitfulness. We have come to share in Christ, if indeed we hold our original conviction firmly to the very end. As has just been said: "Today, if you hear his voice, do not harden your hearts as you did in the rebellion." Who were they who heard and rebelled? Were they not all those Moses led out of Egypt? And with whom was he angry for forty years? Was it not with those who sinned, whose bodies perished in the wilderness? And to whom did God swear that they would never enter his rest if not to those who disobeyed? So we see that they were not able to enter, because of their unbelief.

Therefore, since the promise of entering his rest still stands, let us be careful that none of you be found to have fallen short of it. For we also have had the good news proclaimed to us, just as they did; but the message they heard was of no value to them, because they did not share the faith of those who obeyed. Now we who have believed enter that rest, just as God has said, "So I declared on oath in my anger, 'They shall never enter my rest.'" And yet his works have been finished since the creation of the world.

For somewhere he has spoken about the seventh day in these words: “On the seventh day God rested from all his works.” And again in the passage above he says, “They shall never enter my rest.”

Therefore since it still remains for some to enter that rest and since those who formerly had the good news proclaimed to them did not go in because of their disobedience, God again set a certain day, calling it “Today.” This he did when a long time later he spoke through David, as in the passage already quoted: “Today, if you hear his voice, do not harden your hearts.” For if Joshua had given them rest, God would not have spoken later about another day.

There remains, then, a Sabbath-rest for the people of God; for anyone who enters God's rest also rests from their works, just as God did from his. Let us, therefore, make every effort to enter that rest, so that no one will perish by following their example of disobedience. For the word of God is alive and active. Sharper than any double-edged sword, it penetrates even to dividing soul and spirit, joints and marrow; it judges the thoughts and attitudes of the heart. Nothing in all creation is hidden from God's sight. Everything is uncovered and laid bare before the eyes of him to whom we must give account. (Hebrews 3:12-19, 4:1-13 NIV)

21

Ryan joined Connie at Lake Christian Church Friday evening just as the concert began glad she'd saved a seat for him. It was very much as advertised, a worship and praise gathering, the music a mix of old gospel hymns set to new music and contemporary songs. The crowd was with Jason, their energy high, the gathering creating a nice harmony when singing the old hymns and providing a rocking hand clapping thunder when the music turned lively.

Ryan enjoyed watching Ben's delight as he could feel the vibrations in the small speaker his dad had arranged for him. They were front row center left, as the week before. Music was Connie's button that turned her alive. Her expression softened. She looked happier than any other time he had been with her. She was filling up with energy just being able to offer worship with all her heart. Ryan could feel his own stress peeling away. He wasn't accustomed to singing for a long period of time. He realized at the twenty minute mark it was beginning to change him, the praise words were coming from the core of him. The distractions were dropping away.

Jason pivoted the evening at the forty-five minute mark with a brief thanks and pulled out a stool to take a seat on stage. The musicians settled into a slow-tempo, soft tune as background music. "It's nice singing praise songs together, worshiping as only music lets our hearts fully do. I want to slow us down now for a few minutes, give us time as a body to linger in the Lord's presence. Would you find your seats and join us in the song *Amazing Grace.* We're going to take communion together next. As the emblems are passed during this song, would you take and hold the bread and cup of juice and we'll partake together. I'll be eflection and celebration with a series of nen ending with a scripture."

shers began to pass the communion trays as the he gathered crowd in singing *Amazing Grace*. As the g ended, an usher brought communion onstage and Jason accepted the bread and juice, as the other band members did the same. Jason nodded to the keyboard player; and he changed to the simple melody of *Jesus loves Me* as a soft repeating chorus.

Jason held up the bread and juice he had been handed. "When the church is gathered and shares communion, it's a unique ministry time during the service. Communion is the moment we come into union with Jesus in a special way and it's not uncommon for the Holy Spirit to act during this time to minister to us and often to heal. If you feel his touch – some people feel heat, for others it's like a weight comes off your shoulders, if peace fills your mind – whisper 'thank you' and ask for more. Give him permission to continue ministering to you. He knows what you most need and would like to meet you now." Jason waited until the communion trays had reached everyone. "Thank you. Would you quiet your thoughts, close your eyes if that's helpful and join me now in reflecting on Jesus."

He let the music flow for a moment, then began to read what he had prepared, the text cued up on the monitor for him so he didn't need to use his notes.

"Father, we come to participate in communion with glad hearts tonight.

I remember Jesus.

He laid down his life willingly in order to save me.

He was beaten and scourged, then crucified.

He poured out his blood.

He bore all my sins on the cross.

He took all my sickness and bore all my diseases.

He won the total victory over satan and death for me.

By his shed blood, he forgave my sins.

By his wounds, he healed me.

I remember Jesus lying dead in a tomb for three days.
But death could not hold him.
God raised Jesus from the dead.
I remember Jesus' resurrection.
Jesus is alive, forever!
He is the living King,
Glorified,
Given all authority in heaven and on earth.

I chose baptism and Jesus.
I was crucified with Christ.
I willingly laid down that old life of sin.
My old nature, my sin nature, died on the cross with Christ.
The law that condemned me was also nailed to that cross by God.
I have died to sin.
I was buried with Christ.

And I am alive with Christ.
God has resurrected me with Christ.
God has given me a new nature.
God has seated me with Christ in heaven.
And God has given me his own Holy Spirit.
The Holy Spirit now gives life to my mortal body.
A new covenant has been struck,
You, God, are my God and I am yours.
There is peace between myself and God in Jesus Christ.

I now eat this bread and participate with Jesus' body,
And I now drink this juice and participate with Jesus' blood,
Proclaiming his death and resurrection until he comes again.

Bless the LORD, O my soul;
And all that is within me, bless his holy name!

Bless the LORD, O my soul,
And forget not all his benefits,
Who forgives all your iniquity,
Who heals all your diseases,
Who redeems your life from the Pit,
Who crowns you with steadfast love and mercy,
Who satisfies you with good as long as you live,
So that your youth is renewed like the eagle's.

Praise the Lord! Praise the Lord!
Praise the Lord, all his people!
Amen.

The gathered church echoed his Amen concluding communion. A rustle of movement filled the room as the cups began to be collected. The band shifted to a more up-tempo background tune.

Hearing what Connie spoke about used as the communion reading was effective in a way Ryan hadn't expected, the simple reading moving his heart directly through the events of the cross and making the words of Psalm 103 resonate. He needed to ask Jason if he would be willing to record that same communion reading to video specifically for use in the hospital. With Walter recording a chapel communion service, Jason providing this one, they would be very effective in helping patients take communion in a guided way that presented what communion fully brought to people.

Jason caught Connie's gaze, offered a smile that was very much a private one between the two of them, then he looked back to the audience and made the suggestion, "Would you take a minute to check out your bodies and see what has been healed. Do something you couldn't do before, take off your glasses and read without them, put weight on a sore ankle and check if the pain is gone, whatever it might be. Let's see what the Holy Spirit was doing among us and give him thanks."

Those skeptical among the crowd ignored his suggestion, while those curious to see, followed his advice, some standing, others stepping in the aisle to have some space to move around.

There was a stir in the middle rows on the right side. A young man stood up. "Jason, I busted my wrist playing basketball last week, some of you were there when it happened. The surgeon had to pin it. The constant ache is gone and this brace is suddenly loose, like the swelling has left. Are you telling me this might have just been healed?"

Jason laughed at the young man's surprise. "Yes." He looked around the room. "Where's Scott? Do we have an orthopedic doctor in the room?" He spotted him, now working his way out of a row of people. "Scott, you want to take a look and see what's happened to Taylor's wrist, give us a report after the next intermission?

"Thank you, Holy Spirit. I give you praise and love your quiet way of blessing us. Anyone else notice anything?"

He scanned the room for a moment. "We're going to sing another set of songs, folks and praise God and give the people involved some time to see what's happened. I'll have the doctor give us a report in about half an hour with details. We're in no hurry to rush an assumption. But one thing I do know, the Holy Spirit loves to minister to his people and there's more ministry he's willing to do tonight. Let's let him. Would you stand, find the beat with me and offer God praise, loud praise. We're going to start off this set with *Praise the Lord*, then *Come, Holy Spirit*."

Ryan gave Connie a considered look as she capped her water bottle and set it aside and found the beat of the song to clap along. Ryan hadn't been at Lake services before to know if this was common place or not. Jason had handled it beautifully thus far and had clearly been expecting to see something when he asked the audience to check for what had healed.

Jason set aside the stool, picked up his guitar, caught the tempo with the drummer and the energy level spiked as the audience took his words to heart and sang, voices raised, a hand-raised wave spontaneously moving back and forth through sections of the crowd. As the fourth song ended, Jason brought the set of songs to a close. "Thank you, folks, for the worship and praise you're offering to God." He scanned the room, then signaled to the sound technician and the video screen changed back to the band logo welcome, as the house lights came up. "We're going to take a 15 minute intermission, but before we do, Scott, are you comfortable making a comment on what's happened with Taylor?"

Jason offered his microphone down to the doctor.

"We're heading over to the hospital to get new x-rays. The mobility I see in his hand and fingers, without any accompanying wrist pain, I believe these bones are healed, but we'll let the evidence speak for itself. If anyone would like to see before and after x-rays, stick around for another hour. Taylor's offered to make them public. We'll be back with them shortly."

Shouts of joy and applause echoed through the room. Jason accepted back the microphone. "Thank you, Holy Spirit. We love you. Let's give God a sustained round of applause as thanks, while the band plays what we consider our theme song and then we'll step aside for 15 minutes. We'll have the time on the backdrop so you know when we'll resume."

Connie leaned over as the song finished. "I'm going to dart backstage for a minute, Ryan."

"Sure."

Connie caught Ben's attention and pointed backstage, held out her hand. Ben eagerly joined her.

Ryan thought about what to do with the time, for he wanted to walk around the church before he left, get a feel for how they had converted the building. For now he chose to walk around in the open area between the front row of seats and the platform to stretch his legs. The conversations around him were overlapping and hard to follow with everyone talking, but Ryan caught bits and pieces of those wondering if Taylor's wrist really had healed.

Connie came back to join him after a time, retrieved her water bottle and finished it, repacked it to take back home, then stood looking around, a contented expression on her face. The fifteen minute intermission was counting down on the screen, there were six minutes left. Ryan joined her and leaned over so he could be heard. "A lot of excitement backstage?"

Connie raised her voice to be able to be heard as she nodded. "Gloria just posted an interview with Taylor and Scott as they head off to the hospital. Its excitement crossed with some chaos, which is nice, as I got to do a quick wave hi with Jason on the video blog and consider it our official couple thing for tonight."

Ryan laughed at her relief. "Ben?"

"With his mom. She's been making it a point to pray for him during the intermission after communion, one of those double whammy type moments as it's also a concert of praise music. She's hopeful tonight with reason. I had about a fifteen second glance, but Taylor's wrist looked healed to me."

"We saw a miracle tonight."

Connie smiled. "Yes, we did. Think of a miracle as a healing which finishes in a compressed period of time."

"A useful definition. Think this crowd will believe it?"

"Some will, some won't. It's a church crowd more exposed than most to the idea we are healed at the cross, but it's still not well understood."

Ben came running over to Connie and wrapped a hug around her legs.

"Hey, pretty boy." She hauled him up with ease.

The boy leaned back, comfortable she wouldn't drop him. "Say my name," he demanded.

"Ben."

He giggled and buried his head in her shoulder, then popped back again. "Say it again."

"Ben."

He giggled and disappeared again. Ryan was so startled he felt frozen in place. Sometime in the last ten minutes Ben had received his hearing back. Ben's mom was standing watching her son with tears streaming down her face.

The next time Ben asked Connie to say his name, she giggled with him as she answered.

"What was the first word you heard?" Connie asked him, curious.

"Hi."

"Jesus?"

"He sounded just like how he sounds in my head, too."

"That's good to know."

Ben leaned back, confident she wouldn't drop him. "I told the devil 'go away, in Jesus' name' and stamped my foot cause I was mad at him and my ears popped, like pop, pop, pop cereal and then Jesus said hi."

Connie grinned.

"The devil wasn't listening to my mom and everybody has to listen to my mom, so I told him so, too."

"That was very smart."

"I wanted to hear the music. This is my concert, it's my birthday tomorrow."

"You're going to be seven. I haven't forgotten that."

"You're coming to the party?"

"I already even have your presents wrapped."

Ben's eyes widened. "More than one?"

Connie held up three fingers and got smashed in a gleeful hug.

"You're going to get asked by a lot of people what happened with your hearing. Have you figured out what you're going to tell them?"

"Jesus said hi."

"That will do perfect." She lowered him to his feet. "Go enjoy the music with Jason. The guys will play your favorite song, just tell them which one."

"I can go on stage?"

"Go to the stairs on the side and wave for your dad to come over. Tell him what song you want him to play."

"Okay."

Ben waved his father over and there was a pow-wow that turned into a shout of joy. Word spread from band member to band member as they returned to the stage, preparing for the next set of songs. Jason just stood on the platform looking at Connie, dumbfounded. "Really? This is who else God starts with? Ben?"

Connie laughed.

Time for the intermission passed as Jason conferred with Ben's dad for a long minute, then moved to the front of the stage, signaled the sound engineer to bring his microphone on. "Sorry, folks. We've realized another amazing answer happened tonight. You know Jim on keyboards and many of you know his son Ben. Ben lost his hearing and has been profoundly deaf for over a year. The Holy Spirit restored his hearing tonight. Ben would like us to play *A Joyful Noise* and we're going to oblige him. This band is about to do the biggest celebration set of songs you've ever heard, thanking God for his goodness, for this miracle and Taylor's." Jason choked up trying to finish the thought and paused to wipe his eyes, his grin widening. "When God does two miracles, he's here to do another," he said, his voice husky, but the confidence in that statement clear. "Let's see what else the Holy Spirit has in mind for tonight. Whatever your need, bring it to God. He's here to minister to his people."

The drummer and Ben's dad on keyboards hit the opening chords for *A Joyful Noise* and the celebration started.

****

At the two hour mark it felt to Ryan like the praise was just beginning. The concert had become standing room only as word spread about Ben and the broader Lake Christian Church family gathered to celebrate.

"Guys, lets do the worship group of songs from the Psalms, if you want to reset for that." Jason considered what else to say. "I know its getting late, those of you who have babysitters watching kids at home and early morning Saturday work obligations, I know you'll need to head out in this next half hour. I bless you now, in Jesus name and thank you for coming this evening. Tell your friends what happened here tonight, give God glory by remembering his works to others. Whatever your need is personally, whisper it to the Holy Spirit on the way home tonight. You aren't leaving his presence, he'll be with you as you go. Those of you who want to stay and worship, continue to give God praise and let the Holy Spirit minister as he would like among his church, we'll go as long as the Lord leads us to do so, for now, to the top of the ten o'clock hour."

The band began the opening chords for Psalm 100.

Connie caught Ryan's attention, leaned in close. "We can leave when you like, Ryan. I know your obligations and Jason knows I'll catch up to him later. This kind of night has been in the 'hoped for' column for a lot of months."

Ryan found the offer startling given what had happened and gave her a smile. "The hospital will be in touch on an emergency. For now, I'm good until ten." He nodded to Ben who was front row center, directly in front of Jason so he could be involved with all the songs and his dad on keyboards. "His joy is contagious."

"He's going to be a very tired boy for his birthday party tomorrow," she predicted with a smile.

Ryan loved the worship songs from the Psalms and comfortably joined in on this one, glad Connie had packed the extra water bottles, for his voice was turning hoarse. Some songs were simply better at full volume and this praise song for Psalm 100 was one of them.

Make a joyful noise to the LORD, all the lands!
Serve the LORD with gladness!
Come into his presence with singing!

Know that the LORD is God!
It is he that made us and we are his;
we are his people and the sheep of his pasture.
Enter his gates with thanksgiving,
and his courts with praise!
Give thanks to him, bless his name!
For the LORD is good;
his steadfast love endures for ever,
and his faithfulness to all generations.

****

CONNIE AUGUST

Connie caught Jason's attention and he maneuvered through the crowd around the front of the stage to join her. She laughed as he lifted her off her feet.

"It was pretty impressive, getting to see this evening unfold. God did amazing things," Jason said.

She was delighted with him and how he'd handled the evening. "The first public healings at a Jason Lasting led concert. You can be certain it won't be the last God wants to do." She kissed him because it suited her mood. "Enjoy the late dinner with the guys. I'm going to head home. You need the celebration time and I'm in need of some sleep as I've got birthday party refreshments to bake in the morning. I have a feeling the party is going to turn into a huge celebration as people stop by to see Ben, so I'll be baking more than originally planned. I'll catch up with you tomorrow."

"I'll come find you, help with the cookies, help carry birthday presents to Ben's party." Jason grinned. "It's going to be one incredible party." He nodded toward Ryan. "Let him walk you home or grab a taxi."

She loved the fact he could ignore 8 years of military training to make that suggestion. It was nice simply being a girlfriend. "I'll let him. Try to get some sleep before dawn."

Jason laughed. "I'll try. You were right, about how this feels. It's good to be useful to God."

"It is." She kissed him again just for the joy of it. "Catch up with you tomorrow."

****

RYAN COOPER

"That was by far the best Friday night of my life in more ways than just the obvious one. The music does something to you when it's simply extended praise," Ryan remarked as they walked out of the building with the crowd.

"It's freedom, what you're feeling. Your mind drops away all its worries and comes into sync with your spirit and all of you – spirit, soul and body – gives praise to God."

"That sounds about right." They moved past the crowd heading toward vehicles and turned in the direction of Connie's home. The moon had begun to lose its fullness of last Friday. Ryan judged it to be a little before eleven p.m. The cool air felt good after the heat generated by the crowd, though he was glad for the jacket he'd brought. "This was a milestone night."

"The first public healings at a Jason Lasting led concert. There will be more," she agreed.

Ryan studied Connie thoughtfully. She was happy, content, but not bubbling with joy as others in the crowd leaving with them had been. "You seem…subdued isn't the right word. But a word like it."

"I'm tired mostly. This has been a long time coming. I love the praise offered God, I'm just aware the root of it tonight still rests in the fact people were surprised by God's goodness. This is normal, Ryan, this is what every day looked like in the first century church. We've moved so far away from who we are as God's people that the first glimpse of what should be our normal life sends us into startled celebration. That does make me sad. I want the reality of the Christian life back for its people, not simply the occasional taste. God hasn't changed. God hasn't moved away from that first century church experience. We have."

Ryan realized Connie was in a reflective mood, with more to say, so he retrieved his phone and started a recording, curious to see where their conversation would go tonight. "For the recording which I just started, just to make it official, you weren't surprised Ben was healed tonight."

Connie smiled. "I wasn't surprised. I've been praying for him for months. I knew it would come."

"A profoundly deaf boy received his hearing back tonight and I was there to see the before and after. I'm going to offer for the record — incredible, incredible night."

Connie laughed.

"Also healed tonight was a young man with a broken wrist. The doctors looking at the before and after x-rays are amazed."

"Taylor is walking around shaking hands with anyone who wants to see for themselves that he's in no pain and that his wrist looks normal. That was a beautiful healing, too."

"Do you think there will be more healings on Sunday?" Ryan asked, curious.

"There will be if people come with expectant hearts. I'm hopeful. It's a process. Every healing will raise faith for more. The Holy Spirit has been planning this. I've been one of the pieces in motion, so has Jason, the group of seven and you Ryan. God healed two publicly tonight. He set us up to be ready to pray on Sunday morning for more people. He has a plan unfolding."

Ryan considered that and nodded, pleased. "Ideally, this won't stop for months. What happened tonight is simply the first in a long line of people getting healed."

"That would be ideal and we'll get to that point with this, hopefully soon. They are all easy healings to God. Indulge me for a moment and let me share an observation about God."

He glanced at her and smiled. "Sure."

"God spun a trillion billion stars into the universe and recorded it as five words in scripture, 'he made the stars also'. He slips it in as an aside into the creation story, then waits thousands of years before man has instruments that can tell him, 'those stars in the sky? those are actually galaxies of a billion stars each.' God's humility is showing in those five words as well as his unfathomable power. That's our dad. In five words he shows us both his majesty and his character. 'He made the stars also.' They are my favorite five words in the bible for what they revealed to me about my God. I always ask for what I want to happen. I don't care if what I want is small or if it's massive, because my dad can handle anything I ask. And I've learned to be joyful, but not surprised, when I receive what I asked."

"I love that," Ryan remarked, glad he had her words recorded.

"We'll pray for people on Sunday, pray with boldness. And whatever happens there, we will pray for more people at the next concert. And at some point the fire will catch and people will expect to be healed, will be surprised when they are not.

"The Holy Spirit is sharing Ben's joy tonight and Taylor's, but God also knows the names of every person who walked out of the concert having not received what they also needed. God was present to minister and who received what they needed? A child whose heart was ready to hear Jesus say hi. A young man God chose. That's telling and not in a good way, about where the people of God are at right now. Two is wonderful, but they should have been followed by another four, another eight. God was willing to heal, the problem is still on our side. But it's a seen problem now, something which can be worked on with good teaching, with helping people find hope again that God really is good and hasn't changed. He is our healer."

"How long before the press arrive?"

Connie smiled. "Not long. Tonight is already heavy on social media. I expect reporters will be at church on Sunday, interviewing people, wanting to talk to Ben and Taylor "

"I'd like to come and pray for people as part of the group if you'd consider letting me come and be part of it."

"You'd be welcome, Ryan."

She dug into her pocket and came up with a flash drive. "More homework. As thrilling as tonight was, it's simply one night in what is a year with still around 270 more to go. Remember to get some rest, keep your eye on the long game, keep giving the Holy Spirit time to teach you. This is a marathon, not a sprint. Chicago is a very big city to try to transform. It won't be done overnight, or even in a year. But once George is here, maybe five years makes a big dent."

Ryan accepted the flash drive. "I'll keep studying, teach."

Connie laughed. They were at her home. He waited until she had opened her door before offering a wave goodnight and heading back to his car parked at the hospital.

He chose not to step into the hospital and see Jeff in the ER, wanting a few more hours before he talked about tonight with others, even with family. He walked through the parking garage to his car.

"God, it was a wonderful night, a full experience, but I need time to let it settle before I try to talk through it with you. Bless us, God, all of Chicago and unfold what you have planned."

He drove part way home in silence, then chose at a red light to open his laptop, slip in the flash drive and listen to the first of the audios Connie had handed him.

"Let's start with two scriptures:

"And it shall come to pass afterward,
that I will pour out my spirit on all flesh;
your sons and your daughters shall prophesy,
your old men shall dream dreams,
and your young men shall see visions.
Even upon the menservants and maidservants
in those days, I will pour out my spirit.
(Joel 2:28-29)

And the Holy Spirit also bears witness to us; for after saying, "This is the covenant that I will make with them after those days, says the Lord: I will put my laws on their hearts and write them on their minds," then he adds, "I will remember their sins and their misdeeds no more." (Hebrews 10:15-17)

"Ryan, do you realize we are the only ones who remember our sins and misdeeds? Jesus has died! The new covenant has gone into effect. It is in effect right now on earth. The old one is gone and the new one is ours *right now*. The new covenant says 'I'll be your God and you will be my people,' and God adds, 'I will remember your sins and your misdeeds no more.' That's present day reality. So why are we remembering them when God isn't?

"We have a problem with prayer that comes from our perception of ourselves. We spend our days regretting what we did wrong in our lives, we play our mental list of the top 10 lifetime sins we regret, we hang our heads in shame before God and we pray kind of desperate prayers. We don't live like God isn't remembering our sins and misdeeds.

"Consider the implications. God my Father thinks about me today. He doesn't remember my sins or misdeeds; there is nothing that comes to his mind when he thinks of our relationship that troubles him. We mistakenly tend to think God has forgiven us, but that he still keeps an active memory of our errors in mind. 'She's a good daughter except for the fact she has lied a number of times and there was that breach of the commandments in her 20s and that mess her anger made in her 30s. I would have had to send her to hell if my son hadn't stepped in to take her punishment. I'm so glad Jesus helped her out.'

"That's not happening. God does not remember our mistakes. None of our sins are coming to his mind. Instead, God is thinking 'how can I lavish love on her today? What's the desire of her heart?' The disconnect between the truth—the creator of the universe is our loving dad—and the way we think—I hope God will help me earn an extra twenty dollars to fill up the car with gas before Monday—is the saddest fact in the world.

"It's time we let God be himself in our lives. He's good. It's time we throw open the doors of expectation and anticipation and let God flow his goodness into our lives. God is living in the second covenant. It's time we did so, too. God will thrill us with his love if we will let him be himself."

Ryan smiled as the audio concluded. That was classic Connie. Trying to jar people into seeing God as he was, in love with us and longing for us to expect his goodness.

"Dad, the desire of my heart is to live this, all of it, healing the sick, raising the dead, being able to teach others as Connie has been teaching me, about communion and life and you. I love the fact Connie helps me see you more clearly. Thanks for what this journey has been these last couple weeks. You've refreshed my heart. The songs tonight of praise were from all of me, as a way to say thanks. I love you, dad. And I know I'm loved by you."

22

Ryan listened to the other audio on the flash drive Connie had given him as he walked to the coffee shop to meet her Saturday. It had felt odd waking up with Friday as the recent, but past, experience in his life. He was on the other side of having seen two miracles. The sun had still come up. He'd still been hungry for breakfast. What had changed most was his faith. He not only had faith for miracles now, he had the experience of them and expectation for them. Connie lived differently, with a certainty in her words and he was now understanding why. He was different this morning because of last night.

"I've lost track of which audio number this is. This is a short review note, Ryan. Healing the sick – it's all easy for God. For you, it's either something you've done before, or something new the Holy Spirit plans to teach you how to do. Have an expectation of success rather than failure so you develop a stubbornness about this. Jesus' instruction to 'heal the sick' didn't come with tier one conditions for you, tier two and three to be someone else. We like to quantify difficulty. God likes to say 'see that rock in the middle of the desert? Let's make enough water come out of it to satisfy a million people and all their cattle.' Think of any problem you are facing as it being you and God standing side by side looking at the problem. Then deal with it. You aren't alone. There are no unsolvable problems you will face. Just easy ones and stubborn ones. Be more stubborn than your enemy the devil. You'll make God smile.

"And finally, another simple comment I'd like you to remember. With God we think we have to get every interaction perfect, that because he's a perfect God there's no room for mistakes. So we become so cautious we don't do anything for fear of being wrong. God is actually the opposite; he's very much encouraging us to know him, think with wisdom, but then to have faith to try stuff. He encourages the exploration and the interaction and actually kind of enjoys the detours we end up on because we heard him wrong. He's still walking with us as we're working our way back to the direction he had pointed by a different route, enjoying the detour as much as we would have the original road.

"To paraphrase something Bill Johnson said, 'God had a world without you in it, he didn't like it, that's why he made you.'

"Most people don't realize how much God simply enjoys them. Their way of seeing things, their creativity and personality. He likes your company and the way you enjoy the world he made. Be yourself. Let God be himself. You'll thrive. Your life is about doing good works, because the world needs you. But you will always be more than just your works to God; you will always be his son. Hang out with God. Don't get so busy you forget to just show up and enjoy his company without an agenda. You'll be thankful for that, most of all, when your 120 years reaches its conclusion."

The audio ended. Connie did that well, balanced doing stuff with time hanging out with God. She'd intentionally structured her work life so that there were hours open for her to be with God. The life he wanted was like that, intentionally arranged to give space for God, while doing good. He was pretty certain Connie had decided to live to be 120, there was always a smile in those words. He hadn't decided that question yet for himself, but he was enjoying the process of thinking about it.

****

Ryan bought his coffee and Connie's, her breakfast roll, then chose a table by the window as he was a few minutes early. His phone chimed with a family alert. He tugged it out to check the news. He had a text from Margaret.

"In lieu of finding a creative excuse for why you're coming over, you can bring me some butter and eggs. I'm in the mood to bake. I'm fine, Ryan. It takes more than the mild flu to knock me over."

Ryan smiled and replied with a smile icon and an 'okay', then pocketed his phone, the text message itself a delight. Her perky mood was coming back.

Connie arrived; he handed her coffee and a sweet roll and they set out to walk together. "Thank you for last night. Had I not been there, I would have missed something *amazing*."

Connie grinned. "I loved the evening, too."

"Yet the sun comes up, a new day starts."

She chuckled. "And I've got about ten dozen cookies to bake before the four p.m. party."

"It's weird, the realization life goes on, as if the miracles last night were a speed bump in the normal road."

"You'll adjust, Ryan, to living in a weird split world where you see God do stuff every day and yet the rest of the world continues to go by oblivious to what just happened. After a while you'll even come to accept it's just normal. You tell sickness to go away and it does. You tell a dead person to wake up and they do. Eventually our mind accepts that the full Christian life of doing the same works Jesus did is in fact our new normal life. You'll see a miracle and two minutes later be deciding where to meet a friend for dinner that night and not think anything of it. Even the supernatural becomes normal after you see a lot of it. That's what is in your future."

"Allow me to say how incredible and also fun that sounds."

Connie laughed. "I had one more spirit-prompted thought late last night that might help me clarify the one subject I've been struggling to explain." She dug out a flash drive and handed it to him. "I'm kind of excited about that recording, as I learned some new material, too, as the verses came alive. We'll see what you think."

"I'll listen to it today," Ryan promised.

"I'm going to stop teaching now and let your questions direct where we go next. So to close this period with a final word of advice, I've chosen a scripture which is both a promise and warning. 'Keep your heart with all vigilance; for from it flow the springs of life.' (Proverbs 4:23)

"Keep a humble heart, Ryan, fear God and do good works." She smiled. "And with that, I'm finally at the point where I get to ask the question, do you have any questions?"

He thought the verse was fitting. Ryan considered this to be another milestone moment and reflected on what he wanted to ask. He had a running list of topics on his phone, specific questions he would like her insights on. But for the first question… "What's the one thing you most wish I would remember from all our talks?"

Connie considered it for a time. She smiled. "I really have only one lesson. Believe God is telling you the truth. I just use a lot of words, where the bible needs only a few. We try to wrap our minds around the idea of miracles and the supernatural and stumble at the thought of them happening in our time, in front of us, so doubt healing is for today. If we would instead wrap our minds around the facts God doesn't lie and God is good, we'd draw the logical conclusion there have got to be tons of miracles he wants to do today and go ask him for them all. We doubt his goodness, so miracles surprise us. If we knew his goodness, we would be astonished at anything less than a multitude of miracles wiping out sickness and disease whenever we ask him."

Ryan loved that answer. "Second question. Does this mean our walks are over?"

Connie laughed. "I'll let you buy my coffee and a sweet roll until you've run out of questions or I've run out of answers."

Ryan grinned at the way she phrased it. "That's an offer I'll gladly accept." Spring was finally arriving, his jacket almost not needed and he thought they'd be walking together for most of the spring and summer before he exhausted what he desired to talk about with her. "I've been thinking about ways to implement this at the hospital, how to train the volunteers who work with Walter, how to teach the material to staff who have an interest in the subject. I'd like to run some ideas past you."

"Sure."

Ryan sketched out the plan he was developing as they walked to the hospital, Connie listening and offering the occasional question. He'd finally figured out a way to properly say thanks. He was bringing the material she'd taught him to life at Mercy Hospital. It was the best compliment he could give her.

****

Ryan stopped by the hospital to see if anything urgent needed his attention, transferred the audio file to his phone and took another walk of his own to listen to what Connie had recorded late last night, curious what had her attention after such a rich evening.

"Ryan, I've been puzzling around how to explain something profound about health and there is a passage of scripture that came alive tonight that may be as helpful to you as it has been illuminating for me. To set the stage for this conversation, let me go back to a prior one introducing the subject and then give you this scripture and a couple others and talk briefly about it. Here's how I originally set up the subject:

"My body doesn't go from sick to healed because of my works, any more than my sin nature changed to righteousness because of my effort. People make a mistake when they approach forgiveness of sins as a matter of faith, but the healing of their bodies as a matter of their own works. 'Eat right, exercise properly, see this doctor, take this medication.' They plan their own health regime and govern their lives by those rules they've crafted about how to live. Mostly out of ignorance, they've unintentionally substituted works for faith and as a consequence nullified what Jesus did for them. And then they wonder why they constantly get sick despite what they know about the word of God.

"The forgiveness of our sins and the healing of our bodies are both grace gifts. Jesus paid the price for both of them on our behalf. They are his finished works and his gifts to us. Because of that fact, they can be received only by faith. That really stuns people to hear, to realize what is being said in the scriptures."

The replay of the previous audio stopped and Connie's voice returned. "Okay, that's the context for this audio tonight. Let me read you two passages from first Corinthians, a short one and then a longer one on the same topic.

Do you not know that your body is a temple of the Holy Spirit within you, which you have from God? You are not your own; you were bought with a price. So glorify God in your body. (1 Corinthians 6:19-20)

Do you not know that you are God's temple and that God's Spirit dwells in you? If any one destroys God's temple, God will destroy him. For God's temple is holy and that temple you are.

Let no one deceive himself. If any one among you thinks that he is wise in this age, let him become a fool that he may become wise. For the wisdom of this world is folly with God. For it is written, "He catches the wise in their craftiness," and again, "The Lord knows that the thoughts of the wise are futile." So let no one boast of men.

For all things are yours, whether Paul or Apol'los or Cephas or the world or life or death or the present or the future, all are yours; and you are Christ's; and Christ is God's. (1 Corinthians 3:16-23)

"They are wonderful passages, ones that most Christians are familiar with, at least in part. These are the scriptures most often quoted when people teach about taking care of our bodies and why it is so important. Every Christian wants to take care of their body, the temple of God. It's a love thing as well as one of obedience. We deeply desire to obey God's instruction on this matter and not destroy the temple of God. If that wasn't enough motivation, the sharp warning catches our attention, too; the consequences are serious. If anyone destroys God's temple, God will destroy him! No one wants that.

"Don't read the warning in the verse to mean God is going to take an active action to destroy us. The scriptures are clear that Jesus reconciled all of mankind to God with his sacrifice on the cross. There is now peace between God and man. The verse is rather warning us that God will permit something to happen. Something we are doing is bringing on our destruction and God is not stepping in to stop it. The warning reads as 'If any one destroys God's temple, God will permit the destruction to happen.'

"Our bodies are destroyed by sickness, disease, infirmities, until they accumulate to the point we die.

"Most Christians taking this passage seriously implement some kind of plan to keep their bodies sound, fit and healthy. They have some combination of 'eat right, exercise properly, see this doctor, take this medication, take these vitamins' by which they live. It can be elaborate or a few simple rules they live by like, 'I don't eat sugar and nothing fried,' or 'I never miss my daily walk'. It's a plan that fits the best advice from friends, family, trial-and-error and what they've heard the experts say makes a difference.

"It sounds good on the surface, logical. But without intending to do so, we have removed ourselves from under the cover of Jesus' work of grace and taken ourselves back into the law of works, back to our own efforts.

"Satan blinded the eyes of the church and convinced us to read that passage backwards. He sold the church a works program using the world's wisdom. You don't want to destroy the temple of God? Great! Here's a works program using the world's wisdom. Eat this, don't eat that, exercise this way, see these doctors, take these pills. And we bought the lie. And in doing so, we are destroying the temple of God. Rather than live healed and healthy lives until we are around 120 years old, rather than preserve the temple of God and live holy, we instead live sick, chronically sick and die early, desperately trying to do more 'living right', spending money in ever larger amounts trying to get ourselves healed and stay healthy.

"We have allowed sin and death back into our lives and sickness and disease are destroying us. God will not save us from this error. We must repent—repent means to change your thinking, see the truth and go that direction instead—and come back under grace where we are healed and made alive by the grace Jesus offers. God is not destroying us. Our wrong understanding of scripture has rather kept us trapped under the old law of sin and death.

"Take the passage apart into three sections and you'll see it.

Do you not know that you are God's temple and that God's Spirit dwells in you? If any one destroys God's temple, God will destroy him. For God's temple is holy and that temple you are. (1 Corinthians 3:16-17)

"The very next verses are these:

Let no one deceive himself. If any one among you thinks that he is wise in this age, let him become a fool that he may become wise. For the wisdom of this world is folly with God. For it is written, "He catches the wise in their craftiness," and again, "The Lord knows that the thoughts of the wise are futile." So let no one boast of men. (1 Corinthians 3:18-21a)

"Do you see the incredible wisdom of the Holy Spirit in the fact he placed those verses one after the other? We are told to take care of the temple of God, our bodies and in the very next verses warned not to follow the wisdom of the world as how to do so. The wisdom of the world is folly with God. We simply didn't keep reading the passage. We heard 'take care of the temple' and said 'I can do that!' and jumped up with our own conceived plan or plan from some expert for how to do it. We set out to do so by our own efforts, full of enthusiasm and heart for God, but wrong in our thinking, deceiving ourselves. We stopped reading and have paid a massive price for that error.

"The final section says:

For all things are yours, whether Paul or Apol'los or Cephas or the world or life or death or the present or the future, all are yours; and you are Christ's; and Christ is God's. (1 Corinthians 3:21b-23)

"All things are ours. Life. Health. Strong bodies. Good skin. Youth. They are already given things. They belong to us. They are grace gifts from Jesus. The Holy Spirit is with us to give them to us.

"The first section is what to do – take care of the body, the temple of God. The second section is what not to do – don't follow the wisdom of the world. The third section is how to do it – realize all things are yours. You receive them by faith, by simply believing they are yours as a gift from Jesus.

"Healing is a grace gift from Jesus. Believe it is a gift to you and the Holy Spirit changes you to be healed. You cease working by your own efforts, receive grace, believe it and your body will show over time the fact you are healed.

"Let no one boast of men. We run around proud of how healthy we are because we've eaten this way and exercised that way, boasting of our plan and describing it to our friends who seem to be struggling and don't look as healed and healthy as we are, eager to convince everyone they should try it our way. It's an illusion, that health we display. On the outside we look good, while on the inside we are dying, because we are living in our own works, there is no grace-generated life operating in us.

"Healing and health is by grace alone. When we add man's work plan to Jesus' grace, we fail to gain the very thing we desire. We are healed by grace alone. And we stay healthy by grace alone.

"Let no one deceive himself. When we read the scripture incorrectly we deceive ourselves. At this point just about every Christian in the western world has tripped over this passage."

Connie paused the conversation and Ryan heard pages being turned.

"Here's another passage that goes right at this problem.

Do not be deceived; God is not mocked, for whatever a man sows, that he will also reap. For he who sows to his own flesh will from the flesh reap corruption; but he who sows to the Spirit will from the Spirit reap eternal life. (Galatians 6:7-8)

"The common way this is read is that if you eat fried food and junk food and don't exercise you get what you deserve, disease and death. When in fact the verses are saying exactly the opposite. If you sow to the flesh with a works program of your own efforts, a world's wisdom designed list of dos and don'ts, you walk yourself into sickness and disease, you end up destroyed. You are trying to make yourself healed and healthy by your own actions. You are sowing to your flesh, your old nature. You've come back under law and with it sin and death. If you sow to your flesh you get corruption—destruction. If instead you live by faith and grace, walking with the Holy Spirit and obeying his voice, you will get the very life you are seeking.

"Satan goes to the very verses which give us freedom and uses them to put us back into the world, serving the flesh, into a program of our own works. That satan is a very good liar is obvious to anyone who looks at how he functions. The church over the centuries wasn't discerning what satan was doing, didn't reject the error and has let this deception filter into how we think.

"God respects free will so much God will let us deceive ourselves and end up with destruction. That is a profound reality about God. And a painful reality for everyone struggling with a health problem who thought they could be free of it by doing what everyone around them said was the way to solve this problem. Listening to the world rather than only listening to God is what prevents healing from reaching us.

"For those who have given up trying, don't have an exercise routine at the gym, don't try to stay on a diet, those who simply look with grief at their body and sigh over everything wrong in it, but don't come to Jesus, they are also dying under the world's plan and statistically faster than those who try to ward death off by their own efforts. They are dying because they are still living under works, thinking *if they did go* do something, that is how they would get healthy; they've just paused their works program. They are still living a works program and death is still operating in them, even though their work at the moment is to be a couch potato and eat in violation of the 'rules' they have heard are the right and correct way to live. They are dying because they haven't accepted grace.

"They may not have heard grace exists for healing, or they heard and thought 'that can't be for me'. But without expressing faith to accept grace, they are still dying under the law even though they've given up trying to improve themselves. The world's program of works lives in both our actions and in our beliefs. You have to accept Jesus' grace heals you; you have to hear it, believe it and accept it, before you will walk in that health. Inactivity does not heal you of the error of works. An active turn to Jesus for grace is what saves you and heals you. Not inactivity. A sigh, 'Jesus, heal me', from a person who doesn't think healing is something Jesus has done for them, won't give them the results they need. It's faith in the word of God that brings grace. You need to hear the good news, believe healing is for you by grace, accept it and then you will have that healing grace operating in your life. Your body will show itself healed.

"The Holy Spirit is the Spirit of Truth. He will teach us how to read the scriptures as they are written, he will take us to life and freedom, but we have to let him. We have to let God teach us the truth and be willing to believe it.

"The healing and health we want is here, as a free gift of God's grace. That's the beauty of the gospel, Ryan. What we want is right here waiting for us. All things are ours. It simply takes faith in his grace to walk into it.

"You will keep the temple of God in perfect condition if you simply receive all the things that are yours. Healing, health, 120 years of life. God's blessings to you are a free gift. Stop working. Receive grace. And live."

Connie paused again and he could hear pages turning. "Three other useful scriptures:

For those who live according to the flesh set their minds on the things of the flesh, but those who live according to the Spirit set their minds on the things of the Spirit. To set the mind on the flesh is death, but to set the mind on the Spirit is life and peace. … for if you live according to the flesh you will die, but if by the Spirit you put to death the deeds of the body you will live. For all who are led by the Spirit of God are sons of God. (Romans 8: 5-6, 13-14)

Do you not know that if you yield yourselves to any one as obedient slaves, you are slaves of the one whom you obey, either of sin, which leads to death, or of obedience, which leads to righteousness? (Romans 6:16)

whatever does not proceed from faith is sin. (Romans 14:23b)

Connie paused again, this time for a longer period of time. "Ryan, let me flip to the other side of the coin for a minute. There's something interesting to see. We *are* the temple of the Holy Spirit. The Holy Spirit cares deeply about our body. Corinthians also says, 'The body is meant for the Lord and the Lord for the body.' God designed our bodies, the Holy Spirit is the literal breath of life within us. When we walk with the Holy Spirit having been healed and we're now day-to-day living healthy, what does it look like?

"What the world calls a healthy lifestyle has some truth in it, don't smoke, don't drink alcohol excessively, those are likely to be things the Holy Spirit will also instruct us to avoid. There is a statement David made in the Psalms, 'I will know nothing of evil'. It was how he handled living in the world. He didn't hang around with liars, didn't keep counselors around who disrespected God, didn't permit sinful behaviors to be his lifestyle. That's a good rule of thumb for what to expect the Holy Spirit to also tell us when it comes to how we live in this body. The scriptures pointedly mention a few items, like sexual sins, which are sins against the body. So is there an evil to avoid when it comes to food and drink?

"The Holy Spirit made a point to say that all foods are good and nothing is to be rejected.

The Spirit clearly says that in later times some will abandon the faith and follow deceiving spirits and things taught by demons. Such teachings come through hypocritical liars, whose consciences have been seared as with a hot iron. They forbid people to marry and order them to abstain from certain foods, which God created to be received with thanksgiving by those who believe and who know the truth. For everything God created is good and nothing is to be rejected if it is received with thanksgiving, because it is consecrated by the word of God and prayer. (1 Timothy 4:1-5 NIV)

"If all foods are good as God created them, but then men process the foods a lot, does that make them bad for us? Do we need to care about how processed a food is? How much salt is in it? How much sugar? The surprising answer is no. A healed body isn't bothered by any food, since by definition it isn't sick. We don't need to work to avoid this or that food according to what is in it, have some plan we manage by our own efforts. All foods are yes, unless the Holy Spirit says no. If we're not to eat something, the Holy Spirit will tell us. He is dwelling in us, living through us. Eating what you enjoy and rejecting what doesn't taste good, what you don't want, will actually be you following what the Holy Spirit is creating within you to desire.

"What about eating too much food? Is that something we need to watch? The surprising answer is again no. The Holy Spirit is our self-control. It's one of the facets of his fruit, singular, that marks his presence in our lives. When we walk with the Holy Spirit he's visible in us—love, joy, peace, patience, gentleness, self-control—are showing in our character, not because we're doing anything to bring them out, but because the Holy Spirit is showing himself within us. Self-control over how much we eat is something the Holy Spirit generates within us; it is not our work to measure or control or live according to some number. God is at work within us to will and to want his own good pleasure. We won't want to eat more than God desires as good for us. The Holy Spirit within us will be our self-control. Again, if we're not to eat something, the Holy Spirit will tell us.

> Therefore, my beloved, as you have always obeyed, so now, not only as in my presence but much more in my absence, work out your own salvation with fear and trembling; for God is at work in you, both to will and to work for his good pleasure. (Philippians 2:12-13)

"The original Greek translated 'work out your own salvation' can also be translated as 'work your own salvation out' and that gives the richer picture of what is happening. The healed, healthy, new saved nature inside you is working itself outward and changing your actions and words and lifestyle so that people see the new nature that looks like Jesus. You cooperate with that process, that's how you work your own salvation outward. The Holy Spirit is working and we're cooperating with him.

"Last question. What about being a vegetarian or eating only raw foods? Are there healthier styles of living over others? It would seem common sense that if there was something overall about food and drink God wanted us to follow it would be in the scriptures. But what the Holy Spirit directed Paul to write is surprisingly opposite what you would assume.

> As for the man who is weak in faith, welcome him, but not for disputes over opinions. One believes he may eat anything, while the weak man eats only vegetables. Let not him who eats despise him who abstains and let not him who abstains pass judgment on him who eats; for God has welcomed him. Who are you to pass judgment on the servant of another? It is before his own master that he stands or falls. And he will be upheld, for the Master is able to make him stand. One man esteems one day as better than another, while another man esteems all days alike. Let every one be fully convinced in his own mind. He who observes the day, observes it in honor of the Lord. He also who eats, eats in honor of the Lord, since he gives thanks to God; while he who abstains, abstains in honor of the Lord and gives thanks to God. None of us lives to himself and

none of us dies to himself. If we live, we live to the Lord and if we die, we die to the Lord; so then, whether we live or whether we die, we are the Lord's. (Romans 14:1-8)

"A healed body doesn't care which lifestyle you prefer. Live by grace, honoring God and you'll always be healthy. Be a vegetarian if you prefer, eat meat if you prefer, eat only raw foods if you prefer that. They all give the same result. Healed is healed. Everyone is healed by grace. How you eat and drink is not going to change the fact you are healed. While you remain living under grace, you can't become unhealthy by what you eat or drink. You live a healthy lifestyle by honoring God and walking with the Holy Spirit. The expression of that life as it pertains to food and drink will be as varied as there are individuals.

"The verses rather show us how to handle this liberty. Don't judge someone else's choices regarding food and drink, thinking your choices are better than theirs, for by doing so you will grieve the Holy Spirit. Call living by works for what it is, a sin, but recognize living by grace for what it is, too. Living by grace, healed by grace alone, will be displayed in lifestyles of infinite variations, which are all pleasing to God.

do not grieve the Holy Spirit of God, in whom you were sealed for the day of redemption. (Ephesians 4:30b)

No one born of God commits sin; for God's nature abides in him and he cannot sin because he is born of God. (1 John 3:9)

"We will not sin regarding food and drink if we walk with the Holy Spirit. That's the best news there is in the scriptures and a very comforting truth we can lean against as we sort out our day-to-day walk. The Holy Spirit in us will be leading us in every aspect of our lifestyle to please God, prompting us from within. We are to live in simple obedience to what He says for us to do, when He tells us to do it. We relax, stop our own efforts and let God lead."

Connie paused and then turned the subject slightly. "How can you tell the difference between the person living under works and one living under grace? How can you tell the difference between the person eating a salad because it is their own works program and the one who is eating the salad because the Holy Spirit mentioned have that for lunch? You can't in the short term. You can in the long term. Those sowing to the flesh, living by their own efforts, reap corruption, they get sick and eventually die. Those sowing to the spirit reap from the spirit life. God can see the difference between the two, between the person living under the law and the person living under grace.

"The majority of us have spent our lives living in a mix of our own works and grace. That's what the Holy Spirit most wants to free us from doing. You can't tell where someone is on that spectrum, are they living under law, under a mix, or under only grace, based on an external fact. It's more the direction they are moving that shows the difference. Someone who has been ill a long time, finding grace, gets healed and healthy. Someone under the law looks good for a while as their own efforts yield temporary fruit, but their fruit doesn't last.

"Satan took healing out of the church by convincing the church healings had ended in the first century, then by spreading the thought that sickness comes from God, so if you're sick, blame God. We bought those lies. We lost the truth that sickness, disease and death, are the works of the devil. Then satan convinced the church to accept their own efforts over God's grace for how to get healed and live healthy. Satan's play is readable now, looking back, but it has had time to do enormous damage. Millions of Christians have died early from sickness and disease because satan is a good liar and we didn't read the word of God as it was written, didn't follow the road it presents to grace alone.

"We need to fall in love with the scriptures and the Holy Spirit and let him fix our thinking and our hearts. Only one of us can work in my life; it will be me, or it will be God. My way leads to death, his way leads to abundant life.

"By Jesus' grace to me, I am loved. I am righteous. I am healed. I am rich. I am delivered. I am made whole. He has saved me completely. I am a new creation. I see that truth, I believe God, I rest. I cease from all my own works. These are finished gifts to me and I accept them. As I rest, who I now am, a new creation, comes to the surface for all to see as the Holy Spirit does his work in me. God manifests who I now am. It's a God thing. It isn't my efforts. The Holy Spirit dwelling in me transforms me by his own power. That's grace.

"I am the bride of Christ. Someone so lovely of character and actions, adorned in such beauty, I am worthy of the bridegroom, the first-born son of Almighty God. God has chosen to make me that bride. And I've decided I'm going to let him do so."

Connie paused again. "It is now more than just late, so I'll close the audio here. I thought this passage helpful enough it deserved a late night audio; I just somehow managed to make two other long stops along the way. I hope it helps."

Ryan let the recording end and didn't take the ear buds out, simply kept walking. Amazing. Connie had been looking for the way to show him what she understood and she'd just found it.

He wasn't going to be living the same after hearing this. He might do the same actions as before, but the heart behind them would be different. He'd be doing only what the Holy Spirit desired and letting go of the rest.

"Holy Spirit, would you show me the motives behind what I'm doing? What actions are being prompted by you and which are me doing what I've decided might be good for me to do based on the world's advice? I'd like to get my life cleared out to be only you in how I live. Is there something you would like to tell me now?"

He kept walking and listened. He'd deeply desired a relationship with God which was personal and now he had what he had desired. He leaned into it and as he did so, felt enormous peace flood across him that wasn't in words, but was definitely an affirmation from God. He was on the right path. The Holy Spirit was ruling by the peace in his heart. The joy felt good, the peace. The Holy Spirit had just settled down in his heart like a dove.

The grocery store was up ahead, for he'd been walking in the direction of Margaret's place to bring her the groceries she'd requested. He stepped inside, picked up a basket to carry a few things and felt a nudge, nearly laughed when he saw the apple tied with a red ribbon someone had set on the fruit display. He picked up an apple and then paused, feeling another prompting, 'you sure?' and when the peace didn't change, picked up the caramel sauce too. The peace stayed steady. Shopping with the Holy Spirit was going to be interesting. The only way to unlearn old habits was to simply obey. For the first time in memory he realized he was going to be shopping without thinking about a food label.

****

Ryan knocked lightly on Margaret's door just after 10 a.m. Saturday, carrying the groceries she'd requested. "It's Ryan," he called. He used the key she had given him to unlock the door and let himself in so she wouldn't have to undo her couch throw and get the chair footrest to lower, take the time to stand and get steady on her feet, just so she could cross over to unlock the door when he was holding a key she'd given him.

She was asleep in the chair by the window. That was a good sign. She hadn't been sleeping well with the still lingering congestion. He thought about not disturbing her, putting away the groceries and leaving just as quietly, but knew she would be upset with him later if he didn't at least wake her so she could say thanks, even if he couldn't stay but a minute to chat. "Margaret," he called gently.

He walked over. And saw the truth. She wouldn't be greeting him today. He knelt and checked what he could already see. Her skin was cool, the beginning of rigor had set in. Her tea cup had slipped from her hand to her lap. She only looked asleep. His honorary grandmother was dead in her favorite chair. Sometime in the last two hours, for she was neatly dressed and was having her morning tea.

It wasn't shock he felt or anger at her death. He felt an overwhelming sadness. She had been part of his life for so many years. She had no family left of her own, had been retired for years, he knew she was with Jesus and yet... he didn't want her to go, he wasn't ready to say goodbye.

He leaned over and whispered, "Margaret, in Jesus' name, wake up."

Nothing happened that he noticed, but he didn't speak again, understanding now what Connie had been trying to teach him. Margaret hadn't lived to the fullness of her days yet. God wanted her to live even more than he did. Her color began to change, the gray tones fading and pink tinged warmth returning. Her chest began to rise and fall as her breath returned. God was doing a miracle and he was watching it happen. Ryan felt speechless at first and then richly thankful, his grin so big it felt like his heart would burst with joy. "This is really amazing, God. Thank you," he whispered, feeling that to speak above a whisper would be to interrupt the gift. Having no idea what to expect, the next six minutes that elapsed was another gift. He'd adapted to the truth of what he was seeing by the time Margaret stirred and her eyes opened.

"Oh, Ryan. I'm sorry, I must have dozed off. I was having the most lovely dream."

He leaned forward with a smile and kissed her cheek. "I brought your butter and eggs."

"Thank you, that's perfect timing. I thought I'd make cookies for Jenna's Sunday school class this morning."

She rose from her chair and picked up the tea cup he'd set back on its plate, walked into the kitchen to rinse it out. "Can you stay for the first batch to come out?"

"Sure." He pulled out a chair at the kitchen table. "How are you feeling? How's the congestion today?"

"That nap helped. I'm feeling much better."

She got out the cookie sheets. "What are you grinning about, Ryan?" She lifted her hand to her hair. "Did that nap leave me with half flattened curls?"

"You look lovely. I was just thinking I'd like to get an updated picture for my desk, one of you and me. Maybe Tina could snap one for me when you're next volunteering at the chaplain's office."

"What a nice idea. You can give me a copy of it for my birthday and I'll add it to my wall of photos."

He laughed. "I'll remember."

He turned the open magazine on the table so he could see what she had been reading and asked her about it as a conversation starting point, content to watch her make sugar cookies and listen to what she thought about the Smithsonian's exhibit on early colonial furniture. She'd always loved antiques from that period.

It had been the easiest prayer and smoothest answer to prayer he could remember. Not stressful, not hard and beautiful to watch unfold. God had arranged the details before he walked into the situation for it to be someone he cared about, to not be a rushed situation with others around, it had felt like the right thing to do. There hadn't been any fear with the words. His first resurrection and wasn't that a statement? *Just between us, God,* he decided. *You get all the glory and thanks.* He decided not to tell even Connie for now. What happened on the battlefield stayed there.

He ate two cookies scooped from the first tray and poured himself a glass of milk, teased Margaret about her love of all things cows as he held up his glass with a jersey cow on it. He said goodbye after an hour, kissed her cheek and headed out. A nice Saturday. One he would remember for the rest of his life.

He had a boy's birthday present to go buy and a party to attend.

Epilogue

COMMANDER JOE BAKER

Joe had requested a weekend meeting with the Secretary of the Army and been given a time early on Saturday afternoon. He couldn't remember the last time he had circled through the Pentagon rings to this side of the building. He felt a bit like a proverbial duck out of water, aware of the second glances he was receiving from passing Army personnel.

He was ushered into the SA's office by his military adjunct promptly at two p.m. With a warm smile, the Secretary of the Army circled his desk and offered a hand. "Thank you for coming in, Commander."

"My pleasure, Sir."

The SA motioned to facing couches by the wall of photos every service chief used to impress congressmen and visiting military officers from allied nations and they both took seats. "You've had an interesting seventy-five days I suspect, having seen a portion of your travel schedule."

"I'm spoken to 78 individuals, in person with as many as was practical."

"Are you ready to offer a recommendation?"

"I am, Sir and you'll want it to remain a verbal one."

The SA grinned as he slapped his knee. "That footage was real. They really did a miracle. I *knew* it."

Joe let himself relax and share that jubilee, for it was nice to be able to agree. "I'm convinced, Sir."

"So the question is what to do about it. What's your recommendation, Commander? Do their actions on March 19th, 2016 warrant the awarding of the Silver Star to one or both of them?"

"I'll answer that question in two parts, Sir. They both rendered aid to the injured while under direct fire and mortar attack. Their valor displayed during the battle is that of a Bronze Star, which I'd personally raise to a Silver Star for the number of incidents involved. They were exposing themselves to personal injury and the high probability of death every time they crossed that road. They both have bullets in their vests showing how real that danger was and yet they still kept going out to reach the wounded. The award board of review is highly likely to make a recommendation for the Silver Star, or the lesser Bronze Star, be awarded to each based on that battle footage.

"Now add to that what happened afterwards, the miracle I'm willing to state did happen, both being present for it and their actions certainly go beyond anything the army could reasonably expect from a chaplain or a combat medic.

"They did excellent work that day. But it's my recommendation their names be removed from the list, Sir and no award of any kind be given to either one."

The SA leaned forward, surprised. "Really. This is unexpected. Why?"

"Five reasons." Joe had been thinking about this recommendation in depth for days, searching for what was right to do.

"Regarding the battle itself, they knew if they died the other would raise them from the dead. It was valor, but the kind that comes from being fearless. I'm not sure I want to put them in a position of having to find words to avoid lying every time they are asked a question by someone who recognizes the Silver Star they wear. I know this terrain, Sir. People ask about a Silver Star with both respect and curiosity. I've been asked about what happened, was I afraid, so many times by both soldiers and civilians that I can predict both the questions and the order they will come. It's an honor to wear the Silver Star. But it means the battle it was awarded for lives with you forever. From what they have said, my sense is that neither wishes to carry that obligation.

"Regarding the events after the battle, we weren't intended to see it, Sir, the miracle which occurred. In the normal course of events this footage would never have been archived and reviewed in the detail which happened here. They both sought to help the men in a way which would not get them noticed. It would have stayed at the unit level, fog of the battlefield, those aware something odd had happened quietly not saying anything more. The interviews from the battle, Sir, already show that reluctance to go this direction.

"While the citation for the Silver Star would likely speak only of events during the battle, the fact Sergeant August would be only the third woman to receive the Silver Star since the second world war means reporters will stay curious about this battle for years to come. They'll talk to soldiers who were there that day. You were in that battle, in the convoy diverted to assist the men from the forward operating base. Did you see Sergeant August helping the wounded? What do you remember about that day? If enough guys talk about that day, the fact a miracle occurred starts being more than just a faint rumor, it gets traction. The men themselves don't know they were resurrected from the dead."

"They don't?" the SA asked, startled.

"No, Sir."

"Alright, that's three good reasons. The other two?"

"It's not the only miracle they have done. I can document, if I were to look for further confirmation, nineteen incidents where a soldier is alive and well today who was severely injured or killed on the battlefield."

"19."

"Yes, Sir. Given that, its safe to assume there are also more, but those I can say with high confidence are in the records should the question be pursued. They didn't start doing miracles that day, Sir. They've been helping injured soldiers for the duration of their service."

"The last reason?"

"What do we do about every other chaplain and combat medic?"

Joe simply asked the question and let the SA adjust.

"Why don't you finish that thought, Commander."

"George taught Connie. She wasn't the only one he taught. He's been the lead chaplain of the chaplain corp. And Connie hangs out with fellow combat medics. She taught her friends."

"Just how many know this material?"

"Sir, you get an insider's smile when you ask the question 'do you know the resurrection prayer?' I'd say your entire chaplain corps and most of the combat medics are well versed in what happened that day. They don't talk about what happens on the battlefield. It's been both well taught and kept quiet. My sense of it, both Connie and George are teaching medical staff now, doctors, nurses, paramedics both in and out of the military."

"I asked a question knowing the odds were high you would investigate and then tell me it was battlefield confusion, a mix-up in paperwork. Instead, I'm seeing a terrain I didn't even know was out there and it's happening in my own house."

Joe smiled. "Soldiers are practical, Sir. Reporting up the chain of command a chaplain or combat medic does a miracle means they aren't going to be traveling with your convoy the next day, they are going to be in a room answering question for skeptical investigators. So respectfully, Sir, why talk about it?

"Units and squads are good at keeping secrets. A man learns in his youth that brothers watch out for each other, the army builds on that fact and reinforces it intentionally. Another thing a man learns in his youth is that you don't tell your parents what they don't need to know.

"Why mess up the life of the chaplain or combat medic which just saved your buddy's life? You buy them a drink at the after-hours club, you watch their backs and tamp down any rumor out there. You take care of them. You don't tattle on them."

The SA laughed. "Yeah, I can see the mindset." The SA leaned back and simply thought about it. "We can't not honor what they did."

"They've received the honor they desire, Sir. God knows. Without discussing what I promised to keep confidential, let me phrase it this way. They were like a postman who delivers a million dollar check to a charity. The giver of the gift deserves the thanks. They delivered the letter. God acted. They simply boldly believed and prayed."

"I'm incredibly glad they did. So, no award. No recognition. You're comfortable with that outcome."

"You can't hide a good deed. They've been noticed. Those who saw something are being promoted up the ranks, the ones who heard a rumor and dig for details land on a trail just as I did that leads back to them. I don't think Connie or George will ever set foot on a military base without being given the deference usually reserved for Medal of Honor winners. You don't need to give them an award. The soldiers from the battlefields know."

"That's the most fitting tribute they could receive."

"Yes, Sir."

The SA stood and offered his hand. "My thanks, Commander. For the kind of news which will stay between us. And my, what news it is. I'll see to it their names are scrubbed and don't come out of the review board. You may pass that on to them if you wish."

"Yes, Sir. Thank you, Sir."

Commander Baker took his leave of the Secretary of the Army. Twenty minutes later he walked to his car. He unlocked the door and finished the second call he had made. "Paul, tell her no award is coming. And take her that box I mailed to Ann. It's keys to the beach house, she's welcome to come enjoy Texas as our guest, its my thanks for the audio files. Connie's one solid teacher for a combat medic."

"That she is. And as it happens, I can deliver it in about an hour. We're heading over to the birthday party for a young boy who got his hearing back last night."

"Yeah?" Joe grinned. "That's a nice ending to this investigation right there."

"Isn't it? Stop by next time you're in Chicago."

"Will do."

Joe pocketed the phone, well satisfied with the ending of the matter. He went to meet his wife at their hotel, so they could enjoy the rest of the day walking around Washington D.C. And he thought it might well be worth subscribing to the Chicago Tribune for the next few years, so he could keep abreast of the news happening in the windy city.

****

Further Study

Interested in learning more about the subjects discussed in this story? I highly recommend books by Derek Prince, Randy Clark, Bill Johnson, Andrew Wommack, Reinhard Bonnke, Watchman Nee, Joseph Prince, Robert Morris, Creflo Dollar and others, on the topics of grace, healing and the Holy Spirit. Randy Clark DVDs on healing are very practical resources. I also highly recommend the deluxe edition DVDs by Darren Wilson, *Furious Love, Father of Lights, Finger of God, Holy Ghost and Holy Ghost Reborn*, (the deluxe editions have full interviews included in the extra DVD's, beyond the excerpts in the movies.)

Author Biography

Dee Henderson is the author of numerous novels, including *Taken*, *Undetected*, *Unspoken*, *Full Disclosure* and the acclaimed O'MALLEY series. Several titles have appeared on the USA Today Bestseller list; *Full Disclosure* has also appeared on the New York Times Bestseller list. Her books have won or been nominated for several industry awards, such as the RITA Award, the Christy Award and the ECPA Gold Medallion. For more information, visit www.DeeHenderson.com

Contact information

The Author welcomes your feedback.

Dee Henderson
P.O. Box 13086
Springfield, IL 62791

dee@deehenderson.com

www.deehenderson.com

Books by Dee Henderson

The O'Malley Series
The Negotiator – Kate and Dave
The Guardian – Shari and Marcus
The Truth Seeker – Lisa and Quinn
The Protector – Cassie and Jack
The Healer – Rachel and Cole
The Rescuer – Meghan and Stephen
Danger in the Shadows (prequel - Dave's story)
Jennifer: An O'Malley Love Story (prequel - Jennifer's back story)

Full Disclosure – Ann and Paul Falcon
Unspoken – Charlotte and Bryce Bishop
Undetected – Gina and Mark Bishop
Taken – Shannon and Matthew Dane

Evie Blackwell Stories
Traces of Guilt
Threads of Suspicion

Military Stories
True Devotion
True Valor
True Honor

Various Other Titles
Kidnapped
The Witness
Before I Wake
The Marriage Wish
God's Gift

Books by Dee Henderson (continued)

Short Stories
"Missing" in anthology Sins of the Past
"Betrayed" in anthology [yet to be titled] (coming in 2018)

Companion Books (read one or the other)
Healing is by Grace Alone (non-fiction)
An Unfinished Death (fiction)

Visit the website www.DeeHenderson.com for additional book details.

Made in the USA
Lexington, KY
05 March 2018